the KEEPER *of* HIDDEN BOOKS

MADELINE MARTIN

the KEEPER *of* HIDDEN BOOKS

A NOVEL

HANOVER
SQUARE
PRESS

Recycling programs for this product may not exist in your area.

HANOVER SQUARE PRESS™

ISBN-13: 978-1-335-00577-9

The Keeper of Hidden Books

Hanover Square Press
22 Adelaide St. West, 41st Floor
Toronto, Ontario M5H 4E3, Canada
HanoverSqPress.com
BookClubbish.com

Printed in U.S.A.

For Momma

Every scene in *The Keeper of Hidden Books* makes me recall something I learned in Poland with you at my side and it's made this book all the more special to me. Thank you for those wonderful memories together and for your endless love and support. I'm so lucky to have you.

Also by Madeline Martin

The Last Bookshop in London
The Librarian Spy

PART ONE

Chapter 1

Warsaw, Poland
August 1939

ZOFIA NOWAK SAT BACK on her calves in the warm summer grass while her friend Janina clumsily wound a bandage around her head. The other pairs of Girl Guides sat in a semicircle beneath the oak trees in Łazienki Park, all working to perfect their first aid skills. Not that the looming war on Poland would ever come to Warsaw.

Still, it was wise to be ready and everyone in the city was preparing in their own particular way. For Papa, it was stocking medical supplies at the hospital while Zofia's mother waited in endless grocer's lines to ensure their cabinets were overflowing with tinned food. Posters were plastered all over the city asking men to line up at elementary schools and enlist, and radio stations filled the air with the pulse of patriotic music.

And it was why Helen Keller's *The Story of My Life* was nestled in Zofia's bag, another read inspired by the list of books Hitler had banned in Germany.

Zofia pulled the bandage from her head and repurposed the linen to bind a splint onto Janina's lower leg. "How's that?"

"It feels good." Janina wriggled her limb. "Studying medicine like your father might be a good choice for next year."

Rather than reply, Zofia considered her handiwork.

"Have you decided what you want to do after our final exams?" Janina's voice was gentle as she spoke, but nothing could lighten the pressing decision that weighed on Zofia every day.

This was their last year of secondary school, a final exam away from graduating. They would be eighteen then—adults. The whole world stretched out ahead of them like a runway so they could soar into the future.

For everyone, except her.

"You sound like Matka," Zofia groused.

Though it wasn't really true. Janina's characteristic delicacy was nowhere near the brusque tone of Zofia's mother. Whether she was insisting Zofia dress nicer, be more outgoing, or be more proactive with choosing a career path—something lucrative, like medicine—there was always a demanding air about her mother. Which was precisely why Zofia referred to her in the more formal regard as Matka, rather than Mama.

Janina's mother was a Mama. The type to smile and ask after a test, or to offer hugs on a bad day rather than criticism.

Perhaps that was why Janina was always so kind and considerate. It was that congeniality that started their friendship so many years ago when they were children. Zofia had never been gregarious, more the kind to keep to herself and tuck into a book than drum up conversation with people she didn't know. Being the tallest in class did her no favors, leaving her feeling as though she stuck out like an ugly duckling among baby chicks. On Janina's first day in school, she'd strode over to Zofia with an enviable confidence and shared some of the flower-shaped butter cookies her mother had baked, filling in any silence between them with an animated chatter that made Zofia instantly like her.

Now, Janina moved her leg, testing Zofia's bandage. "If I sound like Matka, then I take back my suggestion." The loosely tied bandage gave and the neat knot slipped free, the band unraveling from her leg. One of the splints tilted over into the grass.

"Being in medicine is not my path, evidently." Zofia collected the splint with what she hoped was an uncaring smile. "I think Papa understands."

Her father was a renowned doctor in Warsaw, specializing in surgeries. His was a name that would be impossible to live up to, especially for a daughter who couldn't commit to any kind of future.

"You love to read." Janina blew a lock of dark hair out of her brown eyes. "Maybe you could study literature." She gasped in excitement and sat up straighter. "Perhaps you could become an author, like Marta Krakowska."

It sounded ridiculous even when Janina said it with such sincerity. While Zofia had no idea what she wanted to do, she did know she was no Marta Krakowska. The author penned epic tales of romance featuring lovers who meet amid the strife of war. Every story was better than the last, each ending in contented happiness for the couple and a little calico cat.

But Zofia didn't believe in romance, and she didn't have the lyrical voice of Krakowska. She was no author, to be sure.

Zofia pulled the other splint from Janina's leg and wound the bandage into a neat ball. "Did you read *The Story of My Life* yet?"

Janina's eyes lit up. "I did. What an incredible—"

"No," a voice called out from the pair beside them.

Their friend Maria shook her head, blond curls swaying, her arm extended toward her Guide partner, who had it wrapped partially to the elbow. "You can't talk about the book right now, when I can barely hear you."

"At the library then." Janina turned her attention back to Zofia with a mischievous glint in her eye. "But you clearly want to change the subject, so let's turn to something more pleasant. Like how much you're looking forward to school tomorrow."

Zofia groaned and Maria turned away with a quiet smile.

Math was tediously dull, the series of numbers lacking any real challenge. Government was dryer than the dust gathering on her unopened textbooks from last year. Even art was awful. While Zofia appreciated the beauty of it, the medium of their application was of little interest to her. Oh, and how she hated, hated, *hated* being subjected to the mediocrity of her own limited skills when forced to try her hand. On and on it went with every class, each one more lackluster than the last.

Except literature. She did enjoy that subject.

At least at university, her courses would be tailored to her future endeavors. Whatever they might be.

Their Girl Guide captain, Krystyna, clapped her hands to get their attention, sparing Janina a sardonic reply from Zofia about just how much she was *not* looking forward to school tomorrow.

"Great job today, Guides." Krystyna looked around the circle of paired-off girls, her head lifted with satisfaction. "War with Germany is coming, and Poland must be ready. At least the Girl Guides definitely are."

Warmth effused Zofia's chest at those words.

The Girl Guides was a scouting organization meant to prepare girls and young women for life with social skills, philanthropic ideals, and the ability to offer aid to the public in whatever form was needed.

If Germany did attack, the Girl Guides' efforts would help Poland.

Zofia was part of the generation of Poles born in a free state after regaining its sovereignty during the Treaty of Versailles. It was something Poland had fought for more than one hundred and twenty years to obtain. From their earliest days, they were fed tales of heroism and bravery until their eyes burned bright with patriotism and their hearts thumped with Polish pride.

Theirs might be a country young in her independence, having only just celebrated twenty years, but she was ready to cut her teeth on victory.

Something the Germans would likely soon learn.

"What does Antek say about the war?" Janina asked as they pushed up from the grass.

Zofia smoothed a hand over her hair to tame her waves back into place after Janina's bandaging attempts.

Like most men and boys in Warsaw, her brother was a self-appointed battle strategist in casting his predictions on the impending incursion. The map he had tacked on his wall was crowded with red-tipped pins representing the German army where they clustered around potential attack points.

"He thinks it'll start in Gdansk." She kept her tone glib. Antek may be one year older than Zofia, but that didn't mean she trusted his assessment. "Maybe it'll happen before school starts tomorrow."

"Zofia," Janina scolded. "You shouldn't say such things."

Zofia picked a blade of grass from where it had stuck to her knee and grinned up at Janina. "Maybe you should come see his map sometime."

Janina's face went red, just as Zofia knew it would. Though the two had been friends for well over a decade, Antek had never noticed Janina until earlier that year. Ever since, he'd made a fool of himself whenever she visited, tripping over his words and giving a funny smile that made a little muscle under his right eye tick.

And as much as Janina protested her own lack of affection for him, Zofia caught her discreet glances and inevitable blushes.

Maria sidled up next to Zofia, her honey-brown eyes as brilliant as Baltic amber. "Are we still going to the library? Papa was recently in Paris and said he'd bring me with him on his next trip. I have to study more books."

"More?" Janina teased.

As any Francophile worth her Parisian silk, Maria knew everything about the city. And, no, it was not enough that Warsaw was considered the Paris of Eastern Europe. She wanted Paris. *The* Paris of all the world.

The trio wandered toward Koszykowa Street, keeping to the shadows where the late-August sun couldn't beat down upon them. They were at the main branch of the Warsaw Public Library nearly every day now, not that Zofia minded.

In previous times, however, they might have gone to the cinema or purchased ice cream from one of the vendors in the park, but the recent lack of coins made such things difficult.

Rumor had it that Hitler ordered all the bronze and nickel coins out of Poland until not a groszy remained, so little things like a single postage stamp or an ice cream were impossible to pay for.

"Can we finally talk about *The Story of My Life*?" Janina slid a pointed glance toward Maria, who smirked.

"Now that I can hear and participate without being wrapped up like a mummy, yes." Her chin lifted slightly, a sure sign she'd had her way.

"What Helen Keller has been able to accomplish in her life is truly incredible." Janina nudged Maria with her elbow. "As I was going to say before."

"That's why I thought this was such a good selection to all read together," Zofia said. It had been her idea for them to read Germany's banned books as a slight against Hitler. Maria and Janina had agreed, but only after Maria accused Zofia of trying to assign them all summer homework. Once Janina was on board, so was Maria. So far this was the fourth banned book they had read.

Zofia turned to regard her friends, almost tripping over a

crack in the walkway. "Did you know she wrote a letter to Hitler and the students of Germany who burned books?"

"Really?" Maria's brows lifted.

A chimney sweep passed, and the three young women immediately grasped for a button on their Girl Guide uniforms. After all, who would turn down an opportunity for good luck with war on the horizon?

When the man passed, Zofia redirected their thoughts from superstition and back to the book. "Miss Keller donated her royalties to German soldiers who were blinded during the Great War, and then Germany burned her books. After everything she'd been through, she persevered and now speaks up for what is right with grace and dignity." Admiration had seeped into her tone, and why wouldn't it? Zofia found Helen Keller to be an astonishing woman even before having read the book on the obstacles she overcame in her life.

They took turns sharing their favorite quotes, Maria's copy marked off with rectangles of perfectly cut paper, and turned down Koszykowa Street. Their voices dropped to a more respectful tone as they entered the library. The vestibule still smelled like fresh paint and plaster, though over a year had passed since the new pavilion had been built.

An employee at the coat check nodded to them as they passed. The poor man didn't have as much to keep him busy in the summer months when the occasional hat might grace the elegant rack behind his desk.

"I'm glad Miss Keller mentioned the lessons of her teacher as well." Janina led the way upstairs. Of course, she would appreciate the educational efforts, when she herself intended to be a teacher.

Two familiar women in matching Girl Guide uniforms descended the steps as the trio was climbing—Danuta and Kasia.

Danuta, the taller of the two, stopped and wilted when she

saw them. "Are we too late for the meeting?" She gave an exasperated look at the blonde next to her. "I told you we'd miss it."

Her friend, Kasia, patted her shoulder and gave her a sympathetic smile. But then, Kasia was never not smiling. "But we completed our final class here. We're going to be librarians."

The two had been talking all summer about the special classes they were taking at the main branch of the library after having finished their final year of secondary school several months before.

"But they were doing first aid." Danuta sighed.

"I'm sure we can get the materials from Krystyna and do some on our own." Kasia looked to them for confirmation. "And there are probably several books you can read for instruction."

Janina nodded. "I'm sure Zofia can ask Dr. Nowak to recommend a few."

Zofia gave a noncommittal shrug. Papa would likely offer a suggestion if he was home, which wasn't often.

"What were you talking about when you were coming up the stairs?" Kasia asked.

"A book by Helen Keller," Maria replied. "We're reading it as part of our book club."

Even as the words came out of her mouth, Zofia practically groaned. Having a club centered around books meant others would likely want to join, and if others joined, their small group wouldn't have the same intimacy where thoughts and opinions could be discussed without judgment. Especially with Danuta, who had a propensity toward trying to outsmart every person, likely due to both her parents being professors.

Danuta gasped in delight and descended two steps, putting her eye level with them. "A book club?"

"What kind of a book club?" Kasia's face brightened with interest.

Zofia gave a quiet sigh.

"We read books that Hitler burned." Maria pulled Helen

Keller's book from her bag, the little tabs bending this way and that from having been crushed inside. "It's an anti-Hitler book club."

Janina wrinkled her nose. "I think we need a better name for the club than that."

"It's not a club," Zofia countered. "It's just talking about a book we've all read."

"Well, if it is a discussion about books, we want to be part of it." Danuta folded her arms over her chest with an air of superiority. "Besides, I've already read *The Story of My Life* and have probably read all the other books you'll be choosing. My insight will be invaluable. Some books can be very hard to understand for—"

"What she's saying is that we'd love to join if you have room." Kasia gave one of her brightest smiles. "And she promises not to interject too much, right?"

Danuta pursed her lips.

"We'll think about it," Zofia said prudently.

The last thing she wanted was Danuta telling them how they should interpret their books.

Danuta opened her mouth to press further, but Kasia pushed off the railing and took her friend by the arm, leading her down the stairs as she called out. "Perfect, thank you."

Hopefully enough time could pass that they would simply forget about the book club.

Upstairs, Mrs. Berman sat at the reception desk. Of all the librarians, she was Zofia's favorite. Not only did she recommend the best books, but she was also always patient with them and even once offered to teach Janina Yiddish.

Zofia knew Janina wished to accept, but her mother wouldn't allow it. Even Janina didn't have all the details, but apparently her uncle was killed twenty years ago for being Jewish. Janina's mother had been so distraught, she'd miscarried her child and couldn't have another one again until Janina was born three years later.

Out of fear for Janina's safety, the Steinmans only celebrated major holidays like Rosh Hashanah and Hanukkah and didn't want Janina telling anyone she was Jewish.

While Zofia wished she could reassure her friend she was safe in this free Poland, violent anti-Semitism and religion-specific segregation were not relegated to the past. In the last few years, Zofia had seen with her own eyes the boycotts of Jewish businesses, the shattered windows in homes and shops, as well as the slanderous graffiti. Even at the University of Warsaw, there were separate benches for Jewish students and limitations on enrollment.

It made her admire Janina's grandparents, who did not hide who they were, and even Janina's parents for engaging in the holidays they did. And it also made her appreciate what Mrs. Berman must have gone through to obtain her role in the library.

The world was full of extraordinary women.

As Maria drifted off toward the foreign language department, Mrs. Berman pulled Janina aside. "There's a new copy of *Ewa* in the magazine and periodical department if you want to see the latest recipe."

The weekly publication offered Jewish recipes and household advice, all written in Polish so Janina could read it as she cooked the recipes with her grandmother, known affectionately to them both as Bubbe. She was the best cook in all of Warsaw, and Zofia was lucky enough to get to taste the results of *Ewa*'s recipes cooked by Bubbe and Janina—with love, as Bubbe liked to add. That was always the most important ingredient.

Once their books had been selected, they went down to the new lending room to check out, each of them with one title of their choosing and each with a copy of Franz Kafka's *Metamorphosis*, their next read for the anti-Hitler book club.

Which, admittedly, was a terrible name.

★ ★ ★

The scream of a foreign alarm wrenched Zofia from her sleep the following morning. She flew upright in a tangle of sheets, her thoughts spinning wildly as the door to her room was flung open.

"It's the air raid siren." Matka's pale blue eyes were wide, her voice shriller than Zofia had ever heard it.

The buzz of planes sounded over the wail of the alarm and sent the windows vibrating in their frames.

Matka gave a shriek and ducked, even though it was obvious the planes were outside.

"Zofia," she cried, "the Germans are here."

Chapter 2

ZOFIA DIDN'T PROTEST AS she was tugged from her room into the living room amid the screaming sirens, barely acknowledging the cool hardwood beneath her feet.

"It's happening." Antek shoved aside Matka's fine lace curtains and bent to look up into the sky.

Matka waved them toward the other side of the room. "Don't just stand there. Get into the study."

They had prepped the room for precisely this moment, for a potential attack from Germany, though no one suspected that would happen. Not on the city of Warsaw.

The authorities had warned them a gas attack would be the highest likelihood and every home should be prepared with an airtight room. The study's single window had been sealed shut with tape and their gas masks waited there with alien-like glass eyes staring blankly at the wall.

Papa rushed from the bedroom he shared with Matka, a pair of binoculars in his hand from when he'd fought in the Great

War. He joined Antek at the window and peered up through the field glasses. "Those aren't German planes, are they?"

"I don't think so..." Antek pointed at the glass, tapping it with a dull thunk. "See the wings, how they spread out horizontally? It looks like a P11."

Papa frowned and handed the binoculars to Antek. "I think the wings are sloping downward."

Antek shook his shaggy brown hair from his eyes and looked again. "The engine doesn't sound like a P11..."

"I want to see." Zofia didn't know a thing about planes aside from the fact that many had been flying for practice over the city in the last month, but she still wanted to see for herself. Down on the street, people gazed at the planes, pointing, and likely having a similar conversation.

Antek handed Zofia the binoculars. She looked through them and her eyes strained against the distorted image. Another set of planes flew by, little more than a flash of gray metal in the lenses. The muscles behind her eyes ached as she lowered the field glasses and handed them back to Papa.

"Aren't they German planes?" Matka moved closer to the window, her curiosity getting the better of her.

"I don't think the Germans would bomb us here in the city." Antek ran a hand through his hair, leaving it standing on end. "They did attack Gdansk early this morning. Exactly as I said they would." There was a note of self-importance in his tone. "But you don't need to worry, our soldiers will put an end to them before they can get inland. There is no way they would attack Warsaw."

Matka chewed her lip and cast another anxious glance outside. "We should go into the study just in case."

Not one person spoke up in agreement. They all loathed the gas room. Matka had insisted they do drills periodically in the stifling area, where they sweated and breathed in each other's hot, dank air until they became dizzy and combative.

In the end, Matka didn't force them into that awful place. Hours later, reports on the radio said Wielun, an area outside of Warsaw, had been struck by bombs, with hundreds killed.

"My parents were right to leave," Matka said under her breath.

A month before when war was just a whispered rumor, her parents had sent a brief one-line note stating they had left their estate and were departing for their summer home in Switzerland. They had not invited Matka or anyone else to join them. But then, Zofia had never even seen her grandparents, and Matka almost never spoke of them.

They didn't like that Papa came from a poor family—Zofia knew that much—and they looked down on their daughter and her husband as though they were paupers, despite Papa's success and established wealth.

The air raid siren wailed to life again, brought on by a new cluster of planes.

Antek picked up the binoculars left by the window and crouched for a better vantage point into the sky. "Those are definitely German—"

An area to the distant right blossomed violently into a ball of fire as thick, dark smoke belched up from the flames.

Zofia remained rooted where she stood, her gaze fixed on the burgeoning conflagration. What she saw couldn't be real.

Her heart didn't beat. Her lungs didn't fill. Her mind didn't believe.

The scene was as detached from reality as a showing at a cinema.

This was Warsaw, a city of culture and learning, not a doorstep for the Nazi war machine.

And yet the sky blackened with smoke, a stark reality she could not deny.

Another thunderous boom shook her from her stupor.

"In the basement now," Matka said with an edge to her voice and for once, Zofia did not argue with her mother.

Papa grabbed his hat and briefcase from where they rested against the table, still there from breakfast. "I need to get to the hospital."

"In the middle of a bombing?" The neck tendons beneath Matka's gold cross necklace stood out like fishing line under her skin. "Don't be ridiculous. We must go to the cellar."

"Get the children to safety, Jadzia." Papa's gaze fixed on hers as if willing her to understand. "I'll be home as soon as I can."

Matka's narrowed eyes said all the things to Papa she didn't put to voice. Another distant boom sent the walls shuddering. "Come." Matka waved at Zofia and Antek, her enormous diamond and sapphire wedding ring winking in the light. They hurried down into the basement where the rest of the building's inhabitants were already seeking shelter. Inside, the air was heavy and damp from so many people. Fat candles set in tins cast a dismal, flickering illumination in the windowless space.

People kept to themselves, their faces pale in the lambent light. No one spoke, not small talk about the day's affairs or speculation about the war. All was silent, save the whimper of a woman from the third floor with a small white dog she clutched in her lap. That, and the distant thuds of bombs detonating as minutes dragged into interminable hours.

Finally, a new siren wailed, the one notifying them it was safe to emerge.

Antek pushed the door open, and Zofia was the first to exit, her legs stiff from sitting for too long. She wandered outside, where the air was thick with dust and acrid with smoke. Emergency vehicle sirens cried out from all over the city, and the sun strained from behind the haze of a bruised afternoon sky.

As impossible as it was to believe, Warsaw truly had been bombed.

The door opened late that night as Papa returned from the hospital. Zofia jumped out of bed and ran out to find him still in the entryway, his head lowered.

"Are you all right, Papa?" she asked.

His head shot up. "Zofia. Of course. How was it here?"

"We were in the basement all day."

Once the phone lines had been clear enough to call, Zofia confirmed Janina and her family were safe. No sooner had she set the phone in its cradle than another air raid siren had launched its piercing call. The remainder of the day had been spent marching up and down the stairs, sheltering through each raid.

She was about to make a comment about how the woman with the white dog was even wearing on Antek's nerves when Papa joined her in the living room. His suit jacket opened slightly as he did so, revealing a red stain on his shirt beneath.

Blood.

"We were lucky," she replied instead.

"Yes." His brow creased. "Yes, we were very lucky." He smiled, the expression tinged with sadness, and she knew what he was going to say before the words came out of his mouth. "You have your grandmother's eyes, you know?"

Zofia nodded, aware that her sky-blue eyes were exactly like those of the grandmother she'd never had a chance to meet. "I know."

He never spoke of his parents, but Zofia knew that his father had left when Papa was a boy. His mother had raised him on her own, until a terrible sickness took several years to kill her. Papa had been there for all of it. Matka said that was why he went into medicine, to help patients so they didn't suffer like his mother had.

Sometimes Zofia thought it was also to keep people from suffering how he did—a boy too young for adulthood, but too old for an orphanage, left alone in the world.

Now, Papa patted her head affectionately, the way he'd done when she was a girl, his warm brown eyes crinkling at the corners in a way that usually made her smile.

That's when she noticed the trail of mud behind him.

"You forgot to take off your shoes." Zofia pointed to his dirty leather oxfords and the grime he'd tracked in. Everyone forgot to take off their shoes from time to time—especially Zofia, sometimes even Matka. But never once had it slipped Papa's mind.

He looked behind him and hesitated before turning back to her with a sheepish smile. "Don't tell Matka."

"Don't tell Matka what?" Zofia's mother folded her arms over her chest and frowned at the mess.

Zofia wasted no time returning to her room, leaving Papa to deal with Matka. But rather than an angry tirade, the hiss of their whispers teased beneath Zofia's door. Curious, she pressed her ear to the door and listened.

"Do you have everything in order, Jadzia?" Papa asked.

"It's not all that bad, is it?" Matka whispered.

Papa didn't reply. In Zofia's mind, she could see his head lower as he pinched the bridge of his nose, the way he did when the stress of life needed a moment's contemplation.

"Jan, tell me." Matka's tone was firm in a way she seldom used when speaking to Papa.

There was a pause before Papa spoke again. "They're targeting the hospitals."

Zofia lay awake each night after that conversation, unable to sleep until her father came home safely. Over the next two days, even Matka grew weary of being sequestered in the overcrowded basement. The air raid siren wailed almost constantly, whether the bombs were overhead or miles away in the Praga district across the river.

The Warsaw One radio station reported the daily casualties of German aircrafts brought down by Polish defenses, and also reported the glorious news when France and England declared war on Germany.

"La Marseillaise" blared through the loudspeakers in the street as Janina, Zofia, and Maria joined the crush of people cheering outside Branicki Palace where the British Embassy was housed. Flags fluttered and flapped in the crowd, offering flashes of red, white, and blue. The Tricolore, the Union Jack, and their own Flaga Polski.

Three countries united against Hitler. The war would be over soon now. Once England and France launched their attacks, life in Poland would return to normal without the infernal air raids and Papa wouldn't be in danger.

Maria threw her head back and sang the final stanza of "La Marseillaise" before the jubilant music was interrupted by a word of caution from the loudspeakers to not form crowds in the street.

It was disregarded by all. No one wanted to be in basements anymore, not with such cause for celebration.

"This means Antek won't go off to fight," Zofia said over the chords of "God Save the King." The concern had been nipping in the back of her thoughts, but she hadn't wanted to give those fears a voice yet. Not until this moment of wonderful security.

"He'll be safe," Janina reassured her with a broad smile. "The war will be over in two days. Maybe three at most."

A man with a charming dimple flashing in his left cheek approached Maria and extended a small French flag toward her with the flourish of one presenting a rose. She coyly accepted it, letting her gaze linger longer than she should. He offered his hand and spun her into a dance while Zofia and Janina clapped along.

Another warning about crowds echoed into the streets, and Janina, ever the rule follower among them, cast a worried glance about. "We should go."

She didn't receive opposition as she usually did. Tension crawled over Zofia's skin. They'd pushed their luck too long. A German bomber would love nothing more than to target a crowd of revelers.

The three of them walked away from the old palace, leaving the celebration behind.

Evidence of what their beautiful city had endured in the last three days was visible everywhere they looked. Trenches gouged in the tender park fields had been widened now that their purpose was truly needed. Buildings on the horizon showed missing structures like errant teeth knocked from a full smile. Even portions of the road were pocked with holes, though drivers easily navigated around the obstacles.

"Guides," a familiar voice called.

They turned to find Krystyna standing near a ditch with a shovel in her hands, a bit of dirt smudged on the gray of her Girl Guide captain's uniform. Around her, various Guides and Scouts were digging a fresh trench into the earth.

"You're just in time." Krystyna pushed her light brown hair back from her sweaty face and indicated a pile of shovels, their tips streaked with clumps of dirt.

In such days of bombing and war, no one was asked if they wanted to help; everyone just did. What's more, they worked alongside one another. The rich dug next to the poor, as did the Nationalists and Socialists, and the Catholics and the Jews. For the first time since the jubilant hope summoned by the signing of the Treaty of Versailles, Poland was completely and wholly unified.

Janina glanced at her pale blue leather sandals, ones that perfectly matched her tailored dress with small flowers dotting the fabric. Her lips tucked into a slight frown.

"You can clean them after." Zofia grabbed her arm and pulled her toward the gaping trench.

The three of them each took up a shovel, the wooden handles worn smooth from use over the last week between the preparation for war and its arrival. Maria nestled the French flag between her hair pins so the Tricolore fluttered just above her coiled blond braid, and they plunged their spades into the dry ground.

After a matter of minutes, Zofia's back and arms ached from the unaccustomed labor and a sore spot on her palm told her she would not escape without a few blisters.

Krystyna joined them, taking up a place near Zofia. "What are you doing tomorrow?"

Her casual question ought to have been their first warning. Krystyna wasn't one for idle conversation. Everything in her life was serious, from her role as Guide captain to her studies in engineering. Likely the trait came from her father who was mayor of the town where she'd grown up.

Zofia also had never been one for small talk. "I feel like you're asking that with a purpose."

Krystyna hefted a load of dirt three times the size of their meager shovelfuls and tossed it behind her. "Mayor Starzyński himself is calling on all Scouts and Guides to help. Digging trenches like this one, putting out fires where we can, that kind of thing." Krystyna stood up and wiped the sweat from her brow with her forearm. "You free to help every day?"

Zofia squared her shoulders, ready to take on any duty for her country. "I absolutely am."

Krystyna glanced to Maria and Janina. "And you two?"

"I'm in if Zofia is." Janina put a hand on her hip. "But you already knew that."

"I can't leave these two alone," Maria chimed in. "I'll be there too. Besides, the fighting will probably only last a couple more days anyway."

Krystyna nodded in approval, then wandered to the other side of the mound to secure Danuta and Kasia's efforts to the cause.

The next day, the girls met up at the same spot to find buckets and shovels waiting for them. Just looking at them made the blisters on Zofia's palms sting.

"If you dug yesterday, you put out fires today." Krystyna glanced at the careful wrapping on Janina's hands. "Let's give those blisters a chance to heal somewhat."

But if they thought getting out of shoveling meant they had an easier task, they were wrong. Putting out fires in Warsaw was no easy feat, especially when the water mains were constantly struck by well-placed bombs. Bucketful after bucketful of sand was used to smother the flames in such events. And in a pinch, even the water stored in the backs of toilets came in handy for small fires inside the homes.

A week went by and still the air raid sirens shrilled throughout the day. People did what they could to save their belongings. They folded up rugs and took down curtains to discourage the spread of fire. Some people even sprinkled sand on their floors, but most at least had a bucketful nearby just in case. And all through Warsaw, windows were taped over to prevent the splintering glass from causing injury.

Polish soldiers began to trickle into the city, staggering back from battle. While women celebrated their return and washed their feet to welcome them home as heroes, Zofia could not help but notice their haunted expressions.

Mayor Starzyński's uplifting speeches to Varsovians came twice daily, encouraging people to dig ditches, to angle broken tram tracks in the ground as tank repellent, to sweep the streets clean of debris every morning. Through his leadership, the water and electricity that were forever going out with each new bombing were constantly being restored.

But aside from their stoic mayor, the Polish government had fled to Rumania, abandoning the country in its time of need. In response to their flight, General Umiastowski had called for the Scouts to join the front line to help soldiers keep the Germans out of Warsaw.

That next morning, Zofia woke to the sound of weeping and

Matka leaning over the kitchen table for support. In her fist was a crumpled letter.

A sickening clench in Zofia's stomach somehow guessed its contents. "Antek?"

"He left last night," Matka choked out. With a trembling hand, she extended the note.

Zofia unfolded it slowly. Smoothing out the wrinkles, she pulled in a steadying breath, and read.

Antek chose to leave in the middle of the night, when he knew no one could protest his departure. His mind was made up and he was determined to fight.

All at once, their childhood rushed back to her—the times he told her stories to get her through thunderstorms, the way he always stood a little taller when he told people she was his sister, the countless hours he spent sharing what he knew as a Scout so she could excel with the Girl Guides. He had always looked after her and clearly meant to do so again now.

She reread the last line again: *Tell Janina and Zofia I'll return a hero.*

Agony tore into Zofia's heart.

Antek was gone.

Chapter 3

ZOFIA'S LEGS BURNED WITH the effort of racing up and down stairs with pails of sand. Her Girl Guide uniform clung to her sweaty back, the gray fabric now rumpled and streaked with soot.

Her efforts were rewarded as the flames on the third floor of the building she'd been helping to save were extinguished. Victorious, she swiped at her slick brow and descended the stairs with heavy steps, succumbing to her exhaustion.

Gunfire popped in the distance where brave Polish soldiers were fighting in Wola, the southwest suburbs of Warsaw and the area of the city nearest Germany. Whatever talk her parents might once have had about escaping had long since ceased. German tanks now had Warsaw surrounded and no one could get in or out. Not even Antek, wherever he was, and whom they'd still not heard from.

Janina appeared at the bottom of the stairs and rushed up, a bucket of sand swinging from her hands.

"Fire's out," Zofia said before her friend wasted her energy.

Janina sighed in relief, her cheeks flushed. Sweat glistened on her brow and she slumped against the wall, letting the bucket drop the last inch to the floor.

The lights flickered and went out, plunging them into darkness, save for whatever sunlight came through a narrow window behind them. They had lost electricity.

Already the water had been cut off an hour before.

"Again?" Janina gave a frustrated groan that Zofia felt in her own soul.

Were it not for Mayor Starzyński's speeches encouraging city workers to stay on top of electricity and water repairs, the city would have been permanently without them by now. But the hours of darkness and the plague of dry taps were beginning to take their toll on everyone.

Zofia settled against the wall next to Janina, grateful for the slight pressure off the balls of her feet. "I have something for you." Zofia reached into her pocket and withdrew a chocolate bar with *E. Wedel* in looping cursive on the front. Saving it had not been easy as food grew more and more scarce. *"Shana tovah."* She handed the treat to Janina as she wished her a happy new year. Rosh Hashanah was a time of avoiding sour or bitter food, favoring honeys and fruits in the hopes it would make the upcoming year sweeter.

Surely chocolate fell into that category when no fresh fruit was to be found and honey was in short supply.

"You remembered." The exhaustion lifted from Janina's face. She held the chocolate in her hands in awe. "Even with everything happening around us, you remembered."

It was something Zofia had done annually since she learned what Rosh Hashanah was and what it meant to her friend. It was a simple gesture, but with so much scarcity and loss recently, its impact was felt more deeply than in previous years.

"Let's get back to the others," Zofia said quickly, before the tears glistening in Janina's eyes could make them both cry.

Outside, the other Guides were gathered in a small cluster, staring toward the neighboring Wola district. The haze of smoke had become ubiquitous, choking and filthy, a byproduct of the constant bombings and the newly introduced incendiary bombs. The latter were usually released in the evenings before the night bombings began.

Incendiaries would be dropped by the hundreds, the sticks clattering to the streets and onto roofs, sparking phosphorus flames that created an incandescent glow throughout the city. Trying to institute a blackout wasn't even worth the mayor's effort anymore.

It was surreal when one stopped to consider the landscape around them. Two weeks before, this had been a city where children laughed and played in the streets, where life thrived with street vendors calling to passersby, and friends—her own friends—meeting one another at the library for new books. Now the world crumbled in on itself, burning away the beauty of Warsaw, and there was no more time for reading than there was food to eat.

A wave of longing struck Zofia then. How good it would be to return to her old life, tucked against the right corner of the sofa with a new Marta Krakowska novel in her hands, her thoughts lost in another world where she knew that in the end, she would be safe and happy.

Shadows of men appeared through the opaque veil of smoke and a bolt of terror caught Zofia and Janina in the same web of trapped fear as the other Guides. They stared into the mists, focusing on the uniforms. Were they Polish or German?

The soldiers marched onward with the dazed, automatic movements of those who had been recently wounded.

"They're Polish," Danuta cried.

That was all the women needed; the adrenaline in their veins launched them toward the soldiers to help. The men limped into the streets, coated in dust and streaked with dirt and blood.

Zofia reached for a man as he tilted toward her, just managing to support his weight before he pulled them both to cobblestones that glittered with slivers of shattered glass. The strong, sharp odor of turpentine emanated from him.

Zofia gritted her teeth to hold him aloft, her body trembling with exhaustion. "Is Warsaw falling?"

Janina threw her a reproachful look. But then, Janina still had faith that Poland would be victorious, just as she believed France and Britain would finally uphold their promise to bring aid.

"We won." A smile curled up from one side of the soldier's mouth. "We were running low on ammunition and had to get creative."

"Turpentine in the streets before the tanks could roll in." A soldier with blood trickling from his temple chuckled. "Once they were there, we added a little fire and..." He imitated the sound of an explosion, his fingers spreading wide in demonstration.

"Then the Germans aren't in Warsaw." Janina's face relaxed with relief.

Zofia didn't share the sentiment as they led the men to one of the many first aid stations being run by the Girl Guides.

The Germans weren't in Warsaw, but they were close. Too close.

How long would their battered city be able to hold out?

The next morning, Matka and Papa met Zofia at the breakfast table with grim faces.

Zofia's stomach plunged. "Antek?"

Papa shook his head, but his expression was no less solemn. "The Jewish quarter was bombed heavily last night."

"No." The word was numb on Zofia's lips. Janina had been with her grandparents that evening in celebration of Rosh Hashanah. Zofia backed away from her parents, toward the front door, and hastily slid her feet into a pair of leather loafers.

"Zofia," Matka said in sharp reproach. "You're in your nightclothes."

But Zofia didn't care. She ran from the apartment despite her mother's shocked cry. Nothing slowed her pace. Not the tightness in her chest or the burning smoke in her eyes. She wound around to the back courtyard of the Steinman's art gallery on Mazowiecka Street, up a flight of stairs, and rang the bell.

Her heart thumped wild and frantic in her throat as she waited.

A minute passed.

Another.

She pushed the doorbell again and repeatedly slammed the heel of her fist against the solid wood.

A shuffle sounded. Footsteps. The lock clicked.

Zofia gasped out the breath she'd been holding. The door swung open and there was Janina. Red eyed with the collar of her white shirt torn, the lapel wrinkled as if a fist had grabbed it and tugged viciously. But she was otherwise safe and unharmed.

Thank God.

"Zofia," Janina choked out. "Bubbe and Zayde."

Saying her grandparents' names was all she could manage before dissolving into tears. Zofia caught Janina as she fell forward, then guided her into the apartment, kicking the door closed behind them.

Inside, the mirrors were covered and Janina's mother sat on the couch, staring at nothing, her right sleeve ripped from the shoulder so it gaped open. She stood upon seeing Zofia.

"I'm sorry, I can't—" Mrs. Steinman rushed from the room, her face crumpling.

Zofia hesitated. "I shouldn't be here."

"Please stay." Janina grasped Zofia's hand, her fingers damp and hot. "We found out this morning. They had received a direct hit, shattering the building and sending all four levels into the basement below where everyone was sheltering. We had just been there. We had just seen them..." Janina's voice cracked.

It was too horrific to even imagine, being entombed by the very place meant to keep you safe. Memories flooded Zofia. Of the Hanukkahs spent with Janina's grandparents, of the many times they found themselves in Bubbe's kitchen, where cookies and wise, gentle words seemed to fix all of life's problems. Janina fell into tears once more and together, they mourned the enormity of such loss.

Janina did not emerge from her home for a week and Zofia missed her dearest friend tremendously. In that short time, without open borders into the city, food grew impossibly scarce. Lines appeared by fresh horse carcasses after bomb raids for whatever meat could be salvaged, and women ignored air raid signals to stand in queues for grocery stores and bakeries. Even when the Nazi pilots strafed the street, the mothers and wives of Warsaw held their ground, preferring to remain in line even at the risk of being shot.

In that one ghastly week, the Soviets attacked Poland from the east and the Polish gold reserves had been sent out of the country. A sure sign of Poland's impending loss.

When Janina finally returned to the Girl Guides, the skin beneath her eyes was swollen and bruised from her mourning.

"We were able to sit shiva for Bubbe and Zayde." She twisted a handkerchief in her hands, the bit of linen etched with deep wrinkles from the force of her grip. "Now work will keep my mind busy so I can't think. Or remember..." Her voice broke.

Zofia caught her friend in an embrace and stayed at her side as Janina threw herself into an endless cycle of digging ditches and putting out fires.

Though melancholy still plagued Janina, a healthier flush returned to her cheeks after only a day. They had just doused the last of the flames on a damaged tram when a tremendous, thundering boom sounded several streets over. The ground rumbled under their feet and dark smoke billowed into the hazy sky.

Krystyna ran toward them. "I need you to go to Świętokrzyska Street. Now."

Zofia recognized the neighborhood where numerous bookstores were interspersed between banks and offices. She didn't wait to be told twice, nor did Maria or Janina, who raced close behind her. They ran three blocks to Świętokrzyska Street, where they drew to an abrupt stop.

The entire area was a wild conflagration. Far more than what could be smothered with whatever sand they had scooped into their small buckets. The inferno raged like a living beast; its breath fanned over them in a scorching heat. Blackened pits marked where buildings once stood and books were scattered throughout the streets, splayed and burning. Scraps of singed pages dashed about in a frenzy, growing smaller as the flames devoured them.

In the distance, rising above it all, was the Prudential Building. Once heralded the tallest building in Europe, it still stood untouched by the tragedy that had befallen Świętokrzyska Street.

"Go." Krystyna's sharp tone snapped Zofia from the horror of the scene.

The bucket was no longer heavy in her arms as she dashed toward the first building and tossed the pailful of sand into the broken display window, spreading the grains on a burning pile of books. It immediately smoldered. A minuscule effort in a herculean task.

Their small contingent continued to fight on, battling the fire one bucket at a time until their throats were raw and their chests clogged from breathing in so much smoke.

A low hum cut through the roar of the destruction, the sound like an agitated bee in flight. Ice prickled through Zofia's veins and lifted the hairs on the back of her neck.

Planes.

An explosion thundered down the street, a fresh blaze expelling from a building they had fought so hard to save only minutes before.

A plane turned and swept toward them overhead. Janina stood several feet from Zofia, transfixed, her eyes wide as the humming grew louder.

"Run," Maria cried from behind Zofia.

Janina didn't move. Zofia shouted at her this time, running closer when the plane opened fire, sending up fragments of burning asphalt as bullets ripped across the street.

The vibration of the engine reverberated in Zofia's skull, sending her nerves quivering in high alert. The plane was practically on top of her now, the pilot's face visible in the glass panel. He smiled—actually smiled—and launched a fresh volley of bullets in their direction.

A shove at her lower back sent Zofia reeling forward, out of the line of fire. She turned abruptly, anticipating a row of bullet holes in the asphalt, and instead found Maria lying on the ground, her uniform bright red with blood.

A scream tore from Zofia, its sound lost in the cacophony of the planes and fire and bullets and all the other hell raging around her. She collapsed on her knees by Maria, desperate to save her friend.

There was so much blood. It glistened over Maria's chest. Her lovely amber eyes were wide with shock and pain.

"Maria." Zofia's hands fluttered over her friend's injuries. "I don't know what to do."

Should she try compressions? Or tie off the wound? But how could you tie off so many wounds at once?

All the first aid training they'd received jumbled within her frantic thoughts.

The helplessness of the moment crushed upon Zofia. Every

second mattered, and they were slipping through the hands of time like the life seeping from Maria's body.

"Someone help," Zofia wailed.

Maria's mouth opened, her teeth red as her lips worked around words that did not emerge.

All at once, her body relaxed back against the broken asphalt, as the brilliant emotion in her eyes dulled into nothing.

Zofia stared in horror.

It had all happened too fast. There hadn't even been a chance to get help.

Someone grabbed Zofia's shirt and wrenched her from the ground. The asphalt puffed up once more amid a hail of bullets, rocking Maria's body with the impact. Zofia was tugged back, her numb limbs limp and powerless.

"Zofia." Her name was screamed in her ear, the voice familiar.

Janina's dark gaze filled Zofia's vision. Above, the sky was blotted out by a corner of a roof. They were in one of the few alleyways that was not aflame.

"Maria," Zofia whispered.

Janina's eyes filled with tears.

"I couldn't save her..." Zofia's voice was hoarse, foreign even to her own ears.

"There was nothing you could have done. Nothing." Krystyna put an arm around Zofia, helping keep her upright. "Janina pulled you to safety, or you would have been lying there with Maria."

Janina?

Zofia blinked in confusion and shifted her focus back to Janina, who stood at least a head shorter. Janina, who had always been petite compared to everyone, but especially so against Zofia's height and broad shoulders.

Janina had dragged her to safety?

How was such a thing even possible when Zofia was so much larger than her petite friend?

As if hearing the question in Zofia's thoughts, Janina nodded and gathered Zofia toward her in a fierce hug.

The pilot did not leave for some time, hovering like a pesky summer fly, waiting for another bite. In the end, they were forced to do as many did—leave their dead in the street until it was safe to return, under the cover of night.

But as they slunk deeper into the alley for a way to escape, they didn't just leave Maria behind; they also left their childhood, their innocence. It had been sloughed off, a husk which was now too small to ever fit again, leaving them raw and vulnerable in this dangerous new world of war.

Whatever happened next, they would never be the same.

Chapter 4

RETURNING TO WORK WITH the Girl Guides the day following Maria's death had not even been a question for Zofia. They had all lost loved ones. They had all experienced trauma. Yet life continued on.

A shadow crossed Krystyna's face when she saw Zofia. The neatness of Krystyna's immaculately coiffed hair and pressed uniform appeared displaced in the war zone in which they now permanently resided. She strode over, feet crunching on bits of fragmented stone and glass. "Have you slept at all?"

Zofia's eyes were gritty and dry with exhaustion and from the tears she'd finally shed. "Have any of us?"

Krystyna put a hand on Zofia's shoulder in a supportive gesture that she'd likely adopted from her father. "Are you sure you are able to continue today?"

This was Zofia's chance to return to the bed she had struggled to drag herself from, to slip back under the covers and block everything out. Temptation tugged at her, but she squared her shoulders. "I am."

Krystyna studied her for a moment, brows knitted together. "Being busy will likely help," she said finally. "And I have a different task for you." She waved over Janina. "Both of you."

When Janina joined them, Krystyna indicated the opposite direction of where they were meant to set up a first aid station that day. "I want the two of you to go to the library. Kasia and Danuta are there and said they need help relocating books."

Zofia hesitated. The Guides would be short staffed with their absence.

"Is this a distraction to take our minds off Maria?" Zofia asked shrewdly.

"Part of leadership is knowing when someone in your care needs a shift of their duties." Krystyna gave a gentle smile. "I've been a Girl Guide leader for three years and plan to be one for the rest of my life. I have a strong feeling this new role will be better for you and Janina both."

Whatever doubts Zofia might have had faded at the mention of Janina, as Krystyna likely knew they would.

With this new set of orders, Zofia and Janina made their way to Koszykowa Street.

It had taken only twenty days for the veneer of Warsaw to crumble away, revealing shells of homes and streets pockmarked from explosions. Graves covered all available plots of land, from parks where children once played to the grassy partitions in the sidewalk in front of stores that were now shuttered. Even on Szucha Street where Zofia lived, makeshift graves had appeared with roughhewn wooden crosses and bits of potted flowers adorning the fresh mounds of earth.

No more birds filled the morning air with their bright, cheerful songs, and the trees they once rested upon were broken and denuded. Many lay uprooted as if they'd been plucked from the ground and tossed aside like weeds.

The library eventually came into view with white columns framing the windows of the second floor and the peaked center with MCMXIII to mark the date of the building's construction. An air raid signal broke the stillness and the two rushed across the rubble-strewn street into the large rectangular door.

It closed behind them with a thud, dulling the cry of the siren and allowing the cool tranquility of the library to embrace them. The tension gripping Zofia's body eased somewhat.

The building was made of metal and wood and stone, like every other structure in Warsaw. A bomb could punch through the exterior, or a fire could lick its way through the stock of books and set it all aflame. But there was something secure and unyielding about the vast grandeur of the main library branch that made it feel impervious to the destruction. Like a child's blanket, its comfort insulated Zofia in a protective shell.

Until that moment, she hadn't even realized the library was open to patrons during the bombings.

If all their time hadn't been spent digging trenches, putting out fires, and collapsing into bed to do it all again the next day, Zofia and Janina would have come sooner.

It was surreal now to stand in the foyer with the wide staircase beckoning them upward.

How had it been only a couple of weeks ago that they lingered on those very steps and discussed the book club?

Now there was no time to read, no thoughts to spare for their former book club. Especially without Maria.

Zofia and Janina went upstairs to the receptionist's desk. The librarian on staff brightened at the sight of their uniforms. "Help has arrived and we can use all we can get. Head to the manuscript department on the first floor of the annex, on the side of the second courtyard." She pointed past several other patrons to direct Zofia and Janina beyond the main reading room.

Their arrival was met with a flurry of chaos.

Papers were piled on every available surface and files were stacked precariously high.

A woman stood in the center of the mess, her cottony white hair billowing around her loose bun like a halo. She blinked up at them from spectacles that magnified her blue eyes to what seemed like three times a normal size. "Ah, you must be the girls Kasia recommended. Zofia and Janina, yes?"

Janina and Zofia nodded.

"I'm Miss Laska," she continued before either of them could speak. "And I am in dire need of some strong hands."

Her gaze skirted over Janina and doubt flickered across her features.

"We're *both* very strong," Zofia assured her.

Miss Laska hesitated and nodded with the perfunctory agreement of a person who didn't have time to protest. She bustled to a shelf. With a gruff jerk, she dislodged a cart from behind it, one wheel protesting with a grating squeal. "I'll need you to fill this with as many manuscripts as you can, then bring them to the warehouse. They say the bombing will be getting worse now that we've had a ceasefire. We need to save what we can."

The ceasefire had been a blissful reprieve for the city—a glorious solitary hour for foreign nationals to leave the city and for Varsovians to indulge in a moment outdoors without fear of bombs or bullets. It had been followed by a shower of leaflets dropped from the bellies of German planes. The city's inhabitants didn't know what was worse—the blatant lie of the letters promising fair treatment upon surrender, or the terrible Polish and garbled grammar. Though they all laughed, the desperate truth of their impending loss sank into their souls in the way a wet chill seeps into one's bones.

Zofia now scanned the mess of manuscripts and thick folders. "Where should we start?"

Miss Laska straightened as she considered the collections. Sunlight played over her face, revealing the delicate brown flecks against her parchment-like skin and the blue-green veins beneath.

"I..." She cleared her throat. "They all are so valuable, so important. I suppose we should start with the oldest ones." Her gaze, however, lingered on a section where the pages were lighter in color. Likely the newer collection.

Janina set a hand on Miss Laska's arm kindly, in the gentle way she always handled people. "We'll do what we can to relocate everything to safety."

They immediately set to work. Once the cart was stacked full of files and folders and bound sheets of loose-leaf paper, Zofia and Janina followed Miss Laska's directions to bring the items to the warehouse.

The wheel cried in protest the entire way down to the hall that connected the main reading room to the warehouse. They pushed through the double doors into the capacious storage area, where the temperature was several degrees cooler and the tinkle of piano music came from somewhere. But what really caught Zofia's attention was the books. Shelves and shelves and shelves of books as far as the eye could see.

The library was large at two stories and had numerous reading rooms with an extensive card cataloging system. Not to mention the various lending libraries throughout Warsaw. But to witness the thousands of books neatly cascading before them in such vast numbers was truly awe-inspiring.

"First time seeing the warehouse?" a male voice asked in amusement.

Zofia spun around to find a man not much older than her leaning against the wall. His dark hair was long enough to touch the tops of his ears, slightly mussed with a confident lack of care, and his thin lips were set in half a smile. The radio on the desk beside him issued the notes of one of Chopin's pieces from a slightly torn screened cover.

"Everyone looks like that the first time they see the warehouse." He pushed off the wall and rummaged in a nearby cabinet. "Or at least everyone who loves books."

There was something to the ease of his demeanor and the way he casually smiled amid all the chaos and strife that made Zofia eye him warily.

Janina, who enjoyed speaking to everyone, clasped her hands over her chest and sighed. "I've never seen anything like it."

"This is just one of the many warehouses." The man withdrew a small can and came closer, his gait as relaxed as his demeanor. "There are several more attached here. One has been designated as housing for staff who have nowhere else to go."

"You mean people are living at the library?" Zofia asked.

He nodded. "A couple hundred. It's why we have an active canteen now. It's not ideal, but it's better than being on the street." He lifted the can abruptly. "Oil." With a wink, he knelt and applied a bit of the glossy liquid to each of the cart's four wheels. "I could hear you coming from halfway across the library."

"That bad, eh?" Janina's face blossomed with color and even Zofia experienced a rush of mortified heat.

"How this thing doesn't drive Miss Laska mad is beyond me." He stood up and gave them an easy smile. "I'm Darek."

His gaze settled on Zofia first and the skin around his eyes tightened as if he was studying her.

"That's Zofia," Janina said helpfully. "And I'm Janina."

"Well met." Darek took Janina's hand and kissed it before doing the same with Zofia.

The whisper of his lips left a quiet warmth lingering on Zofia's skin. She didn't know if she liked it, and she didn't want to expend the energy to sort out her feelings on the matter.

They might be in a room full of books, tangled in a moment of magic within the library, but the world outside was on fire and filled with death and loss. And Maria…

An ache welled in the back of her throat.

This was not the time for flirtation or befriending someone who could well be the next body in a makeshift grave outside Zofia's window.

"We need to get back to work," she announced.

Janina turned and widened her eyes, a sure sign Zofia was being rude.

Darek chuckled and waved his hand dismissively. "I understand. I work at the University of Warsaw Library and know how busy it can be."

"Then what are you doing here?" Zofia asked.

Janina gave her an exasperated look.

He grinned, clearly unperturbed by her question. "Mrs. Mazur is my aunt."

Zofia didn't know who that was, but nodded anyway. "Thanks for fixing the cart." Though really her appreciation was expressed for Janina's sake rather than Darek's.

A crash sounded on the radio, earsplittingly loud. Static crackled where music had once been. Darek returned to the device and fiddled with the knobs.

Zofia turned away and wheeled the manuscripts to one of the rear shelves, away from the man who smiled too readily and regarded her with too much interest.

The radio broadcast didn't come back on again, too damaged by the bombing at its main station. There was much to be missed in the newfound silence, most especially Mayor Starzyński's daily speeches and his profound love of Warsaw as he delivered necessary doses of courage and support.

Zofia and Janina were sent to the library again the following day, this time helping Kasia with the youth reading room on the second floor.

While one or two patrons occupied the many desks in the main reading room, Zofia was surprised to find a number of children sitting at the wide tables in the newly constructed children's area. Several of the small patrons wore rustic necklaces with a bit of twine and a leather tag stating their name, their parents' names, and their home address. The homemade tags were a common sight in Warsaw. While macabre, such things were entirely necessary amid the bombing.

Kasia smiled and waved Zofia and Janina over. "We were just selecting places we wanted to visit." She turned to the children. "Who wants to show Zofia and Janina where you would go?"

The kids all spoke up at once and enthusiastically held up magazines and books with images from all over the world, from tropical beaches to chic city streets.

"I want to go back here." A girl of perhaps six or so unceremoniously shoved her blond curls off her face and pointed to the magazine of a beach Zofia recognized.

"Gdynia?" Zofia asked.

The child nodded. "We had to leave early because of the war." Her dark brown eyes remained sullen. "We even left our bags."

Zofia had heard of many people who ended their vacations prematurely as men were called up for the impending attack at the end of August. The trains were so packed with people eager to get home, luggage was abandoned.

Suddenly, the globe lights that hung overhead from the grid-like ceiling flickered and went out. Several of the children shrank into themselves, their eyes wide and fearful. The girl who had just spoken of Gdynia started to cry.

The air raids were hard on everyone, but there in the youth reading room, the muted light from the windows illuminated the terrified faces of those who had been dealt the toughest hand—those who had been robbed of a childhood.

"The power appears to be out," Kasia said in a cheerful voice. "Good thing we have so many windows to still see by. Janina, will you read a story?"

Janina, who had never outgrown her affinity for fairy tales, leaped at the chance and selected Zofia's favorite story to read.

One about the mermaid of Warsaw who lived in the Vistula River. After a fisherman saved her from a nefarious evildoer, she vowed to protect the city for all of time. Even the staunchest naysayer spoke of tales of the mermaid, swearing they'd seen her cresting the choppy water of the Vistula River.

The idea of an intrepid mermaid prepared to fight for their city had always intrigued Zofia. Much to her immense disappointment, however, she had never been so lucky as to catch a glimpse of Syrenka.

Zofia wondered now at the mermaid, and what she might think of the attack on her beloved city.

The electricity didn't come back on and the water faltered soon after. Parched throats could only be soothed by the pumps scattered through the city, but their number was insufficient. Warsaw was dark, thirsty, and hungry.

No one spoke of France or England coming to their aid anymore. Whatever vestiges of hope remained now lay on the brave Polish army who defended their borders with dwindling supplies and wounded men.

In only a matter of days, Hitler unleashed his power upon the tortured city that refused to yield to his demands for capitulation. The force of his wrath came in with the cry of an air raid siren as the early rays of dawn colored the smoky sky with streaks of violent crimson.

Matka threw open Zofia's door as she had done nearly a month ago with the first bombing. "We must get to the basement."

"I have to go to the library, Matka. It's Monday." Despite Zofia's protests, an uneasy sensation crawled up her spine.

Whatever intuitive warning teased at Zofia's awareness apparently plagued Matka as well, and she shook her head vehemently. "No."

There was no explanation or threat, just a simple, single word. And it was effective.

Zofia quickly followed her mother to the door of their apartment when the first bomb struck, its force making the building shudder against the impact.

Matka cried out and shoved her into the hallway. Before Zofia could process what happened, they were racing down the stairwell with the other tenants as plaster sprinkled from the ceiling like finely sifted flour.

They moved in a group as one, flowing as salmon do to the basement below and cramming into the door two at a time. The bombs were seldom so close.

Nor were they as frequent.

All day, bombs whistled and crashed nearby, while distant ones landed with a muffled whump. Bullets rattled almost incessantly in the background, sounding as though they were right overhead.

But each target struck with that earth-rattling blast was not their building. Zofia hated the relief of knowing they had survived yet another assault when it likely came at the expense of someone else's demise.

The little girl who lived downstairs from Zofia pressed her face into her mother's house robe. "If I die, I want to be with you."

The words were a stark reality in their stuffy hovel lit by only a single carbide lamp. In the space between them, Matka grasped Zofia's hand and held on to it tight.

Zofia looked at her mother, their eyes locked with a fear neither dared to put to voice. Not only for their own lives in the swaying building that could easily collapse in on them, but also for Papa, who worked out of a makeshift hospital. And for Antek—always for Antek—whom they'd still heard not a word from.

Zofia and Matka huddled together, physically closer in terror than they had ever been in affection. For once they did not notice the rasp of their empty bellies as Matka clutched her little gold cross necklace with her free hand and fervently prayed for the onslaught to finally be over.

But as the little carbide lamp flickered out and bathed them in darkness, as the hours dragged seemingly without end, and as the merciless bombing continued on and on and on, those prayers seemed futile.

Chapter 5

THE AIR WAS ON FIRE. It burned as Zofia tried to drag a mouthful into her lungs, to steady herself as she took in her surroundings. Or what was left of them.

Infernos raged out of control on every side of her, towers of flames scrambling up a smoke-blackened sky. Death was all around, those who were strafed trying to flee and what was left of bombing victims. Cries rose in the air, of injury, of loss, of madness for this scene that lay before them.

Matka stood mutely, her fingertips patting over her chest and throat, as though trying to reassure herself she was real. That this was *real*.

And how could it be?

How could this be Warsaw? A city where Chopin concerts were given amid the vibrant and plentiful blooms in Łazienki Park. A cosmopolitan city of learning, of the arts, of safety.

Wind whipped at them, flecked with ash like whirling snow,

and brought with it more odors than Zofia cared to identify. Bile rose in her throat.

"Zofia," a deep, familiar voice called her name.

A figure emerged from the smoke, tall and slender, a medical bag bumping limply at his side.

Papa.

She couldn't even say his name as he rushed toward her and Matka, catching them both in his long-armed reach and bringing them into a tight embrace. All of Zofia's life, Papa had been calm and composed, his emotions neatly concealed beneath a patient resolve. But now that stoic man sobbed against them, his thin body wracked with shudders.

There was no way to tell how much of the city was left, but at least in this moment, the three of them were safe.

Zofia paced the length of her small bedroom, catching the corner of her mattress at each pass.

The phone lines were still as dead as they had been several days before the bombing, and Matka stationed herself at the front door like a warden to keep Zofia from running to Janina's house.

Worry twisted knots in Zofia's stomach. What if Janina was hurt? Waiting for help?

A knock came from the front door, a subtle two-rap sound that Zofia knew without question. She was out in the living room before Matka could even undo the lock.

Zofia grabbed the handle and threw open the door despite Matka's protests. Janina stood there in a clean dress and not a scratch on her.

Zofia gasped out a cry of relief.

"Mama and Papa would be livid if they knew I was here," Janina whispered, as if her parents were within earshot rather than several blocks away. "But I had to make sure you were safe." Tears swam in her large brown eyes.

"Your parents are unharmed?" Zofia confirmed.

Janina nodded. "Though I think they may kill me themselves when they find I'm missing now."

"Hurry home, Janina," Matka said firmly. "And be safe."

Janina left after a quick embrace, determined to keep her parents from worrying. In her wake, black marks scuffed the floor where she had walked. Zofia realized, upon inspection, it was rubber from Janina's shoes, melted by the heat of burning city streets.

No more bombs fell through the night or the next morning, so Zofia dressed in her Girl Guide uniform and went to the library to help.

Amid the destruction that had transformed her homeland, the library had thankfully remained fully intact.

Ever punctual, Janina arrived at the same time as Zofia and she huffed out a relieved breath. "It's still here."

They hastened to the reception desk, grateful to find everything inside appeared unscathed by the brutality of the attack. There was no electricity, of course, but they hadn't had that since before the bombing anyway.

Mrs. Berman turned from a patron she'd been speaking to and smiled wanly at them in greeting. "Janina and Zofia, I'm so relieved to see you are both safe. Your families…?"

Janina nodded. "All safe, thank you. We're here to help in any way we can."

An expression shadowed Mrs. Berman's pretty face. "They'll need your help at the Krasiński Library. It was struck last night, and the librarians are trying to save what they can."

It was about half an hour's walk to Krasiński Library, where the opulent building held the Krasiński family's impressive book collections they had generously opened to the public. Now, the central area of the structure—what was once the reading room, reference collection, and museum—had been reduced to broken beams and stone with priceless collections buried beneath the debris.

Not bothering to ask for instruction, Zofia led Janina to a damaged area where no one else stood yet. She moved aside a massive splinter of wood and rolled away a block of stone. The corner of a book peeked out from the detritus. Carefully, she lifted it. Half of the book fell away, little more than ash that sifted into dust at a mere touch.

Zofia held the crumbled remains in her careful hands, helpless.

These books were Poland's legacy. Generations of learning and foundational ideas were penned in these pages. The centuries of fighting for freedom, names of heroes that might have been lost to history were they not painstakingly written down. What might be forever erased from the world's knowledge with the destruction of just a single book?

She regarded the demolition before her.

And what of hundreds of books? Thousands of books?

Zofia spotted another cover beneath a layer of dust and reached for it, her hands as gentle as if handling a brittle autumn leaf. This text remained intact as she freed it and drew a cloth over its face, smearing soot away to reveal rich green leather beneath with a bit of gilt lettering.

Janina held out her hand. "You find them and I'll clean. It'll go faster that way."

It was a good and effective system, one they continued for several hours until a female voice interrupted them.

"May I help?"

"Yes." Without so much as a glance toward the woman, Zofia retrieved another book and then a second for the newcomer. "We can go twice as fast with two of you cleaning these off. But you must be careful, as they are very fragile."

She straightened with a book in hand and froze. The woman had brilliant red hair and eyes as blue as a stretch of Polish summer sky, a perfect match to the kerchief wrapped elegantly around her head so only a sweep of red bangs were visible. There was only one person whose features were so striking, so unmistakable.

Marta Krakowska.

The author of *A Rose for Poland*, *Lilac in Summer*, *Lilies in the Valley*, and so many more that Zofia had read over and over again in the last several years.

"This is for me?" Miss Krakowska indicated the book in Zofia's hand.

Zofia could only nod. Behind her, Janina mouthed the author's name, as if Zofia was completely blind and didn't know who stood in front of her.

Miss Krakowska turned the book in her hands and tsked, her brows pulled down in genuine hurt as she lovingly wiped the cover clean.

"You're Marta Krakowska." Zofia swallowed.

The woman looked up, those brilliant blue eyes locking with hers.

"And you're here." Zofia wished she could recall the idiotic statement as soon as it left her lips.

"Like you, I want to save books." Miss Krakowska's gracious reply was followed by a sorrowful glance at the destruction to Krasiński Library. "I cannot imagine Poland without our wealth of literature." She shifted her gaze to the stack of books set aside, the ones that were unable to be salvaged—little more than a spine or a partial cover with most of the pages missing. "So much has been lost."

"We're saving what we can," Janina said. "And most are salvageable."

"I mean the other libraries that have been destroyed as well." Miss Krakowska turned the book in her hands and solemnly ran her rag over the soiled cover. "The entire Military Library has been obliterated. The University of Warsaw Library had suffered massive damage to several of its collections despite the effort of those who tried to save them. They have attacked us at our heart, my girls."

Janina shot Zofia a look and mouthed "Darek," reminding her that he worked at the university's library. Zofia might not be entirely keen on the man, but she certainly didn't wish him ill and hoped he was not injured.

With a heavy sigh, Miss Krakowska set the book among the growing stack of others they'd saved. Zofia handed her another dust-covered text and turned toward the rubble once more to continue her search.

"How did you know you wanted to be an author?" Janina asked abruptly.

Though Zofia pretended not to have heard, she knew Janina had asked on her behalf.

"Writing and telling stories have always been part of me," Miss Krakowska replied. "It soothes a part of my soul that would otherwise be left wild and bereft." She hesitated. "Are you asking because you want to be an author?"

Zofia busied herself with extricating a couple of books from the debris. Her hands were gritty with smears of grime and her Girl Guide uniform looked as if she'd romped about in a coal bin.

"Not me," Janina answered truthfully. "Zofia."

Zofia turned back to them, cringing slightly. Miss Krakowska had joined them to help save books, not give advice on becoming an author. Zofia handed Janina one of the excavated books, hoping her pointed stare would convey the full extent of her mortification over Janina outing her to Marta Krakowska, of all people. When Zofia gave the other book she retrieved to Miss Krakowska, humiliation burned in her cheeks.

Miss Krakowska accepted the damaged item. "Ah, so it is you who wants to be an author. The young lady who handles books as a mother does her newborn babe?" In a quieter tone meant only for Zofia, she said, "I knew you to be a lover of books the moment I saw you. It was why I joined you over the other groups where men are using shovels to liberate these precious tomes."

"I suppose I'm still trying to figure out what I want to do after I finish school." Zofia dug her toe into the ground, a habit from her childhood that only emerged when she was uncomfortable enough to want to writhe out of her own skin. She caught herself in the act and stopped.

"You'll know when you have a story to tell." Miss Krakowska nodded sagely as she set to work with careful cleaning. "Books are the perfect conduit to convey a message to the world. It could be an idea that blossoms into a way of life. It could be a new theory for mankind to explore. It could be a journey of life that few have trod. When you have something to tell, it will simply burst from you and you won't be able to stop it."

Janina regarded the author with rapt attention. "And how do you write such strong and powerful emotion?"

Miss Krakowska's hands stopped moving over the book. "Pain." Her chest lifted with a hard inhale beneath her black coat. "When one has experienced the rawest sentience and passion, when you have died a thousand deaths and have learned to tame that agony into prose, that is how great emotion is written."

"I have had much loss," Zofia murmured. Her heart brimmed with the enormity of all she'd suffered recently, when Maria was killed before her and the incessant ache of worry for Antek. There truly was no greater sensation than that of anguish and grief.

Miss Krakowska patted a hand at Zofia's shoulder. "You are almost there, my girl. Almost there."

Her words took Zofia aback.

Was she not yet there now? How much more must be endured before her soul was primed to create?

But Miss Krakowska distributed no more bits of wisdom as they continued in silence. They worked until it was almost dusk. Through their toils, Miss Krakowska remained visibly pained over each book that was unearthed and pronounced wholly destroyed. When they bid her good evening, she did not respond, but instead took a small notepad from her handbag and sat among the ruins with her pen swiftly flicking over the page.

"I don't believe what she says," Janina remarked when they were out of earshot.

Zofia turned to her friend. "No one writes emotion like Marta Krakowska."

"Because that's been her experience. Not every author would agree with it." Janina put her hands on her hips. Her nails were dark with soot and left finger-length smudges on her gray uniform. "I don't want you looking for things to wound your heart to make you a viable author."

Zofia gestured to the crumbled city around them. "I don't have to look very hard."

"I miss the way things used to be." Janina spoke quietly as she voiced the words they all thought and scarcely had the courage to say. "I miss school, and going to the cinema, and getting ice cream at the park." Her voice grew husky with emotion. "I miss meeting Maria at the library, and I miss our anti-Hitler book club."

"That really is a horrible name," Zofia said with forced mirth.

Janina gave her a sad smile.

Zofia ached for things to return to how they had been, so much that it was too painful to dwell on. But wishing for their previous life back was as useless as imagining herself an author someday. Zofia had no story in her to tell, only the ache of loss that apparently a woman of Marta Krakowska's caliber did not deem worthy.

The notice of Warsaw's capitulation was announced the next day, followed by a ceasefire. The bombings had finally come to an end.

Zofia stayed in her house that day as Nazi troops swept into the city like locusts, swarms and swarms of round-helmeted soldiers marching in droves. Their motorbike engines reverberated off broken stone walls and their tank treads ground rubble to dust.

But what would Hitler do with the city he had finally conquered?

By the time Matka allowed Zofia to leave the apartment again, Krasiński Library's surviving books were as recovered as was possible. Instead, Zofia turned back to Koszykowa Street to offer her aid to the Warsaw Library if it was needed. She was nearly there when the shuffling steps of countless boots filled the air.

Heart racing, she turned to the sound and found an army headed toward her. Not ones with polished jackboots and chins notched high in smug victory. This was a sad procession, comprised of exhausted soldiers who moved without proper formation, and kept their hats pulled low over gray faces. Their coats were belted against the October chill. Some men limped, while others cradled injuries.

Poland's defeated army.

Zofia exhaled a shaky breath. These men had not always been so downtrodden. Stories from the battlefield were on everyone's lips lately, whispered behind the enemy's backs. The intrepid soldiers who refused to retreat even when they were outnumbered, the cavalry who managed to hold back a Nazi army with their sabers and rifles, and the ones who were relegated to clever and creative tactics when their ammunition had run out.

What Poland's military lacked in arms with their antiquated tank trains, underdeveloped aircraft, and limited guns and ammunition, it made up for in courage.

If the war could be won on bravery alone, Poland would have been victorious.

That knowledge made the sight before her even more bitter.

"Where are they being taken?" Zofia asked one of the Nazi soldiers in German.

He was young, not much older than her. His pale brows rose in surprise. "You speak German."

Her father was from Poznań, the area of Poland once part of the German empire, where almost half the occupants still spoke the language. But this lout didn't need to know that, and she continued to stare, awaiting his reply.

"They're going to work camps." The Nazi turned his attention back to the slow march of conquered men. "Nothing you need worry yourself over."

Zofia stood there a moment longer, studying every face that passed her, desperate for the familiar visage of her beloved brother. Of course, if he'd been in Warsaw, nothing would have kept him away from home. Not when he knew how much they worried.

"Excuse me." She caught the arm of a passing Polish soldier.

He turned his gaze on her, brilliant blue-green eyes the color of sea glass.

"Did you work with any of the Scouts?" she asked, desperate for information on any of them. "The ones who arrived from Warsaw."

A muscle flexed in his jaw and he tried to press onward.

"Please." Zofia dug in her handbag and produced the heel of bread Matka had sent for her lunch.

The Polish soldier pushed away the food and his chin trembled, a grown man fighting to hold back tears.

Fingers of fear curled an icy grip around her heart.

"Why did they send them?" the soldier asked, his voice breaking. "So young. Completely untrained. Too eager and unskilled. Those poor boys." His throat flexed around a silent sob and his nostrils flared as he drew in a hard breath. "Why did they send them?"

Zofia shook her head, unsure what to say. She pushed the bread into the man's limp hand until his fingers closed over it. Then she ran to the library on Koszykowa Street, her chest tight with the very real understanding that she had spent the last month trying to avoid.

They would likely never see Antek again.

Chapter 6

ROWS OF NAZI TROOPS filed past with their ridiculous goose steps, their jackboots striking the pavement so loudly it could be heard above the victorious German music. Zofia and Janina crouched by one of the many blown-out windows in a shelled building on Ujazdowskie Avenue.

The men marching by were not the troops who had been at war. Their uniforms were brand-new and perfectly pressed, their faces absent any markings of battle. It was all a facade, made to look as if the German defeat of Poland had been effortless.

"Remind me again why we are doing this?" Janina whispered from where she peered over the window frame.

"To look our enemy in the face." While Zofia had wanted her words to be said with conviction, a tremor filled her voice.

The Nazis were an impressive force, exactly as they were intended to appear. They filled the street, all rigid with discipline like tin soldiers rather than real men of flesh and blood.

"Do you remember when all the Jews were sent into Poland

from Germany?" Janina asked, her voice small and nearly inaudible over the German music blaring from the speaker in gross display of triumph.

The previous autumn, trains from Germany had deposited countless Jews who had been expelled from Germany. Though many didn't even speak Polish, they were considered of Polish descent due to their ancestry. Some didn't even have families who could take them in, and those who did were so distantly related, they were little more than strangers. Soon after, a massive attack against the remaining Jews rippled through major German cities, targeting their businesses and houses, leaving many innocents beaten and arrested.

"Do you think what happened in Germany will happen here?" Janina turned away from the window and hugged her legs against her chest, her back pressed to the wall.

Zofia met Janina's worried gaze. "I won't let anything happen to you."

All their lives, they had protected one another. No matter what, Zofia would continue to do so now.

But Janina did not appear reassured. "What if you don't have a choice?"

Above them, flags the color of violent blood snapped in the wind, rippling the swastika overhead. The Nazis continued to march in an endless stream and a shiver rippled over Zofia.

The city had running water and electricity again, the chief focus of the Nazis upon their entry. Though Hitler did not stay long after his victory parade, his soldiers remained to do his bidding. They skulked through the streets like jailers, seeing everything, barking at everyone.

Several days later, an alliance between the Soviets and Germany had them splitting Poland among themselves, two predators ripping apart their prey. Warsaw fell into the German side, now dubbed the General Government, and many began to plot their escape to Soviet-owned soil.

One of Zofia's teachers once quoted: "Better the devil you know than the devil you don't." Having been under Russian occupation for decades before gaining their independence, Poles at least knew what to expect from them.

While Warsaw waited to see what the Germans would do with their control, Zofia and Janina found succor once more within the comforting walls of the Warsaw Library. This time, however, without their Girl Guide uniforms. Krystyna had sent them all messages individually declaring that their weekly public meetings were canceled indefinitely. The recent murder of over a dozen Boy Scouts in Katowice by Nazis meant any Scout or Guide wearing a uniform was in danger.

None of those young victims had been more than fourteen years old.

Mrs. Berman was at the reception desk when Janina and Zofia arrived and greeted them with a smile. "I've heard you two were invaluable in your assistance at the Krasiński Library."

"And we met Marta Krakowska." Janina beamed at Mrs. Berman.

"School isn't open yet and we have nothing but time on our hands," Zofia said. "Can you find something for us to do?"

Mrs. Berman's features relaxed with gratitude. "Your help would be very welcome. I'm afraid we've been short staffed and reassessing our inventory with so many books having not been returned this last month…" Her solemn expression indicated she knew very well why most of those books hadn't been returned. "It's been an enormous task."

Zofia stood a little taller. "Put us to work."

"Go to the warehouse." Mrs. Berman lifted a stack of papers and tapped it on the desk, straightening them. "Mrs. Mazur will know exactly what to do with you."

"Oh, that's Darek's aunt," Janina said. "Do you think he'll be down there?"

Zofia snorted in disgust. "We're here for books, not boys. And he was very fresh, kissing our hands like that."

"You know all men kiss the hands of ladies. He was being polite."

"He was being flirtatious."

Janina rolled her eyes, more with affectionate teasing than irritation. "You could have been nicer to him. Besides, I want to ensure he remained safe after the university's library was bombed."

Zofia pursed her lips, not wanting to think about Darek or the way the warmth of his mouth had tingled on the back of her hand for some time after. There was far too much else to occupy her thoughts. Like how much Warsaw had suffered, and what they might still lose. Like what could happen to Janina and her family and Mrs. Berman and all the other Jews in Poland if the Nazis treated them with the same hate as the ones who lived in Germany.

Thankfully, the only person in the warehouse upon Zofia and Janina's entry was not Darek, but a woman. As they approached her, Zofia noticed her chin-length brown curls, half swept back and pinned to reveal an oval-shaped face. She was busily stacking books in a cart.

"Mrs. Mazur?" Janina ventured.

The woman looked up, startled. "Can I help you?"

"Mrs. Berman told us we could help you with the inventory," Zofia replied.

The small lines around the woman's green eyes put her likely around Matka's age and the set of her thin lips was reminiscent of Darek's. "The destruction of our city has cost us a lot of our stock. And many of our people." Her constant motion stopped for a brief moment, as if pausing in remembrance before continuing. "Many books were taken from the library and not returned. Some went to the front line for soldiers, others went to hospitals, and then there were those that were destroyed."

In an instant, she plucked a stack of paper neatly held together with a metal clip and passed it to Zofia. "This contains a list of missing books. There are often duplicates through the warehouse to replace the ones no longer available within the main area of the library. They need to be found, and that's where you come in. You'll see the shelf location for each." She indicated a column on the list.

Janina peered over Zofia's shoulder at the page. Sure enough, each item had a series of numbers listed by the title.

Mrs. Mazur pushed the half-empty cart away and called over her shoulder, "Good luck."

Incredibly enough, Zofia and Janina did have good luck. The store of books was so plentiful that each book on the list had an extra copy within the warehouse, some with two or three more copies. The hours flew by as they returned the titles home to their designated shelves within the library, and Zofia and Janina left after a long and satisfying day with several new books to read.

They were only able to volunteer for a couple more days, as the schools were soon opened.

No matter how hard she tried, Zofia could not summon the same excitement for lessons to begin as Janina.

She didn't prepare her outfit with the same level of care as Janina on their first day either. Zofia's uniform wasn't pressed, but it was without any stains and perfectly sufficient, though the disapproving twist of Matka's mouth that morning suggested otherwise. But then, she was always disapproving when it came to Zofia. Even amid a war. Even with her thoughts distracted by Antek's disappearance.

Janina was lovely in her crisply ironed uniform with perfectly shined shoes and a confidence that turned many heads on their way to school. Including several of the Nazi soldiers who loitered on the street with lit cigarettes and lewd comments.

“I could use a proper Polish welcome,” one of them shouted in Polish when they strode by.

Zofia bristled, but Janina shook her head, her fresh curls bouncing. “Not today, Zofia. Please.”

Bitterly, Zofia swallowed down her retort and spoke with more optimism than she felt. “Let’s just get to school.”

Janina shot her a side glance. “I never thought I’d see you so eager to return to classes.”

“I’m eager for life to be normal again. Even if that means sitting through another of Mrs. Paszek’s mind-numbing math instruction.”

Yet even school proved to be a far cry from normal. The windows were still boarded up and the once-thick row of trees outside was markedly absent, leaving the stone building feeling strangely nude.

The number of students was noticeably smaller than before. Half of what they were before the bombing. The other girls were all standing in clusters, with several of them staring at Janina.

A twitch of unease told Zofia their attention had little to do with Janina’s pretty curls.

Oblivious, Janina slipped her bag from her shoulder as they entered the building, ready to settle her items on the floor beside her desk. Several people were already sitting in their places, the gaps between them apparent, including the one in front of Zofia where Maria once sat. A flash of hurt and rage lashed through Zofia, so all-consuming it nearly blinded her. Maria should never have been in Warsaw. Her father should have taken her and her family to Paris before the first bomb fell.

But who could have known what would happen?

A delicate touch on Zofia’s forearm pulled her away from such thoughts. Janina’s face was sympathetic for their shared loss. She gave a slight nod to Zofia. They could do this.

Together.

Fortunately, the school day opened with a lesson on German

writers, and Zofia found distraction in the beauty of how easily words could twist her away from haunting memories.

She was lost in an engrossing passage from Friedrich Nietzsche when giggles suddenly sounded behind her, interrupting her thoughts.

Perturbed, Zofia turned and noticed three girls pointing at Janina's hair with apparent mirth. Shifting back in her seat, Zofia glanced at the back of Janina's head and found wet balls of paper clinging to her dark curls.

Janina continued watching their teacher, unaware she was being made into a joke. Those lovely, glossy curls were there because Janina's mother had spent an hour carefully rolling her hair the night before. Zofia knew Janina never slept well on those rollers, but she did it anyways to look nice.

And now the other students were being so cruel to Janina just because of how beautiful she looked on the first day of school. Not wanting her to understand what had happened, Zofia began swiftly picking the wet wads of paper from Janina's hair.

This made the girls laugh all the harder.

Janina turned in her chair and the class erupted with cruel glee. Understanding dawned on Janina and her face went first pale with horror and then bright red with humiliation.

"Enough." Their teacher clapped at the front of the classroom.

"You're all idiots," Zofia hissed behind her and tossed the last piece to the ground. It landed with a sodden plop.

Janina lowered her head over her book, her mouth pressed into a hard line. But even before her telltale sniffle, Zofia knew Janina was focusing more on not crying than she was on Nietzsche.

"You don't belong here, Jew," someone called from the back of the class.

The words must have hit Janina like a slap, for she flinched as if she'd been struck. Never in all their time at school had anyone made Janina feel like she hadn't belonged. Any days she spent away from lessons for Hanukkah or Rosh Hashanah were done without explanation or harassment. She had always been among the most popular, liked by everyone and easy to get along with.

Before the Nazis invaded their city, they had all been friends.

Zofia rose from her chair, mouth opening to fire back an insult when their teacher slapped a ruler on the desk with an audible smack that captured the attention of her class. "I said enough."

Clearly the offense was with the disruption and not the context. The realization made Zofia's cheeks burn all the hotter.

The remainder of the day, she sat with her fists clenched so tightly that her short nails bit into her palms. She couldn't imagine what it cost Janina to remain at school after suffering such humiliation at the hands of people she once called friends. Despite her passivity, the three girls behind them had whispered throughout the lessons, their words hissed with malice. When their last lesson finally came to an end, Janina practically leaped out of her chair to leave.

Zofia walked at Janina's side, putting herself between her friend and the three instigators as they walked to the classroom door, nearly free. Finally.

One of the girls, the taller of the three with pockmarked cheeks, maneuvered in front of Janina and spit at her, the glob landing just before the toe of Janina's glossy shoes.

"Jew." The girl's upper lip peeled away from the word.

Zofia launched herself at their classmate, her knuckles slamming into the other girl's pert little nose, exactly like Antek had shown her. Blood spurted from the girl's face amid a yowl of pain. An ache lanced up Zofia's arm, but she didn't let that stop her. She attacked again, flinging another punch with her left, this time catching the girl in the mouth before someone yanked her away.

"I don't think you'll need a tetanus shot." Papa turned Zofia's hand slightly as he examined it in the overhead light, as serious as any physician. A box of plasters and a nearly empty bottle of ethanol rested on the kitchen table beside them.

"Do not tease her as though she isn't in trouble." Matka folded her arms over her chest.

Papa's brows lifted as he regarded Matka's pacing form. "She isn't in trouble."

"Excuse me?" Matka's eyes flashed like the ancient basilisk of Old Town. Zofia would rather be turned to stone from such a beast than face her mother's wrath now.

But Papa was unperturbed as he resumed his assessment of Zofia's hand. The skin beneath her split knuckle was already beginning to darken with a bruise.

"She did what was right, Jadzia." Papa's hazel eyes were reproachful as he regarded Zofia's mother.

"She is not allowed back at school," Matka reminded him.

Zofia looked away, desperate for space from the intimacy of her parents' squabble. There was a clear view through the window now that their radio had been relinquished to the Nazis per their orders. Failure to comply promised fatal consequences, and Matka hadn't wanted to take the chance. The street below revealed a smooth pavement now, the bodies once buried there after the bombings having been exhumed and relocated.

As though none of it had ever happened.

"We have to stand against what is being done to our Jewish friends and neighbors," Papa said. "The persecution from the Nazis is already starting to show itself here on the streets of Warsaw. If you read the *Courier*, you'll see the poison they're pouring into Polish ears."

"It's just a paper," Matka fired back. "One with poor spelling at that. In times such as these, we must look after ourselves."

"I hope that is not how you truly feel, Jadzia." Papa twisted in his seat to look at her. Disappointment laced his tone, and though it was not directed at Zofia, she still winced at its barb.

Matka huffed and left the room, the rapid click of her heels echoing on the wooden floors.

Papa's hands were gentle as he dabbed at the cut on Zofia's hand with the ethanol one more time. "You did the right thing."

Zofia watched his careful administration, barely feeling any sting. "I know."

There was pride in his smile. "Where did you learn to punch like that?"

"Antek." Saying his name aloud was its own kind of blow, one that hit in the softest part of her chest. "There was so much blood."

"There always is with head wounds." Papa affixed a plaster to her knuckle and spoke slowly, as though choosing his words with great consideration. "School will not be the same under the occupation. I believe there are some schools being organized, some that are done in secret. Perhaps those might suit you better."

Zofia lifted a shoulder in a noncommittal shrug. "We plan to see if Danuta can get jobs for us at the library for the time being." Zofia and Janina had discussed it on the way home as they came up with ways to avoid ever going back to school again. Danuta had an uncle who helped with staffing at the library and might be imposed upon, assuming Zofia's parents didn't keep her locked in her room forever in punishment after the teacher phoned them.

Papa tilted his head, a sign he agreed with part of what she said. "Promise me you won't neglect your education."

How could she make such a promise with a future so clouded with uncertainty? And yet, she never could resist an opportunity to please her father and so she nodded. "I promise I won't neglect my education."

The next day, Danuta stared across the glossy reception desk she was minding while one of the librarians went for a fresh cup of coffee. She tapped one rounded nail on the polished wood. "We can't just hire everyone."

Janina gave a breathy laugh, small and friendly. Entirely unperturbed. "We're not *everyone*."

"And we have been helping with the library since the bombing," Zofia added, less inclined to shield her irritation. "We can take librarian classes like you and Kasia did."

"That's only if you've completed secondary school, which it sounds like you won't be doing."

"If you don't give me something to do, I'll be left with my mother all day." Zofia leaned across the table. "We'll do anything for a chance to work here."

Danuta's brows lifted. "Anything?" A slow smile spread across her lips in a way that made Zofia's stomach clench.

"Yes," Janina confirmed. "Anything."

Danuta swept her braid over her shoulder with a flourish. "I want to be in the book club. Me and Kasia, actually. We both want to be in it."

Her words caught at a wound in Zofia's heart that was still tender and raw. "We don't have the book club anymore. Not since..."

Maria.

"Too bad." Danuta adjusted the pen and notepad again, though neither was out of place. "We probably don't have any jobs."

"We can start the book club again." Janina's warm brown eyes found Zofia's, growing more desperate.

The terrible encounter from the day before at school flashed in Zofia's mind, and something deep inside her winced. Janina needed this.

Zofia sighed. "Fine. We're currently reading Franz Kafka's *Metamorphosis*."

"Wonderful." Danuta's face broke out into a wide grin. "And fitting since I've already read it. I'll go talk to my uncle."

Chapter 7

WORKING FOR THE LIBRARY was different than volunteering, their tasks being more detailed and given with higher expectations. Zofia was placed in the warehouse with Mrs. Mazur, who appreciated her no-nonsense demeanor, while Janina worked with Kasia up in the youth reading room. Every day at four, they met in one of the rooms on the upper floor with one of the instructors, Dr. Bykowski, to be educated in librarian studies. It wasn't the full course since they had yet to complete school, but enough to orient them in the library.

The canteen that fed the employees lodging in the library during the siege had remained open for library employees, a free lunch to help stretch their meager wages. In the following three weeks of their employment, Zofia and Janina found themselves there on lunch breaks. Zofia ladled sour rye soup into a bowl and took a piece of bread and a hard-boiled egg.

Janina followed suit. "My parents registered us with the city as Jewish."

Zofia tried to keep the concern from her face, but couldn't stop the bubble of worry from rising in her thoughts. "You don't have to move, do you?"

They both had seen the Jewish quarter, now prickling with barbed wire around the perimeter and plastered with warnings of disease. More of the poisonous slander to turn the Poles against the Jews.

Janina shook her head. "We haven't been told anything about relocating. I'm sure we'll be fine." She slid into a chair at an empty table. "And at least now with being at the library, my work card will prevent me from being picked up for forced labor."

The forced labor mandate ordered all Jews between the ages of fourteen and sixty to work unless they had proof of employment, such as the one now always on Janina's person.

Already there had been terrible stories about Jews being made to perform abysmal tasks under the name of "forced labor," like cleaning the floor with their underwear, then being made to put them back on, or old men having to move the heavy rubble left behind after the Nazi bombardment—useless tasks that had no purpose but to demean.

Indignation burned inside Zofia, hotter than the phosphorus flame of an incendiary. The Nazis would pay for what they were doing, and she would be there to fight them every step of the way.

Zofia squelched her rage for Janina's sake and dropped into the opposite chair. "How have your parents been?"

Janina lifted a spoonful of soup, holding it to cool as steam curled from the pale brown liquid. "Papa was able to get money out before they restricted our access to the banks. Your father gave him the idea. I think there's someone he's working with to secure the store for Papa as well." She blew on the soup again and then took a careful bite.

Janina's father owned one of the more prestigious art galleries on Mazowiecka Street. The area known for fine art and jewelry shops had grown popular with Nazis recently, as priceless pieces could be bought for a steal with the overinflated purchasing power of the reichsmark.

"It isn't right how your family is being treated." Zofia picked up her own spoon, but while she usually loved the tart saltiness of the fermented rye-based soup, disgust curdled away her appetite.

"Mama says we must make do with life as it is now," Janina said. "Has there been any mention of Mayor Starzyński in the *Courier*?"

The mayor had been arrested at the beginning of the occupation, then released, then arrested again. Only there was no immediate release the second time, and many suspected the worst.

Papa received the *Courier*, that vile newspaper printed by Germans. *Better to know your enemy*, he stated. But even as he skimmed through the slanderous articles about how Jews wanted to steal land, food, and wealth from Poles, his jaw grew tighter. Even worse was the number of people who believed those repugnant stories.

"There's been no mention of Mayor Starzyński." Zofia stirred her soup, moving it around the bowl. "Though I doubt they would publicly make him a martyr."

Much as she didn't want to think of it, he was likely already dead, killed in private, away from public eyes. Mayor Starzyński had been a hero during the siege. Acknowledgment of his death would incite the masses.

"I hope you're not discussing any book club matters." Danuta settled into the chair beside Zofia.

Kasia remained standing, her tray in her hands. "Do you mind if we sit with you?"

"Of course not." Janina edged over to make room for Kasia, who joined them at the table.

"I scheduled the conference room for Friday afternoon for us, the one in the new pavilion." Danuta bit into her bread and swallowed. "So everyone has three more days to read *Metamorphosis*."

"She read it again last week and has been so excited to discuss it with the anti-Hitler book club," Kasia explained.

"We really need a new name," Danuta added around another mouthful of bread.

Zofia didn't bother to hide her sigh. The club had never been named anything and she hadn't wanted to invite any of them, especially when the meeting would only be steeped with memories of Maria. Zofia opened her mouth, but Janina nudged her foot under the table, a silent warning. After all, they couldn't lose their jobs at the library, especially not when Janina's was so important now.

Zofia plastered a pleasant smile on her face, though it felt tight and brittle. "We can also discuss the name on Friday if you like."

Metamorphosis was not a long book and once Zofia set aside the discomfort of reading it without Maria, she very much enjoyed the strange story. Admittedly, a man waking up as a giant beetle wasn't initially Zofia's idea of a fun read, but there was so much more to the thematic layers of the novel.

Friday came quickly and whatever intimacy had existed within their little club now evaporated in light of the expansive conference room and rows of hard-backed wooden chairs. Squares of overhead lights flickered on in the ceiling, while the sun streamed in from the abundant line of windows along the side wall.

Danuta went to the podium.

"No." Zofia dropped her bag on a chair, the telltale, hollow clunk of a bottle muffled from its center. She ignored Janina's curious expression. "If we're doing this, it's on the same level, so we can talk as equals."

Danuta shrugged and the four of them pulled the sturdy chairs into a semicircle.

"This book was gross." Kasia wrinkled her nose with a laugh. "I can't imagine being a bug."

"What do you think your family would do if you woke up like Gregor?" Janina asked.

Kasia tilted her head, her expression almost dreamlike. "My mother would make sure I was well cared for. She wouldn't hide me away like Gregor's family did."

Zofia could see how Kasia would be well cared for. Her mother was a nurse at a convalescent home, a woman whose heart was made of gold. Her father had been a soldier in the war, now serving in a camp. But when he'd been in Warsaw, he was the kind of parent who was always laughing and enjoying time with his family.

Janina's parents would also help her if she woke up as a giant bug. Zofia already knew that. For her, however, Matka might disown her; Papa would want to study her. Antek would have definitely helped her.

Antek and Janina, of course.

A pang of longing struck Zofia for her brother. Still, there had been no word from him, as if the war had swallowed him up.

"I think the point of the novel is about more than what family would do to help." Danuta looked up at the ceiling thoughtfully. "It's about how being the one who's responsible for everything is overwhelming and, at times, isolating."

The thoughtful response was intriguing to Zofia, not only how Danuta skillfully dodged answering the original question about her own family, but also her depth of perception. Even more, it opened the conversation for the group to explore this layer of Kafka's great work.

The discussion went from the support of loved ones to the sacrifices people will go to for their family, the way Gregor did. It was a telling conversation that demonstrated Danuta's obvious avoidance of the discussion of her parents and a hardness in her gaze when Kasia continued to praise her own mother's constant affection.

Maybe Danuta's life stung with constant disapproval the way Zofia's did with Matka. And perhaps that might be why Danuta was always so keen on trying to flex the strength of her vocabulary and comprehension.

The hour flew by more swiftly and enjoyably than Zofia had been expecting.

"Kasia, why don't you choose the next book?" she offered. "We can each take turns, but it has to be one that Hitler doesn't want anyone to read."

"Quickly," Danuta added. "Before they ban all our books here too."

Zofia frowned at her. "You shouldn't joke about such things."

But Danuta wasn't smiling. "I wasn't joking."

A chill skated down Zofia's spine.

Kasia clasped her hands in front of her chest, her lips pressed together in consideration. "How about *The Time Machine* by H. G. Wells?"

Antek had loved H. G. Wells and the collection of his books still remained back at the apartment.

But it was also an ideal moment to reveal what Zofia brought to the meeting.

"I thought at the close of each of our discussions—" she dug in her bag and produced the bottle of Baczewski, a brand of vodka so famous, that it had been genericized so the name and the spirits were synonymous "—we should toast to Maria."

Zofia thought Janina would balk at doing a shot of vodka on their lunch break before going back to work, but she surprised them all by being the first to reach for the bottle. And anyway, they weren't drinking copious amounts. No more than anyone might take with a bit of pepper for a stomachache, or to brace oneself for walking outside on a particularly icy day.

"To Maria." Janina put her lips to the bottle and drank in

a single hard gulp. Danuta was next, then Kasia, with Zofia going last.

"Schnell." The German order for someone to hurry cut through the quiet conference room. It came from outside the door.

The four looked at each other. Thus far the Germans had left the main library branch alone. The University of Warsaw had not been so lucky, as their library had been commandeered by the German police. Rumors were horrible: a tailor's shop had been assembled in the reading center, and motorcycle repairs were being done in the manuscript room. Most egregious was the auditorium, which had been turned into a stable with the luxurious reading tabletops being used as horse stalls.

And now the Nazis were in the main branch of the Warsaw Library.

Zofia opened the door to find a Wehrmacht soldier with Miss Laska stumbling ahead of him, paper clutched in her hand and her glasses slightly askew.

"I don't understand." There was a frail tremble to Miss Laska's voice and wisps of cottony white hair fluttered around her head. "I don't speak German."

Zofia motioned for everyone else to leave and approached Miss Laska. "What's going on?" she asked, speaking Polish out of precaution.

"Zofia." The older woman gripped Zofia's arm in a viselike hold, shoving her slightly away. "You don't need to be here."

The Wehrmacht soldier regarded them with a cold, hard stare.

Zofia stood her ground. "What's the meaning of this?"

Miss Laska released Zofia, her tiny body suddenly more diminutive than before. "I don't understand this man. He keeps yelling and I tell him I don't speak German." She thrust the list at Zofia, half of the page crumpled from where she held it tightly in her fist. "I don't know what this is."

Zofia took it from her and recognized the heavy German font. Quickly, she skimmed over it and her heart gave a little stutter.

These were books to be removed from the library's shelves.

Banned books.

She looked up and found the soldier staring at her with narrowed eyes. Her shock had been too great to remember to keep her features blank. Now he knew she spoke German.

It would be a mistake she would not make again.

"These books need to be removed from your library," the Wehrmacht soldier said.

Zofia lowered the list and stared at him. His dark hair was combed over with so much pomade, it gleamed like plastic beneath his cap and his eyes were a flat gray.

"What are you going to do with them when they're taken off the shelves?" she demanded in German. Were they going to be piled into a bonfire and set ablaze like the ones in Berlin six years ago?

"It is none of your concern."

"It is my concern." She gestured to Miss Laska, who was watching the exchange, spectacles still lopsided. "Why else would you be aggressive with an old woman over some books?"

He was unperturbed by her remark. "These books pose a risk to Polish-German relations and must be omitted from your lending floor."

"Your abysmal treatment toward an old woman is what will ruin Polish-German relations," Zofia snapped back. "She is a kind woman who is gentle—"

He moved so fast that Zofia didn't see his fist until it forcefully connected with the side of her jaw and sent her reeling. Miss Laska cried out and when the world stopped spinning long enough for Zofia to reorient herself, she found the older woman in front of her, blocking the man from Zofia with her own fragile body.

Zofia lurched to her feet. The right side of her face ached in pulses that matched her heartbeat, but she edged ahead of Miss Laska protectively.

"Give him what he wants," Miss Laska whispered.

Zofia glared defiantly at the soldier and replied in Polish, "He wants our books."

"It isn't worth your life to protect them."

Wasn't it?

Zofia regarded the list. There were well over a hundred book titles. If they were destroyed, the knowledge within those texts would turn to ash with them.

Like all those destroyed books at Krasiński Library.

She recognized a few titles, ones that promoted socialism, and acceptance of all, books that encouraged fraternity and love. Without that, what was left?

Hate.

The vodka burned in her stomach, though her outburst hadn't been inspired by the mouthful of alcohol. It had been borne of indignation, from witnessing the suffering of others and blazing with impotence at the injustice of it all.

The Nazis had already taken so much, and now they wanted Poland's books.

"I think we should speak with Dr. Bachulski about this," Zofia said in a hard tone. The softspoken library director would know what to do. But Zofia didn't have the authority to be the voice behind this decision.

Miss Laska understood the director's name despite Zofia speaking in German, and came to Zofia's side, nodding vigorously. Zofia led the way down the hall to the reception desk to ask after Dr. Bachulski when a group of Nazi soldiers emerged from the main reading room.

They held the director pinned between three of them.

Dr. Bachulski, usually so well composed, was flushed about the face, his eyes flashing behind thick glasses and his graying hair was mussed. "Don't let them take it." His shoulders wrenched as he tried to pull from their grasp. "They want the Social Museum and if they have it, I vow we'll not see even a pamphlet from it again."

Zofia and Miss Laska drew up short.

The Social Museum was a newer piece to the library, filled with artifacts and details about life during the Great War as well as other various historical pieces from Poland's past.

"Don't let them have it," Dr. Bachulski cried. "Don't let them have any of it."

He was led swiftly to the stairs, his glossy leather shoes skidding over several steps. The soldiers tightened their grasp on him, so he remained upright without pulling them down with him.

The officer leading the Nazi soldiers stopped at the top of the stairs and glared at every patron and employee within his line of sight. "If any of you think about opposing our rules, you'll be joining your director in Pawiak."

At the mention of Warsaw's prison, the breath squeezed out of Zofia. The glossy-haired Wehrmacht soldier beside Miss Laska skewered her with a look that needed no translation.

"Fine," Zofia said through gritted teeth. "I'll get you the books."

Zofia strode home at a clipped pace, not caring if she aroused Nazi suspicion. Let them see her. Let them encourage her wrath.

She needed something more than the November air to cool the anger flooding her body. The afternoon had been spent beneath a Nazi shadow as she pored through the detailed card catalog to identify books that required removal.

They swore the books she was to remove would eventually end up safe behind closed doors, but she expected they'd land in a pyre. Likely a similar fate was being meted out for the contents of the Social Museum, which had begun to disappear one box at a time.

It was then she noticed that the sidewalk under her feet was now smooth, fully repaired from the devastation of the siege. No doubt through the efforts of Jewish men and women commandeered for forced labor.

At the corner of a fence, a burned-out candle remained, a slip-up of otherwise efficient German cleaning after All Saints' Day on the first of November. The somber holiday was all the more so this year with candles lit throughout Warsaw for their many dead. While the Nazis were thick in the streets that day as they cast each other wary looks, they did not attempt to quell the mourning. The next morning, however, there wasn't a single candle visible on the streets.

Except for this one: a lone hollow glass bowl left behind with a pool of spent wax and a withered blackened wick. It was a reminder to Zofia that efficiency was not perfect. Not every *i* could always be dotted, and not every *ł* slashed with a middle tilde. The Nazis would have a weakness and somehow the Poles would find it.

Despite the events of the day, Zofia's mind continually wandered back to the conversation the book club shared about *Metamorphosis*, though she couldn't understand what exactly was prodding her thoughts like a sore wound. Not until she returned home that evening to find Matka sitting at the kitchen table, looking out into the street.

"It's about time you're home." Matka rose, her face tense. "Sit and I'll warm your dinner."

Zofia did as she was told and Matka rushed about the kitchen, heels clacking over the tiles. From the first bombing, her mother had swept the family to safety like sheep herded from a wolf. Despite strafed breadlines and a lack of electricity and water, she had kept them from going hungry. When the Nazis marched into Warsaw and "generously" opened their kitchens to the starving citizens with fanfares of celebratory accordion music, she still went. She had endured the humiliation of their propaganda film crews to obtain that food for her family when many others had turned away in disgust.

And she had done it all entirely alone.

Papa had been busy with his work. Antek was gone to war. And Zofia…

Zofia had been selfish in her insistence of fighting Matka at every opportunity.

And if Matka would have turned into a giant bug, like Gregor in Kafka's *Metamorphosis*, Zofia grudgingly had to concede to herself that she might not have been better than Gregor's family in her mother's care.

Suddenly Zofia understood the recurrent sore spot in her mind that had been opened by their discussion of *Metamorphosis.* It was her own shame for how she had regarded her mother, the woman who incessantly sacrificed for the family.

Zofia thanked her mother for the food and readily answered questions about her day when Matka asked. But she didn't tell her mother about the library director's arrest or the books that were taken.

Despite the appearance of strength, there was a fragility to Matka these days. It was in the quiver of her fingers when she pinched a cigarette between her fingers, and in the way her muscles tensed at the slightest sound. It was also in the desperate gleam in her eye every time Zofia left the apartment, as though Matka feared she might not return.

However, Zofia fully intended to tell Papa of the events at the library. She needed an ally in this war and knew no man stronger than her own father to have at her side.

Chapter 8

THERE WAS NO MORE room for books.

Zofia peered into the open cavity in the hardwood floor of her father's study where piles of books now occupied the once-hollow space. Papa handed her a copy of *All Quiet on the Western Front*.

She eyed the book judiciously. "We can't fit that in here. There's no space left."

"That can't be right." Long hours at the hospital during the siege, and now his forced continuation to work for the occupation, had etched hard lines in his brow. They creased deeper into new paths of weariness as he sat back on his heels and ran through a careful mental calculation.

"You gave me twenty-three, which is three more than you estimated would fit," Zofia explained. "There isn't room."

Papa examined the cover in his hands and his lips pinched hard together. It wasn't easy for him, she knew. Books had always been his dearest friends. In each text, he'd always said there was a world to be explored and loved. They had gotten him through the days after his mother's death and through the trenches of the Great War.

How could he possibly choose one from the other to leave behind?

Especially when they had included Antek's H. G. Wells collection beneath the floorboards. Those titles weren't on the list at the library yet, but with the books having once been burned in Berlin, Zofia was certain there would be another round coming at some point.

Already there had been a call out to civilians to give up their private book collections. But without the same fatal threat that had been paired with the order to relinquish their radios, most people ignored the notice.

"There must be somewhere else we can hide this." Papa extended *All Quiet on the Western Front* toward her, his hazel eyes brimming with such hope, she couldn't say no.

"I'll manage," she conceded. "But only this one." Surely there was a place in her room to hide the book, maybe a floorboard or two might be loosened like those in Papa's study.

He patted her cheek affectionately and got that familiar sad look about him when she reminded him of his mother. Though he didn't say as much, she knew he was thinking it—that she had her grandmother's eyes.

She would take special care to ensure the book was completely hidden in her room. The odds of their home being searched were slim, but it was better to take precautions. Especially with the Gestapo setting up their headquarters across the street at 25 Szucha Street. Papa said the proximity made their apartment less likely to appear suspicious, but Zofia's skin still crawled with unease nonetheless.

The bookstores throughout Warsaw were affected too, their windows now filled with pictures of Nazi heroes and ugly swastika flags rather than the glossy covers of new books. Their shelves had likewise been purged of the list of texts the library had been forced to remove; 156 titles in all.

Papa fit the floorboard into place over the collection of hidden books. "You know the excuse of infectious disease in the Jewish quarter is a lie," he said abruptly.

The schools had closed down again, this time citing the spread of illness under the implication that it had come from the Jewish area of the city.

"It's all propaganda to make Poles think Jews are spreading disease." A muscle worked in Papa's jaw. "It's not true. I suspect that conditions may become worse for our Jewish brethren, that this is only the beginning." He was speaking slowly, thoughtfully, the way he did when he wanted to ensure the weight of each word.

"What do you mean?" she asked. "Is this because of the armbands?"

The *Courier* had recently announced that on the first of December, all Jews above the age of ten would be required to wear a white armband with a blue Star of David on their right arm.

"Yes." Papa folded the rug back over the replaced floorboards and pushed to his feet. "As well as the dissemination of all these lies. If too many people live in one location, as in the cordoned-off Jewish quarter, it can indeed breed disease. If that happens, I've been in correspondence with a man named Dr. Weigl with whom I worked during the Great War. His letters are in the second drawer of my desk, tucked in a seam at the top."

Hidden.

Zofia's pulse kicked up a notch.

Papa went to his desk and pressed his long fingers on the smooth top, directly over the drawer he'd referenced. "Make sure you stay in communication with him. If not for you and your mother, then for Janina and her family."

Prickles of gooseflesh rose on Zofia's arms.

But all the questions that immediately rose within her were

silenced by the rumble of a covered truck pulling into the Gestapo Headquarters. Papa slid to the side of the window, bringing her with him, and stared at the building across the street. The hooded vehicle was not the first to arrive there that day. It likely would not be the last, and something about that seemed to cause Papa great worry.

People did not hide their interest as Zofia and Janina walked down the street.

"Everyone is looking at me." Janina adjusted the white band on her arm.

This was exactly why Zofia had insisted that she accompany Janina from her home to the library. Usually they met at Savior's Square, a good halfway point that led them to Koszykowa Street. The square was open and lovely with the impressive Church of the Holy Savior rising up into the sky in all its elegant splendor.

Yes, going to pick up Janina from her apartment was twice as much walking and the December wind stung Zofia's cheeks, but she would not have Janina go out for the first time with her armband alone.

Zofia discreetly glared back at a boy who stuck his tongue out at Janina. "Not everyone is staring."

For those who regarded the brilliant white band against Janina's black coat with hostility, there were far more who continued on their path, their focus tucked on the movement of their feet. Zofia wondered which of them did not approve of the armbands, but were resolved to smother their objections.

"How do you think the children will react to it?" Janina asked.

Zofia considered the small group who still gathered in the youth reading room every day to hear Janina read to them. She was so engaged in the books and made a new voice for each character in ways that made the children smile and laugh.

"I don't think they will care," Zofia answered honestly. "But there might be questions. Let's think of some answers you can give them as we walk."

As they talked, Janina seemed to allow herself to be distracted by the conversation. At least until a Nazi brushed past them, intentionally pushing Janina as he did.

Zofia nearly said something to him, but stopped when he approached a wooden cross with flowers and candles set up at the intersection of Polna Street and Koszykowa Street. Crosses and stone shrines to saints had popped up at most crossroads in Warsaw, organized by the staunchly Catholic community in silent protest to the recent closures that limited their time at churches to only two hours on Sunday morning.

A woman prayed in front of the cross, a green-and-yellow sprigged kerchief tied around her head. The Nazi shoved her out of the way and knocked the cross and candles to the ground. There was a quiet pop as the candle's jar broke, sending beads of hot wax spattering the surrounding area. Before the woman could protest, he stomped the cross with his booted foot, splintering it against the cobblestones amid crushed flowers.

The sight was not uncommon. No more than the spectators who bore witness in silent indignation.

Zofia hated that fear, the stink of it as pervasive as fire smoke had been in September. Even she had fallen prey when she gathered the listed books after the library director was dragged away. He'd been in Pawiak Prison ever since, and Zofia could gather no information regarding his release.

The rage of it all simmered under her skin, burning hot in her veins.

Zofia pulled Janina away from the scene. If nothing else, it was a diversion from the prying eyes on her new armband.

After leaving Janina upstairs at the youth reading room, responding to questions they had anticipated on their walk over, Zofia rushed down to the warehouse. Trepidation crawled down her spine as she did so. Fulfilling the General Government's list had left her unsettled. Every day she waited for the presentation of another.

She didn't think she could comply with another order.

Darek was in the warehouse when she arrived and she swallowed a groan, with no choice but to stand near him as she deposited her coat on the rack.

He grinned at her. "Zofia, right?"

She nodded, but didn't address him back. He didn't need to know she had remembered his name. It would only encourage his attention.

"Is my aunt here?" he asked.

Zofia left the scarf wrapped around her neck to ward off the chill in the warehouse. "I'm not sure yet. I've only just arrived."

He held out a brown-wrapped parcel. "I brought this, if you wouldn't mind giving it to her—it's a book."

Zofia glanced down at the package. "I can do that."

He handed it to her, studying her carefully as she accepted the item. A wave of self-consciousness rippled through her. "Why are you looking at me like that?"

"Your face," he murmured, as he tilted his head with an intense focus. His eyes were a warm, rich brown, like velvety milk chocolate. And far too probing for her liking.

She stepped away from him, ready to drop the book he'd given her. "What about my face?"

He didn't reclaim the distance she'd put between them, but he did continue to stare. "It's perfectly symmetrical. I mean *perfectly.*"

It was her turn to stare.

Symmetrical?

"That is the strangest compliment I've ever received." She refrained from adding that it was the only compliment from a man she'd ever received.

But then, her face wasn't one to warrant praise. She had heavy brows that punctuated her expressions more than she liked, sharp features, and a strong jaw to go with her strong opinions. Her wide mouth was the only thing soft about her, which she'd inherited from her mother. Except what looked elegant on Matka simply made Zofia appear sullen.

Darek shook his head slowly, his eyes fixed on her. "No, what I mean is...you are absolutely beautiful."

Zofia didn't mask her irritation. "I already said that I would give this to Mrs. Mazur. You don't need to flatter me."

To her surprise, a flush spread over his cheeks. "I've just never seen anyone whose face is so perfect."

"No one's ever said that before," she said wryly. If the jests were to come, let them be sooner rather than later and end his charade.

But his expression didn't change. "Other people don't look at things as I do."

She nodded, ready for the conversation to end.

"Do you think you might want to have dinner with me sometime?"

This took her aback. "Why?" she asked in a feeble effort to stall. How was she to possibly respond to such a question?

"Because we have to eat." He lifted one shoulder in a simple shrug and ran a hand through his brown hair. It fell perfectly back into place.

Heat flushed in Zofia's cheeks. The Jews were being forced to wear armbands on the street, opening them to hostility that the General Government had encouraged with their inflammatory newspaper. People were being arrested for harmless infractions like owning a radio, and books were being stripped off the library's shelves. This was no time for romance or falling in love. This wasn't a plot in a Marta Krakowska novel. This was real life.

"I don't think this is the right time for such things," Zofia replied.

Darek grimaced. "No—you're right."

Janina would be upset with Zofia for being so curt with him.

Zofia sighed and tried again, more gently this time. "It's just that with the General Government controlling us, and the way they are treating my friend's family…and all the Jews in Warsaw…"

He nodded. "You're right. It was a horrible idea. I shouldn't have even asked."

Zofia tried to give him a little smile.

Maybe that was going too far, because he still pressed on. "Something is bothering you. I could tell as soon as I saw you. What is it?"

Zofia shook her head, not wanting to talk about it, and picked up a stack of damaged books that would need to be replaced once library funding was approved.

"Are the Nazis back in the library?" he asked.

"No, but they're still doing their damage anyway, aren't they?" Vitriol made her statement come out harsh.

"Did you see the Copernicus statue?"

Zofia frowned in confusion.

"The plaque was changed to claim he is now German instead of Polish." Darek scoffed with disgust. "But there's something we can do to stop them."

Zofia gave him her full attention. "And what is that?"

"Maybe we'll discuss it more another time." Naturally, when she finally wanted him to stay, he turned on his heel and left.

Several days passed at the library, but Darek didn't come back again and Zofia refused to ask Mrs. Mazur after him. If word of Zofia's interest came back around to him, he would never leave her alone.

Once upon a time, December had been Zofia's favorite month. She and Antek would have festooned the apartment with sparkling decorations while Papa hauled a crisp-smelling tree into the living area. And then there was Hanukkah, which she'd often celebrated with Janina and her family enjoying Bubbe's delicious recipes, all made with love. The holiday, often referred to as a

Festival of Lights, was extraordinarily dark in 1939. Zofia had seen as much in Janina's dulled demeanor, and felt it in her own diminished spirit as well.

Any attempts at celebration were further hindered by the newly implemented rationing that limited their butter and sugar and other necessities for baking through the holidays.

It was a particularly gray day in December when Zofia noticed Mrs. Mazur whispering with the librarian from the magazine reading room. The librarian left and Mrs. Mazur put a hand to her mouth.

Unease slithered low in Zofia's belly and she quickly went to her supervisor. "What is it?"

"Oh, Zofia." Mrs. Mazur lowered her hand to the desk. "They've fired everyone who is Jewish."

The blood drained from Zofia's face, leaving a coolness in her cheeks. "When?"

Mrs. Mazur's brow flinched with grief. "Just now."

Zofia didn't stay to hear another word. She raced out to the hallway connected to the main reading room and abruptly stopped at the sound of trudging feet on the stairs. A line of men and women descended single file, a white armband with a blue star on each of their right arms.

"They can't do this," Zofia said, her voice too weak to be heard.

Then she caught sight of Mrs. Berman and Janina behind her.

"They can't do this," Zofia repeated, louder now.

Janina shook her head adamantly. "Don't get yourself dismissed over this."

"I don't want to work here if this is how Jewish employees are treated."

"It wasn't the director," Mrs. Berman said under her breath.

Zofia followed the discreet flick of her gaze to where a stiff-backed elderly man watched them, his face calm with cold indifference.

"Stay at the library," Janina begged. "For the two of us. You can sneak books to me and we can talk about them."

Zofia clamped her back teeth together, forcing herself to stay silent, letting the rage blaze inside her as whatever thread of control was holding her together threatened to snap.

A somberness hung over the library. Even though Janina had been in a different department than Zofia, the pain of her absence was poignant.

A hooded truck turned down the street behind Zofia on her way home after the long, heartbroken shift at work. It pulled into Gestapo Headquarters and a frisson of fear shuddered through her. The deep rumble of the engine was unsettling, the way it reverberated ominously in her chest, and left choking exhaust in its wake.

She quickly entered her building to escape its menace and climbed the stairs.

The uneasy feeling from seeing the Gestapo's hooded truck did not abate. In fact, the closer she came to her apartment, the stronger the sense of dread.

Something wasn't right.

She raced up the last few flights of stairs to her apartment. Fingers shaking, she pushed the key into the lock and the door swung open.

A figure was curled into one corner of the couch, illuminated by every light in the house.

Matka.

Zofia let the door close behind her with a slam. Matka's head snapped up at the sound. Her hair was disheveled, the neat updo from the morning jutting up in uneven bumps and wild, wiry strays. The cosmetics she dusted on her lashes to darken them now ran in watery black on the puffy skin beneath her eyes.

Zofia's bag slipped from her shoulder and thunked to the

floor. Without bothering to take off her shoes, she rushed to her mother.

"Is it Antek?"

Matka didn't reply.

"Answer me," Zofia demanded. "Is it Antek?"

Her heart was in her throat, its beat thundering in her ears. *Don't let it be Antek. Don't let it be Antek. Don't let it be—*

"Your father," Matka choked out.

Zofia's whole world fell away and she staggered back. Reeling. Uncomprehending.

Her gaze went to Papa's study, where the light had been left on. She ran, his name a mangled cry on her lips.

Matka's wracking sobs followed her as Zofia drew to a stop at the threshold. A lamp had been tipped over, its beam cast crookedly across the floor. Papers that were usually piled neatly were scattered off the desk.

The bookshelves were completely empty.

"Papa," she called, her voice breaking.

"He's gone." There was a flatness to the way her mother spoke, a statement of an inarguable fact.

Zofia shook her head, but even as she did, the truth sank in. Her chest went so tight, she couldn't breathe properly. She gasped in a mouthful of air that didn't seem to take and the surreal slant of light across the floor wavered as her knees gave.

The wall caught her, holding her upright until she could regain her bearings.

"He's been arrested." Matka was at her side somehow.

"How? What happened?"

"They didn't say." Matka clutched the cross at her neck. "They knocked so hard when they came that they nearly broke down the door. I tried not to let them in, but they forced past me and to the study and—" She put a hand to her chest and dissolved into fresh tears.

Something caught Zofia's attention behind the desk, amid a

carpet of churned papers. She stepped forward and found a single book remained, green leather with a glint of copper at its center. Lifting it, she examined it. A bullet was lodged in the cover, as if the book had caused such offense that some soldier felt it necessary to shoot it straight through the heart.

That's when she remembered the letters.

She glanced up and found Matka gone, the sound of her weeping echoing from the living area. As silently as possible, Zofia slid open the second drawer. Its contents were missing, disemboweled onto the floor. But that wasn't what she wanted. Instead, she slipped her hand up to the construction of the drawer, fingertips skimming the rough wood there until they met a smooth expanse of paper.

She pinched her prize and dislodged it, finding the correspondence from Dr. Weigl. The pages trembled in her hand as she slid to the ground, weighed by the burden her father had left on her shoulders, and by the realization that he had known this day would come.

Chapter 9

WHEN THE POLISH POLICE opened their doors the following morning, Zofia was already there, waiting to inquire after her father.

The police officer picked a piece of lint from the sleeve of his blue uniform, barely listening as she told him of her father's arrest. He leaned to the side of his chair with disinterest. "If your father had books that were confiscated, he likely is in Pawiak Prison."

"They weren't confiscated, they were stolen," Zofia corrected.

"Pawiak Prison," he repeatedly dryly, then sipped from a mug and idly examined the paper in front of him, ostensibly done with her.

Knowing she would get nowhere with the police, she left the building and made her way to the block-shaped prison, fully prepared to do whatever necessary to secure her father's freedom. The interior was dark and desolate, the Nazi presence oppressive and all-consuming.

Somewhere in those walls, Papa was sitting in a cell amid the frigid December temperature that dropped several degrees inside the prison.

A Gestapo officer behind a desk lifted a brow at her.

Zofia stepped forward, her back straight. "I was told my father, Jan Nowak, is here."

The man's eyes lowered to peruse a stack of papers. With a perfunctory flick of his wrist to the final page, he looked up with a short nod. "*Ja*, he is here."

"Why?" Zofia demanded. "He has done nothing wrong."

"If he didn't do anything wrong, he wouldn't be here."

She stared at him, refusing to be so easily put off. "What can I do to get him out?"

"That is impossible."

"Nothing is impossible."

"Perhaps he was arrested for being insolent." The man's mouth thinned into a hard, unforgiving line. "What did you say your name was?"

Zofia clenched her teeth to keep from throwing a nasty remark in his face.

"He is allowed to receive parcels," the guard finally said, as if offering her a prized concession. Anything to make her leave, most likely.

With no other options, she accepted the unfair compromise and returned that afternoon with a box containing food from her own rationed allotment, a heavy scarf, Papa's thickest coat, and woolen socks. At least her father could be fed and warm until they found someone to set him free.

Later that night when her mind had cleared somewhat, she withdrew the hidden letters from Dr. Weigl and composed a message to him, fully aware that the correspondence would be read by discerning eyes.

Dr. Weigl,

Continuing my father's endeavors, please correspond with me going forward. It would be best to reach me at the main Warsaw Library branch at 26 Koszykowa Street.

With Sincere Appreciation,

Zofia Nowak

The library was often in receipt of so much mail that a letter from the doctor would not stand out, certainly less so than at their home on Szucha Street.

Christmas passed with sorrow replacing ceremony. Even if they had tried to celebrate, it would not have been the same without Papa and Antek.

The library was closed briefly for the holidays. Without work to occupy her time and desperate for a distraction, she read *The Time Machine*, losing herself in a fantastical world set in the future. In that story, she discovered she enjoyed H. G. Wells's writing. Partly for the connection to Antek, but also for the entertainment of the tale itself and the journey into a world she could never have dreamed up on her own.

And she never would have read it had Kasia not recommended it for their book club.

After the holidays, a new face awaited them back at the library. Herr Nagiel, a slender short man with a severe part and a thin turtle-like mouth.

"He's the new German commissioner of the library," Miss Laska whispered to Zofia as they gathered in the main reading room. "You should tell him you speak German."

Zofia said nothing as the man took his place before the crowd of employees he'd assembled.

He brushed at the lapel of his dark suit then addressed them with a self-important lift of his head. "There will be some changes going forward."

Zofia's palms prickled with sweat and the crowd around her shifted uneasily.

If Herr Nagiel noticed their agitation, he didn't acknowledge it as he continued, "We will need all English and French books to be removed from the floor. They will no longer be available to lend to readers. German books will be separated and placed in a new reading room for Germans only."

Nür fur Deutsche.

For Germans only.

Signs bearing such verbiage were sprouting all over Warsaw like weeds. They were on the front seats of trams, displayed at the best hotels and restaurants, and scribed in bold writing on the windows of the most elegant shops. They were not as offensive as the other notices declaring 'Entrance is forbidden to Poles, Jews, and dogs' that were just as prevalent throughout the city.

Now such signs were going to infiltrate the library.

"There will no longer be budgets approved for purchasing more books." Herr Nagiel stared out at the crowd as though willing someone to challenge him. "And there will be staff reductions coming as well as closures of smaller branches and reading rooms."

A pall fell over the employees and any face that might have been brightened by holiday festivities was now gray.

Miss Laska gestured to Zofia to go to Herr Nagiel after they were finally dismissed. But Zofia had no interest in putting herself to quick use for the Germans.

Before stricter rules could be implemented, the book club gathered again. Not in the conference room, as that might call attention to them, but in a warehouse toward the back of the building, one seldom used. The day of their meeting, Zofia slipped Janina into the warehouse just before the library closed.

"It's so good to be here again." Janina breathed in a deep inhale, her eyes closed.

Zofia knew what Janina was smelling, that wonderful musty, dusty scent redolent of paper and ink from countless books all stored in one area. It was an aroma she took for granted after working around it every day. Seeing the pleasure it wrought in Janina renewed Zofia's appreciation.

Kasia and Danuta arrived together and embraced Janina warmly. There was no hesitation in accepting her as they always had, nor was there any mention of Janina's armband, which she had insisted on still wearing once inside.

"I confess, being someone who doesn't care for science fiction, I wasn't looking forward to this book." Danuta shot a look at Kasia, who flushed slightly. "But it was really excellent."

"I hadn't expected to like it either, but I really did," Zofia admitted.

"The entire time I was reading it, I couldn't help but imagine having my own time machine," Janina said. "But I wouldn't go as far into the future as the Time Traveller, nor would I go as far back. I would have gone just a few months into the past. Maybe even a year, to see if the world could be altered with one small change."

She didn't have to elaborate. Zofia had felt the same way reading the story, wishing to wind time back to June 1939. Knowing what they all did now, they could warn everyone to escape. Maria would be alive and so would Janina's grandparents. And if Zofia could convince her parents to leave Poland, Antek would never have gone to war and Papa would not be in an icy cell in Pawiak Prison.

"This was a particularly impactful book to read right now," Danuta added. "This is a story about making the choices you know are right, even when the rest of the world feels confusing and disorienting. It's knowing who you are and choosing kindness and love; like the Time Traveller did."

The shuffle of approaching feet sounded during her last few words and she quickly went silent. The footsteps did not stop.

"Take off your armband," Zofia mouthed the instructions and indicated Janina's armband.

Janina's eyes bulged and she shook her head vigorously in vehement refusal. "I could be arrested," she mouthed back.

"Is someone here?" a male voice asked in Polish.

Better Polish than German. Even still, while most employees at the library were trustworthy, there were several who looked out for themselves before anyone else. Polish did not necessarily mean safe.

They all remained silent, pressed against the wall of books about nature, wishing to disappear. Zofia edged closer to Janina and leaned her body in front of her friend, obscuring the armband.

The footsteps were on the other side of the aisle now, the man's trousers visible. Janina trembled with a fear so tangible, Zofia wanted to attack whoever was coming with her bare hands. The man stopped and turned, the toes of his shoes pointing toward the aisle they were in, and stepped forward.

Darek.

He appeared at the end of their aisle, jerking back slightly in surprise. "Why didn't you answer when I called?"

"Shhh..." Danuta hissed through a finger against her lips.

Darek scanned the surrounding area. "Why are we being quiet?"

"In case the Germans come," Zofia replied frostily. "Why are you here?"

Janina relaxed at her side, no longer quaking in fear.

"I was coming by to see if my aunt needed any help." Darek glanced down at Danuta, who held a copy of *The Time Machine* in her hand. "I love that book. Was that what you were talking about?" He searched their faces. "It is, isn't it?"

"Yes," Kasia replied. "We've been picking out books banned by Hitler to read."

"The anti-Hitler book club, I think is what you called it?" Danuta asked, looking quizzically at Zofia.

Darek grimaced. "That's a horrible name. And a dangerous one too."

"That was never the name." Zofia threw her hands up in exasperation. But he was right about it being dangerous now.

"We were supposed to choose a new name at our last meeting," Kasia added. "But that was the day we received that list."

She didn't have to elaborate on to what she referred. The weight of the list would hang in their minds for all eternity.

"What about…?" Darek searched the air as he thought. "What about the Bandit Book Club?"

"The Bandit Book Club?" Janina repeated.

"Yeah, because of how the Reich refers to people who fight against them as bandits." He leaned casually against the bookshelf. "Seems fitting, doesn't it?"

"I love it." Danuta nodded. "The Bandit Book Club it is."

"I'm going to have to join now." He hooked a hand in his trouser pocket. "Since I named the club."

Zofia slid a look at Janina. But rather than receiving any solidarity from her friend, Janina nodded enthusiastically.

"We need to figure out what to read next," Kasia said. "Why don't you choose, since you're our newest member."

"Well, if we're reading books that Hitler is banning, we might as well start with our own recent list." He plucked the copy Zofia had been forced to work on from his pocket and ignored her strange look as to why he had it in the first place.

He pinned his index finger on the rumpled sheet. "Let's do *All Quiet on the Western Front*. There should still be some copies in the warehouse."

"Perfect." Danuta turned her attention to Zofia. "Shall we adjourn this meeting?"

Zofia pulled the bottle of vodka from her bag and held it aloft. "To Maria."

They all took a hearty drink, including Darek, who accepted the bottle from Janina and swallowed a mouthful before handing it back to Zofia. While it was unlikely he knew who Maria was, he had the good sense not to ask.

In war, there were bad people, but there were also those who were good. It was all about who one chose to surround themselves with. The Time Traveller knew that in *The Time Machine.* But even more impactful, was how one chose to act. It was a lesson Zofia vowed to remember for however long the occupation might last.

There was no fanfare as 1939 become 1940. Zofia continued to search for someone who might help free her father from Pawiak without avail. No one in the city could find a way to rival the Nazis. None were even willing to try. Nor was there any word from Dr. Weigl.

Despite being forbidden to see her father, she assembled a weekly box with warm clothes and food in the hopes it might at least bring him some comfort.

The winter had been brutal, its icy grip on Warsaw exacerbated by the fuel shortages with electricity alternating availability between houses based on location and building number, leaving everyone without at some point. She could only imagine how miserably cold the cells at Pawiak must be.

When the library opened again in 1940, Zofia found Miss Laska upstairs packing her belongings from the overly crowded desk in the manuscript room.

Zofia rushed forward to help lift a particularly heavy binder the older woman was fumbling. "What's happened?"

Miss Laska took a handkerchief from the pocket of her sweater and dabbed the pink tip of her nose. "I've been told I am no longer needed."

Zofia's mouth fell open. Miss Laska had worked for the library since 1907, when it was first assembled with donated materials from the city's residents.

"That can't be possible." Zofia shook her head. What would happen to Miss Laska with no income? And what would happen to the library without Miss Laska?

Herr Nagiel came into the room and addressed Zofia in German. "Ah, there you are, Miss Nowak. Please follow me." He nodded toward Miss Laska and switched to Polish. "Thank you again for your recommendation, Miss Laska."

Zofia shot her a look, but the older woman lowered her head to her task in silence. It was impossible to be angry when Miss Laska was only looking after Zofia, more so than she did for herself.

Herr Nagiel took Zofia to one of the reading rooms in the new pavilion, one of the larger, grander ones. The shelves had been emptied and stacks of books were in piles on the floor.

Herr Nagiel surveyed the room before regarding Zofia. "I know you've been studying under Dr. Bykowski, whom I understand is quite the expert in library education."

Zofia clenched her jaw so hard, her teeth ached, and nodded.

Herr Nagiel narrowed his eyes with interest. "Why have you not registered on the *Deutsche Volksliste* as *Volksdeutsche*?"

The German list was open to Poles whose origins had anything to do with Germany. It was an opportunity for Poles to live a better life, receive better rations, have higher paying jobs—all at the cost of their souls. Such collaboration would never be any kind of enticement for Zofia. She would rather starve than lump herself with her enemy.

"I'm fully Polish," Zofia replied. "The *Deutsche Volksliste* would not accept me."

Herr Nagiel gave an emotionless shrug. "I expect you to have this reading room ready for German residents as soon as possible. You'll be joined by several others who speak German as well, but you may begin on your own now."

Zofia later learned that nearly a third of the library's staff had been let go. Anyone too old was instructed not to return, as were newer employees who didn't understand German. If Miss Laska had not spoken up on Zofia's behalf, she too would have been turned away.

The wages at the library weren't much and most of what Zofia brought home went toward food with little left over. Still, she saved every groszy she could manage. After all, whatever money Papa had left them would not last forever.

She studied the box she assembled for Papa now. His last scarf was in there as well as a warm pair of woolen socks. There was not much food, sadly. A heel of bread and a few boiled potatoes, plus whatever vegetables could be found, which amounted to a few miserable-looking carrots. Zofia and her mother wouldn't eat for the rest of the day for the food put in there. Not that Matka had an appetite lately anyway.

With Antek gone and Papa arrested, Zofia's elegantly thin mother was slowly wasting away. She stared at nothing from the lace-curtained window in the kitchen, and plucked at the gold cross on her necklace with restless fingers. The tailor-fit persimmon dress that once swung around her calves as she rushed about now hung limp on her frame.

There was a part of Zofia that was angry at the grandparents she'd never met for having abandoned them all. Matka's parents had left without any thought for the family, and moreover, they'd left without any thought of her. As difficult as Matka could be at times, as much as Zofia even wondered if her mother truly loved her, Matka never would have abandoned Zofia or Antek the way her own parents had deserted her.

Zofia tied the package with a simple string. "I'm going to deliver this to Papa."

Matka did not reply. Zofia had not expected her to.

"I'll be back soon," Zofia reassured her anyway, and slipped from the apartment. She inhaled deeply, finding it easier to breathe in the Polish winter air that scalded her lungs than in the stuffy apartment where the heavy silence made the space seem unbearably small.

She walked the distance to Pawiak Prison. No matter how much she prepared herself for it, the awful desolation within still struck her anew as it did every time she entered. The ugly, flat gray walls, the harsh lighting that left the closed-off world ensconced in shadows. Despite the extreme cold, the odor of unwashed bodies and sickness was enough to make her empty stomach turn.

The guard sitting at the entry glared at her and she glowered right back, thrusting the box toward him. "I have a package."

"For?"

Irritation flared in Zofia. The man knew who her father was. This very guard was the one who took her parcel every week. "Jan Nowak," she answered with as much patience as she could muster.

He didn't move from his position. "He's not here."

Zofia continued to hold out the package with its simple string tie. "What do you mean he's not here? Since when? Where did he go?"

The guard shrugged and turned his attention to the newspaper on his desk.

"Where is he?" she asked, her voice trembling.

The guard ignored her.

She slapped her hand on the desk, over his paper. "I said, where is he?"

The man looked up at her, his gaze colder than the January wind off the Vistula. "Unless you'd like a cell here as well, there is nothing I can do for you. Your father is gone."

Exhausted with hunger, beaten down by helpless indignation,

this was just one more offense in a string of many. She would get no more from this man, she knew that well enough.

All at once, the fight bled out of her. She gripped the parcel to keep it from slipping from her grasp and exited the building. Rather than make her way home immediately, she remained where she stood, rooted in place by the weight of such news. The world blurred with hot tears and an ache lodged in her chest like a stone.

Your father is gone.

What did that mean? And what could she possibly do?

But no matter how many times those questions cycled in her mind, the answers did not come.

Chapter 10

ZOFIA HELD THE NEWEST list of forbidden book titles in her hands. Three months had passed since she'd been told her father was no longer at Pawiak and life had only become more difficult. Work had been taxing in her efforts with the German reading room and the overall library with its limited staff. Even the Bandit Book Club hadn't had the opportunity to meet in a while due to how busy they'd all been.

"This comes from Dr. Gundmann himself, do you understand?" Herr Nagiel's chin quivered with emphasis.

Zofia stood in the youth reading room, where she'd been dividing her time with the warehouse and the lending room after several more layoffs left the entire library with barely any employees. The youth reading room was her favorite. Children were coming in more often now, seeking stories of adventure and fairy tales to distract them from the horrors of life around them. There was something magical about seeing how stories could so quickly transport those desperate children to another time and place.

At least the odious task of setting up the opulent German reading room was complete, over which Herr Nagiel had implanted himself as its chief operator as though he had done all the work.

He wagged a finger at her now. "Not one item on here remains in the catalog, *ja*?"

"Of course," she replied.

Satisfied with himself, he turned abruptly and left, taking the weight of oppression with him.

Zofia breathed a little easier.

He wasn't as bad as some of the German authorities and thankfully their library was not subject to the kind of looting that plagued the Krasiński Library. Rumors had circulated about ancient texts that had survived the bombing being ruthlessly taken away, crated in boxes that were too small, damaging the priceless books and artifacts.

And at least the main library branch was still open. Most of their lending libraries were closed, as was the National Library, whose employees continued to work without pay, sacrificing their chance at a livelihood to care for the books. It was an act of passion in a time when everyone's bellies were empty.

Zofia regarded the list in her hands. There were hundreds of items. Not only book titles, but author names, meaning each name could be equal to half a dozen different titles or more. Many of those named were Polish and Jewish.

Was it not enough that the Germans had taken their museums, silenced their music, and commandeered their printing presses? Now Hitler was taking away their literature as well.

Pretty soon, there would be nothing left of Poland.

Zofia went to the warehouse and found Mrs. Mazur there, already running her finger down a catalog booklet. Zofia pulled a booklet from a stack and opened the rectangular catalog. As she trailed down the carefully printed inventory offered at the library, she noted the strike-through of a pen from the previously removed books.

"Herr Nagiel said he wants every item removed from the catalog," Zofia reported.

"I'm well aware," Mrs. Mazur said distractedly.

Zofia leaned a little closer. "But he didn't say anything about actually taking them off the shelves."

Mrs. Mazur paused and a smile curled over her lips. She glanced around before replying. "We can leave at least some on the shelves and give them duplicates from the warehouse."

At least on the main floor, they might still be read by those who knew how to find them.

Mrs. Mazur struck out a line of text from the catalog and lifted her chin a little higher. However small it may be, they would take all the victories they could win.

Zofia met Janina outside her apartment on Mazowiecka Street after work that afternoon to accompany her in shopping for the family's weekly rations. Rain pattered down around them and the wet cold seemed to seep into Zofia's bones despite her umbrella. But she wouldn't miss coming to meet Janina, the same as she always did these days after the pogrom in March.

The violent Polish attacks against Jews had started on Good Friday and continued for several days, the perpetrators not only acting with impunity but also at the goading of the Nazis.

The violence had stopped for the most part, and while Janina didn't live in the Jewish area, by recent law, Jews could only shop at Jewish-owned businesses. This meant those living in blended neighborhoods like Janina and her family were forced to go to the Jewish areas of town, where roundups and beatings were frequent.

It was one of the many laws meant to endanger and demoralize the Jewish population. Like keeping them from riding trains, limiting the wealth they could keep on hand, and barring them from restaurants and cafés.

A note of melancholy weighted Janina's usually bright demeanor.

Zofia noticed her friend's mood immediately. "What's happened?" She glanced back at the shop window of the Steinman's art gallery.

The glass was still in one solid piece, absent the blue Star of David thanks to a Polish Socialist friend of Zofia's father who purchased the shop from Mr. Steinman to keep it safe. Thus far they had been successful in the ruse.

"It's my mother." Janina kept her head down as she spoke.

"What happened? Does she need something?" Zofia stopped and turned back to the apartment.

Janina caught her arm and pulled her forward. "She's fine now. The Nazis picked her up with some other Jewish women and took her to the Żoliborz district, where she scrubbed a house from top to bottom until midnight. Apparently, it was being given to a German family soon to arrive."

Zofia could only imagine how frightened Janina and Mr. Steinman must have been when Mrs. Steinman didn't come home that night. And Mrs. Steinman who was always so lovely and kind, being forced to clean until the middle of the night… It was more than Zofia could stand.

She swallowed down her bitterness and instead squeezed Janina's arm with all the sympathy welling within her. "Your mother is safe now?"

Janina nodded. "Thankfully she was not sent to one of the work camps or to labor in Germany."

Many were not so lucky. Jews and Poles alike were being caught in roundups; most were never seen again without ever even having a chance to say goodbye to their loved ones.

It was not enough for the Reich to take their food and coal and valuable book collections—they were also taking people.

"How are things at the library?" Janina asked, clearly eager to change the subject.

Zofia never volunteered information about the library when she knew how desperately Janina missed it. But still Janina always asked, genuinely interested in how the books were being cared for and if any lists might be coming out again.

They skirted around several chairs in front of a café, all empty due to the rain. As they turned the corner, they hugged the building for whatever protection the eaves could offer.

A man appeared suddenly, taking the corner from the opposite direction at a clipped pace. There was no time to stop as Janina careened into him.

The man wore a belted jacket and a garrison hat with an eagle at its peak.

A Wehrmacht soldier.

Janina drew back in horror and Zofia edged toward her in a protective motion. His bloodshot eyes slid first to Janina's armband, then to the open doorway where she stood in its threshold. He swayed on his feet a moment.

"Jews aren't allowed in cafés." His words had a slight slur to them.

Janina gaped up at him. "We weren't in the café."

His lip curled, revealing a slightly crooked front tooth. "Don't lie to me."

"She's not lying." Zofia spoke in German and shifted so she stood closer to the soldier, putting herself in front of Janina. "We were trying to get out of the rain by walking under the eaves."

"Jews don't belong in cafés, bringing in their filth and contagion." Color rose in the soldier's cheeks.

Heat blazed through Zofia. "They do not bring contagion or filth," she countered. "It's all lies you spread to make people hate the Jews. It's disgusting."

The man drew up so he was an extra inch taller. "Are you calling me disgusting?"

He threw the challenge at Zofia's feet. A warning sign blared in the back of her mind, but her blood was roaring too loudly in her ears to listen.

Rage scalded her veins for what they had done to Maria, for what they had done to Papa, for what they were now doing to Janina and her family and every other Jew in Warsaw.

The injustice of what they endured every day knocked around in her brain like a boulder. The beatings, the forced labor, the reduced rations, the loss of jobs, of freedom, all of it and so much more. And no one around them was saying a thing to help. Not one person.

How could she *not*?

"Yes, you are disgusting." Zofia enunciated every word with distinct clarity. "What you have done to this city and what you are doing to the Jews, innocent people who are—"

Suddenly, his fist shot out. But it wasn't Zofia he struck. The blow slammed into Janina so hard that she staggered back against the side of the café doorway. His gun followed, a pistol withdrawn from a holster at his side, the glossy barrel pointed directly at Janina's face.

Zofia gaped in horror.

"No." The word tore in a harsh cry from her. "No. Please. Forgive me."

She had thought standing up to the Nazis would make others see their wrongs, that her voice might incite a series of others to join her. She had anticipated the punishment.

But Janina…

Never had Zofia considered that Janina would be punished in her place.

"What's one less Jew?" the Nazi demanded, his cold gaze fixed on Janina.

People walked past them, like water parting around a rock in the middle of a stream, their gazes averted out of fear of their own implication.

"No, please," Zofia pleaded, her voice breaking.

Janina didn't move from where she stood, staring at the gun. A simple flex of his finger and she would be dead.

Like the fifty-three innocent men on Nalewski Street in November, or over one hundred men in Wawer in December who were executed in retribution for the deaths of two German officers.

Like the many Scouts throughout the war who were slain for no reason at all.

Janina was one young woman, easily made an example of.

"Please don't do this," Zofia cried.

The Wehrmacht soldier glared at Zofia even as he kept his pistol trained on Janina. "Would you die for her?"

"Yes." Zofia did not hesitate with her reply. "Yes, I would die for her."

The gun was still pointed at Janina. Malice knotting the drunken soldier's expression.

Zofia licked her dry lips.

"Please kill me instead," Zofia said louder.

The man's mouth flinched, his upper lip curling. "Get on your knees, you Polish swine."

She knelt before him, icy rainwater soaking into the knees of her tights.

"Please kill me instead," Zofia said again.

He jabbed the pistol hard against her forehead. Metal grinding against skull. The pain of it was intense enough to make her eyes water, a ridiculous note of discomfort when seconds from now, she might die.

Because, yes, she truly might die.

The realization hit her suddenly as she waited for what may come. The Wehrmacht soldier's belt buckle was eye level, portraying an eagle looped in a circle with words arching over it: *"Gott Mit Uns."*

God with us.

She might have snorted at the absurdity of such words were her life not precariously teetering toward a violent end.

He pushed the pistol harder, shoving her forehead back. She clamped her eyes shut in anticipation. The odor of wet metal clung to the damp air.

Matka would know the exact prayer in a time such as this, a rapid whisper on her lips that ended with the sign of a cross.

But Zofia just chanted, *Oh God, Oh God, Oh God.*

The pressure lifted from her head for a quick moment and then a solid weight slammed into her forehead with enough force to throw her to the ground. She caught herself on the rain-soaked sidewalk, her eyes flying open to spots of white blooming and winking in her vision where the hard metal gun had struck her face.

The Wehrmacht soldier sneered down at where she lay. "*You* are disgusting."

With that, he holstered his gun and stepped over her as if she were a piece of rubbish.

Zofia pushed to her hands and knees, but could rise no farther than that. Her relief lasted only a flash of a second before the ease of her muscles went taut once more.

The humiliation.

The injustice.

Her own impotence.

She stayed rooted to the ground, curling her fingers to keep from leaping to her feet and launching herself at the cocky, drunken soldier. Fists, feet, fingernails, teeth, she wanted to tear into him like a beast and make him pay for what he'd done.

And yet she could do nothing but remain where she lay.

"Zofia."

She looked up, realizing Janina was at her side.

Janina caught Zofia's face between her palms and tears shone in her dark eyes. "Zofia, you could have been killed."

Janina.

She had almost been killed.

Because of Zofia.

"You—" Zofia couldn't force the words out from beyond the ache at the back of her throat. All the fight drained from her as she reached for her friend, drawing her into a solid embrace. "Oh, God, Janina, I'm so sorry."

Janina clutched her tightly, two people drowning in a river of people that continued to part around them. "You didn't know."

But Zofia was beginning to learn.

There was no way to stand up for what was right when it came to the Nazis.

Chapter 11

GUILT PLAGUED ZOFIA'S THOUGHTS during the day and pried her eyelids open at night. Janina accepted her apology every time they saw one another over the next two days, but her forgiveness was never enough to assuage the awful realization of what could have happened.

After a particularly difficult night with hardly any sleep, Zofia sat at the kitchen table, staring at her breakfast. She was fortunate to have the dark bread and marmalade on her plate. Many did not have much to eat on account of the rationing system and the złoty losing most of its value with the new exchange rate.

Matka shuffled into the kitchen, her blond hair wild around her head, not yet having seen a brush that day. She wore her night robe still, sloppily belted at the waist. That was a new low, even for this broken side of Matka.

She found more and more reasons to stay at home these days, fluttering about the windows like a trapped bird.

Zofia knew what she was doing, and who she was looking

for through the lace-curtained windows. She was hoping her son and husband would come home.

She indicated the food in front of Zofia. "Make sure you eat all of that. You'll need your strength." The corner of her mouth tucked downward as if she were on the verge of losing a tearful battle. "We have to move."

Zofia stared at her mother, certain she had not heard her properly. "What?"

"Germans will be living here soon. We must find somewhere else to go."

Somewhere else to go. As if such a thing was easy with so many houses still damaged from the bombing the previous September. Glaziers had been kept busy, trying to replace boarded-up windows with actual glass, and structural repairs were impossible for builders who were occupied with projects for the General Government.

Zofia eyed her mother warily. "Where will we go?"

Matka threaded her fingers into her tangled hair. "I don't know."

In the past, Matka would have taken charge with maddening authority. She would have ordered Zofia to begin packing the items from her room immediately and Zofia would have been irritated by the inconvenience.

She missed that Matka.

Now between gathering their food and working at the library, Zofia would also need to find them a new place to live. Where was she going to scavenge the time?

Zofia leaned her head back in frustration and her hair fell back from her face.

Matka woke up suddenly, snapping back into life with her keen eagle's eye focused on Zofia. "What is that?"

"What is what?" Zofia leaned forward quickly so her wavy hair swept forward like a curtain.

Her mother didn't answer, but swooped across the room and

pushed Zofia's hair back from her brow, exposing the bruise left by the German's pistol. Matka sucked in a hard breath. "Zofia, what's happened to you?"

It looked bad; Zofia knew that. A round bruise from where the barrel of the gun pressed into her skull and an angry purple, black, and red contusion covering half of her forehead where the pistol slammed into her face.

She'd tried to keep it hidden from Matka under her unruly waves. There would be too many questions she didn't want to answer.

"It's nothing." She leaned away from Matka and shook her hair back over her injury.

"It is *not* nothing." Her mother reached for her again, but this time her touch was light as she exposed the bruise. She sighed softly as her gaze wandered over the injury. "You don't have to tell me. I know you wouldn't anyway."

There was a note of sad resignation to her mother's statement.

Guilt nipped at Zofia's conscience. This new Matka was fragile and possessed a gentle, self-sacrificing nature. It was a foreign terrain that Zofia didn't know how to navigate.

Her mother's fingers slid lower to Zofia's face, cradling her cheeks between dry, warm palms. "I have failed you, Zofia." Matka's face flexed with silent pain. "I have been so consumed by what I have lost that I have forgotten to pay attention to what I still have." Her eyes locked with her daughter's. "You."

Zofia lifted a shoulder in a nonchalant shrug, uncertain how to respond. What could be said to such a thing?

And how to react to so much…affection?

"You're all I have left." Matka wrapped Zofia in an embrace, skinny arms and a skeletal body pressing hard to Zofia's, her mother's messy hair rasping against her face.

Awkwardly, Zofia patted her mother's shoulder.

"I vowed I would never treat you the way my parents treated me." Matka finally released her. "I'll find us a place this afternoon. I won't let you down," she said the last part with vehemence, with a significance Zofia didn't fully understand.

"What do you mean by that, Matka?"

But Matka only brushed Zofia's hair back again. She gave a muffled sound, like a sob, and covered her mouth with her hand. Her wedding ring sparkled on her slim hand, the band now too big and twisted on her finger from the weight of the gems.

True to her word, by the time Zofia returned home from the library that afternoon, Matka's hair was washed and styled, her dress pressed and snugly belted against her thin waist, and an apartment had been secured. Whatever wealth Papa had left for Mama likely helped in procuring a place with expediency.

"It's a two-bedroom apartment on Krucza Street." Matka brought a box into Zofia's room. "You know, the street that used to sell cheap women's clothing. It's not ideal, but most of the windows are intact."

"I think that sounds perfect," Zofia said encouragingly.

A light smile flitted briefly over Matka's face.

Once her mother left, Zofia sneacked into Papa's office and took out the hidden letters and books, dispersing the latter between several boxes to ensure they remained inconspicuous.

Matka made dinner that night—potato cakes and goulash. Peasant food, she had once called it. Zofia had always enjoyed such fare. The savory goulash, thick with chunks of vegetables and tender meat along with the shredded potatoes sizzled in fat until golden. It was more potatoes and less meat with almost no fat for frying the cakes, but still enough to set Zofia's mouth watering.

"Your father loved this food." Matka smiled sadly and slid a potato cake onto her plate. "He said it reminded him of home."

"He grew up in Poznań, right?" Zofia knew the answer, of course. But when she and Antek were young, they found asking Matka questions about Papa sometimes started her talking, sharing stories about his life that he never told them. Sometimes she might even share stories of her own, living in a massive manor filled with priceless pieces of art and going on lavish trips around the world. Once upon a time Zofia had envied Matka's stories until she had realized Matka was often left on her own under the charge of some new, uncaring governess.

"In Poznań, yes. That's how he knew German to teach it to you." Matka fell silent after her reply, staring at the food on her plate. "Are you nearly done packing?"

If Zofia weren't so hungry, she might have lost her appetite at such a question. After all, how could an entire life be boxed up in only one day? Though it had to be done, one day was all they had. But while she had a single room to pack, Matka had the rest of the house.

"Do you need help?" Zofia toyed with her fork when silence blanketed the room. They were not a family who asked for aid. Or accepted it.

Matka studied the untouched potato cake on her plate. "I haven't…" Her gaze wandered toward the closed door of Antek's room.

Zofia was still raw when it came to Antek. They both were, but Matka was also so defeated these days.

The task would be best left to Zofia. She balled her hands into fists under the table. "I'll do Antek's room."

While Matka would never ask for Zofia's help, nor did she decline it now. After the dishes were cleaned from supper, Zofia drew in a deep breath and opened the door to her brother's room. There was an unmistakable scent within—the clean aroma of soap and a tinge of sweat—the way Antek smelled. Zofia hadn't been prepared for the blow it delivered, one that came packed with memories of laughter and life lived at one another's side—a love that only siblings knew.

A hand settled on her shoulder. She looked up to find Matka next to her.

"It still smells like him in there," Zofia said.

The delicate muscles of Matka's throat squeezed in a hard swallow. "I know. But we must pack what he'll need when he comes home."

If he came home.

But Zofia didn't voice her misgivings.

Together, they took the boxes and carefully packed Antek's belongings.

His model planes were left where they hung from the ceiling, the broad map of Europe spread on the wall, its pins still poised for a Polish victory against the German invaders. Let the new occupants know that those who lived in this home before were Polish patriots, with pride and love for their country.

The next day they left their home. Zofia didn't look back as they drove from 16 Szucha Street in a carriage with all the belongings they could fit piled around them. Matka did though. She turned completely around and watched the ornate, art deco–style building slowly slip away, the way one does with a beautiful sunset they can't take their eyes from.

Perhaps that was a fitting way to look at it. For the sun truly did set on their former lives that day, leaving them blanketed in the darkness of a home with small windows, two of which were still covered with boards. The living area was a quarter of the size they were used to and Papa's desk that Matka refused to leave behind took up most of their dining room.

A soft rap at the door interrupted their unpacking. Zofia answered it to find a petite woman with threads of silver shimmering in her black hair and fine lines creasing the corners of her eyes. In her slim hands, she held a covered dish, heavy pottery dotted with cobalt blue flowers and yellow centers.

"I'm Mrs. Borkowska, your neighbor." Her thin lips pulled into a smile. "There isn't much of it, but I brought you some borscht. It's so hard to figure out supper when you're getting settled. And anyway, I wanted to welcome you and let you know I'm right down the hall if you need anything."

Matka appeared beside Zofia and thanked the woman.

"That was kind of her," she said, shutting the door after their new neighbor departed.

And it truly was, especially with food so scarce. They hadn't even thought of what they would eat with so much ahead of them for the evening. Though exhausted, they continued to go through boxes into the evening when the pulse of German music sounded in the distance, followed by cheers and laughter. Despite her mother's protests, Zofia went to the window to look at a distant bar filled with Nazi officers.

They gathered in the street and sat at tables, oblivious of the darkening sky as they drank from mugs of beer and tossed back glasses of vodka. They were partying as Warsaw suffered, while families were forced from their homes, while people were left without employment, while violence ensued from their prejudice.

The anger came roaring back again, prickling at her palms and the back of her neck. It built in her like a scream, one that threatened to make her explode—one she couldn't expel.

Matka yanked the newly hung lace curtains closed and turned her back to the carousing. "Best to ignore it's even there."

But when lying awake that night, haunted by the sounds of merriment from their conquerors, the ember of fury in Zofia's heart glowed hotter and brighter until she could scarce stand it any longer.

Darek was in the warehouse of the library when Zofia arrived at work the following morning. She moved quickly, needing only to gather a new collection of books to bring up to the children's library and then she could leave his presence.

His crooked smile melted away as she approached. "What happened to your face?" He reached for her, but she drew back.

"Zofia," he tried again. "Tell me what happened?"

She shouldn't. She should walk away, leave him alone in this warehouse. Except the emotion of everything that happened welled in her like a tsunami. It pounded in her brain and left her heart aching.

"Nothing and everything," she managed, and swept her hair over her face.

"Sounds like quite the paradox." The playful flirtation came out flat and his brown eyes were dark with worry.

"*Everything* has happened and there's *nothing* I can do about any of it." Her reply was harsh. "I'm not in the mood to talk."

"You can do something about it, you know?" Darek glanced around.

"I tried." She indicated her forehead. "Confronting them didn't work. Janina was almost shot because of me."

"But she wasn't." It was a platitude, and did nothing to assuage Zofia's torment.

"When do we fight back?" Zofia demanded. "When do we stop tolerating the persecution and the oppression?"

"If you really want to help, it takes true discretion." His empathetic smile softened his words. "Impulsive behavior is what gets people killed."

Zofia understood that now more than ever before.

"I can talk to someone," he said in a low voice.

The weight of despair lifted slightly at his words. Was this what he'd alluded to before? She knew people were fighting back. After all, this was Poland. They had never accepted defeat in the past and wouldn't now.

She just needed a way in and it looked like Darek was the key.

"I can be discreet," she assured him. "I was a Girl Guide for years before we were told we couldn't hold meetings anymore."

A thoughtful expression pulled at his brows. "You should know that this work can be dangerous."

Four days ago, she'd been kneeling in the rain, begging a Wehrmacht soldier to kill her. She smirked. "I'm not concerned."

"Those who care about you are." His stare held hers too long and an unaccustomed warmth spread through her chest.

"It's them I'm fighting for," she replied. "Those who care about me."

"Like Syrenka, our mermaid protecting the city." He nodded slowly. "I'll see what I can do. In the meantime, I was told to give you this."

He pulled something from his jacket pocket and handed it to her. "See you at the next book club meeting?"

The envelope was creased and battered, marked from a hard journey. She accepted the letter from him and nodded. "Next week on Thursday."

"I'm looking forward to what you thought of *All Quiet on the Western Front.*" He inclined his head and departed, giving her privacy to read the message.

Ms. Nowak,
I'll do what I can to send several vaccine doses to you when they are ready. Your father was a good man.
Dr. W

Dr. Weigl had finally written back, and not through the mail system. Which meant whomever Darek had been speaking to was part of the same underground organization as Dr. Weigl.

And who Papa had likely worked with as well.

Several days later, Zofia was welcomed into the Gray Ranks, an underground resistance group of Boy Scouts and Girl Guides that worked with the Polish Underground State to fight their Nazi oppressors. Her code name: Syrenka.

Doubtless the name of the Warsaw mermaid had been Darek's suggestion. She was sworn in to her role in a windowless basement, wearing the Girl Guide uniform she'd hidden away several months before, pressed beneath the weight of her mattress to smooth out the wrinkles.

On the left side of her chest, she proudly wore her Scout's cross, pinned on with a hidden safety pin. The metal cross was wrapped in laurel with a lily at its center, and inscribed with "Stay Alert."

She took her vows, promising to uphold the original ones she made years ago with the Girl Guides, in addition to serving the Gray Ranks, keeping the organization's secrets, following orders, and not shying from the sacrifice of her life.

Darek was there in a small collection of people. Several she did not know. The ones she did included Danuta, Kasia, and their former Guide Captain, Krystyna, who swore her in.

Much as it plucked her guilt, Zofia did not tell Janina of this decision. Not because she couldn't keep a secret, but to ensure her safety.

Today. Tomorrow. The day after tomorrow.

It was a motto Zofia tattooed onto her heart with purpose.

Today's endurance under the occupation.

Tomorrow in preparing for the fight for freedom.

And the day after tomorrow for the new, free Poland they would live in once more.

Darek approached her after she was sworn in and firmly shook her hand. "Now you're a real bandit, Syrenka."

She held herself taller, full of renewed purpose and an undeniable pride for Poland. For the first time since the Nazis marched in their victory parade down Ujazdowskie Avenue, Zofia felt hope.

Chapter 12

ZOFIA HAD NEVER DONE anything without Janina before. The secret of being with the Gray Ranks lodged itself into the forefront of Zofia's mind every time they were together, a nagging thought she couldn't put voice to. Not when knowing about the organization might threaten Janina's safety.

So far, Zofia's time with the Gray Ranks had been a lot of training in how to evade capture, how to respond if caught, and which official forms and cards to have on her at all times. She also helped with the distribution of the clandestine newspapers and sticking anti-Nazi messages around Warsaw when no one was looking.

But it was still too risky to share with her friend. Anything that drew Janina outside of her home was dangerous. As it was, Zofia was anxious about having her attend the book club, but Janina refused to miss it.

They were back in the library warehouse minutes after closing time, in the section on Poland's plants and wildlife in the farthest warehouse. Zofia glanced around, her ears sharp for any misplaced sound.

Janina nudged her. "Don't worry."

But Zofia did worry. Jews were no longer allowed in libraries, not even as patrons.

After the fear of almost losing Janina to the Wehrmacht soldier's wrath, Zofia was not inclined to take any chances. The tables had suddenly turned with Zofia erring toward the rules and Janina shirking them. But then, if Zofia was trapped indoors as often as Janina, she would likely be doing anything to get out as well.

Danuta, Kasia, and Darek came around the corner. Kasia gave a squeal of delight when she saw Janina and embraced her. "I'm so glad to see you. I hoped you would still be able to come."

Danuta even gave Janina a hug, and Darek gallantly kissed Janina's hand. But as he did so, he slid Zofia a wink.

The flirt.

The five settled on the ground and formed an intimate circle to keep from having to speak too loudly.

Darek leaned forward with his elbows on his knees. "What did you think of *All Quiet on the Western Front*?"

The normally talkative group went quiet. Zofia had found the story to be a difficult read, with graphic battle scenes from the Great War. What made the story even harder to absorb was the protagonist who was German, especially in their current state of affairs as Hitler swept through Europe. First Belgium had fallen, then in mid-June, France capitulated as well.

A brief silence lingered before Kasia spoke up. "It made me appreciate what Polish soldiers endured in their efforts during the attack." She spoke slowly and cautiously, the way she always did when giving her opinion on books, as if worried she might say the wrong thing. In this particular case, her perspective carried a sorrowful weight, given that her father had been one of those men fighting.

Darek caught Zofia's gaze and the flood of memories rushed at her from the night she was sworn in to the Gray Ranks. Everyone in the book club knew of her involvement except Janina.

Zofia's cheeks went hot with guilt. Janina obviously mistook the flush on Zofia's face from Darek's attention and gave her a knowing smile. Zofia swallowed a sigh.

"It was a brutal read," Danuta said. "But I think it's precisely the hard reality people who don't fight need to know, to understand what sacrifices are made. And that sometimes even soldiers who seem strong on the outside are still reeling from what they saw and experienced."

"What about you, Zofia?" Darek asked.

"I had a hard time with the book, but not because of the gruesome details." Acid churned in her stomach. "Have any of you wondered if this man is now an officer here in Poland, forcing Jews from their jobs or executing Poles in the streets?" She shook her head. "It's impossible for me to get past that to see anything else."

"You need to see beyond the nationality of the protagonist and look at the person," Darek interjected. "It's like Danuta said, the power of this perspective is a man at war, it's someone who is making an enormous sacrifice. And it also pulls down the filtered veil so people who want war can see it in full reality. It's stark and it's raw."

That he agreed with Danuta jarred Zofia.

She looked to Janina, who clasped her hands in her lap. "I agree on both sides," she offered diplomatically. "It is hard to open our hearts to sympathy for someone who is our enemy. But it's also important to understand what the men who protected our country went through. Even our fathers."

Whatever outrage ignited in Zofia with the idea of any sympathy for their enemy dimmed at the realization of what Papa must have lived through fighting in the Great War. He had witnessed firsthand those difficult scenes depicted in the book. She recalled suddenly the reverence with which he'd held the very book she now possessed. The Germans had been his enemy in his past and present and he clearly saw through it to regard the poignance of what was written on the pages.

Perhaps someday Zofia might be able to as well. But now was not that time.

As Zofia pulled the bottle of Baczewski vodka from her bag at the end of the meeting, Kasia spoke up. "Let's do *Brave New World* by Aldous Huxley next. I've heard it's a fascinating read."

"Another science fiction piece?" Danuta lifted her brows.

Kasia grinned. "Don't act like you didn't enjoy the last one."

"I liked it." Janina played into her role as peacekeeper and made the decision for them all. "I'm sure *Brave New World* will be just as good."

Zofia insisted on walking Janina home after book club. The *Courier* was doing its job well with turning Poles against Jews and the armband Janina wore was a beacon. Fortunately, aside from a few derogatory remarks, she was generally left alone.

Janina hesitated before going upstairs once they reached her building. "I have a favor to ask."

"Anything."

"Can you bring a couple novels by Marta Krakowska on our next shopping trip?"

"I thought you read them already."

Janina looked down. "They're not for me. Mrs. Rosenberg who runs the grocery store said she can't get anything new to read. Not with the libraries and bookstores closed to us. She didn't know I don't work at the library anymore and she asked—"

"I'll bring them," Zofia promised.

The next time Zofia met up with Janina to do her errands, she brought three of Marta Krakowska's books in the bottom of her shopping bag. They were from the library, from the stash stripped from the shelves to appease Herr Nagiel. It had been almost too easy to smuggle them out of the library, even past the guard at the front who looked over everyone's belongings day in and day out. He'd gotten lazy in his search of the employees and Zofia had taken advantage.

At least this way the books were still being put to their intended use by getting into the hands of readers.

The grocery store was just inside the Jewish quarter with "Rosenberg" written in lavish script above the plate glass window, one of the few to have survived the bombings. It was the store Janina's grandparents had frequented their entire lives.

"Janina and Zofia, my darlings," Mrs. Rosenberg called when they entered. Her short dark hair was set in a fashionable wave and her lips were always painted a pretty shade of pink.

Janina shared a look with Zofia and grinned at Mrs. Rosenberg. "We have something for you."

"Oh?" The older woman peered dramatically into their baskets.

Zofia pulled out the library books and Mrs. Rosenberg clasped her hands in front of her chest. "Oh, girls, you warm my heart with this kindness." She accepted the books and dabbed at her eyes with the corner of her apron. "I cannot tell you what this means to me."

But she didn't have to tell them; her ebullition and the shine of her delighted tears said more than words. Inasmuch as it brought Zofia joy to see what those three small books had done for Mrs. Rosenberg, simultaneously it made her ache for the many forced to go without.

When Zofia and Janina returned to the shop again, Mrs. Rosenberg pulled the books from under the counter. "I confess, I read them in three days."

"Three days?" Zofia asked in shock.

"You're an even faster reader than Zofia," Janina said with a laugh.

"A book a day." Mrs. Rosenberg beamed. "I'd love something else. Do you think you can find *Gone with the Wind*?"

The book hadn't appeared on any removal lists, but was a very popular item. With Mrs. Rosenberg reading so fast, it would be easy to borrow a copy for a few days. "I can do that."

"And more Marta Krakowska," Mrs. Rosenberg added with a shy smile. "In Yiddish. My mother isn't fluent in Polish and is desperate to read the same books I am so we can talk about them."

Yiddish books might be more difficult to smuggle out, but Zofia nodded anyway. "I'll see what I can do."

The next week, Mrs. Rosenberg asked for additional books for her friends, both in Yiddish and Polish. Soon Zofia was sneaking a book or two from the library every day as well as checking out the ones that hadn't offended Nazis enough to be pulled from circulation.

Several weeks later, Zofia came into the library's lending room with two books to check out and discovered Mrs. Mazur working there—a role they all took turns sharing these days with their limited staff.

In addition to the two legal books in hand, Zofia had a forbidden copy of *Brave New World* tucked in her bag, bundled in her sweater. While June had left everything warm, the warehouse was still cool enough to warrant long sleeves.

Mrs. Mazur took the two books and settled them on the counter. "What are you doing?"

"Checking out books." Zofia kept her tone innocent.

Mrs. Mazur eyed the checkout log and tapped the sharpened point of her pencil over several entries. "You've borrowed fifteen books since last Thursday."

Zofia tried to swallow, but found her throat too dry.

Had she really checked out that many?

Perhaps she had been a little overzealous.

"What are you doing?" Mrs. Mazur repeated and arched a

brow as she indicated the room with a pointed expression. "I suggest you answer me before anyone else comes in."

"I've been borrowing books for other people," Zofia admitted.

"Other people?" Mrs. Mazur tilted her head. "And they aren't patrons?"

"They were," Zofia replied slowly. Carefully. "But they're no longer allowed to come."

Understanding lifted Mrs. Mazur's features. "I see." She slid the books toward her and lifted her pencil once more. "In that case, I'll check these out under my name to keep from arousing suspicion."

Time tumbled by quickly as work occupied most of Zofia's days and whatever free hours she had in between were delegated for her sabotage efforts with the Gray Ranks. Their contribution to Polish resistance was more pranks than violent acts like blowing up railways, yet it afforded Zofia some satisfaction to at least be fighting back in some way. With the other men and women she'd taken her vows in front of, she slipped fake copies of the *Courier* into newsstands, dropped paint bombs made of burned-out light bulbs on German signs, and stood watch while others stole gun holsters from Nazis in cafes, and removed the swastika flags from buildings.

Through it all, she continued to deliver weekly books to grateful recipients in the Jewish quarter as the heat of summer was swiftly replaced by the crispness of fall. And every time, Zofia was amazed that Janina always greeted her cheerfully when they met to do shopping for the Steinmans.

Prior to the war, Zofia never was as optimistic as Janina, but even now with this occupation, where Jewish rations were cut to half of the meager allotment Poles received, where their curfew ended an extra hour earlier, Janina continued to find reasons to smile.

"I wish I had your happy demeanor," Zofia said.

"You always say that." Janina grinned and nudged Zofia with her elbow. "You just have to think of the things that are going well. Like how I get to see you every day even though I can't go to the library. And how the books you bring to share with the Jewish quarter make everyone light up. And also that I'm able to still be part of the Bandit Book Club."

Two small children appeared on the walkway ahead of them, hands clasped, bags slung on their shoulders as they hurried to school. They were young Poles, of course. School was banned for Jewish children and public education for Poles no longer extended beyond the fourth grade. Lessons were limited to teaching children to count up to five hundred and understand enough German to follow order.

An officer approached the children and they both obediently handed their bags to him.

"They must be looking for books," Zofia said under her breath. "As if children are smuggling illegal texts to school." She steered Janina down another street to avoid the officer, very aware of the weight of her shopping basket and her own smuggled illegal texts nestled beneath a cloth. Chills rippled over her skin at the risks she was taking, at how easily she might be caught.

Janina leaned closer to Zofia. "I've heard there are schools still being taught for older students. In secret."

A memory flashed in Zofia's mind about Papa telling her that very thing when he implored her not to give up on her studies.

"Could you attend as well?" Zofia asked.

Janina did not reply, which was answer enough. She could not. It was risky enough to teach in a secret school for Poles. Let alone if a Jewish student attended.

Zofia exhaled through her nose in consternation. "Then I have no interest in attending either."

An old woman abruptly ran toward the main part of the street and cried, *"Łapanka."*

Roundup.

Zofia and Janina froze, trying desperately to figure out which direction the roundup would come from. They all knew those taken were never seen or heard from again.

The old woman screamed her warning a second time, the echo reverberating off the cobblestone street. A Gestapo officer appeared suddenly in front of her. In a single motion, he pulled his gun from the holster at his side and fired it at her face. She dropped to the ground, unmoving.

There had been no notice, no preamble. Nothing. Alive and shouting one minute, and dead the very next.

Zofia shoved Janina toward an alleyway. If nothing else, Zofia's work papers and training with the Gray Ranks would help her out of this. Janina, however, would surely be hauled away.

The main street filled with people crying and screaming in confusion, stepping over the woman who had lost her life trying to alert them. Papers were checked with brutal efficiency, men were shoved against the wall and searched—only to be pushed toward the hooded trucks, their faces white with shock and their pockets turned out.

"My daughter," a woman screamed. "Save my daughter."

The woman nudging her daughter from the crowd was familiar, someone Zofia saw in her apartment stairwell often visiting with her neighbor. And then realization caught—they were the daughter and granddaughter of Mrs. Borkowska.

The girl squeezed between the mass of people and stood there, sobbing, hand reaching for her mother, Mrs. Borkowska's daughter. If the child remained there, she would be taken with the others and Mrs. Borkowska's granddaughter would be gone forever.

But if Zofia was caught helping the girl, it would put both her and Janina in terrible danger. Zofia's head pounded. She needed an answer immediately without having any time to think.

Chapter 13

THE LITTLE GIRL'S CRIES were drowned out by the piercing whistles and the shouts of those being herded up. Zofia glanced down the alley and confirmed Janina was on the other side, where she could easily slip into the next street that was not caught in the roundup.

She was safe.

Quick as a Nazi strike, Zofia grabbed the little girl and pulled her into the alley to where Janina hid in a deep doorway. "You need to be very quiet," Zofia whispered fiercely.

The little girl sniffled and looked back. "But Mama."

"Your mama wants me to take you to your grandmother's house." Zofia nodded as she spoke, hoping to be more convincing.

Though the girl's large blue eyes were still plagued with uncertainty, she quieted.

The chaos of hundreds of voices lasted about another twenty minutes and then, after the rumble of truck engines departing, the street fell into an ominous silence. Janina and Zofia shared worried looks, uncertain if it would be safe to emerge.

"Stay here," Zofia said softly as she crept from their hiding place. Of the three of them, she was the least vulnerable.

She slowly slipped to the end of the alley and peered down the smaller street where they had just been, the one that led to the larger Polna Street, where the roundup had occurred.

The old woman's body was gone, sawdust sprinkled on the telltale blood left behind, as though murder could be so easily blotted away. On the street were discarded items, scarves, dropped baskets, a shoe.

A bit of paper tumbled toward Zofia with something written on it. She snatched it before it rolled away. The message was hastily scrawled.

Papa, they have taken me in a roundup. Tell Mama I love her. And I love you too.

An address was hastily penned beneath.

A breeze rippled through the open, empty street, sending other scraps of paper skittering over the cobblestones. Zofia raced around, grabbing at them as swiftly as she could so none would be lost, each one crammed into her pocket for safekeeping.

Once she'd gathered them all, she returned to the alleyway. "It's safe," she said quietly.

Janina and the little girl emerged, eyes wide as Zofia joined them.

"I thought something had happened to you," Janina said under her breath.

Zofia lifted several of the crumpled notes from her pocket, keeping them cradled in her palm. "I had to gather these before they blew away."

One was unfolded enough to make out the heartfelt goodbye within and the address below.

Janina pulled in a soft breath and nodded in understanding. Together, they walked back to Krucza Street, to the apartment across the hall from Zofia's to deliver Mrs. Borkowska's granddaughter to her as well as the bad news about her daughter being caught in a roundup.

Mrs. Borkowska looked at both Zofia and Janina, her gaze lingering on Janina's armband before falling to her granddaughter. She accepted the girl with an admirable strength of spirit, her voice even and calm as she told her to prepare the table for the evening's meal. But Zofia noted the glimmer of tears in the old widow's eyes before they left her.

"Do you want me to go with you to deliver the messages?" Janina asked as they made their way back to her home.

Zofia was dreading going to each of the addresses wadded in her pocket and bearing witness to the hurt of each stranger's loss. But she also knew the danger in bringing Janina.

"I would feel better if you were safe at home," Zofia replied.

"I thought you might say that," Janina said with chagrin. "And you're probably right."

Once Janina was secure in her own apartment, Zofia set out on the painful task of delivering the notes to their loved ones and the knowledge that they would likely never be seen again.

Herr Nagiel shared the joyous news that more lending libraries and reading rooms would be reopening in Warsaw. Even better, this allowed for the rehiring of many employees, including Miss Laska.

Zofia rushed to her, embracing the frail older woman as if she were made of delicate bird bones. She seemed to have shrunk since Zofia saw her last. The furlough had left Miss Laska in poor health. Her cottony white hair was thin enough to show her pink scalp beneath, and her usually immaculate appearance was marred by a slight hole in the sleeve of her cranberry-colored sweater.

Zofia had managed a few visits after Miss Laska was let go, and left food as often as she could spare. But with helping Janina, working at the library, and her efforts with the Gray Ranks, there had been little opportunity to do more for the older woman. Seeing Miss Laska in such a state snagged at Zofia's conscience. Surely there was more she could have done, or more of her own rations Zofia could have sacrificed for the other woman.

Miss Laska didn't notice the burden of Zofia's thoughts as she regarded the aisles of books. "Oh, it is good to be back." Closing her eyes behind her thick lenses, she deeply inhaled the scent of thousands of books in one breath. "It still smells exactly the same."

"Will you be working in the manuscript room again?" Zofia asked as they made their way toward the warehouse closest to the main reading room.

"Partly." Miss Laska looked about as she replied, rapaciously taking everything in, as if she expected it all to disappear. "I'll mainly be running the reading room on Traugutta Street."

They pushed into the warehouse where Mrs. Mazur rushed about, her steps erratic, her normally neat hair flying about her flushed face.

"Zofia, I need your help right away." She cast a desperate look at Miss Laska, a colleague who had been a friend of hers for at least two decades, and slowly shook her head—a silent message for the older woman to stay away.

Zofia gently guided Miss Laska through the doors they had entered through only a second before and spoke loudly. "I think you may need to check the manuscript room."

Miss Laska cast a worried glance between them, her steps hesitant even as she played along. "Yes, I'll see to that."

"This new list needs to be removed at once," Mrs. Mazur said in a firm, authoritative voice, the one she used in case someone was listening, and handed several pages to Zofia. "Not a single one is to remain from our catalogs, do you understand?"

Though her tone was uncharacteristically hard, her wink said what words could not.

They would approach this new list of forbidden books as they had the last. All those with duplicates were to be sent in a cart in sacrifice to satisfy the demands. Those without duplicates were mis-shelved in seldom-used aisles. The Germans didn't spend much time in the warehouse, which gave Zofia and Mrs. Mazur opportunities to salvage banned books. But at least in this case, if their actions were somehow brought to light, Miss Laska's absence absolved her of any implication or guilt.

Zofia and Mrs. Mazur worked side by side, pulling and shuffling where it was needed. Some of the books on the list were questionable. Like one on birds with the unfortunate title of *Our Enemies and Friends*, which likely was what caused it to land on the list.

When they were done, hundreds of books were stacked in boxes awaiting their fate, whatever that might be. A Wehrmacht soldier entered the warehouse with a group of boys in khaki Hitler Youth uniforms. Their footsteps were in time with one another, a line of future soldiers for the Reich.

Apprehension rippled over Zofia. The children's presence was unsettling.

The boys stood along the boxes as the Wehrmacht soldier addressed Mrs. Mazur and Zofia. "It has been brought to our attention that books sent for destruction are being kept by drivers for resale. Going forward, these items meant for disposal will be damaged to prevent further theft from happening."

"Destruction?" Zofia echoed in horror. "We were told they were being held in warehouses."

"Some are, yes," the soldier replied with disinterest. "But not all." He waved in a "go" motion.

The boys launched at the boxes like a pack of wolves. They cracked the spines in their hands and wrenched the books in half, discarding the two sides to the ground like ruined carcasses.

Zofia sucked in a hard breath at the devastation. These were books people once cradled in their hands or held against their chests in anticipation of spending hours poring over them. They were cared for by countless patrons before being returned to the library for safekeeping. And now they were treated like unwanted refuse even though that very day readers had asked for some of those specific titles.

Even worse, it was rumored that this was being done throughout all of Poland. Zofia recalled the losses at Krasiński Library, those precious texts forever removed from the world.

The Wehrmacht soldier flicked his hand at Zofia and Mrs. Mazur, dismissing them.

They went to the opposite side of the warehouse where a delivery of new books for the German reading room had recently arrived, the sounds of literary carnage almost imperceptible from where they stood.

"What if the books we've held back are the only ones left in all of Poland?" Zofia asked quietly.

Mrs. Mazur withdrew several items from a box onto an already crowded table. "I've had the same thought."

"We need to find somewhere else to keep them." Zofia leaned closer. "Are there any warehouses in the library where Herr Nagiel would never think to look? Maybe one that was damaged?"

Mrs. Mazur nodded slowly, her eyes narrowed in thought. "There was one on Świętokrzyska Street that was destroyed in the bombing. It had a cellar..."

"That could work." Zofia's breath quickened. "We'd have to sneak them a couple at a time, properly hidden in case of an inspection. It could go quickly with help."

"Know anyone willing?" Mrs. Mazur's smile said she already knew Zofia did.

Before Zofia could bring the idea up at the next meeting of the Bandit Book Club, the loudspeakers on the street interrupted a chilly October day, announcing the movement of all Jews to the Jewish quarter and the relocation of all Poles currently living there.

Zofia immediately went to see Janina, who answered the door with red-rimmed eyes and a pink-tipped nose. "They're making us move."

"I hate this for you." Zofia hugged her friend. "You should come stay with us."

Janina shook her head. "I don't think that's a good idea."

Zofia was not so easily deterred. Once she convinced Matka, she could encourage the Steinmans to stay with them.

"Do you want help packing your room?" Zofia asked instead.

They started that afternoon, going through a lifetime of memories in Janina's room—the matching red ribbon to the one in Zofia's nightstand from a set they shared that first year of their friendship, a copy of *The Story of My Life* from that summer before the war when they were still the anti-Hitler book club, complete with Maria as their only other member. While they carefully boxed up Janina's life, her parents scoured the new map of the Jewish quarter to determine where they might find a place to live.

By the time Zofia returned home, she was exhausted and incensed. It was unfair that the Steinmans should have to move from a home that Janina's parents had lived in since the day they were married. It was unfair that Zofia and Matka had to leave the place filled with memories of Papa and Antek. All of it was so achingly unfair.

Zofia closed the door to her apartment and toed off her shoes.

"Why didn't you tell me?" Matka demanded.

Zofia started and faced her mother, whose eyes flashed with anger. In the past, Zofia might have wondered what new thing she'd done to irritate her. But recently, they'd grown closer, sharing meals and even details about their days, and the accusation in her mother's voice stung.

Zofia dropped her bag to the floor beside her discarded shoes. "About what?"

"About the roundup," Matka said with exasperation.

Zofia slid her gaze from her mother's.

"Mrs. Borkowska commended your heroic deed this afternoon as she regaled me with a story about how you saved her granddaughter at considerable risk to yourself." Matka stopped and put her fingertips to her mouth, as if suppressing a sob. "Why would you not tell me?"

"Nothing happened. I didn't want to worry you."

"I worry about you every day." Matka paced the floor, her stockinged feet thudding with every step. "Especially when you take Janina to the Jewish quarter to get her rations."

"She's my friend and I intend to protect her." Zofia approached her mother. "Have you heard what is happening? All the Poles have to leave the Jewish quarter and all the Jews have to relocate there. Everyone. Including Janina and her family."

Matka sighed. "Don't be so dramatic. It's for their own safety, to protect them from Polish abuse."

"Is that what the *Courier* says?" Zofia's chest went tight with indignation. "You do realize it was the Nazis who encouraged Poles to engage in those pogroms over Easter."

"And what about the typhus outbreak?"

"Matka," Zofia exclaimed in horror. "It's all lies to drive a wedge between Poles and Jews. And if the Jews do begin to suffer from typhus, it's because they are all being squeezed into too little of an area for so many people. Have you seen the map? It's far too small for everyone. The *Courier* may refer to it as a quarter, but it's a ghetto."

Matka pursed her lips.

Zofia shook her head in disbelief at her mother. "Surely you know this. You and Papa discussed it often."

At the very mention of Papa, Matka's pale blue eyes went brilliant with pain.

"We can't let Janina and her parents go there," Zofia said. "Maybe they can move in with us—"

Matka stared at Zofia in shock. "Absolutely not."

Zofia lowered her voice, "I don't trust this. It's not being done to keep Jewish families safe."

"They've been told to relocate, just as we were." Matka shifted her weight to one skinny hip. "We can't go against these rules. You saw what the penalty was for something as simple as failure to comply with turning in our radio. Death."

Whatever exhaustion Zofia had felt was singed away with her renewed rage. "They're not radios. They're people. Friends."

Matka folded her arms over her chest.

"The answer is no."

Whatever relationship had started to blossom between Zofia and her mother wilted that day. Meals together fell into silence once more and they drifted through the tiny apartment like strangers.

Zofia stood outside the Steinman's former apartment the day of their move into the ghetto. They bid their farewells to the building, not only to the home where Janina's parents had lived since they'd married, but also to the shop below.

They'd already had their furniture and larger items sent ahead to the apartment on Próżna Street that they'd found earlier that month. It was a good area with nice apartments that overlooked Grzybowski Square. Zofia hoped they would be comfortable there, maybe even happy. If one could be happy when forced to leave their home. She knew herself how painful it was to turn away from a lifetime of memories.

"Thank you for being here for Janina." Mrs. Steinman embraced Zofia, enveloping her in the familiar powdery spice scent of Shalimar. "But you shouldn't come with us."

Janina looked at Zofia, eyes wide with a silent plea not to leave as Mrs. Steinman released her. Zofia remained where she stood at her friend's side.

Mr. Steinman cleared his throat. "Zofia, it may not be safe."

She stiffened at the realization he meant it might not be safe for them, for Janina. Zofia shook her head, refusing to put her friend at risk. "I'm sorry, Janina. I can't..."

Janina nodded in understanding, her face strained against a flood of tears she was obviously trying to hold back.

Zofia's throat ached with emotion, hating how this felt like goodbye. "I'll come see you when you're settled."

And by that, she referred to their next book club meeting to discuss *Brave New World*.

Janina nodded again, this time with a whisper of a smile.

Though Zofia did not accompany the Steinmans, she did join the Poles who watched the procession of Jewish families on that final moving day. Some bystanders hurled insults, others talked among themselves, regurgitating the vile words of the *Courier* in their praise for keeping Poles and Jews safe from one another.

And still others watched with pallid faces, their cries of outrage smothered behind pinched lips. Like Zofia, they likely had learned the hard way how futile it was to stand up to the Reich.

When Zofia was able to enter the ghetto the next day to visit Janina and her family, she found the area so thickly packed with people that there was scarcely room to walk. All along Leszno Street, vendors sold their wares from carts with everything from bread to the white armbands with a blue Star of David that Jews were forced to wear. The area where Janina lived was fortunately less crowded and much nicer. Janina met her outside the building with a smile that soothed some of Zofia's worries and together they climbed the stairwell.

A little boy no older than five rounded the stairs as they reached the landing. He wore suspenders over a pressed shirt which was neatly tucked into a pair of brown trousers. His black hair was glossy beneath his newsboy cap and his dark eyes were rimmed in thick, long lashes.

He skidded to a stop and flashed a grin up at them, a dimple winking in his right cheek. "Miss Janina." He swept off his cap and offered an elaborate bow. When he stood, he regarded Zofia with a coy expression. "And who is your lovely friend?"

Janina ruffled his hair as he shifted his adoring gaze to her. "Mouse, this is Zofia. Zofia, this is Mouse. He lives in the apartment across from ours."

Mouse put his cap over his chest reverently. "You are beautiful, Miss Zofia."

"Watch out, he's a charmer." Janina plucked his cap from his hands and settled it playfully askew over his mussed hair.

"I'm only a charmer if the ladies fancy being charmed." Mouse spun around and winked at Zofia.

"Off with you." Janina nudged him, but he paused to catch Zofia's hand, bending over it and planting a kiss with pomp and relish.

Janina shook her head as his footsteps clambered down the stairs. "That one is going to be trouble when he grows up." With a laugh, she pulled Zofia toward the large oak door to the Steinman's apartment.

While their new residence was smaller and barely held all the personal effects they'd brought with them, it seemed in good repair and even had all the windows still intact.

After showing Zofia around and doing her very Janina-best to allay Zofia's concern, Janina pulled on her coat so they could leave for the library.

"Where are you going?" Mrs. Steinman asked, though she hadn't even turned around.

Janina always said her mother had a sixth sense when it came to her getting into trouble. It wasn't the first time Zofia had witnessed the phenomenon herself.

Janina widened her eyes at Zofia.

"We're going to meet some friends," Zofia replied casually, lying for Janina since she was never any good at it.

"Where?" Mrs. Steinman turned in her chair to look at them.

Zofia hesitated. Jews weren't allowed in parks anymore or in cinemas or restaurants, or really anywhere except the ghetto.

"My apartment," Zofia said with conviction in the hopes Mrs. Steinman would not press further.

After all, Zofia couldn't very well tell her that they were going to the library after hours to meet with a secret book club that read books Hitler was stripping from Poland's shelves.

Zofia tried not to think of any of that as Mrs. Steinman studied her, just in case her sixth sense extended to reading minds. A shot sounded in the distance and made Mrs. Steinman's decision in an instant.

"You're staying here until we know it's safe to venture out," she said, turning back in her seat. Even Zofia knew when she spoke with that crisp note to her tone that there was no arguing with her.

The Bandit Book Club members were very understanding when Zofia showed up alone, and all were amenable to changing the date so Janina could join them. It did help that Kasia hadn't finished *Brave New World* yet, citing it to be extraordinarily scandalous. They also agreed to help transport books to the damaged warehouse on Świętokrzyska Street, much to Zofia's relief. After deciding to meet the following week, they adjourned.

But on the afternoon of November 16, when the book club was going to meet again, Zofia found the gates to the ghetto closed. Normally that didn't happen until nine in the evening, when the Jewish curfew began, but they always reopened at five in the morning.

"What's going on?" she asked the guard in German.

He gave her the long-suffering look of a man who had repeated the same message many times that day. "No one is allowed to enter or leave the ghetto anymore."

Zofia shook her head. "I don't understand."

"The ghetto is sealed," the guard replied bluntly. "And it will not open again."

Chapter 14

ZOFIA REFUSED TO ACCEPT that there was no way into the ghetto to see Janina.

When asking sweetly hadn't worked, she'd resorted to pleading, which eventually turned into an attempt to bribe her way in. The twenty złotys were all she had on her, meaning she would likely have no way to get out, but she was desperate to see her friend one last time. It might be her last opportunity until…

Until when? Until the war ended? Until someone finally defeated Hitler and bothered to help Poland?

Zofia knew Poland's history. The previous occupation had lasted 123 years.

She might never see Janina again.

After years of spending nearly every day together, constant companions in joy and sorrow with dreams that were built together—the thought was too large and awful to acknowledge.

How could she get food to Janina? How could Zofia fulfill her promise to protect her friend?

And how could Zofia get by every day without her friend's infectious smile and optimism and everything else that made Janina who she was?

It hadn't mattered how much Zofia had on her anyway. The guard would not be swayed. She would not be allowed in. Defeated, she left, making her way to the library. A tear spilled down her cheek, immediately going cold in the brutal November wind before she could swipe it away.

Someone called her name.

She didn't turn and instead marched determinedly onward.

"Zofia." This time the man's voice was right beside her, close enough for her to recognize Darek. He frowned with concern. "What is it?"

She shook her head, unable to speak.

"What's happened?" He caught her shoulders in a gentle grip and turned her toward him. The warmth of his brown eyes, so full of compassion and empathy, was her undoing.

"Janina." It was the only word she could choke out before the wall of her control crumbled beneath the weight of her loss. The tears flowed too fast to stop.

Darek said nothing as he pulled her into an embrace. Any other time, she would have jerked away. But as his arms came around her, the strength of her legs gave way and she collapsed against him. He caught her and held her as she sobbed at the futility of their situation.

Where the rest of the world was cold and spinning out of control, he was warm and solid. She clung to him, and for that moment he was the only thing keeping her standing.

At least until her tears slowed, and what she was doing dawned on her.

She leaped back. "I'm sorry. I shouldn't..."

He shook his head and a lock of hair fell over his forehead. "Don't worry, I won't tell anyone." His attempt at a grin came out looking as miserable as she felt, and his expression immediately sobered. "I know what happened at the ghetto. Everyone has been talking about it."

"There has to be something we can do," Zofia said. "Darek, I didn't even get to say goodbye." The tightness of her throat squeezed out anything more she might have said.

Darek shoved his hands in his coat pockets. His gaze lowered to the ground, but not before she saw the wounded look in his eyes shift to thoughtfulness, as if he was working through the problem.

Her problem.

They walked in silence into the library as the last of the day's patrons were finalizing their selections before closing. Kasia and Danuta were already there for the book club meeting when Zofia and Darek arrived in the warehouse.

Kasia jumped to her feet when she saw Zofia and threw her arms around her. "I heard about the ghetto being sealed."

Zofia nodded mutely and sank onto the floor beside Danuta.

"This war is costing us everything." Danuta's eyes were bright with pain.

Just after their last meeting of the Bandit Book Club, Danuta's parents had both been arrested like Zofia's father had. Danuta had moved in with Kasia and her mother shortly after, but she'd had a note of melancholy about her ever since.

"*Brave New World* was…um…" Kasia flushed bright red beneath her blond waves. "Well, it was an interesting read."

"It was scintillating, to be sure," Danuta jumped in, coming to life as she shifted her focus from grief to the book discussion. "But also a fascinating world to consider. To have no discomfort, no sorrow, a world completely controlled by science. Yes, it is an unnatural state of life, but it was an interesting one nonetheless. I found myself often wondering as I read through it if I would take Soma to get through the occupation."

The little tablet mentioned in the book would allow them to mentally escape from the horrors they'd experienced. It would ease the pain of loss and smother that burn of rage and indignation.

Zofia shook her head. "That would be too easy."

"It's supposed to be easy," Darek pointed out.

"I want to feel everything we've been through." Zofia fisted her hand. "I want to be enraged by injustice and let myself mourn for those who are lost. How can we see wrong if we let ourselves go numb?"

Until that moment, she hadn't realized how necessary the intensity of her anger had become.

"And by taking away pain," Kasia added, "they also eliminated the opportunity to love."

Their discussion dipped into a brief, but awkward discussion on the romantic lives of the characters before shifting to various other themes of the book. None, however, were as poignant to Zofia as the realization of how important that fury inside her had become.

"Why don't we read Helen Keller's *The Story of My Life* next?" Darek suggested when they finally ran out of the many topics to discuss about *Brave New World*. "I read an article on her once in the library's newspaper when it was still being published and she seems like an amazing woman."

"No." Zofia said the word too fast, too harshly. "We already read it, when it was just me, Maria, and Janina." Her voice tapered off. None of them were in the group now except her. "Although, if no one else has read—"

"It's already been chosen." Darek gave an easy shrug. "And I've already picked a book before. I think it's your turn, Zofia."

She frowned down at the floor and thought about the most recent list of books to be destroyed. "How about *The Doll* by Bolesław Prus?"

"I just put that one in the hidden warehouse," Danuta said. "It was very thick." She rubbed her hands together in anticipation. But then, Danuta was the kind of reader who could miraculously devour a book like *The Doll* in just three days.

"We'll never meet again if we read that one now, not with how busy we've all been." Kasia winced.

It was true. Already their meetings were spread further apart now with only one copy of the forbidden books to share between them. That and limiting their meetings was prudent when the Bandit Book Club was so dangerous. If caught, they would all be arrested. Possibly even killed, made into an example for others. After all, they were not only reading books that should be destroyed; they were discussing ideals that Hitler was determined to pull out by the roots, to stamp out of existence until minds were left without free thought.

Zofia shivered. "Then how about *The Street of Crocodiles* by Bruno Schulz?"

"*The Doll* is not *that* long." Danuta rolled her eyes.

"Then you can select *The Doll* when it's your turn," Zofia offered.

Danuta brightened at that and nudged Kasia. At least they knew what was in store for them when it came to the next book they were going to read.

Zofia had been so focused on helping Janina and her family settle into their new apartment in the ghetto that she hadn't had an opportunity to see the hidden warehouse on Świętokrzyska Street for herself. Several days after meeting with the Bandit Book Club, Zofia found a chance to make her way to the warehouse, the copy of *Brave New World* wrapped in a bulky red scarf in her bag.

In truth, she had been holding off on going to the ruined warehouse. The last time she'd visited that street, many of the bookstores had been in flames with burning pages skittering across the ground, like animals in flight.

Even worse was the memory of Maria being strafed by the

pilot, his laughing face still etched in Zofia's mind. She stopped at the exact location now, staring at the bare asphalt as if expecting to see a demarcation there. Perhaps a bullet hole or a stain of blood. Something. Anything.

But, no, the paving was new and smooth, blanketing yet another atrocity.

The ache of loss was a weight Zofia carried with her every day. Not only for Maria but also for Papa and Antek. And now for Janina.

Going through life without her dearest friend was like losing her right arm, the absence poignant and felt with every movement.

The lending library on Świętokrzyska Street was little more than a shell of a building. While the property still belonged to the Warsaw Public Library, the lack of funds kept it in a sorry state.

Zofia entered from the rear of the building through the courtyard to avoid arousing suspicion. The previous May, the small patch of land had bloomed with purple and white lilacs and left the air heady with their perfume. Now, the soil was disturbed from exhumed graves, recalling the horrors of the attack on Warsaw.

Inside the building was cold and damp, stinking of mildew and the acrid reminder of fire damage, even a full year since the flames were doused. Whatever books could be salvaged had been cleared out long ago, but resources couldn't be spared to divest the remaining debris and rubbish.

Lumps of indistinguishable detritus littered the floor and smoke left soot blackening the walls. The former lending library appeared entirely inhospitable and certainly beyond repair.

It was perfect.

Zofia descended the steps and unlocked the warehouse door. It stuck slightly, but yielded beneath the force of a strong shove. Inside were rows of dusty shelves, the corners frosted with cobwebs. There was a stale odor of disuse, but it did not stink of mildew like the building above. Whatever books were stored here would be safe.

A series of small windows near the top of the warehouse let in weak streams of sunlight through panes that were opaque and milky with grime. Outside, grates in the walkway covered these windows, obscuring them from view. Most likely it was how they had been protected during the blasts that had shattered the other windows in the library.

If nothing else, those narrow windows provided enough light to see by in the otherwise dark space.

She made her way through the large expanse of the warehouse to the back where three shelves were filled with books. Franz Kafka, Helen Keller, Albert Einstein, Ernest Hemingway, H. G. Wells, and so, so many more.

Her fingers trailed lovingly along their glossy spines, resplendent in various jacket covers and leather bindings. Here they would be kept safe, a treasure buried under the noses of the very men who would see them destroyed. She withdrew *Brave New World* from her handbag and settled it against *The Time Machine*, then took a step back to survey their collection again.

One book at a time.

Janina would be proud.

When Zofia exited the dilapidated library, she intentionally turned the opposite way toward Marszałkowska Street, which met Próżna Street, where Janina now lived. As she approached, a wall blocked Zofia's path and obscured her view of the ghetto. It was made of mismatched brick, rubble taken from bombed homes, and rose more than three meters high, making it impossible to see over. Coils of barbed wire twisted over the barrier and bits of broken glass embedded at the top glinted wickedly in the sun.

She drew closer to the wall and put her hand on a rough

brick, chipped at one corner. It was icy under her palm, offering no comfort or explanation. The sounds of the city moving on behind her reverberated off the structure, keeping her strained ears from picking up anything that might be happening on the other side.

What was going on in there?

"Hello?" she called out. "Can anyone hear me?"

"Get back." The German command was delivered with such malice, the hairs on the back of her neck stood at attention.

She lowered her hand and looked at the Wehrmacht soldier approaching in swift strides. His eyes were gray as gunmetal and just as cold.

"Get back," he repeated, reaching for his gun holster.

Zofia looked at the wall one last time and stepped away, her task abandoned but by no means forgotten.

The following morning at the library, she was asked to go through the main reading room to gather books left behind by readers. Winter had resulted in an influx of new patrons despite the increase in the monthly library fee from fifty groszys to one złoty. With the electricity alternating between streets, some patrons sought a warmer place to spend their afternoons. Others were looking for a replacement for their previous pastimes as all the museums were now closed, theaters only offered vulgar shows, and the cinemas were poisoned with propaganda movies created by Nazis.

Only pigs went to the movies.

That's what they said often among themselves in the Gray Ranks, sometimes even painting it boldly across the face of a cinema advertisement. Zofia had attended movies there occasionally, but only to participate in minor sabotage.

Once they'd set fleas loose on the occupants, another time there had been smoke bombs set off mid-viewing, and one rainy Friday night, they had sprinkled itching powder onto the seats and stayed a good half hour to watch everyone squirm and scratch.

Patriotic Varsovians sought a different escape now from their new reality where friends were locked behind a ghetto wall, or jobs had been stolen by *Volksdeutsche*.

"Excuse me."

Zofia turned to find a man behind her. His tweed jacket was buttoned at the waist and his beard was neatly trimmed. "Do you have *The Invisible Man* by H. G. Wells?"

She pulled a discarded book toward her and slid it onto the cart. "Unfortunately, we can no longer offer books by H. G. Wells per direct orders from the General Government."

"More and more books are disappearing from your shelves," the man said irritably. "It's wrong to limit books and education."

"There are many wrongs in this new world," Zofia muttered under her breath.

"I'd hoped to read it to my son," he continued. "It was one of my favorites when I was his age. I have often found myself wondering what I would do if I became invisible."

"Hopefully you would use such an ability to better effect than Griffin."

"Ah, so you have read it, as you know the protagonist." The man grinned at her as she lifted a stack of books from the table. "Can you imagine such an ability now? What might be done?"

In truth, it made her heart clench to consider the possibility of having that kind of power.

She could slip past the guards of the ghetto and see Janina. Or she could travel to Germany, sneak her way into whatever grand building Hitler resided in and end the war with a single gunshot.

When Zofia didn't answer aloud, the man gave her a little smirk as if he understood exactly what she was thinking. Likely he was envisioning the very same thing himself.

"Well, perhaps when this war is over, I can read *The Invisible Man* to my son, as well as the rest of H. G. Wells's books."

She thought of *The Time Machine* where it lay nestled against *Brave New World* in the warehouse beneath the destroyed lending library. It was ridiculous to have the book on hand and not be able to lend it to patrons. But at least after the war, they would still have the book to offer.

Whenever that might be.

"That would be good." Zofia forced a smile, a bright congenial one like Janina would have given. "After the war."

The man departed with a friendly nod and left her to gather the remainder of the discarded books to return to the warehouse. Once the cart was full, she guided it from the large room, one wheel squeaking.

Mrs. Mazur wasn't in the warehouse when Zofia arrived, but her nephew was.

"I recognize that squeaky wheel." Darek turned away from a stack of books he'd been going through and slid one into the bag at his side, likely meant to be smuggled into their hidden warehouse.

"The squeaking didn't start until it was full." Zofia slowed the cart, grateful to stop the grating sound.

Darek went to the cabinet and, as he'd done before with Miss Laska's old cart, he knelt by the wheels and dabbed a bit of oil on each.

"Don't they keep you busy at the university library?" she asked.

He straightened with the oilcan in hand. "Absolutely, but I had a reason to come here today."

"To fix my squeaking wheels again?"

"No, but you're welcome for doing it anyway." He winked.

She moved the cart front and back, the glide of the wheels smooth and wonderfully quiet. "I admit you are handy to have around. Thank you."

He returned the oilcan to the cabinet. "Even handier to have around when you hear what I have to say."

"I'll be the judge of that." It came out almost playful and she immediately put her attention to reordering the books on the cart to avoid meeting his gaze. "Out with it, then."

There was a familiar comfort to the way they bantered with one another, each replying without pausing for thought. And though she'd never admit as much to him, she rather enjoyed it.

She lifted a book to shift it to the cart's lower shelf when he replied, "I have someone who can get a letter to Janina for you."

The book slipped from her hand and slapped to the hard ground with an audible smack. She looked up, ignoring the fallen book. "If you are teasing me—"

"I would never tease you about something so serious." His brown eyes were filled with sincerity.

"How? Who?" Zofia shook her head.

"Several pharmacies are still open in the ghetto that are owned by Poles." Darek bent and retrieved the fallen book. "I know someone who works at Kijewski's and has a pass into and out of the ghetto on a regular basis. He has agreed to transport the message to her and bring you one in return."

Zofia knew the pharmacy on 21 Zamenhof Street, now caught in the walled net of the ghetto. Her stomach clenched. "For how much?"

These days, her salary at the library wasn't enough to afford food for herself, let alone Matka. But somehow Matka managed to find ways to keep them from starving. Likely money Papa had set aside before he was taken, but even still that wouldn't last forever.

"There is no cost," Darek replied.

"No cost?" Zofia regarded him skeptically.

He shrugged, a look of nonchalance pasted on his face. "All you have to do is write the letter to Janina and I'll make sure she receives it."

Nobody did anything for free now. Not when danger lurked at every corner.

Everything had a price.

Darek lifted his hands, palms up in an innocent gesture. "There really is no cost. Janina is my friend too, if you remember. Just write the letter."

Zofia couldn't turn away his offer. Not when it might be her only opportunity for communication, her solitary chance to say goodbye.

"Thank you," she said. "Truly, this means so much to me."

"I know." There was a lightness to his face when he smiled, something boyish that called to attention how very handsome he really was.

Zofia pushed her hair back self-consciously, curling her fingertips behind her ear to secure her waves into obedience. "I should put these books away."

"I can help you." Darek took the cart. "It's my day off."

"You should be enjoying the afternoon," she protested. "Spending it with your friends."

He didn't relinquish the cart and grinned at her instead. "I am with friends. You and the books. You and…" He lifted a random book from the cart, then smirked as he read the title. *"The Fundamentals of Flatulence."*

Zofia laughed for the first time in a very long time. His cheeks went red and she felt bad enough that she rescued him. "Have you read *The Street of Crocodiles* yet?"

"Kasia has it still, but I have been reading *The Story of My Life* while I wait for her to finish."

"What do you think?" Zofia put a hand out to stop the cart on the aisle where she needed to shelve several books.

Darek obediently stopped alongside her. "It made me realize that I need to go back to school. I quit when the university was closed, but now…" He glanced around and leaned toward her when she selected a text. "Now there are other options."

Yet another reference to the secret schools Papa had spoken of.

"I've been thinking of attending them as well," Zofia said. "I only have one year remaining of secondary school."

She didn't know why she'd said it. Likely for a number of reasons. For the reminder of how Helen Keller had touted the importance of education in *The Story of My Life* and how Zofia had promised Papa she would complete her schooling.

After work that day, she sought out her former Girl Guide captain for information on the clandestine schools. As usual, Krystyna did not disappoint and by that evening Zofia was already enrolled. It was precisely the kind of thing she was bursting to tell Janina about, and now she could. In a careful, roundabout way, of course, just in case the letter fell into the wrong hands.

As promised, Darek came the next day for the letter. Zofia had stayed up late into the night, burning far too much of a candle that was supposed to last a week to get the wording just right.

In careful description, she explained how hard she tried to get into the ghetto and the futility of her efforts. She also detailed life in the library, naming people by their initials only and referencing things in a way Janina would understand, but that a stranger might not.

No sooner was the envelope out of Zofia's hands than she was already anxious for Janina's reply. Days went by without any notice from Darek, each one more fraught with angst than the last.

Despite Zofia's diligence with her work at the library and her efforts with the Gray Ranks that involved sneaking itching powder into a batch of clean underwear to be delivered to the Wehrmacht barracks, her nerves were starting to fray to nothing as she waited for Janina's reply. Finally Darek met her in the warehouse one frigid morning two days before Christmas.

"Sorry it took so long." He spoke in earnest, obviously realizing how agonizingly long she'd been waiting. "My contact only goes into the ghetto a couple of times a week and unfortunately I wasn't able to get away from the university library until now."

He handed her a letter, the strong scent of pomade clinging to the sealed envelope. Zofia brought it to her nose and sniffed.

Yes, definitely pomade.

Darek gave an unexpected laugh. "My friend smuggles your letters in his hat. He slips the envelope into the liner in a small slit there. I take it the letter smells like pomade?"

"I don't care what it smells like so long as I have news from Janina." She held the letter in her hands, eager to read its contents. "Thank you for this."

"My friend said he'd be willing to take another letter if you respond."

Zofia eyed Darek. "Why is your friend being so accommodating?"

"He knows what this means to you."

Somehow Zofia doubted the messenger cared as much as Darek implied, but she was genuinely grateful for the opportunity to correspond with Janina.

Without making Zofia wait any longer, Darek bade her farewell and slipped away, leaving her to read in private.

No sooner had the door slammed closed behind him than she slid her finger under the envelope flap and withdrew the letter.

Chapter 15

Letter from Janina

December 15, 1940

Dearest Z,
I was so excited to receive your letter. I should have known you would find a way to communicate with me beyond these sealed walls. You asked how conditions are here. With most people, I would not be so candid, but I know your question was asked out of concern, so I'm giving you an honest reply.

Yes, it is crowded and continues to become more so. People are sent here from villages outside of Warsaw but have nowhere to live once they arrive. The lucky ones are able to take up residence with another family in a small apartment. Otherwise, they are forced to live on the streets. Despite the overcrowding, more and more people continue to be brought into the ghetto. We are far more fortunate here in the Small Ghetto, as it's called. Those in the larger side are crammed into tiny apartments.

There is even less electricity here than before and I'm constantly shivering. The rations have only gotten more meager after we were locked in here as well. We receive the worst quality items; the carrots are pathetic strings and the potatoes are small and sometimes full of rot. The bread is also made with potatoes and, I think, sawdust. Mama is beside herself as she tries to collect enough rations to see us fed each day. Regardless of if she succeeds or not, we are always hungry.

Papa has been able to find work excavating bricks from buildings that have fallen in on themselves; there are quite a few here that have not been repaired after the German attack on Warsaw. It's brutal, miserable work, and every day he falls asleep as he's eating dinner. It breaks my heart to see him so exhausted.

However, you'll be glad to know I'm finding ways to cope in the best way I can—with books.

I managed to bring my small library with me. I'm grateful to not have been stopped and searched as many were. Any books found in such investigations were confiscated. With all the libraries closed, my neighbor was so desperate for books, she asked if she might borrow one.

Much in the way it was with Mrs. R at the grocery store when you brought books for her, my neighbor asked if a friend might borrow a book as well. The next thing I knew, everyone was asking for books.

That was how it started.

Since then, I have taken to carrying a suitcase up and down these crowded streets, playing something of a librarian in my own right. Dr. B's instruction in our library studies has been integral to keeping track of all my books, which are precious commodities.

Before I leave the house, I know who is seeking a particular book of mine, or perhaps which others I intend to suggest to my readers. That is how I determine what to put into my suitcase for the day. It's ridiculously heavy, but the effort is worthwhile when I see what joy these books bring.

Like our own library, people can't receive their new book unless they give me the previous one they borrowed. It's been a good system overall so far. It's like I'm running my own library. I think Dr. B would be proud.

I've gotten all my books back so far, aside from Mrs. G across the hall who has had The Time Machine *for far past her allotted lending window, but she's such a dear, I don't feel comfortable prodding her.*

Selling secondhand wares has been a big business here. Sometimes I can even find books. I saw our favorite librarian, Mrs. B, one morning while looking for new stock. She was with another fellow bibliophile, a quiet man who used to publish books in Hebrew and has sought to amass a library of books in Hebrew and Yiddish. Apparently, he has so many already that they fill most of his three-bedroom apartment and he has to sleep in the hall.

Mrs. B said she's looking for children's stories in any language she can find, but especially Yiddish. It's for her own sort of library as well, but this one is for children. Remember the old library we used to go to near my grandparents' home? That's where she intends to establish this new wonder.

Now when I'm not running around the ghetto with my suitcase library, I'm assisting Mrs. B setting up her special project. She's asked several other girls to help as well, but I'm the oldest. We have been repairing books in poor condition and organizing everything into catalogs. We should be opening soon and I can hardly wait.

Carpenters are renovating certain areas with moving compartments, so toy shelves can be flipped to reveal a row of book spines. It's truly incredible.

The children here are a sorry sight. With no school to occupy them and so many without parents, they have taken to begging on the streets. It makes my heart physically ache to see them abandoned and in need. Soup kitchens try to feed their empty stom-

achs, but there are so many children and not nearly enough food. Mrs. B hopes that when the library opens, we can provide a safe place for them to escape into books.

I am uncertain if our communication will be able to continue, but your letter brought me such comfort. It was so wonderful to know that the book club has continued to meet and I did get a laugh out of imagining poor K blushing so much. I will try to find a copy of Brave New World *here. Please tell the bandits I think of them often. You are forever in my thoughts, Z, as is your family and everyone we both know and care for. It made me so happy to hear Miss L has been asked to return to her position.*

If you are able to reply, I would love to receive another letter. However, I understand correspondence may be difficult. I will also try on my end to find a way to reach out to you.

While it is a disheartening thought, I fear if I remain here forever and am never able to communicate again, I would be remiss not to say this now: When your brother returns home, tell him I love him too.

I know you weren't ignorant to the relationship blossoming between us. It breaks my heart to imagine never seeing him again either.

Best of luck with completing your last year of school. I'm so proud of you for deciding to return. Don't worry too much about where the future will take you or what career you should choose. Just go about it one day at a time.

I miss you tremendously and think of you always!

Also, Mouse sends his affectionate greetings. He happened upon me writing this and has blown a kiss to the letter, the little charmer. I've promised to share his endearments and now I have done so. I tell you, this boy is a character!

All my love,

J

Zofia reread the letter three times, processing all the details between the candid lines. In her mind, she could perfectly see the library on 67 Leszno Street, where Mrs. Berman from the Warsaw Library would be opening a place for children to come and read. How very like her to put children's education and interest before even her own safety. And Antek… Zofia pressed the letter to her heart. Janina did love him.

After one more read through, Zofia finally replied by the flickering flame of a stub candle. If only it was possible to send food with her reply. Barring that, Zofia added all the złotys she could spare into the letter before sealing the envelope in the hopes the money would find Janina and somehow help.

Chapter 16

CHRISTMAS WAS DISMAL THAT year with Zofia and Matka scarcely talking, the barrier between them as thick and hard as ice. The only cracks that began to show came with the letter they received just after the holiday.

That horrible, soul-crushing letter.

The Pawiak Prison letterhead stamped on top preceded a generic message stating in cold, stark words that Dr. Jan Nowak was dead.

No explanation, no condolences, no details.

The walls between Zofia and Matka came down for a brief interlude, a moment of holding one another, bodies shaking with grief as they mourned the loss together. It didn't last long, barely enough time for their tears to dry and each to wander to their own room to ruminate over Papa's death.

The grim news hadn't been unexpected, of course. Not when they'd heard nothing from him. And yet the force of it had been devastating and whatever sense of closure Zofia had longed for rang hollow.

Returning to work after the new year had been an anticipated reprieve, not only from the chill that had frosted between her and Matka once more, but also from the weight of mourning.

Darek met Zofia in the warehouse upon her arrival, a broad smile pulling at his lips. "Did you have a nice Christmas?"

She didn't want to answer him, to wilt his happiness when there was so little to be had. Nor did she want to mire herself once more into what she was trying to escape.

"As well as can be expected," she replied blithely. "Yours?"

"Good. I spent it with my aunt." He looked down at the ground in a shy manner. "I have something for you."

Zofia's mouth fell open with embarrassment at her own empty hands. "I didn't—"

"It's nothing special, I..." He shrugged and dug a folded page out of his pocket. "It's just a drawing."

She accepted the paper and unfolded it. There, in smooth, dark lines and gradient shading, was an image of Zofia and Janina, their heads bowed close together as if whispering candidly between each other. In the image, Zofia's hands rested lightly on the bottle of vodka and beneath it were the words "To Maria."

At the bottom right was a signature, a large *D* with a squiggle of a name.

The likenesses of herself and Janina were perfect all the way down to the scuff on Zofia's right shoe where she absently nudged it into the ground while lost in thought. The artistry was done by a hand of awe-inspiring skill.

Darek rubbed the back of his neck, his gaze carefully fixed on her. "Losing people is hard, I know. I thought this might be a good way to always have them with you. Until you can see Janina again, of course. I'm only sorry I didn't know what Maria looked like."

Zofia regarded the drawing once more, her appreciation magnifying with his explanation, with the understanding of who had created something so poignant just for her. "You drew this?"

Darek nodded. "Do you like it?"

"It's incredible." She pressed it gently to her chest, over her heart, and looked at him with a fresh perspective, as a true artist. "Thank you."

His fingers were long and tapered, graceful for a man, capable of unfathomable talent. "Do you have the letter?" Darek asked, drawing her focus back up to his handsome face where his cheeks had flushed at her praise.

She nodded and pulled the envelope from her handbag. "Maybe I can also send some food…?" She hesitated, unsure if she was going too far in her request.

Darek didn't appear to be concerned. "I'll have my friend see what he can do. If he can bring food, I will provide it."

"You are doing so much to help me. Is there anything I can do for you?"

She recalled how once he had called her beautiful and her pulse skipped a little faster. He might ask her to accompany him to dinner one evening? Or even for a kiss?

Such considerations shouldn't be appealing.

But he shook his head. "I don't do anything to solicit favors. I just want to help where I can."

A moment lingered between them, layers peeled back to reveal the genuine altruism and a man who drew like a master even as he remained almost shyly humble.

He cleared his throat. "They're forcing the police out of the library at the university, so I'll be busy there for a while as we set things back to rights. There has been considerable damage. In addition to everything else, the Germans started using the card catalog boxes to mail items home and left the cards scattered everywhere."

His anger banked just beneath the surface as he spoke, his eyes bright at the offense. "If the letter comes and I cannot deliver it myself, I'll find a way to get it to you," Darek vowed. And by the intensity in his gaze when he spoke, she knew he would.

January ushered in the start of 1941 amid a frigid flurry of ice and snow. The occupation had been in place for more than a year and their lives were all the worse for it. At least classes had officially begun, which provided a welcome distraction for Zofia from the cases of books the Hitler Youth continued to destroy on a regular basis. Rumor had it that several trucks filled with books were left at the Warsaw Security and Note Printing Works for pulping. Most likely from one of the numerous schools throughout Warsaw that had been divested of its libraries.

She went to Krystyna's apartment on Wilcza Street for the clandestine first class of her last year of secondary school. No one else from their small group had arrived yet.

Krystyna's home was modest, but tidy with a large table set with five chairs in the dining room. Three pictures hung on the wall, men in Polish uniforms depicting two from the Great War and one in the current uniform of the men who had defended Warsaw only a year before. A somber black ribbon draped over the corner of the last image.

Lace curtains were drawn over all the windows, keeping people from seeing inside while still letting in ample light.

"Please take a seat." Krystyna indicated a chair at the oval-shaped dining table. "The others will be joining us over the next fifteen minutes."

Their arrival was intentionally staggered to avoid notice. A group of young women entering the house at the same time was cause for suspicion. As it was, there would only be five of them in total.

The other four girls were from their dissolved Girl Guide group, though Zofia had never been close with any of them.

Krystyna waited until they were all settled, then handed an embroidery hoop, needle, and thread along with a design to stitch.

Zofia accepted hers with dread.

"If we receive a visit from the Nazis, we need to pretend to be sewing," Krystyna explained in her authoritative manner. "What we are doing is very dangerous. Know that coming here to receive this education puts you at risk of arrest or deportation. Perhaps even worse. However, learning a trade is not illegal. You'll each need to start this embroidery before our next meeting."

They all nodded, knowing what they were doing was in defiance of the General Government, that this secret education was one more way to stand against the Nazis.

The skin around Krystyna's eyes tightened with approval. "Then let us begin."

They met three times a week, alternating locations. Some days they met at Krystyna's apartment, other times at the home of their former principal, and sometimes in various people's cellars.

Sometimes they were even sneaked into the library when Herr Nagiel was about his tasks that took him from the building from noon until three every day like clockwork. Those were the riskiest days of all, but the ones they all cherished the most. There, Krystyna had access to science and mathematics texts smuggled temporarily from the German reading room which she had Zofia translate for the other students.

They couldn't have books on them for class, but it didn't mean they didn't receive assignments to be read if the texts could be found. And often, they could be, despite constant regulations and destruction by troops of Hitler Youth groups.

The task to find a certain textbook had Zofia out in the middle of a particularly unforgiving February evening where the bitter wind filtered through the layers of coats and scarves to nestle deep in her bones. Snow had sifted over the street the day before, coating the rooftops the way flour once dusted hot loaves of fresh bread. Zofia's mouth watered at the memory.

The road carved a river of dirty slush between the walkways, leading to Gebethner's Booksellers, an eight-story Gothic-style building set at the corner of Zgoda and Sienkiewicza Street. Zofia had not gone to the location since before the war and now found the bookstore set in the first story to be nearly bare.

"Hello," a young woman greeted Zofia upon her entry. Her blond hair was bound back in a careless updo and she smiled as she casually leaned on the counter. "I'd offer to help, but there's not much to be done with our limited stock."

"This is even worse than the library," Zofia said in quiet awe.

The woman scoffed. "I don't think anything can be worse than the library. There are almost no books left to check out."

"Not through our choice," Zofia said testily.

"Nor through ours either," the woman replied as she came around the counter. She had full hips despite the ration and let them sway like a hypnotist's pendulum when she walked.

"We have all the authorized books here." She indicated a shelf on her right. "General Government–approved children's stories." It was the smallest of the three sections with tales Zofia recognized as similar to their collection at the Warsaw Library. *Robinson Crusoe*, *Nick of the Woods*, and of course *Grimm's Fairy Tales.*

"Then we have the books on the General Government and those on German language and conversation models." These two sections made up the largest assortment by far, the covers brand-new, their spines crisp and unbroken. The woman made a face. "Published right here on the second floor with express permission from the Reich. And our last section." She indicated a shelf on cookbooks. "For the abundance of food crowding our pantries."

Zofia pointed at the cover of *One Hundred Potato Dishes.* "Well, this one at least seems appropriate."

After all, potatoes supplemented their meager rations. Boiled potatoes for breakfast, lunch, and dinner, sometimes with a limp carrot or a pathetic fish that was more scales and bones than meat.

The woman gave a scornful laugh and rested her bottom against a shelf of German books. "So what are you here for? If it's a book in German, you must know it takes months to receive any special orders. We have specific rules to follow in procuring our stock through Germany's booksellers only." She sighed dramatically. "It's an enormous hassle, so I'm hoping you're here for something else."

Zofia looked over the cookbooks. Beyond the joke of the potato recipes, there was a stark ugliness to the other covers of these "approved cookbooks." The *Sugar-Factory at Home* to create one's own sugar. *Making of Honey from Carrots. Vegetable Gardening for Home Consumption.* Those pathetic titles highlighted how much Poland had been going without while Nazis gorged themselves on generous rations.

"Krystyna sent me." Zofia spoke in an even tone.

Based on the conversation, she assumed the store's lone employee had no love for the Nazis, but then few Poles did.

A smile lightened the woman's face. "In that case, you now have more than four lackluster options of books available to you."

The tension around Zofia loosened. "I'm looking for a textbook on physics."

The employee pushed off the rack of books and strode by, curling her finger in a beckoning motion. "This way." She stopped at a locked curio and withdrew a key from her pocket. The locked door clicked open and she shifted a hidden wall, revealing several rows of textbooks.

She pursed her lips, then plucked one with a blue spine free, her smirk sinister. "I hated this one. If you told me three years ago these textbooks would be contraband, I never would have believed you."

"If you told me that I would want to finish school badly

enough that I'd risk my life to attend clandestine classes, I never would have believed you," Zofia retorted.

They shared a bitter chuckle. This was not the world they had been born into. It was not a place in which anyone was meant to live and truly thrive.

"That will be fifty złotys."

The cost was dear. Fifty złotys was a quarter of Zofia's monthly wages from the library. When the same fee could afford a kilogram of lard, the sacrifice for a single textbook was high indeed.

At least now she had the necessary book for class in her pursuit to honor Papa's wishes. That made the price worthy.

As it turned out, physics was no more interesting to Zofia in a clandestine setting than those classes had been in public school. And yet, the impact of what she was doing made her appreciate the opportunity to continue learning.

Their occupiers meant to see all Poles blunted with insufficient education and stripped bare of their heritage by robbing them of their history and culture. This was yet another means of standing against them, by sharpening her wit and honing her knowledge. All the better to combat their enemy.

If the Nazis were doing this to the Poles, what were they doing to the Jews?

Suddenly the inability to have an update from Janina, the absence of her dearest friend, and the stretch of distance between them that felt worlds apart broke Zofia's heart anew.

When Zofia returned to the library the following day, she was met with chaos. Boxes of materials from Krasiński Library were piled in the warehouse as part of a new initiative to make a collective State Library in Warsaw. The three parts of this were to be a university library with German books, a National Library with Nazi-approved Polish material and the third was comprised of the special collection from the Krasiński Library. The latter of which was unceremoniously dumped at the main library branch without details on what any of the boxes contained.

In short, the project was a mess that left the reduced staff in a frenzy of confusion. Zofia opened a box to figure out where to place these new items. Inside, she found history mixed with mathematics, incorporated with old manuscripts and even a faded children's book. What was worse, the items had been crammed into the box, resulting in crumpled pages and two broken spines.

The barbarians.

"It looks as bad here as it does at the university," a familiar voice said from behind Zofia.

She turned to find Darek behind her, his dark hair ruffled from the wind and his cheeks pink. He gave her a smile and she felt her own lips lift in return.

"I have something you've been waiting for." He glanced about before withdrawing two letters from his coat. "My aunt said this one came for you yesterday, but she didn't trust leaving it here."

Zofia accepted the first envelope and found it to be from Dr. Weigl stating the vaccines were ready and he would be sending a couple doses along as soon as it was safe to do so.

"And one from Janina." Darek presented the letter to Zofia.

She hugged the letter to her chest. "I appreciate this so much more than I could ever say."

A shadow crossed Darek's expressive eyes.

"What is it?" Panic slid over Zofia like ice. "Janina, is she all right?"

"Yes." Darek held out his hands, palms toward her in a calming motion. "There have been rumors that the pharmacy will be shut down soon and reopened on the Polish side only."

Zofia's fingers instinctively tightened around the envelope, as if she could hold on to her means of communication just as fiercely.

"I'll try to meet with my contact more often to ensure your letters are delivered expediently," Darek promised.

Zofia nodded her thanks. As soon as she had a moment alone in one of the back rooms, she opened the envelope and read Janina's newest letter.

Chapter 17

Letter from Janina

February 10, 1941

Dearest Z,
I'm delighted to have heard from you again and hope this letter makes its way to you. Each bit of communication through these sealed walls is truly such a gift.

I wish I could say things have improved here, but they continue to grow worse. Food is becoming more and more scarce. A black market has opened for the purchase of food and other goods, though the cost is exorbitant. The man your father recommended to take over Papa's business has continued to send money, and through that, we've been able to be fed. Few people are so lucky.

In the Large Ghetto, many people do not have enough to eat, their bodies whittled away to little more than bones, the bellies and feet swollen with the extent of their starvation. More and more

Jews are being forced into the ghetto and people have stopped being generous with their living space. There are so many people who have to live on the street with little to no food. Z, they're starving, many of them children. It's so awful. I hear them crying out at night, begging for food. They are so piteous, even the guards do not reprimand them for being out past curfew.

My parents have opened our home to these new people coming into the ghetto and have allowed three families to live with us. Can you imagine it? Four families in our small apartment! Everyone is respectful of the other's space thus far, though Mama did notice some of our food goes missing from time to time. We've taken to sleeping with anything edible tied in a bundle beside our bed to ensure nothing more is taken. Food is far too precious a commodity.

Mouse still lives across the hall, but his father was killed, shot for no reason whatsoever by a random bullet fired into a crowd as Nazi entertainment. It's a sick game, and one that is played often. Our intrepid, charming Mouse has deemed himself the "man of the house" and has become a smuggler to obtain food for his sister and mother. Boys like him manage to wriggle through holes in the wall, ones made larger with loosened bricks. I worry for him. Those boys are not well treated when they are discovered. He is, of course, confident he will never be caught.

Seeing the children is the hardest part of being in this awful place. I continue to deliver books from my suitcase, which is looking very battered these days. As are the books, if I'm being honest. The pages are worn and dirty from so many hands with so little access to soap. But I spend most of my time at the children's library. The small patrons who come in break my heart. Sullen and quiet, not at all how children should be. It is impossible to tell how old they are without the plumpness of youth. Their faces are those of old men and women, their eyes flat from hunger and witnessing the horrors of this new life.

Every day they come to the library, seeking to feed their appetite with distraction through books even as their bellies remain empty.

I read for the ones who cannot yet read themselves and their eyes devour the brightly colored pictures. One little girl told me the books make her forget the gnawing ache of cold and hunger.

We work with the orphanage and the children's hospital to bring stories to keep up their spirits. Sadly, the books that go to certain areas of the hospital that are rife with typhus require us to leave the books there for fear they will spread the illness. Contagion is already so hard to quarantine as it is. But those children are so immensely grateful when they do receive new books that we can never deny their requests.

Every day tears at my soul to see the suffering of those who are so small and vulnerable, but how could I possibly stop when I know what my efforts mean to them?

Mrs. B has been teaching me Yiddish. She says I am a quick study. Truth be told, I think your instruction in German has helped me considerably in this endeavor. It's remarkable how similar the languages are. I was even able to read a book in Yiddish to the children the other day. Bubbe would have been so proud of me. That realization left me with tears in my eyes by the time I finished the book, and the children soothed me with hugs. How fiercely those thin arms can squeeze when offering comfort and love.

Enough on the children, or I fear this letter won't be legible for all my tears.

Instead, I have to tell you about Mrs. G. I finally worked up the gall to ask her for The Time Machine. *She confessed she has been copying it, would you believe it?*

The novel is her husband's favorite since he was a boy. They are older and Mr. G can barely afford to feed them both, let alone have the funds left over to purchase a book. So, Mrs. G was copying it onto scrap pages she managed to acquire. She showed her work to me, and it's exquisite. Each of the letters was painstakingly copied in a hand so neat, it appeared to have been printed by the finest press.

I offered to give her the book, but she refused, saying it was nearly done and graciously wanting it to remain in circulation so that others might enjoy it as much as her husband. She did, however, allow me to help her create a cover for it and sew it with binding like Dr. B showed us.

The Gs are such good people, always giving what they have to others, even if it means some nights they don't eat, themselves.

I was there when she presented it to him for his sixtieth birthday. Oh, Z, when he opened the gift and he saw what his wife had done, his chin quivered and his eyes filled with tears. His voice was so thick, he could scarcely speak to say it was the most beautiful present he'd received in his whole life.

Isn't it so heart-achingly perfect what books mean to people? It made me miss the Bandit Book Club tremendously—all those hours we spent discussing what the characters and stories meant to us. I wish I could join all of you again.

I suppose the gift for Mr. G also reminds me of your brother and how much he loves The Time Machine. *My heart still holds out hope of his return, as I'm sure yours does too.*

There I go crying again.

I miss you tremendously. But I don't wish you were here. I wouldn't wish anyone was here, even that awful girl from school whose nose you ruined with that well-placed punch. Instead, I wish we had our own time machine, that we could wind the days backward to the point where the war had never started. From there, we would find a way to stop Hitler in his tracks, and then in this moment, we would all be safe and warm and full.

It is that thought I leave you with, one of comfort and normalcy and love, as I sign off on this letter. I think of you always, my dearest friend.

With love,

J

Zofia shed tears of her own as she read the letter. For the desolate life Janina had described, for the children who endured such suffering. Zofia couldn't imagine Mrs. Steinman, who took such pride in a clean and lovely home, dealing with so many people crammed into the apartment, worrying about theft. Just as it was impossible to imagine little Mouse stepping up as man of the house when he was so very young.

When Zofia wrote back this time, she shared the news of Papa's death and the strange new library system. But outside of that, she tried to find positive aspects of life to include—like the beautiful picture Darek had drawn of them and the way Danuta was so eager to discuss *The Street of Crocodiles* after reading it first, knowing it would be a while until they could meet again. In this moment in their lives, Zofia realized it was she who needed to be positive for Janina.

Chapter 18

ZOFIA TUCKED HER HANDBAG closer to her, cradling the hidden book within under her arm as she passed the column where announcements were attached near Świętokrzyska Street. The execution statement of several detainees was plastered there, highlighting the awful news in bold font. The victims of the Nazi's latest punishment were sentenced for killing the notorious collaborator and famed actor Igo Sym. All of those innocent victims had come from Pawiak Prison. People who were no more guilty than Zofia's father had been.

The horror of it stayed with her as she rushed across the street toward the hidden warehouse.

Even this atrocity of executing innocent Polish prisoners paled in comparison to what was happening in the ghetto where Janina was. Papa's prediction about the spread of typhus in close quarters had come to pass. As soon as Zofia finished Janina's letter, she'd replied to Dr. Weigl asking him to hurry with the vaccines, discreetly specifying a need for at least three. One for each of the Steinmans. She only hoped he wouldn't be too late.

The quiet of the dilapidated lending library assailed her. Somewhere within, a plinking of water dripping echoed off the cold, empty walls. Down in the warehouse, sunlight streamed in through the narrow windows at the top, illuminating the rows of shelving, over a quarter now filled with books whose duplicates had been brutally destroyed. Zofia liberated a copy of *With Fire and Sword* by Henryk Sienkiewicz from her bag, the first of his trilogy of novels set in seventeenth-century Poland, and settled it next to Sienkiewicz's *Quo Vadis.*

Quo Vadis was a brilliantly written love story set in ancient Rome, where an officer fell in love with a Christian woman and their romance led to his conversion to Christianity. It was Matka's favorite book, which meant a copy was also buried under the loose floorboards in Zofia's bedroom where she concealed what was left of Papa's once-extensive library.

A thunk came from above.

Zofia went still.

A steady crunch sounded, like footsteps over the gritty main floor.

Zofia locked the air in her lungs, too afraid to even exhale lest whoever was upstairs might hear her. As if she could freeze in place and be made invisible by silence.

Had someone seen her enter? There would be no reason for anyone to be in the ruined building otherwise.

The footsteps slapped down the stairs and her heart hammered so hard against her ribs, it was surely audible.

Her thoughts swirled like bits of ice in a blizzard, disorientating and too frenzied to catch. Where could she hide? What could she say as an excuse? Had she locked the door behind her? She couldn't recall…

The scrape as a key slid into the lock and a click echoed in the open warehouse. Whoever it was had a key.

The door swung open. "Zofia?"

Breath exhaled from Zofia in a rush. "Darek?"

"I didn't mean to scare you." He hastily locked the door behind him.

Zofia put her hand to her chest where her heart fluttered like a trapped moth. She remained where she stood, her back pressed against the empty shelving behind her.

"I'm sorry." Darek approached and gave her an apologetic smile. His gaze fell on the small collection of Sienkiewicz's works and his features lightened. "That's fitting." He held up *The Deluge*, the second book of the author's trilogy, and added it beside the first.

"I've always liked Sienkiewicz," Zofia said thoughtfully when she was recovered enough to speak. "His research really shows how hard Poland has fought, and how turbulent our past was before we finally earned the shortlived freedom we enjoyed before the occupation."

Darek's jaw flexed. "And why we still continue to fight." His head dropped to his chest and remained there, a look of defeat despite his vehement declaration.

Concern prickled over Zofia. "Darek, what is it?"

He finally looked up at her, his eyes bloodshot with tears. "I was part of it."

"Part of what?"

"Igo Sym." His lips parted and he drew in a harsh breath, then turned away from her. "I didn't pull the trigger this time, but I was integral in his execution, to seeing it carried out. The Home Army sought me out for the task. I couldn't say no…"

This time.

"There will be more executions of Nazi collaborators?" Zofia asked through numb lips.

"And more innocent Poles killed in retaliation." His finger ran over the spine of *The Deluge*. "Igo Sym was tried in an underground court with the Polish Underground State for his cooperation with the Nazis and found guilty, sentenced to death. We knew the General Government would retaliate by killing Poles who had nothing to do with Igo's death. We knew many innocent men and women would die for one man's meted justice."

That was the way of things now. One Nazi's demise exacted the toll of a few dozen Polish lives.

They all knew as much. It was the cost of fighting back. And the detail of the information Darek shared now was dangerous. The Nazis had held those Polish hostages for three days while they offered Warsaw the chance to come forward and confess who had killed the actor.

"Why are you telling me this?" she asked.

"Because I had to tell someone." He turned to her, the haunted look in his eyes boring into her soul. "It's like I have a coal burning inside my chest keeping it locked inside me. And I trust you."

If Janina were there, at that moment, she would have opened her arms to this man who wore his heart in his long-lashed gaze and try to heal him. But Zofia was not that woman.

"You are fighting for a free Poland." She didn't look away from the intensity of his stare as she spoke. "You are fighting to give us our lives back, to give us what our parents and previous generations fought and died for. Freedom. And I want to join you."

She was desperate to do something more than delivering underground newspapers or putting stickers on walls or pestering cinemagoers. This was what she'd hoped to be doing in the fight against the Reich.

"It's only men who are tasked with executions right now." Darek ran a hand through his dark hair and the silky strands fell effortlessly back into place. "Even if it wasn't, I can't put this burden on your shoulders."

She reached for his hands and held them in her own. Charcoal dust had settled into the grooves of his fingertips, reminding her of the talent of his artistic skills. Those hands that could create such beauty were now being wielded against the enemy as a weapon.

"What you are doing for Poland is noble," she whispered fiercely. "You are fighting for us all."

Their hands remained clasped for a long time, the silence between them intimate and comfortable. He had trusted her with the enormity of his secret and she would never betray him.

And someday, she would find a way to join. To fight.

It did not take Zofia long to adapt to life in school once more. Krystyna was a proficient teacher and the small class size meant there was an opportunity for lessons to move along at a quicker pace. For the first time in years, Zofia was challenged by the instruction rather than watching the minutes slowly drag by.

One day, during a lesson on Polish history, Krystyna flipped over one of the paintings of the soldiers from the Great War to reveal a map smoothed along the back of the canvas. The girl beside Zofia jumped slightly at the thump of the painting bumping the wall.

They were all on edge after the latest rumor about a secret class being found out by the Gestapo. The officers shot the professor and arrested the remainder of the students, who were never heard from again.

It was a reminder of the danger they courted, but also the importance of that risk. They were lucky to have someone to instruct them in every subject. Most secondary education had to be taught by multiple people, which made clandestine schools even harder to navigate with either the teachers rotating locations or the students.

But then, most instructors were not like Krystyna.

Maybe it was all the surprising educational tools she had nestled in the decor of her home that made her teaching so fascinating. Or perhaps it was how her face lit up with each new subject, instructing it as though it was the greatest story ever told. Regardless, she made the lessons enjoyable.

"As we all know, prior to gaining our independence following the Great War, Poland was divided between Prussia..." She indicated a shaded area of the map with the butt of her pen, then swept toward another location. "Russia." Then on to another. "And the Habsburg monarchy." The glint in her eye and the quirk of one brow spoke of a scandalous tale from history soon to follow. "Now, what you might not have known about the monarchy—"

The rumble of an engine beneath the window made them all pause. They waited in agonizing silence to see if it passed.

It did not.

The engine cut off. Whoever it was had parked at their building.

Krystyna calmly turned the painting back around, revealing the solemn-faced soldier once more, as though his conscience was weighted down by the secret he carried.

Footsteps thundered up the stairs, their echoes banging through the small apartment.

Krystyna glanced around the room to ensure nothing else was out of place. But then, she was always good about setting things to rights as soon as she'd used one of her hidden instructional tools. "Ladies, if you'd please take out your needlework."

The code word meant they also had to hide anything pertaining to their lessons. Zofia folded up her notes and slipped them into her shoe. The girl beside her remained frozen where she sat.

Zofia nudged her and the girl quickly folded her own notes with shaking hands before similarly tucking the paper into her own shoe.

A knock thundered from the door. Zofia leaped at the ferocity.

Krystyna set aside her own needlework and calmly approached the door. The bird stitched into the center was almost complete, each bit of thread on the little ringed plover perfectly sewn with a back that likely mirrored the front. All around Zofia the other girls had loops that were just as neatly embroidered.

Stomach sinking, Zofia examined her own embroidery hoop. With an arthritic foot sprouting from its breast, and an eye that hovered at the top of its head rather than near the beak, it scarcely resembled the delicate birds that darted about on the shores of the Vistula River.

In hindsight, she ought to have asked Matka to help her. But that would have required talking to Matka, which Zofia was still not feeling gracious enough to do.

The letters from Janina only fueled Zofia's anger at her mother for not allowing the Steinmans to live with them instead of being forced into the ghetto. Because Matka didn't want the apartment too crowded or to take on the risk, Janina and her family were living in hell.

Boots thudded over Krystyna's glossy wood floors as four Wehrmacht soldiers and an officer appeared in the doorway of the living room, their expressions hard and calculating.

The girl beside Zofia trembled like a leaf in a brisk wind and Zofia found her throat was suddenly too dry to swallow.

"Good afternoon, gentlemen—you've arrived just in time for our embroidery lesson." Krystyna held a hand up, presenting her students with their innocent hoops.

"I would like to look around further," the officer said in smooth Polish.

"Of course." Krystyna took a step back against the wall, her skirt intentionally covering a glass with scratches on it to indicate measurements. The item was seemingly benign, but inviting any amount of suspicion was unwise.

The soldiers walked around the table slowly, examining the embroidery over each woman's shoulder. While they did this, the officer went to the paintings on the wall and reached to lift the one with the map.

"Please, sir." Krystyna put a hand to her chest, her light blue eyes imploring. "Have respect. My grandfather died during the Great War and that painting is all I have to remember him by."

A shadow fell over Zofia, and a body suddenly blocked her from seeing if Krystyna's request was fulfilled. Zofia tried to angle her embroidery toward her chest so the man standing over her wouldn't see how bad it was.

She looked up, meeting him in the eye—a distraction and a challenge all at once. He was young, around Antek's age, with pale lashes and a wry twist to his lips.

He plucked the hoop from her hands before she could think to tighten her grip. Her stomach knotted, waiting for him to call out their entire ruse. The folded notes lay awkwardly under her heel, the corner sharp where it pressed at the arch of her foot. She had brought them all down with her wretched needlework.

Krystyna did a double take at the embroidery and her face paled slightly.

"Look at this." The soldier held Zofia's mutilated embroidery in the air.

Then, to Zofia's great surprise, he burst out laughing. He jutted a claw-like hand from his stomach and rolled his eyes up in his head, imitating Zofia's bird. The others roared with laughter. Even the officer chuckled.

But amid the mortified heat blazing in Zofia's cheeks at their mockery, there was still a live wire of fear running down her spine.

"Enough, enough." The officer waved his hand at the soldier. "Let me see it."

The soldier gave him Zofia's embroidery hoop. The officer studied it for a long moment, then regarded Zofia. "This is yours?"

Zofia nodded. *"Ja."*

The stoicism on his face broke in a brief chortle of laughter and he shook his head. "You need a *lot* of work."

"Which is why she's here," Krystyna chimed in. "Zofia has

only recently joined my class. The others were just as rough when they first started." She gave a proud smile. "Soon they'll all be skilled embroiderers."

The officer regarded the other hoops with an approving nod. "Very well. Continue on." He gestured toward the door and the entourage departed, leaving heavy silence in their wake.

None of the girls moved until the roar of the car began again and rumbled its way down the street, resuming its prowl through Warsaw.

All eyes turned toward Zofia and she wished she could melt into the floor.

Krystyna picked up Zofia's embroidery and gave a sad shake of her head. "I think next time, I'll sew this for you first." Her mouth flexed as if she were trying not to smile, then she finally laughed, the sound husky and deep. "I loathe the Nazis, but that man did a perfect impression of your bird."

Even Zofia couldn't help but chuckle at that.

After their mirth died away, the girl next to Zofia lifted her large, sad brown eyes up to the soldier's portrait from the Great War. "I'm sorry about your grandfather, Krystyna."

"Oh, my grandfather is alive and well, working as a cobbler in Praga." Krystyna gestured in the direction across the river. "I don't know who this man is, but the frame fit my map perfectly when I bought the painting several months ago."

"You look as though someone has walked over your grave," Mrs. Mazur said when Zofia joined her in the warehouse that afternoon following her lessons. "What happened?"

"The Wehrmacht came to Krystyna's today for an inspection." Zofia rolled her eyes at the foolish mistake that might have gotten them killed. "I thought my awful embroidery skills were going to put us all in Pawiak, but in the end, it might be what saved us."

"It couldn't have been that bad."

"We're supposed to be learning how to sew and, well..." Zofia pulled the hoop out of her bag and passed it to Mrs. Mazur, who burst into laughter.

"Maybe it *is* that bad." She wiped moisture from the corners of her eyes. "It's a good thing you are so adept at your work here. I don't think you have a career in sewing."

"Have I received any parcels?" Zofia asked, pointedly ignoring her mirth. There had been enough at her expense for one day.

All at once, seriousness fell over Mrs. Mazur and she was back to being the efficient authoritarian. "In the top drawer of my desk, behind the rejected budget suggestions. I figured no one would look there. I've also already called Darek over."

No sooner had she said his name, Darek rushed into the warehouse and practically jogged toward them. "Are they here?"

Zofia went to the drawer and nudged aside the budget ledger. She and Mrs. Mazur had spent months putting together a budget plan to recoup lost books—Hitler-approved ones, of course—as well as acquire necessary supplies that were nearly gone. The proposal hadn't even been glanced over before the General Government rejected it. Zofia's fingertips brushed beneath the cloth-bound book and caught the smooth side of a wrapped parcel.

She pulled it out and peeled the paper from the box, revealing a dark blue box sealed with a white strip. "Prof. R. Weigl" was printed in red and beneath that "Vacc. Ty.exanthem" in white letters on a red background.

The typhus vaccine.

Inside the box were three glass bulbs with liquid at the bottom. Enough for Janina and her family.

For the first time in longer than she cared to remember, Zofia's spirits soared. That was until she caught Darek's sorrowful expression.

She shook her head, not wanting to hear whatever tragic news he meant to deliver.

"The pharmacy has already closed down, Zofia."

"No." Disbelief and horror knotted in her gut. "There has to be some way for him to go back, to bring this to them."

Mrs. Mazur cast an anxious glance at her nephew. "Perhaps you can take them and just ask…?"

Darek nodded, and though the doubt in his gaze was unmistakable, he accepted the vaccines. "I'll see what I can do."

With that, he slipped away, taking all of Zofia's hopes with him.

Chapter 19

THERE WAS NO SLEEP to be had as Zofia waited to hear if Janina and her family received the vaccines. Three days passed of distracted work, distracted lessons, and even a distracted book club where they were finally able to discuss *The Street of Crocodiles* by Bruno Schulz.

While Zofia had enjoyed *The Street of Crocodiles*, finding it both surreal in a dreamlike way and almost overwhelmingly descriptive, she had been too caught up in her own thoughts about Janina to offer much insight. Especially when Danuta articulated her opinions with such eloquence and pinpoint accuracy. There was much comparing of Schulz to Kafka and the depth of evocative imagery Schulz's work brought to life. Outside of those details, there was little point in Zofia offering her own bumbling take. In the end, they let Danuta choose and no one was surprised when she selected *The Doll* by Bolesław Prus.

On the morning of the fourth day, Zofia was staring out the window, lost in a constant jumble of worried thoughts as raindrops chased one another down the pane. *The Doll* lay open before her on page one, its content read five times over without a single word processed. But how could she read or even think when her mind was so fogged from tossing and turning all night?

A knock came at the door, startling her.

"Who could that be?" Matka emerged from her room and rushed to the door before Zofia could even stand. She pulled the door open and her slender shoulders stiffened with surprise. "Zofia, you have a visitor."

Zofia rose from her chair and peered around her mother. Darek offered Zofia a shy smile. His dark hair was soaked from the rain and droplets glistened like crystals on his wool coat.

"Please, come in," she said quickly and ushered him inside.

Matka lifted her brows and Zofia found herself grateful that at least her mother's displeasure was silent. There would be questions later, but they would be worth every tortuous second.

The room fell into a stark silence.

"I have to finish something in my room." Matka's performance was an awkward one, but Zofia appreciated her departure nonetheless.

Her door snicked closed, but Zofia suspected Matka pressed her ear to the crack to listen.

"I'm so sorry for coming here," Darek said. "My aunt gave me your address and I knew you'd want to know right away."

Zofia nodded. "Yes, of course. What is it? Were you able to get the vaccines to Janina?"

"Yes." Relief shone in his eyes. "My contact was able to administer the shots himself, and I was able to bring you this as well." He pulled a folded paper from his pocket. There was no envelope this time, just a hastily torn page from a ledger that had been folded in half. "It's the last now. There isn't a way for him to go back into the ghetto with the pharmacy closed."

Zofia nodded, overcome by a contrasting mix of joy and sorrow. "Thank you," she managed. "Thank you for this gift, for all you've done for Janina, for me..."

His lips parted, as though he meant to say something, his eyes unreadable for the first time since Zofia had known him, shadowed with an emotion she couldn't name. All at once, his expression smoothed into a good-natured smile. "I'm glad to have helped." With that, he turned and saw himself out.

As soon as the door shut, she read Janina's letter.

Dearest Z,

You are an angel, and so is your messenger. I don't know how he was able to find us in this chaos, but thankfully he has. We have all received our inoculations for typhus, which will make my efforts at the children's library all the more helpful. The ghetto borders are shifting and we were made to leave our home. Our new location is more cramped with far too many families in one place. But I am too rushed to go into any of that.

Forgive me, but I cannot say more as there is no time. Know that you might well have saved us all with this vaccine. Thank you. I have cherished your friendship these long years and will always hold you in my heart.

With eternal love and affection,

J

Zofia stared at the scrawled words as the desolate reality sank in. This was likely the last communication they would ever share.

PART TWO

Chapter 20

Seventeen months later
August 1942

ZOFIA OPENED THE LIBRARY'S copy of *One Hundred Potato Dishes* and cringed at the offensive new library stamp glaring up at her. The previous one had depicted a fighting mermaid, but the Reich now claimed all books as theirs. They managed to strip off the original Warsaw Public Library stamp and replaced all books with their own: a swastika and an eagle accompanied with the words "Staatsbibliothek Aht. I." This abomination infiltrated not only the more contemporary collections, but also manuscripts and artifacts that dated back to the fourteenth century.

This was yet another set of the abysmal new laws in place to transfer the Polish libraries into the full control of the General Government.

Zofia shut the book and forced a smile, handing it to the patron. "You'll need to return this in two weeks."

"I won't need two weeks." The woman took the book with a look of chagrin. "I wish we could get copies of Marta Krakowska's books again."

Zofia gave her customary response to the popular lamentation. "We can only hope to have those on our shelves again soon."

There were, of course, Marta Krakowska books stored in the hidden warehouse, waiting to be lent out once more after the occupation.

A man stepped forward after the woman departed with her cookbook. "Do you have a copy of *Anna Karenina*?" he asked.

"I'm afraid Tolstoy has been removed from our catalog," Zofia replied.

After Hitler turned on the Soviets and consumed their portion of Poland a year before, all Russian books had been banned from Poland as well. If Hitler continued to take over the world, there would be no books left to read at all.

At least not legally.

In fact, they did have a copy of *Anna Karenina* by Leo Tolstoy. It had been the Bandit Book Club's most recent read. They only met every five months or so now, or however long it took for them to read the single copy they shared. Sometimes faster, if they could find multiple copies in the secret bookshelf at Gebethner's. As the days pressed on, the Nazis grew more violent, more cruel, and therefore the book club became ever more dangerous.

She'd spent much time at the bookstore in the previous year with so many texts needed for her education. Fortunately, she'd been able to sell them back when she was done, as promised by the woman at Gebethner's. In January, Zofia had taken the final test for her secondary education. It had been done in her former principal's home with him watching sternly as they all sat at his dining room table. When she'd passed, she was awarded a voucher that could be exchanged for a certificate of completion after the war. Papa would have been proud.

The patron in front of Zofia sighed. "There are hardly any books to choose from anymore."

There were plenty of books, of course. But they were from a very curated list.

Zofia said nothing. After all, the choice was not hers. Especially with the numerous lists that kept coming, each one condemning books for destruction. She and the others saved what they could, hiding them among newspapers when the Wehrmacht kept a closer eye on them, and secreting them in boxes when left unsupervised.

The hidden warehouse was nearly full now with only one empty shelf remaining. Soon they would have to acquire boxes to stack along the walls.

Mrs. Mazur came into the lending library to relieve Zofia. "Time for you to head upstairs."

Zofia grabbed a pile of children's books that had been returned as she slid from the stall and allowed Mrs. Mazur to take her place. Upstairs in the youth reading room, the large table was crowded with patrons.

More and more children were appearing at the library as time went on. Many of them were desperate for distraction, to read about faraway places they could not go, or to transport themselves to mythical lands that could still tease at their dulled imaginations. They wanted stories where villains were vanquished.

But books were more than a means of escape for these children; they offered another life to live. They offered hope.

Unfortunately, not all the books could withstand the amount of love they received. With so many people reading now and so few books to be had, they were often returned with the pages torn, dirty, and soft from use. But those items weren't pulled from circulation until they could no longer remain intact. Not when there hadn't been any budgets approved to purchase new books since before the war.

An older girl entered the children's area with her four small sisters trailing behind her. The five of them all had messy blond braids and narrow faces. It wasn't the first time Zofia had seen this group. Sadly, theirs was not an uncommon sight.

Many fathers were prisoners of war, leaving mothers to work in factories or in restaurants to eke out a mean wage to support the family. That meant the older children assumed the task of motherhood at far too early an age. Though they could attend school up to the fourth grade, many did not have time between laundry, cooking, housekeeping, and getting the younger children to their lessons.

Ewa was the oldest at around eight years old and busied herself adjusting socks and smoothing hair on the other four before turning her attention to Zofia.

"What story would you like to read today?" Zofia indicated the stack of books she'd carried from the lending room downstairs. They were some of the more popular stories that were usually already borrowed and thus unavailable.

The girl studied the books, her lips pursed in thought. Three of the selections had more pictures than words. They would be an easy choice. But Ewa was always pushing herself a little harder and instead selected the thick copy of *Robinson Crusoe.*

Two months before, the girl would never have been confident enough to select a book with chapters.

Every afternoon for the last six months, Zofia had assumed a rotational shift at the youth reading room after months in the lending area. It was at the time of day that school let out for the younger children, and their older siblings assuming adult roles took them to the library for something to do. The library was more than entertainment; it was a refuge.

But while the younger children received an education, the older ones often did not even know how to read. Janina had inspired Zofia to focus her attention on the children, and Zofia put herself to the task of teaching the older ones how to read.

If only there was a way to reach out to Janina once more, to let her know the positive impact she'd had on these young lives, even with a wall separating them.

Through it all, Zofia had not stopped her efforts in trying to help Janina and her family. Few organizations were available to offer aid or food, and even those who could were overwhelmed. Without an address, Janina and her family couldn't be helped.

Eager for a distraction from her frustrating inability to save Janina, Zofia handed Ewa the book and settled back in her chair to listen to the girl's careful, overly enunciated reading. Ewa's sisters pressed closer, enraptured by the eldest, who they clearly held in high regard.

On the way home later that evening, Zofia stopped by Traugutta Street where Miss Laska would be closing up the small reading room there. The older woman worked the library entirely on her own most days, a task she never once complained about.

Zofia pushed through the door and found herself in a room framed in by shelves, the offering of books meager compared to how they had once been.

"Zofia." Miss Laska shuffled toward her. "You didn't have to come." She smiled, her upper lip pulling down slightly to hide the eyetooth she'd recently lost.

"You always say that." Zofia set her bag aside and took a heavy box of books from the table to the back room. Its weight would have been impossible for Miss Laska to manage.

"And you always say you enjoy my company."

"I do enjoy your company." Zofia returned from the back room and put her hands on her hips. "What can I do?"

"Well, since you're here..." Miss Laska gave another shielded smile, but wasn't fast enough to hide a flash of the redness of her receding gums. Zofia had noticed them becoming worse with the passing months.

"I can't seem to reach this shelf to water the plant. I fear the poor thing will die of thirst." Miss Laska pointed up to a plant with limp waxy leaves, its stems crinkled with dehydration.

But what truly caught Zofia's attention was the massive bruise that showed on the older woman's forearm.

"Miss Laska, what happened?" Zofia gently clasped the librarian's arm before she could pull her sleeve down. The bruise covered the length of her forearm and was dark as night with a sickly green-yellow discoloration framing the injury.

Miss Laska's skin was soft and delicate beneath Zofia's fingers, as if it might tear if handled without the lightest touch.

"Oh, I just hit it on a table." Miss Laska waved off Zofia's concern. "I bruise easily these days. It happens with age."

"And the sore on your other arm?"

Miss Laska sighed like a child caught lying, and reluctantly pulled up her other sleeve to reveal a wound on her elbow that was no closer to healing than it had been a month ago.

"It isn't age," Zofia pressed. "It's scurvy."

One of the books in Papa's hidden collection was about medicine. After noticing Miss Laska's wound was not healing and that several older librarians at the main branch were suffering from similar afflictions, Zofia looked up the symptoms.

"Scurvy," Miss Laska scoffed. "I'm no pirate on the high seas. Though that would be quite the adventure."

"But you aren't eating properly either." Zofia retrieved her bag. "I suspected this might be an issue and brought you some cabbage and potatoes. You need to eat this in addition to the bread rations you receive."

Miss Laska began to shake her head, protesting the extra food.

"Please, do it for me." Zofia pushed the small sack toward the older woman's hands until she finally accepted it. They were black market goods procured at a steep price, but a worthwhile sacrifice. "I want you to be healthy."

Miss Laska reached out with a cool, dry hand and clutched Zofia's fingers. "You do too much."

But really, Zofia felt she didn't do nearly enough.

On the way home from the reading room, she altered her path to ensure she strode by the ghetto wall.

Though the ghetto had shifted to exclude Janina's home on Próżna Street, the border hadn't moved far. Zofia walked past her friend's former home, still able to recall every room of the small apartment, and tried to imagine what it must have been like with four families living within. A new wall was erected halfway down the street in the same hodgepodge mix of various brickwork scavenged from demolished buildings.

It was just as tall as the previous one, and still impossible to see over. But she didn't need to glimpse the other side to know the horrors that lay there. Her other senses were keen enough.

The stink of rot exuded through the wall, and the pops of gunfire rang out at all hours. The cries for food, for help, and for the loss of loved ones were impossible not to hear no matter how many people rushed by pretending otherwise.

The smells and sounds were even worse in a farther area of the ghetto, past the bridge built the prior year over Chłodna Street that connected the two parts of the ghetto. There, the stench was strong enough to make Zofia retch. Not only rot but the unmistakable odor of death.

Every time Zofia passed that bridge, she looked up, hoping to find Janina among the crowd moving swiftly over the structure. Anyone who stopped as they crossed earned a sharp reprimand and sometimes was even shot at. Likewise, guards remained on Chłodna Street shoving Poles aside who stood too long. Zofia had borne more than her fair share of aggressive nudges away from that bridge.

The sky had gone dark while Zofia was helping Miss Laska.

The journey home would take just under half an hour and curfew was quickly approaching. While it would be faster to take the trams, the risk of a roundup was too great. It wasn't unheard-of for trams to be ordered to stop as Wehrmacht soldiers entered from either side and arrested every person trapped within.

No, it was better to walk if it could be helped.

The summer night air was a delicious reprieve from the heat earlier that day and she let her thoughts wander as her feet followed the familiar path home.

Perhaps that was why she did not notice the person in the courtyard of her apartment as she approached the back door.

A shadow moved near the only tree, amid a whisper of rustling grass. The hair stood on Zofia's arms and she took an instinctive step back.

She froze, caught between the impulse to dash up the stairs, risking them coming after her, or asking who they were. Before the split second of contemplation passed, a figure stepped from behind the tree.

"Zofia." Though the soft voice was merely a whisper, Zofia would recognize it anywhere in the entire world.

Her heart clogged her throat and her reply came out in a rasp as she uttered a single name. "Janina?"

Chapter 21

JANINA STEPPED FROM THE shadows into the light of the waning moon. The silvery glow fell on a face Zofia knew well, though thinner now with gaunt cheeks and hollows under Janina's dark eyes. Despite the hard life that Zofia had only glimpsed through letters, Janina was still as lovely as she'd ever been. Her hair was pulled back in a neat knot and her dress and sweater were in good repair.

Zofia stared, incapable of doing anything more.

A year and a half of separation had passed between them, after a lifetime at one another's sides.

Zofia had mourned the loss like a death, forcing herself to come to terms with Janina's absence to keep from becoming overwhelmed by the constant hurt. Especially knowing they were only several blocks away from one another. So close and yet so completely inaccessible.

And now, like an apparition in the early-August night, there she was: Janina in the flesh.

As much as Zofia wanted to cry out and hug her friend, the city had eyes everywhere.

Instead, she cleared the emotion clogging her throat. "How good of you to come and visit from the country, cousin. Please, after you." She indicated the door, her voice too thick to say anything more.

Janina lowered her head and strode forward with steps so quiet, only the shush of grass announced her movement. The key to the door trembled in Zofia's hand and it took several attempts to finally get it unlocked. They walked up the stairs in silence, Zofia forcing herself to keep a steady pace.

As they climbed, Zofia's mind whirled with questions.

How had Janina gotten out of the ghetto?

Where were her parents?

Was she on the Polish side to stay?

The last thought was almost too painful to consider. She couldn't bear to have Janina leave again after finally reuniting.

Zofia opened the door to her apartment and quickly drew Janina inside. Once the door was closed, she threw her arms around her best friend, relieved at no longer having to hide her emotions. There was so little to Janina now, just ribs and a jutting backbone as they embraced.

A sob choked from Zofia's throat.

"I thought I'd never see you again," Janina said, her voice thick with tears. "And your father. Zofia, I'm so sorry, I—"

The door to Matka's room flew open. "What's going on? Who—" Her gaze landed on Janina and she sucked in a breath.

Zofia drew her friend into the open living area as they both wiped at their tears. In the lamplight, the sallowness of poor health showed in Janina's complexion and there was now a flatness to her brown eyes. Her skin seemed to stick to her bones, aging her well beyond her twenty years.

"I shouldn't be here, but with curfew approaching..." Janina's voice trailed off. "I didn't know where to go. I couldn't be caught. I didn't even know if you still lived here."

"Janina?" Matka said her name with wonder. "Is that Janina Steinman?"

Zofia spun around on her mother and stopped short. Tears shone in Matka's eyes.

"Janina, is that you?" she asked again. "How—"

Janina nodded solemnly. "I'm working with an underground agency delivering messages between the ghetto and the Polish side." She gestured helplessly to her overlarge coat, her legs skinny where they jutted beneath. "I know I don't look the same. I've lost some weight and..." Her voice grew weaker as she spoke, fading into nothing.

Matka shifted slowly forward, as if in a dreamlike state, her eyes reflecting the horror of Janina's shocking appearance. "My God, Janina." Her voice broke. "I'm so sorry, I'm so sorry, I'm so sorry. I didn't know..." Matka, who bent down to no one, save God, sank onto her knees in front of Janina, humbled in a way Zofia had never before witnessed.

Poor Janina backed up, clearly uncertain of what to do.

"Matka." Zofia spoke gently as she took her mother's hand, helping her to standing. "We need to get Janina something to eat and drink."

"And bathe," Janina added. "If I may. I'd love to please bathe."

"Yes." Matka shook her head as though bringing herself back to awareness. "Yes, of course. I'll put something together."

Lice was something Zofia was quite familiar with. Sometimes the children who came into the library had the pests crawling in their hair. As a result, they always kept a bottle of pyrethrin in the bathroom.

Zofia helped comb it through Janina's dark hair, pausing from time to time to crush one of the vermin or scrape away nits.

The gasoline-like odor stung their noses, but Zofia ignored it as much as she ignored Janina's embarrassed apologies.

"This is not your fault." Zofia sprinkled another dose of the pyrethrin into Janina's thick hair. "The Nazis did this when they ordered far too many people into too small a place."

"That hasn't even been the worst of it." Janina stared into the distance.

"Do you want to tell me?" Zofia asked.

"Yes." She blinked away tears. "And no. I don't even know where to start."

Tension knotted in Zofia's chest. "Your parents… They are still safe?"

Janina nodded. "Yes, but I'm not sure for how long."

Zofia exhaled with relief and continued combing her hair without nudging for anything more. After years of friendship, she knew no prodding was needed. Janina would share when she was ready.

Pots clanked about in the kitchen as Matka put together a solid meal of potato pancakes and their few precious boiled eggs. She had insisted after they both saw how badly Janina's hands shook when she ate the bread they had given her.

"There is nearly no food in the ghetto," Janina said at last in a monotone voice. "Our rations can't keep anyone alive, so we turn to the black market, but all the food there has become so expensive, few can even afford it. Everyone is desperate for something to eat. Everyone. People sell fake food that isn't edible on the streets so they can buy real items for themselves. Others wait outside stores and steal food from patrons, cramming it into their mouths as they run away. Still others will keep the corpse of a loved one in their home for weeks to avoid having to give up the person's ration card."

Zofia's hand kept moving through Janina's hair even as she internally reeled at the awfulness of what her friend described.

Food was hard to come by for Poles, with the rations unable to sustain anyone, but at least black market food could be procured. Every train that pulled into the city bore country folk with vegetables and even meat hidden in suitcases and on their person. Zofia had once bought sausages from a man who had twined links of them around each of his calves beneath his trousers.

"People are dying every day, dozens of them." Janina swallowed. "From typhus or starvation, but no one has the money to afford to bury them, so bodies are left on the street, naked so they can be taken away and buried at the expense of the Judenrat who manages things in the ghetto. And Mouse…"

Zofia stopped combing Janina's hair, her stomach going tight. "What happened?"

Janina sniffled and when she answered, her voice trembled. "The children who smuggle food in for their families are punished without mercy. The guards shoot at them, like hunters blasting a flock of birds. I was there when Mouse was shot, when he died."

"No." Zofia turned her head aside as if doing so could shield her from the terrible truth of poor Mouse's death. The boy had been so *alive*, so full of zeal with his charming demeanor and incessant flattery.

Janina pulled in a shuddering breath. "I'm sorry, I… I shouldn't be telling you all this."

"There is nothing you shouldn't tell me." Zofia put a comforting hand on Janina's shoulder. "Unless you don't wish to. I want to know, to see how I can help."

"Can you find a way to smuggle my parents out?" Janina turned around and looked at Zofia with wide, hopeful eyes. "There is a resistance group in the ghetto. I joined them in the hopes they would help find a way to free my parents, but recently there have been roundups where people are being taken by train somewhere. We don't know where yet, but we don't believe the glib excuses about resettlement in the east. They beat us and humiliate us and work us to death. The Nazis are too cruel to offer such mercy." Janina grasped Zofia's hand in a hard grip. "I can't let them take my parents."

Zofia didn't know of anyone who could offer aid, but now that she had an address for Janina, Darek may be able to find a way to help. But if he didn't, then what? Zofia clenched her teeth. She couldn't let Janina down. Not with something like this.

Janina released Zofia's hand and tears swam in her eyes. "I know it's asking a lot. And you've already helped so much with the typhus vaccines. Do you know they were going for five hundred to a thousand złotys only several months later?"

Determination rose in Zofia. "After all you've been through, there is nothing I won't do for you. I'll find a way to get your parents out."

Janina studied her, more worried than hopeful now.

"I will find a way," Zofia repeated.

Somehow, she would.

Janina turned forward once more, her voice reverting back to the detached monotone. "We all work in factories and are good workers. I think the owners will fight to keep us from the roundups for a while, at least if the rumors are to be believed. Papa makes brooms and Mama and I both sew at a place called Toebbens. The owner beats us for any mistake, but we do at least receive some food. I regret that the job keeps me from working more at the children's library as my hours at the factory are long."

A tug in Zofia's heart sent it spiraling downward. Janina spoke as if she intended to go back.

"You don't have to return there," Zofia said. "You can stay here."

But Janina shook her head. "I need to be back by morning for work."

"Please don't," Zofia begged. They were finally together. Too much time had passed with them apart to be separated again.

Especially knowing the appalling conditions Janina would be returning to.

"I have to." She hugged her legs to her chest. "Mama and Papa are there. I can't leave them."

Resolve settled over Zofia and she began to do a final comb-through of Janina's hair. "I'll find a way out for all of you."

After several washings, the odor of pyrethrin was gone from Janina's hair. She ate with relish afterward and Zofia offered Janina her bed to sleep in while she took the sofa. Janina had tried to refuse only once before her gaze fell on the soft blanket and thickly fluffed pillow. Her protests died away after that, and Zofia could only imagine what conditions Janina was forced to reside in.

The night was a restless one for Zofia, filled with the anticipation of Janina leaving again. That, and wracking her brain to find a way to help the Steinmans. Morning came far too quickly. Matka insisted Janina wear one of her dresses and gave her food to put in her handbag.

When she finally left and closed the apartment door behind her, a hollowness resounded in the small apartment. As the sun rose over their defeated city, Zofia's dearest friend had slipped out of her life yet again.

Matka chewed at her thumbnail, a habit she once chided Zofia for. "Janina shouldn't have gone back."

"She doesn't have a choice." The truth of those words lodged in Zofia's chest like a stone. "I am going to find a way to get her and her parents out of there."

"Good." Matka nodded. "Once they are out of there, they can live with us." Her mouth twisted. "The way they should have done a year and a half ago."

Zofia lifted her brows, certain she had heard incorrectly. "Have you seen the notices around the city warning death to those who are caught harboring Jews?"

"I have." Matka's fingers nipped the little gold crucifix at her neck and her chin notched up higher. "And I should have listened to you before. I made a mistake and now it's time to correct it. Zofia, we will do whatever possible to get Janina and her family out."

And Zofia intended to do exactly that.

Chapter 22

A NOTICE WAS POSTED on the door when Zofia went to work later that day, announcing a temporary closure of the library from August 11 to September 10 to assess the overall operation and the collections on hand. Any books checked out were required to be returned by the twenty-fifth.

Unease twisted in her stomach. This did not bode well.

Herr Nagiel had personally questioned the staff recently about every nuance of the library, ranging from the materials delivered from the Krasiński Library to how books were checked out and tracked. They had also been asked after several missing books from the lists of those meant to be destroyed. It was the latter that made Zofia's blood go cold.

After the attack on Warsaw in September 1939, the inventory had been too scattered to track properly despite their best efforts. Some were damaged and others were lost, and many that were returned were overlooked. Hopefully any confusion stemming from that time meant the inventory in the hidden warehouse would be overlooked.

Mrs. Mazur joined Zofia beside the announcement and scoffed. "They say the closure will be temporary."

"You don't think it will?" Chills prickled over Zofia's arms. They'd only recently begun to hire employees back in the last year. People like Miss Laska, who had no one else to provide for them.

"We're scarcely funded as it is with barely enough to pay wages. And we all know those aren't substantial. Look at how horrible this past winter was."

The winter had indeed been miserable. Without fuel, there was no way to heat the large, open building. They were forced to wear coats and scarves, their breath freezing in puffs. Without electricity, there was no light, so the operating hours had to be reduced to only cover times when the sun was up.

Summer had been better, at least until now.

"Is Darek supposed to be by today?" Zofia asked.

"Not that I'm aware of." Mrs. Mazur tried to hide her grin. "But he'd be happy to know you asked about him if you'd like me to let him know."

Zofia's cheeks went hot with the understanding that the message might be miscontrued. "No, that's not necessary."

Though Darek hadn't called Zofia beautiful again or said anything else so direct, she was still aware of his interest.

Which simultaneously intrigued her and terrified her.

There were already too many people in her life to protect, too many people she had failed to save. Her heart bore the brunt of those losses.

She couldn't afford to open herself up to any more.

No, it was better that she and Darek remained as they were, especially when her focus was needed for getting Janina and her family out of the ghetto.

With that distraction rattling like a pebble in Zofia's brain, she took her place in the lending room and the minutes dragged like days until she would see Darek at book club that evening and petition him for help again.

When the summer sun finally sank in the sky, Zofia waited for the rest of the Book Club Bandits to arrive. A lone candle flickered on the warehouse floor, far enough away from the books to avoid an accidental fire. The door to the warehouse opened and Zofia recognized the long-legged stride over the hard floor as Darek's.

She jumped to her feet as he came into view, propelled by the pent-up energy brewing inside her. "I saw Janina." Her words rushed ahead of her. "I saw her and she looks terrible and she needs help."

Darek caught her hands. "Zofia, slow down. How did you see Janina?" His back straightened and he cast a quick glance around. "Is she here?"

Zofia shook her head and inhaled slowly to rein in her emotions. "She's back in the ghetto, but she's asked for help to get herself and her parents out. I think she's worried that if they are sent east they'll never come back to Warsaw. You know important people with the Gray Ranks. Is there anyone doing anything to help the Jews out of the ghetto?"

The Polish Underground State had over a dozen different departments to oversee. Law, education, culture, newspapers, employment, and everything in between. It was also the Polish Underground State that condemned collaborators to death in secret courts.

Surely there had to be a department established to help Jews from their terrible plight.

Darek rubbed his hand over the back of his neck. "Let me check with a few people."

An ache gnawed at her chest. There had to be something they could do to get Janina and her family out of the ghetto.

Danuta appeared with Kasia at her side. "Someone didn't finish the book in time." Danuta nudged her friend.

"To be fair, *Les Misérables* was a very long book." Kasia gave an exaggerated grimace, followed by a self-deprecating laugh.

"It could have been longer." Danuta tossed her braid over her shoulder and settled on the floor. "I intend to read every piece of classic literature I can get my hands on."

"I lost interest during the part about Waterloo." Kasia pulled out a mound of sad-looking purple yarn.

"What's that?" Darek asked.

"It used to be a scarf." Kasia dug around in her bag and produced two knitting needles. "My mother and I have been using old items to re-knit into hats for children."

Danuta raised a brow. "It's August."

"It'll be October soon," Kasia replied cheerfully. The needles clicked together, starting the base of a little purple cap.

"I found it interesting how Victor Hugo opened the story highlighting the injustices of the world and the book's importance until such terrible times no longer exist," Zofia offered. "It's sadly fitting today though it's been decades since the book was written."

"Things have become worse, rather than better." Darek picked at a loose bit of rubber on the edge of his shoe. In previous days, he might have plucked it free and tossed it aside. Instead, he smoothed it down as if it might fuse together once more. Rations were limiting all their wares.

"We can't let ourselves be brought down by that kind of thinking," Danuta said in a crisp tone. "Let us instead focus on the theme of *Les Misérables*, the beauty of redemption. Fontaine was an exquisitely illustrated character, one you would judge on the surface if you didn't know her story."

"I loved Fontaine," Kasia added wistfully, her needles never slowing down. "She did everything for her daughter. It's that kind of love that makes me so desperately want to be a mother someday."

It was easy to see Kasia having a child and raising it with affection and compassion like her own mother.

"She truly did love her daughter," Zofia agreed. "It's so heartbreaking what was being done behind her back."

Danuta gave a patient smile at the interruption and continued. "The story was spun for us in such a convincing manner that when Valjean told Fontaine she was absolved of her guilt, I had tears in my eyes. Likewise, when we saw how Jean Valjean was so wonderfully forgiven by the bishop. Rather than focus on their ugliness, or casting judgment on these characters, Hugo gives us the rare insight to see what they've done and why they should be forgiven."

It was perfectly said and the way Danuta strung the explanation together left a profound impact on Zofia as she considered Matka. But could Zofia forgive her mother for not offering refuge to the Steinmans when they were first sent to the ghetto?

"I really enjoyed seeing Valjean become Monsieur Madeleine and all the good he did," Darek added.

Zofia nodded in agreement. There were so many characters one cheered for in the book that fell outside the scope of a classic hero. Victor Hugo truly wrote a masterpiece with *Les Misérables.*

The discussion continued on to address the French uprising, one of the many in France's history. It was a theme that resonated with them given their own Polish past filled with uprisings. There was much to be mulled over and their conversation lasted until just before curfew.

"For our next book, I'd like to propose something Russian," Darek said.

"Russian?" Danuta arched her brow. "Do you know something we don't?"

Darek shrugged. "I was at Gebethner's and was talking to the woman who works there."

The memory of the woman flashed in Zofia's mind with her curvy figure and red lipstick. Something uncomfortable twinged in Zofia's chest.

Oblivious, Darek continued, "She said the Germans have been purchasing more books lately, something they generally do before they're deployed. She also overheard them speaking about the Soviets. I think Hitler is going to attack Stalin next. Which is why *War and Peace* would be a timely book."

"Tolstoy." Danuta nodded approvingly. "And a story where Russia defeats a rapacious despot infiltrating their lands. I support this suggestion."

Kasia dropped her knitting and covered her ears. "Don't ruin the story."

Danuta threw her hands up in exasperation. "It's Napoleon. We all know what happens to Napoleon."

"At least this one doesn't mention Waterloo," Darek teased. "That battle came after Russia booted Napoleon out."

Kasia shook her head, the pleasant smile returning to her lips as she took up her knitting once more. "Then I'm in support of reading it as well."

Within the week, Darek notified Zofia that there were no departments in place to offer aid to the Jews from their perilous situation in the ghetto. One that grew worse by the day.

Zofia strode by the ghetto most afternoons, finding paths to different areas of the walled enclosure to keep from attracting notice. On that particular day, she was on Dzika Street—or Wildstrasse, as it was renamed in German. Not that any Pole worth their patriotism called it that. The houses on the even side of the street were all visible, but the odd-numbered ones had been swallowed up within the barrier.

There, the stink of black smoke from a train belched up into the summer sky and the wail of children and women rose above the din of everyday sounds. Those on the Polish side strolled by, their focus fixed intently on the cobblestones. But Zofia absorbed it all. The pierce of whistles in the air, the German orders barked to hurry, the cries that no empathetic heart could ignore.

These were likely the deportations Janina had spoken of.

Not that Zofia thought those trains truly went to the east. She didn't believe that any more than she trusted the closure of the library would be temporary. Already patrons were fearfully asking where they might go and the mothering children were trying to find new refuge for the unfair burden of their sibling wards.

Zofia stared at the ghetto wall, wishing she could see through the unyielding barrier. Was Janina waiting for that train? Her parents?

Finding someone to help was taking too long. In her desperation, Zofia had gone to Krystyna earlier that day, but she didn't have any contacts that could help either.

"You're not looking away."

Zofia glanced beside her to find a boy not much older than Mouse had been. Her heart gave a violent wrench. "How could I?"

The boy studied her with large doe-like eyes, his sweaty brown hair tucked under a cap, revealing a widow's peak beneath the brim. "Lots of people don't look. They've got their own problems. No wages, no food. The Nazis trying to arrest us every chance they have."

He pulled something from his pocket. "Read it and pass it on to people who matter. People who don't look away."

She glanced at the paper titled *Protest*, then returned her gaze beside her once more, but the boy had disappeared as quickly as he'd arrived. At a discreet glance of the pamphlet's contents, she found it to be a plea to Poles to stop ignoring the atrocities being committed against the Jews.

Her pulse hammered faster. This was a call to action. Finally.

But it was dangerous to have in her possession, like holding a hot brand.

A quick scan of the area revealed a Polish police officer in his customary blue uniform walking toward her. Zofia casually folded the paper, and slid it into her purse.

Once she was home, she read the leaflet in its entirety, devouring the plea for help, for Christians to step up in a world that had gone silent while Jews were dying. Zofia agreed with all of it except where the author reflected her personal views toward the Jews as enemies of Poland's economic and political structure. While the nationalist attitude still prevailed, at least there was someone willing to do something to help.

And Zofia needed all the help she could find.

With no name attached to the pamphlet, it was difficult to pinpoint the author, and once more, Zofia's inquiries were met without success. Work at the library was not going well either.

Herr Nagiel's usually benign personality had become abrasive regarding the numbers and figures reported back to him, his fleshy face often an unnatural shade of red. But working through inventories had been helpful for Zofia and Mrs. Mazur, who found they were able to mark certain books as having not been returned by patrons while slipping them out of the building to store in their hidden warehouse.

Several days after reading *Protest*, Zofia returned home from a grueling shift at the library to discover Matka was not alone. A woman with dark hair bound back in a twist at the nape of her neck sat at the table with a slice of precious bread in front of her. Matka set down a teapot and turned to welcome Zofia.

The damp aroma of linden flowers clung in the air from the tea substitute steeping in the pot.

"Ah, here she is now." Matka smiled at her, the way she'd done when Zofia had been little, before years of being a disappointing daughter had left Matka's lips pulling down instead of up. As if Zofia was not grimy from shifting boxes all day.

Dust and dirt lingered in powdery imprints on her dark green dress and the dampness of sweat had left her wavy hair wilder than usual. In all, her appearance would normally encourage a few disparaging words from Matka.

Zofia paused in the entryway, wary of her mother's reaction as much as she was of the woman in their home.

Matka waved her over. "Zofia, please come and meet Veronica."

The dark-haired woman smiled and nodded.

"I'm sure you read the piece called *Protest*," Matka said.

Both women stared at Zofia.

She did not reply, uncertain of the stranger.

"I found it in your handbag," Matka replied.

Irritation scraped over Zofia's frayed nerves. "You went through my handbag?"

"Only to get your ration cards." Matka cast a self-conscious look at Veronica as she spoke, her cheeks going pink with embarrassment. "You were already asleep and I didn't want to wake you. Not when you work so hard."

"What did you think of the leaflet?" Veronica asked. Her eyes were deep blue, the skin around them tight as she regarded Zofia.

The request seemed one of a personal nature for someone with whom she'd only just been acquainted. But Zofia had thoughts about the writing and was not one to quell her opinions.

"I'm relieved there appears to finally be someone willing to help the Jews." Zofia squared her shoulders and approached the stranger. "People have been looking away for too long, pretending they don't see what is happening. However, I feel much of the conviction of the piece was dulled by the author's clearly nationalist attitude toward Jews."

"Zofia." If Matka's cheeks were pink with embarrassment before, they were crimson now.

But Veronica didn't seem offended. "That's an interesting observation."

"I presume you are the author?" Zofia's blood roared in her ears.

Veronica gave a tight-lipped smile.

"I have a friend who is in the ghetto with her family," Zofia rushed. "Do you know anyone who can help sneak them out?"

"Your mother has already discussed the matter with me," Veronica replied. "And I do."

Zofia swallowed her surprise. "When can we expect them to be freed?"

"Hopefully in a day or two," Veronica replied coolly. "So long as there are no complications."

A "day or two" could mean a roundup or two. Zofia suppressed a shiver at the thought of how many complications could arise.

"And what of the other people trapped in the ghetto?" Zofia asked. "My friend and her parents are just one family."

Veronica's narrow brows lifted. "You're ambitious."

"I'm not silent." Zofia quoted the pamphlet and notched her chin a little higher, the way Matka did when she came upon something offensive.

"In that case…" Veronica's forefinger silently tapped the table beside her plate of bread. "Would you like to help?"

Zofia's breath caught. *This.* This was what she had been wanting since the start of the occupation, to do something more than just stand idly by. She longed to be a participant, actively working against the persecution.

"Yes," Zofia replied fiercely.

"Good." Veronica gave another tight smile. "I'll be in touch."

Matka pulled something from her pocket and approached Veronica. A set of ruby and diamond earrings caught the light as they slipped from Matka's slim hands into Veronica's palms. "To cover any costs."

Zofia said nothing until after Veronica left. The woman hadn't eaten her bread and Zofia was glad for it. Her stomach rasped with hunger after her long shift at the library.

"I haven't seen those earrings before," Zofia said casually.

Matka nudged the bread plate closer to Zofia in silent invitation. "Your father bought a considerable number of gems before the attack, knowing they would be easier to hide than money. It's kept us alive."

That explained how Matka was always able to find food for them and pay the rent and utilities on their apartment, despite Zofia's limited wages. A lifetime ago, Matka would have worn those brilliant gems, sometimes even replacing the little gold cross at her throat with a string of pearls or sparkling diamonds. Now, it put food in their stomachs, which would only be hungry and empty again the following day.

Zofia slid into the chair, still warm from where Veronica had occupied it, and sank her teeth into the coarse bread.

"I gave Janina several items as well." Matka moved around the kitchen, cleaning without stopping to regard Zofia as she spoke.

Some of the tension in Zofia's stomach relaxed. Hopefully it was enough to keep Janina and her family from the deportations until they could be freed.

In a way, those ruby and diamond earrings glimmered with a similar note to the silver candlesticks in *Les Misérables*. Papa had unintentionally helped Matka when he left her those earrings in the way the bishop had knowingly done when he gifted those silver candlesticks to Jean Valjean. It gave her the opportunity to right a terrible wrong, to alter her path to one that would help others.

And soon, Janina and her family would be safe. So long as there were no complications.

Chapter 23

HERR NAGIEL WAS FIRED. It was quite a sight to witness him slinking from his office with a box of his effects clasped in his stubby hands. The victory, however, was short-lived. Dr. Witte, the Warsaw deputy of the *Hauptverwaltung* in charge of Poland's libraries, hadn't even waited for Herr Nagiel to depart the building before bringing forward the two women who would take his place.

They were both middle-aged with crisp, black business dresses, their short blond hair sculpted into perfect curls. Neither wore makeup, no doubt to please their Führer, and their plain features made it hard to distinguish one from the other.

"This is Frau Schmidt and Frau Beck," Dr. Witte said as the two women stepped forward. Side by side, Frau Beck was slightly taller, an unhelpful feature if one was without the other.

Dr. Witte nodded at the two. "They will be managing the German reading room going forward and will be overseeing the daily operations here. I expect you to comply with their requests."

The two wasted no time asserting their power once Dr. Witte was back in his office.

"You will each be given a log to record your daily work." Frau Beck's voice was high-pitched and edged with condescension.

The Hitler Youth group entered the main reading room and the boys withdrew plain black notebooks from a box, distributing one to each employee.

"If you do not do as you are asked, you will be released from your duties here." Frau Schmidt had a deeper, rasping voice, her Polish heavily accented with German.

"And going forward," Frau Beck said with a nod to Frau Schmidt, who finished for her, "logs of Polish books are to be destroyed."

The loss of Polish book catalogs was an unexpected blow. Zofia numbly accepted the notebook from a boy whose expression was blank with bored disinterest. The cover was stiff and cold.

"To confirm, you mean the log of approved Polish books?" Mrs. Mazur asked.

Frau Beck narrowed her eyes at the warehouse supervisor who had given decades of her career to the Warsaw Library. "Considering all unapproved books should have been destroyed, I would assume the answer to your question is rather obvious."

Frau Schmidt shook her head in obvious irritation. "Anyone else?"

If there was, certainly no one felt welcome to ask.

Mrs. Mazur pulled Zofia aside as soon as they were in the quiet of the warehouse. "If something happens to me, my key to the hidden warehouse is near the back beneath the third shelf to the right."

Zofia frowned. "If something—"

"Herr Nagiel was asking about books missing from certain

collections before he was dismissed." Mrs. Mazur drew in a deep breath. "I think that might be why he was relieved of his position."

Which meant the Fraus would shift the full blame on Mrs. Mazur's shoulders.

"Promise me you'll see those books in readers' hands again when Poland is free," Mrs. Mazur said. "Promise me."

A prickle of unease raked over Zofia's skin, but she nodded.

"It's just a precaution," Mrs. Mazur added with a smile Zofia was sure she meant to be reassuring.

The next few days swept Zofia into a frenzy of removing books, shifting them around, tweaking inventories, and appropriately updating her work log to report her efforts while concealing her more clandestine actions. It was evening when she left the library at the end of the week, the sky was darkening from the pink-and-orange hues of a summer sunset into a gray-blue dusk.

"Excuse me." A man approached quickly. "I'm not able to make it to the reading room on Traugutta Street to return this in time. Will you accept it here?"

Zofia took the book from him. "It's a good thing you didn't exert the effort to go there—it would have been a waste of your time. The Traugutta Street branch is closed to patrons. All the library branches are right now."

The man tilted his head in confusion. "But it's not. I was there just yesterday and checked out another book. Miss Laska chided me about getting something new when I hadn't returned one that was overdue." His cheeks colored beneath his dark beard. "Lucky for me, she was lenient, but I didn't want to let her down."

Zofia glanced about to ensure no one had overheard what he'd told her and responded in a quiet voice. "Then you can return the favor by telling no one what you've just told me."

His face changed with the seriousness of her tone and he gave a solemn nod. "I swear it."

Zofia looked at her watch. There was still time to make it to the small reading room, especially as Miss Laska had a tendency to be slow at shutting down the library. Guilt nipped at Zofia. She hadn't been there to help the last few days as she had assumed Miss Laska wasn't at the library.

Zofia rapped on the door and Miss Laska shuffled over to open it. In her delight, she forgot to shield her smile, displaying the missing tooth.

"I wondered where you've been." Miss Laska touched Zofia's arm as she entered the library.

Miss Laska appeared to be in good health. The yellow tinge to her skin was replaced with a rosy hue since Zofia had been delivering cabbages and potatoes to her a couple of times a week. It was strange that Miss Laska had forgotten the library was supposed to be closed. She usually had such a keen mind. Perhaps stress had finally begun to take its toll.

Zofia closed and locked the door behind her. If anyone were to come in, they could always claim to be working on the inventory, an innocuous excuse for their presence there. "Miss Laska, the library was supposed to be closed this last week."

"Oh, that." Miss Laska waved her hand. "Why should we close the library when people need books? I've seen more of Warsaw's youth in this library after the occupation than I ever did before. These books are good for them. Not only their minds that Hitler is trying to inhibit, but also for their souls. We can't take that away."

She wasn't wrong. Every day they witnessed patrons turning away from the library in disappointment at the doors locked against them.

"Why can't we just keep it open a little longer?" Miss Laska asked, her eyes overly large and pleading from behind the thick lenses of her spectacles. "No employees of the main library ever come here but you. It would likely be months before anyone noticed."

"You don't know these new women who have taken Herr Nagiel's place. They are shrewd, exacting women who leave no stone unturned. It would not take them months to realize a reading room was still in operation, and they would not take kindly to orders being disobeyed."

"I'm an old woman with a bad memory." Miss Laska made her voice wobble with a feeble undertone and blinked rapidly like someone who'd suddenly forgotten where they were.

Zofia clapped softly. "An excellent performance. Unfortunately, you'll find no empathy from those two. We're not even allowed to have a catalog of Polish books anymore."

Miss Laska grumbled something under her breath, appearing fully lucid once more, and went about her normal tasks of putting items away. Zofia watered the little plant that was already looking in a sorry state with just a week of no water.

"Do you want me to move this so it can be watered more easily?" Zofia asked.

Miss Laska shrugged. "I prefer it out of the way." She stiffened suddenly.

Zofia practically dropped the watering can as she ran to the older woman. "What is it? Are you all right?"

"I'm better than all right." Miss Laska's blue eyes gleamed like marbles. "I've had an epiphany. What if we had a library for patrons that Dr. Witte didn't know about? We'll have our own catalog of books to offer, and we'll keep a private coded checkout log. This would be the ideal location to use since it's so out of the way, everyone seems to forget about it. And I can finally put these back into circulation." She waved for Zofia to follow her and indicated a stack of boxes labeled with supplies. There were pencils, ink, and stamp pads. An extraordinarily large amount of stamp pads.

Curious, Zofia pulled open a box and saw *War and Peace* sitting on the top along with a novel by Marta Krakowska and *Gone with the Wind*. She sucked in a breath. This was a treasure of books that should have been destroyed.

Miss Laska laughed, the sound something like a cackle. "I may seem like a sweet old woman, but I refuse to follow rules that don't suit me." She folded her skinny arms over her chest. "I was quite the rebel in my day, always causing trouble for the Russians. I don't plan to be any more compliant for the General Government."

"That's a great idea," Zofia said. "But we should store these in a safer location, and I know just the place."

Once more, Zofia was skirting curfew as she hastened home. The idea to run a secret library out of the small reading room was perfect. They would only offer it to their loyal patrons they could trust, and books would be selected from a handwritten catalog, one with their full stock. Not only those that were Hitler-approved.

After all, none of this was sanctioned by the General Government.

A shadow moved behind the tree in the courtyard and Zofia's heart skipped. "Janina?"

Janina stepped around the tree, shielded by the darkness cast by a shy moon. Zofia waved her over and quickly ushered her inside the stairwell and up to the apartment.

Janina cast a longing look around the tidy, comfortable living area, and said quickly, "I can't stay. There are several roundups slated for tomorrow. Have you received the new identity cards for my parents?" The desperation in her gaze squeezed at Zofia's heart.

"I have." Zofia recalled what Veronica had written on a note of paper, one that had to be memorized and burned immediately after. "You need to go to All Saints' Church—"

"All the pastors have been made to leave the ghetto." Panic pitched Janina's voice.

Zofia grasped her hands. They were like ice despite the warm night. "It is not a pastor you need to find, but a woman who tends the garden. She has the documents you need to escape the ghetto, including the bribe. If you can get out tomorrow, I will wait for you."

She had been warned about the people who loitered around the ghetto, waiting for Jews who happened to offer a high enough bribe to the gate guards to slip free. These Polish "greasers" hid in the shadows as they lay in wait like vultures, ready to descend on anyone with a haunted expression or a gaunt face. They extorted and robbed without mercy, blackmailing them for being Jewish, often finding ways to locate them afterward to continue their cruel games. Once the Jews no longer had the means to pay, the greasers would notify the Nazis of their presence.

That would not happen to Janina or her parents.

"Yes, tomorrow," Janina said with finality. "There's a home at 14 Franciszkańska Street I can use to exit. The basement is connected to the ghetto and they let people come out for a price. They work with the resistance, which is how I'm able to get in and out of the ghetto."

"I'll wait all day if I have to," Zofia vowed.

Finally Janina and her parents would be free.

Chapter 24

IT WAS FORTUNATE THAT Zofia was already scheduled to be off the next day when Janina and her parents would be escaping from the ghetto. Zofia packed a small bag containing some food, a stack of złotys in case additional bribes were necessary, and a book that hadn't yet been banned. The novel was a pithy tale about a missing key to a safe. By the end of the first chapter, she'd already figured out who had taken the key and was now simply reading to confirm her assumption.

Essentially, it was a disguise to make her appear to be enjoying the summer weather without suspicion if she had to remain in place for a while.

She went to the small bakery beside Franciszkańska Street and spent far too much money on a soft, white roll. Her fluttering nerves released their hold on her appetite the instant the warm baked good was in her hand. For so long, she and her mother had been living off coarse bread with beet marmalade or cabbage-and-potato soup.

They almost never had meat or items sweetened with real sugar anymore. And bread like what was steaming in her palm was merely a fond memory from the past. She sat in the shade of a poplar tree and inhaled the tantalizing yeasty aroma before savoring every bite of the roll.

An hour passed.

Then another.

And another still.

"This bench taken?" A man around Zofia's age sat on the seat beside her without waiting for a response. "Good book?"

She didn't bother to answer him.

He snapped open a copy of the *Courier.* The front page showed a home with the door left open to convey its vacancy. The story was typed in a font large enough to read from a distance at a quick glance. A Jew had been found, hidden in someone's apartment on Krucza Street, only a few buildings away from Zofia's home. Harboring a Jew had fatal consequences. Everyone knew it. Warnings were plastered all over Warsaw.

Out of the corner of her eye, Zofia caught some of the article. The offending family had been slain there on the street and the rest of the building's inhabitants had been arrested or executed as accomplices.

Zofia's stomach churned with nerves once again, but she dropped her gaze back to her book.

After several minutes passed, the man lowered his paper and regarded Zofia. "You waiting on someone?"

She slid him a slow, long-suffering look, the kind deserving of any person intentionally seeking to interrupt a reader. "Actually, I'm trying to read."

The man put up his hands in surrender and backed off the bench.

Another chapter slid by.

The guilty party she'd anticipated in chapter one proved to be true by chapter forty-three. With a sigh, she closed her book, wishing she could have *War and Peace* with her. She had finally gotten past the ballroom scenes and the battle was just beginning.

Movement across the street caught her attention.

Janina appeared with her mother in tow. The ghetto had greatly changed Janina's beautiful mother. Even from a distance, Zofia could see the haggard lines etching her lovely face and streaks of silver glinting in her dark hair. Zofia hesitated, waiting for Mr. Steinman to join them, but he did not appear.

Janina strode confidently over with a little wave at Zofia, as if she was meant to be there in her stylish blue dress and red sandals. Mrs. Steinman, however, cast a furtive glance back and forth on the street, her bag clutched to her breast like a mother with a new babe. When she walked, her steps were quick and quiet, her back slightly rounded, as if she could make herself small enough to disappear from view.

Except rather than make her invisible, her demeanor called the attention of every passerby.

Panic charged through Zofia. In Mrs. Steinman's attempt to not be seen, she was putting a target on their backs. Zofia rose from her bench, keeping her actions smooth and casual.

"Mrs. Zieliński." She used Mrs. Steinman's new name as she approached. "You need to smile and act like everything is fine," Zofia whispered.

"Yes, of course." Mrs. Steinman stretched a smile across her lips that looked as awful as lipstick applied without a mirror.

Zofia turned to Janina and embraced her. "My dearest friend. How is Mr. Zieliński?"

Janina's composure broke for only a fleeting fraction of a second. Her nostrils flared slightly, imperceptible to anyone but Zofia. She licked her lips. "I'm afraid he won't be joining us. He's on a business trip for the General Government." Though she kept her demeanor nonchalant as she said it, pain shone in her dark eyes. She shifted her attention to the ground and cleared her throat. "I believe we'll be late if we don't leave now."

Mrs. Steinman's face crumpled, the sorrow at their loss too heavy to mask.

Zofia stepped closer, adjusting Mrs. Steinman's collar, and whispered, "I'm sorry, but you must keep smiling."

Mrs. Steinman's face pulled into a smile that looked more like a grimace.

It was unfair that she should have to swallow her grief and play at happiness when it was obvious her husband had been taken in the roundups. And Zofia hated being the one to tell her to do so. To show her sorrow in public where people were looking for those who were distraught and scared was dangerous.

Zofia squelched her own grief for Mr. Steinman, putting the news away into a place within herself she could come to later to mourn. Head up and face bright, she led them down the street, discreetly gazing about to ensure they weren't being watched. As soon as their steps touched the cobblestones, someone sidled up next to Zofia.

"Did you finish your book?"

She looked up to find the man who had sat next to her on the bench, and frowned.

"I see you found some friends." The man's gaze cut to Mrs. Steinman and Janina. Zofia's heart stopped, caught momentarily in a grip of fear.

"The book was interesting," she said quickly. "I guessed who had taken the key early on. If you want to—"

"Your friends are Jewish." The man's statement made a ball of ice form in Zofia's chest.

She laughed, and the sound came out in a strangled pitch, as foreign as if it had emerged from a stranger's mouth. "Don't be ridiculous."

Mrs. Steinman's face contorted and silent tears ran down her face.

"I'll stay quiet about it." He grinned magnanimously, revealing yellowed teeth. "For a fee."

The bag at Zofia's side was suddenly very heavy where it hung on her shoulder, at the knowledge of how many złotys she'd been given in the event of such a thing happening. "How much?"

"Two thousand złotys."

Though she had it on her, Zofia still balked. That was ten times her monthly salary at the library. This crook intended to make that amount in a day, by recognizing and then exploiting people who were helpless and hunted.

No wonder they were called greasers. These oily men were the basest humanity had to offer.

"Let's go in the alley." She nodded toward a gap between the apartment buildings.

Her mind raced as they shuffled toward the alleyway. He would keep quiet now, but for how long? What if he recognized Zofia on the street and tried to get more money? What if she came back to help someone else and he did this again because he knew her face?

Cold fear prickled in her veins as she led the greaser into the shadows along with Janina and Mrs. Steinman.

What if he saw them at a later date and turned them in?

The calm demeanor Zofia had managed to maintain thus far began to crack. Her heart was pounding too hard. The air she dragged into her lungs wasn't enough and left her lips tingling for oxygen.

Refuse littered the narrow walkway, not only bits of discarded rubbish, but also a few bricks that appeared to have tumbled from the building. They stepped over them and went deeper until they were blocked from the view of the street by an alcove.

The greaser turned his greedy eyes on Zofia and thrust out his hand. "The money."

An idea struck Zofia and her stomach swam with acid.

"She has it." Zofia nodded to Janina.

The man turned to Janina.

"Oh." Janina recovered quickly. "Yes, it's here. A moment..."

She rummaged through the small bag at her side. While he was distracted, Zofia moved without thought.

Because if she allowed herself to think, she might not be able to do what was necessary.

She knelt down and curled her fingers around a solid brick, her grip so tight, the edges cut into her palm. Using every ounce of her strength, she slammed it into the back of the man's head.

At the impact, something cracked, reverberating up through her arm. She dropped the brick in horror and stepped back as the man crumpled to the ground.

Mrs. Steinman's lips opened, but Janina clapped a hand over her mother's mouth before she could scream.

"Let's go," Zofia hissed.

The three of them rushed back toward the street.

"You need to smile, Mama," Janina whispered fiercely. "Remember when I was little and I was horrible at telling jokes, but you would always laugh at them regardless? You tell me that story all the time. I need you to do that now."

Mrs. Steinman nodded and gave a chuckle as they made it out to the street.

"Do you recall my name day celebration when we went to Gdynia?" Janina asked her mother, clearly instigating a conversation meant for people to overhear. Especially one about a Christian tradition that someone Jewish would not normally celebrate.

As they talked, Zofia's mind probed back to that fateful moment in the alleyway.

Had she killed him?

Either answer terrified her.

If he was still alive, he could find her or report her. Zofia could be arrested and jeopardize Mrs. Steinman and Janina. If they were forced to talk, Veronica could be implicated as well as anyone working with her, including Matka. All of it could crumble because of Zofia's rash decision.

And if he was dead…

A shudder rattled through her.

She had never killed a man before. As the daughter of a renowned doctor in Warsaw, she had once entertained the idea of turning toward a career in healing. How far she had fallen from such aspirations.

And yet, as horrible as the idea was that she had taken a life, she truly did hope the greaser was dead.

No one else took notice as Zofia, Janina, and Mrs. Steinman went through the city toward Zofia's apartment. Janina chattered on behind Zofia, recounting every name day she'd ever celebrated to her mother, who answered with overly bright enthusiasm. Though they managed to keep a normal pace, Zofia's heart pounded as if she were sprinting.

Finally they rounded the corner to Krucza Street and slipped up the stairwell as silently as was possible. Matka was waiting for them when they came in the door, perched on the edge of the couch like a bird ready to take flight.

"Thank God you're safe." She made the sign of the cross and rushed over. First, she touched a hand to Zofia, a watery look of relief in her eyes, then she welcomed them all deeper into the apartment. The curtains were partially drawn and the light filtering through the lace was muted, dimming the room.

"Please come in." Matka beckoned them with the congeniality of someone hosting a dinner party and swiftly shut the door. "We have some food for you and clothes, whatever you need." Matka drew back, regarded the three of them. "I thought Mr. Steinman..."

Janina pulled in a shaky inhale. "I told Papa not to go to work today, that there would be roundups. But he worried if he didn't go and we couldn't escape, he would be fired and there would be no way for us to have food. As soon as I left to get the documents we needed..." Her voice broke. "He went to work."

"And there was a roundup." Mrs. Steinman's speech was staccato, breathless. "It was too late to save him. The train had already left."

If they had been one day earlier, Mr. Steinman would be here with them now. One day.

"It's my fault." Janina swallowed hard and looked away. "I should have found a way to come sooner. There could have been something—"

"I should have offered for you to live with us from the start," Matka said miserably. "You never should have been in the ghetto."

Mrs. Steinman put her hand to her chest, composing herself. "No. We would never have accepted. We made the decision early on to put our names on the list of Jews knowing we would likely go into the ghetto. If you had tried to save us then..." Mrs. Steinman reached for Matka, comforting her even as her own world was falling apart. "You likely would have been found out and we all would be arrested now."

Matka's eyes welled with tears. "You are safe now," she said determinedly. "We'll make sure you stay safe."

Some of the tension from Mrs. Steinman's face relaxed with her grateful smile. There was no real safety for anyone anymore. And though she surely was aware of that, it was doubtless good to know that there were those who still cared, those who truly meant to help.

That evening while Matka went through her closet with Mrs. Steinman to ensure the other woman had enough clothes, Zofia found Janina staring out the window. The apartment was nearly dark, lit by a single candle. Janina's face was turned away, blanketed in shadows.

Zofia slid into the chair across from her and put a hand on hers in silent comfort. After all, now was not the time to ask if Janina was all right. Her father had been deported and they would likely never see him again. Zofia understood how very not all right Janina was feeling, especially after losing her own father.

"The trains aren't going east." Janina's voice was quiet, just above a whisper, her gaze still locked on the street below.

In the distance, the pulse of music mingled with laughter as the Wehrmacht and Gestapo officers celebrated at Bar Podlaski with its brothel on the second floor.

Zofia frowned. "Where are the trains going?"

"To camps that were built to kill." Janina's hand twitched under Zofia's and she pulled it away to rest in her lap. "Only the people in the organization I'm working with know about it right now." Janina's brow pursed into a furrow. "They bring the Jews by train to a platform where they're welcomed with live music to quell their fears. Then they pretend everyone will have a chance to shower. That's how they do it, with a poison gas dropped into a room, killing hundreds at a time."

Zofia stared at her friend in horror.

"Mama doesn't know." Janina's eyes were bright with tears when they met Zofia's. "I don't want her to…" She broke off and swallowed thickly. "They took the children and elderly first, so we had our suspicions. By the middle of August, we couldn't run the library anymore because…" She drew a shaky breath. "There were no children left."

"People need to know about this," Zofia said vehemently. "The Allies. Surely they will come to help."

Janina shrugged. "They are being informed. Time will tell." The flatness of her tone said it all: they anticipated as much help from the Allies now as when Poland was first attacked in September 1939.

"I'm going back tomorrow," Janina said.

"No." Zofia sat up in her chair, her body tense. "Janina, you could be caught in a roundup, you could be…"

She couldn't finish that terrible thought. It was too awful to even consider.

"We're going to fight, Zofia." Janina spoke low and quiet through gritted teeth. "We're going to make them pay."

There was no winning against the Nazis. If the Jews in the ghetto were all as overworked and underfed as Janina and Mrs. Steinman, they didn't stand a chance for victory.

"It's too dangerous," Zofia protested.

"It is. But I would rather die fighting. I want vengeance for Papa." Her voice went thick with tears. "For Mouse. For all the children who never had a chance to really live. I attended a poetry reading in the ghetto titled *The Little Smuggler* by Henryka Łazowertówna in tribute. There wasn't one person not crying by the time she'd finished her poem. We were all thinking of children we knew who had died trying to provide for their families." Janina glared outside, her eyes fixed on the German-only bar where the Nazis reveled. "I will make them all pay."

"Then I'll go with you."

Janina swung her gaze to Zofia and shook her head. "Keep Mama safe. Help other Jews like you've helped us. And see what you can do to acquire weapons and support from the Home Army, from the Gray Ranks."

Guilt twisted in Zofia. "How did you know I belonged to the Gray Ranks?"

Janina lifted a brow. "Because I know you better than I know myself, and it's impossible that you wouldn't find a way to join an organization determined to fight back. Just as I'm doing now."

Zofia nodded, fully understanding that Janina wouldn't be any more discouraged from the path than Zofia was from hers.

"I'll see what I can do," she promised.

But as she went to sleep on the couch that night, the conversation tumbled around in her thoughts. Because no matter how much aid or weapons Zofia was able to procure, she could not rid herself of the fear that Janina and those who fought with her would not survive the battle.

Janina slipped away from the apartment the next day as soon as the curfew was lifted, a thick envelope of newly drawn-up documents for Jews still trapped in the ghetto hidden within the false lining in her handbag. Those birth certificates, baptism papers, marriage certificates, and identity cards from Veronica were authentic, once belonging to Poles whose deaths were not reported so their identities could be transferred. Life saved by death.

Zofia left not long after to collect a delivery of blank identity cards from a nearby baker for Veronica. She delivered the box behind a healthy lilac bush in a courtyard on Hoża Street exactly as she had been instructed.

Her task for Veronica complete, Zofia snagged a copy of the *Courier* from a newsboy and hurried toward the library. Most Poles read the Nazi-controlled paper, but not for the slanted stories. The obituary section was always of the greatest interest, to learn if someone they knew had been killed. Zofia scoured that page on her way to Koszykowa Street for any mention of a man found dead in an alleyway.

There was none.

Her stomach knotted.

She put the newspaper in her handbag and entered the library.

One of the Fraus stood beside the guard at the front door scowling at her watch. "You're late." The heavy German accent seasoned with self-importance indicated she was Frau Schmidt.

Zofia glanced at her own watch. "I'm supposed to be here at nine."

A victorious smirk peeled at Frau Schmidt's thin lips. "It's two minutes past. You must be prompt." She punctuated the last word with a sharp clap.

Zofia muttered an apology that stuck in her throat and headed toward the warehouse to see what her primary assignment would be that day. As she approached Mrs. Mazur, the stiffness in the woman's back indicated she knew she was being watched.

"You need to pull these books from the shelves to inventory

them," she said curtly. "Ensure all your actions are recorded appropriately in your log."

"I have it here." Zofia pulled the black notebook from her handbag. The cover creaked when she opened it. The majority of the smooth, grid-lined pages were blank. Ready for anything she wished to write.

With new notebooks being so rare these days, it was a shame to use the treasure for recording labor time for the Fraus.

The list awaiting Zofia from Mrs. Mazur was one with books previously pulled for destruction. Was it a trick?

Zofia's heartbeat skipped.

A rhythmic thump rumbled through the warehouse, the sound of a dozen or so boots marching in unison.

"Mrs. Mazur?" Frau Beck's shrill voice rang out. "Come forward at once."

Mrs. Mazur closed her eyes, took a deep breath, and slowly exhaled. When she opened her eyes again, her expression was calm, as though silently saying, *I have been expecting this.*

Zofia strode forward with her, but Mrs. Mazur shook her head and held her hand back in a mute demand that Zofia remain behind, hidden by rows of shelves. Then, back straight and head held high, Mrs. Mazur strode like a queen toward her ill-fated destiny. A gap above the row of books allowed Zofia the opportunity to follow Mrs. Mazur's progress to the front of the room where Frau Beck waited with an army of Gestapo agents.

Such a show of force for one mid-sized, middle-aged Polish woman was ridiculous and unneccessary.

"You are accused of stealing property from the General Government." Frau Beck narrowed her eyes at Mrs. Mazur. "Illegal books have gone missing on your watch."

Zofia pulled in a hard breath. *She* had been the cause of most of those missing books. The warehouse had been her idea. It had been her who always pushed the idea of taking "just one more" to store away.

And what would happen to Darek if Mrs. Mazur was arrested?

"I have done nothing that goes against my conscience," Mrs. Mazur replied evenly.

"Then your conscience has sealed your fate." Frau Beck waved her hand and the men swarmed forward. One punched Mrs. Mazur in the face, sending her stumbling backward.

Zofia clapped a hand over her mouth to smother a cry.

Another man lashed at Mrs. Mazur with a rubber truncheon, striking her hard enough in the shoulder for the thwack to reverberate in the large room. Two Gestapo agents lifted her from the ground and half carried, half dragged her to the door.

"I regret nothing I've done," Mrs. Mazur shouted, her voice strong and defiant.

And Zofia knew those words were not only meant for Frau Beck and the men who had beaten an unarmed woman before hauling her to Pawiak.

Those words were meant for Zofia.

Chapter 25

WHILE MRS. MAZUR WAS the only one arrested that day, she was not the only employee of the library to be relieved of their duties. Miss Laska was included on the list of employees to be let go. Not that she would go without a fight.

The Association of Small Businessmen pooled donations every month and raised a considerable sum for Warsaw's libraries. Those funds were distributed between employees who had been furloughed as well as current employees to ensure the meager wage was at least enough to provide adequate food and housing. Whatever was left after those employees had been cared for was applied toward the preservation of the main library building. Zofia petitioned the group to ensure Miss Laska received her fair share of income.

If nothing else, it would keep the older woman in her apartment and with enough funds to fulfill her ration card.

Only three days had gone by and already Mrs. Mazur's loss was powerfully felt in the warehouse. Her massive presence seemed to grow even larger in her absence, not simply in the extra work that fell on Zofia's shoulders, but how desperately she missed Mrs. Mazur's guidance and support.

Zofia salvaged the key Mrs. Mazur had mentioned from under the shelf when it was finally safe to do so. Upon examination, she discovered an address attached to it, one she would be able to visit the following day when she was off from the library.

At home, Zofia found Matka and Mrs. Steinman with a deck of French cards playing a lively game of Pan.

"I win again," Matka crowed.

"Only because I let you." Mrs. Steinman winked at Zofia as she spoke. "As I'm a gracious guest."

There was a flush to Matka's cheeks Zofia had not seen in years. All brought on by the companionship of Mrs. Steinman.

In the week Janina's mother had been living with them, she too had regained a healthy complexion and her eyes lost their dullness. Zofia heard her tears at night as Mrs. Steinman mourned her husband and worried for Janina, but during the day, Mrs. Steinman slipped a mask in front of her sorrow and gave way to Matka's intentional distractions.

Today's endeavors apparently involved baking a pie crust with only potatoes, which was cooling on a rack by the oven. It was a success in that it remained intact. How it tasted had yet to be discovered.

An insistent knock came from the door. Zofia froze, as did Matka and Mrs. Steinman.

"Yes?" Zofia called out warily.

"It's Mrs. Borkowska from across the hall." The woman's pleasant voice came through the door.

Zofia locked eyes with Mrs. Steinman and nodded to her bedroom. Mrs. Steinman moved stealthily in her stockinged feet while Matka cleared away the game.

"What do you need?" Zofia called to the door.

Matka craned her neck at Zofia in disbelief at such rudeness.

Zofia rolled her eyes and made a show of walking heavily to the front door and opening it just wide enough to accommodate her frame. "I was washing dishes," she offered apologetically.

Mrs. Borkowska gave an impatient smile. "I'd like to come in."

A tightness seized Zofia's stomach. "Perhaps another time. Our house is not in a state to receive visitors."

Though Matka was behind her, Zofia could feel her mother's glare burning into her back. Matka had always taken such pride in the appearance of their home.

"I'm an old woman living alone with a six-year-old granddaughter." Mrs. Borkowska laughed. "You haven't seen a messy home until you've viewed mine. I'm afraid I must insist." At the last part, she scrabbled around Zofia with surprising speed and edged her way into the apartment.

"Jadzia." The older woman nodded to Matka and surveyed the immaculate room with a lift of her brow as Zofia closed the door. "I need to speak frankly with you both." The urgent whisper of Mrs. Borkowska's tone brought Zofia to a heightened awareness. "I know you're hiding a Jew here."

"Excuse me?" Zofia asked, blinking her eyes with feigned innocence.

"Don't play coy with me," Mrs. Borkowska scoffed. "I've lived too long to be a fool. Jadzia, how could you? Have you not seen the news where the residents of an entire apartment building are killed because one unit was hiding a Jew?"

Matka didn't lower her gaze. "I don't know what you're talking about."

But she knew. They all knew. The stories were common in the *Courier.*

Mrs. Borkowska pressed her lips together. "I'm going to say this one time only. You are harboring a Jew. I know you are.

She cannot stay here. My granddaughter is all I have left in this world, do you understand that? *All* I have left."

Matka strode closer. "We don't—"

"Don't lie to me, Jadzia," Mrs. Borkowska snapped. "I can't have you jeopardizing my granddaughter's life. Or mine, for what would become of her without me?" She gave a defeated sigh. "I will give you all the food I have for the woman you're hiding and I will give you some money as well. But she cannot stay here."

Zofia's pulse raced as she met Matka's gaze from across the room.

"I don't want to do this." Mrs. Borkowska pulled in a pained breath and let it hiss out through gritted teeth. "But you must understand I have to protect my granddaughter."

Again, Zofia and Matka said nothing.

"If you do not find another place for her to stay…" The older woman's eyes closed as if she was waiting for a blow. "I will have to report you."

"Excuse me?" Zofia blinked, unable to believe kindly Mrs. Borkowska had issued such a threat.

"After Zofia saved your granddaughter, you would do this?" Matka's eyes blazed.

Mrs. Borkowska dropped her head. "I don't want to, but you saw what happened to the apartment on Krucza Street last week. I can't let that happen here. Please find another place for your friend."

With that, she slipped out of the apartment. Several minutes later, a knock at the door revealed a small parcel containing several cooked potatoes, a jar of beet marmalade, and a loaf of bread along with five hundred złotys in crumpled, old bills. The latter was likely more than Mrs. Borkowska could afford.

Apparently guilt came at a high cost.

But Zofia would not turn down the offering. They would need it to find accommodations for Mrs. Steinman.

★★★

The next day, Matka went to see Veronica about another place for Mrs. Steinman to live while Zofia pulled out the small, handwritten address Mrs. Mazur left with the key—which was now hidden beneath the floorboards with Papa's book collection.

The address was for a tenement house a block away from the library. Zofia climbed the stairwell, her curiosity piqued as she considered what the address might reveal. Was it a new contact for the library? Or maybe a stash of books Mrs. Mazur had been keeping?

Zofia rapped softly on the door.

Or maybe it was—

Darek opened the door, his brows lifting in surprise. "Zofia?"

His face was wan and solemn, his gaze filled with his grief.

"Your aunt," she began.

He stepped back and opened the door wider, inviting her in. Zofia didn't hesitate and entered the apartment.

The scent of paint lingered in the air and several canvases were propped against the wall. The scenes on them were a transformative blend of life before the occupation and the chaos wrought by the Nazis' initial attack. Tranquil streets morphed into rubble, lush vegetation and trees on one side of the portrait were rendered a barren wasteland on the other. No detail was spared, not on the fiery blasts spewing ash and black smoke into the sky, or the carnage left behind. The scenes were so real, they pulled Zofia back to that moment in time, flashing her into a nightmare.

"It's a project the underground has commissioned," Darek said shyly.

Zofia pulled her gaze away and found Darek watching her with his sensitive brown gaze, his hurt quiet but blatant.

"Your aunt…" Zofia's voice caught. "Have you had any news?"

"I don't expect any."

Zofia nodded soberly, recalling when her own father had been arrested.

"How did you know where we live?" Darek asked. "Where I live," he corrected in a pained whisper.

"I didn't realize you shared an apartment with Mrs. Ma— your aunt." Zofia glanced around, seeing past the canvases now. The curtains were a delicate touch of lace and portraits lined the walls. Likely all painted by Darek's own hand.

As if in confirmation, she noticed the prominent *D* on the right corner of those images followed by a flourish of a signature.

A table with two chairs sat by the kitchen window, a copy of the *Courier* spread in a patch of sunshine. The newspaper lay open to the obituary section.

"It's been just the two of us for a while." Darek stared toward a portrait Zofia recognized as a younger Mrs. Mazur. "My parents drowned when I was a boy along with my brother. My aunt was my mother's only sibling and she and my uncle took me in." Darek nodded toward another painting of a man with a hard jaw and slightly crooked nose. There was a fierceness to his gray eyes. "My uncle fought with Piłsudski himself in his Strike Group at the Miracle of the Vistula." Pride edged into Darek's voice, a tone Zofia had never once heard coming from him. Not even when she'd praised the artwork he'd drawn for her. "A problem with his heart took him from us several years before the German attack. After that, it was just my aunt and me."

Meaning he no longer had any family left.

"I'm so sorry," Zofia said softly.

He nodded in the way one does when their throat is too tight to offer words.

She took his hands in hers. His graceful fingers were dotted with flecks and smears of red and black, evidence of the art he'd been creating.

"Let me know if I can help with anything, Darek. Please."

It was a pithy condolence, but then weren't they all? There was nothing that could be said to ease the hurt of such a terrible loss.

Zofia let go of his hands, opened her arms, and stepped closer, pulling him into an embrace like Janina would have done. He fell against Zofia with a shuddering breath and clutched at her in his grief.

She held him for a long moment, supporting him in the way he'd supported her once before. His body was warm and the scent of paint lingered with something pleasantly spicy.

"I'm sorry." He stepped back and briskly wiped at his eyes. "I'm sure you have more to do with your day than check in on me." He glanced back at the canvases. "Besides, I have more work to do."

Zofia had never been good at reading between people's words. Being a blunt person herself, she took what was said as truth. But now she hesitated, uncertain if he wanted her company still, or the privacy to mourn.

"Thank you for coming." Though he put a gentle hand on her arm, there was a finality to his tone.

Zofia slowly stepped toward the door, watching his face for an indication he wanted her to stay. Because she would, if he needed her.

But his eyes were as shielded and blank as his expression now.

When had he learned to do that, to mask the emotion in his gaze when all of his feelings had shone so brilliantly in his eyes before?

"I can stay..." Zofia tried.

Darek shook his head and opened the door. "How did you say you got this address again?"

"It was with the key to the warehouse your aunt had stashed away in case something happened."

A corner of his mouth lifted. "Of course."

Miss Laska was surrounded by books when Zofia joined her at the reading room later that day. The older woman's head snapped up at Zofia's arrival, her large eyes bright with excitement. "I've already had several dozen people come by and they all requested certain books."

She withdrew a handwritten list and waved it at Zofia. Several dozen would be a lot of books to transport. Fortunately, the hidden warehouse was only one street over from the reading room, far enough away to avoid Nazi suspicion. It would make moving the items less risky.

A knock sounded at the rear door, three quick raps and a single slow one.

Miss Laska checked her watch. "That should be Ewa now. Here."

She handed a copy of *The Mysterious Affair at Style* by Agatha Christie to Zofia. "Can you please deliver this to her? By the time I make my way there, she might be gone. You know the impatience of youth." She gave a good-natured chuckle as Zofia accepted the book and went to the rear door.

On the other side of that door was Ewa, the girl Zofia had spent several months teaching to read. She leaned against the wall, her face tilted dreamily up at the late summer sky with a whimsical smile, so lost in her thoughts she had not heard the door open.

"Ewa?" Zofia said gently.

The girl started and a blush crept over her cheeks. She was thinner than when Zofia saw her last when the library closed over a month ago.

"Come in." Zofia waved her in as Ewa withdrew a copy of *Alice's Adventures in Wonderland* from her bag.

"Have you read this one?" Ewa handed her the book.

Zofia glanced at the cover depicting flowers surrounding a teacup. "I haven't yet, no."

"Oh, you must. It's the most fantastical story about a girl who happens upon a new world by going into a rabbit hole. There is a tea party with a mad hatter, and a queen who plays croquet with flamingos." Her eyes sparkled with the afterglow of a good book. "My sisters loved it."

"I think they weren't the only ones." Zofia lifted the Agatha Christie novel. "Is this for them too?"

Ewa flushed. "That's for me. They are all in school this week, so it's something to read when I queue for our rations. We're only able to check out one book at a time, so I give myself one book a week just for me."

The rule had been set in place by Zofia and Miss Laska. Which meant it was a rule that could be broken.

"Have you read *Peter Pan and Wendy*?" Zofia asked.

Ewa shook her head.

"Miss Laska," Zofia called out. "Can you please bring a copy of *Peter Pan and Wendy*?"

A departing shuffle answered Zofia as she withdrew a check-out log with "1932" in neat script on the cloth cover. That had been Miss Laska's idea, to backdate the ledger by a decade so it would predate the invasion and thus make the records of little interest to the Fraus.

Zofia found Ewa's name on the first line of the ledger listed only as Ewa B. After marking the book as checked in, she issued *The Mysterious Affair at Style* to her as well as *Peter Pan and Wendy*.

Right on time, Miss Laska entered the room with a battered copy of *Peter Pan and Wendy*, the gilt lettering partially rubbed away at the center.

"This was always a favorite when I read aloud to the children before we had the youth reading room." Miss Laska handed Ewa the book.

"Two books?" Ewa's eyes widened as she accepted the item like a gift, cradling it to her chest alongside the book she'd checked out for herself.

"Don't tell anyone." Miss Laska put her finger to her lips.

Ewa hugged the books tighter against her and shook her head. "I wouldn't. I… This means so much to me." Her brows furrowed. "We can't afford books, but they're such a wonderful way to take our mind off…well, everything. When the library closed, it was like our world went dark. And you've found a way to light it up again."

She set the books aside and caught Zofia in a fierce hug and then Miss Laska in a gentler one. With a large smile, she deposited her books into her bag and slipped out the door.

Miss Laska watched her leave with a twinkle in her eye. "She is why we're doing this, Zofia. For her, and everyone out there that these brigands have robbed of a childhood."

Zofia returned home to find Matka and Mrs. Steinman sitting at the table by the kitchen window, their faces creased with worry.

"Was Veronica able to find something?" Zofia asked.

The older women exchanged a look.

"Yes," Matka answered hesitantly. "But not until tomorrow evening."

Tomorrow evening was too late. Mrs. Borkowska was a woman of her word. And even if she wasn't, the risk was too great to leave to chance. The earlier joy of working with the secret library cooled as the familiar anxiety and fear slid into Zofia's thoughts.

There had to be somewhere Mrs. Steinman could stay, somewhere that wouldn't attract the attention of the authorities, somewhere out of the way.

But where?

Chapter 26

THE BEDDING WAS EASY to mask in a laundry bag along with several other items that Zofia insisted on carrying. Mrs. Steinman was forcedly pleasant as they walked to the hidden warehouse, discussing the topic of name days once more. Zofia led her toward an apartment building to avoid suspicion, but at the last minute, turned down an alley leading to the courtyard of the demolished library.

Mrs. Steinman's steps faltered.

"Trust me," Zofia said under her breath.

It was all the encouragement Mrs. Steinman needed and followed Zofia into the charred building, her footsteps careful on the rubble-strewn floor. Zofia led the way to the basement-level warehouse and withdrew the key.

After a hearty shove on the door to unstick it, they were inside. The bookshelves were completely full now with several boxes piled up near the far wall.

Mrs. Steinman gasped in awe. "What is this place?"

"We've been given lists at the library of books to remove from our shelves for destruction." Zofia settled the laundry bag of bedding and supplies on the floor in the corner. "We give them only the books for which we have duplicates. The rest we've been storing here."

"Zofia," Mrs. Steinman breathed. "This is incredible."

"It's been a combined effort by several of us at the library." A pang of sadness cut through Zofia for Mrs. Mazur.

She pushed the hurt aside and directed Mrs. Steinman toward the bedding on the floor. "I brought extra blankets. It can get chilly in here and the floor is hard. I know it isn't ideal."

"It will be perfect." Mrs. Steinman's gaze swept to the books. "May I choose one to read?"

"Of course," Zofia replied. "But you can't have a light down here or someone might see through the windows."

Mrs. Steinman nodded as she stepped forward and surveyed a row of books. "I understand."

"I'll be by tomorrow afternoon with the new address."

Zofia scarcely slept that evening. No one had ever stayed overnight in the warehouse and she wasn't sure what Mrs. Steinman might face. Was it cold? Did vagabonds take shelter in the more complete rooms of the lending library upstairs? Would Nazis bring their dogs by?

It was one thing to hide books, but to hide a person, especially someone so dear to her—well, it was another thing entirely.

Zofia found an excuse to go by the next morning, bringing some bread and a bit of what passed for coffee these days. The watery brown liquid was still warm when Zofia entered the warehouse. She was relieved to find Mrs. Steinman perfectly safe with her nose buried in a copy of *Gone with the Wind*.

"Did you sleep well?" Zofia asked.

"Yes, the street outside was quiet." Mrs. Steinman held up the book she was reading. "Have you read this one? It was very popular in the ghetto. I know Janina even had a copy she lent out, but I never had the time to read it." She put her hand to her chest. "What an amazing story."

Her words were a balm to Zofia's ruffled unease. These books that were supposed to be destroyed were now bringing pleasure to a reader once more. After the horrors Mrs. Steinman had endured in the ghetto, she found some reprieve from her pain in literature and it was truly a beautiful thing to behold. "You can bring it with you this afternoon if you like."

Mrs. Steinman gave a gentle smile. "I would like that very much, thank you."

Zofia left Janina's mother nestled in the pile of blankets with the book cradled in her hands.

When Zofia arrived at home, Veronica was at the kitchen table, this time with a steaming cup of coffee in front of her.

Veronica nodded her head in greeting. "I've come with the address for this afternoon. But I also come with some news." She shifted in her seat, putting her body toward Zofia to give her full attention. "My organization is now fully dedicated to saving as many Jews as possible. Your help delivering documents has been beneficial, but would you also be willing to escort people from the ghetto to safe houses?"

The greaser who Zofia had attacked immediately rose to the forefront of her mind, the way his body lay crumpled in the alleyway, how that sickening crack reverberated up her arm. The obituaries never indicated a body found in an alleyway. What if he was still loitering around the ghetto wall? What if he remembered her?

"I hope you'll say yes." When Veronica spoke again, it made Zofia realize how long she'd been quiet.

"As of now, there are no volunteers to take on this role." Veronica looked at her hands in her lap. "We do know it's dangerous."

"Dangerous?" Matka echoed. "How dangerous?"

But it wasn't danger for herself that concerned Zofia; it was danger for the men and women she would be smuggling out of the ghetto. And yet it would be worse for them to have everything in place to escape, but no one to help them navigate to safety.

"I'll do it," Zofia said. "But I need an exact time to meet them so I don't attract attention by waiting too long. And I'll need ways to disguise myself to avoid the possibility of being recognized."

Veronica's lips parted in understanding as the benefit of these important requests apparently dawned on her. "We can do that. I'll have some items sent to you."

Mrs. Steinman was transported to her new location with an elderly couple who welcomed her in with kind smiles and promises of security. It was enough to melt some of the tension gripping the mucles at the back of Zofia's neck. Within a couple of days, a box arrived for Zofia containing several wigs, a pair of glasses that obscured most of her face, some scarves, and a hat that would not only block the sun, but also her facial features.

A scrap of paper between the scarves indicated a time the following morning with a mention of the Twarda Street ghetto entrance and an address to go to afterward. "Magda will be wearing blue socks" was written in the neat script toward the bottom.

When the time came to meet Magda, Zofia slid on the oversize glasses and wrapped a dark gray head scarf over her hair. She also borrowed one of Matka's more dowdy dresses. The effect left her looking older and decidedly not herself.

The entire way to Twarda Street, Zofia's heart pounded so hard, she had to constantly force herself to slow to avoid becoming too winded. Especially when she spied a familiar figure walking toward her.

Kasia's eyes met Zofia's as they approached one another, first in recognition followed immediately by confusion, then a blank expression erased the furrow from Kasia's brow. She continued on as if they truly were strangers.

Zofia breathed in relief as she arrived at Twarda Street and stopped to fiddle with the bag at her side as if looking for something. It was nearly eight in the morning, meaning she could still be at work on time after completing her task.

Although she knew the importance of appearing nonchalant, she could not stifle the constant worry pressing at her back. She scanned the area for the tenth time in only a matter of seconds, looking for *him*, for the man who she had struck with a brick.

Her mouth was dry at the thought of seeing him again. What if he confronted her? What could she possibly say to excuse what had happened?

Movement at the ghetto gate caught her attention as a woman approached one of the guards, and slipped something into his hand. He looked away and stepped closer to the street, putting his back to her while simultaneously blocking anyone's view.

The woman rushed from the gate, a pair of blue socks pulled up to her shins. A child of about ten held her hand, the girl's thin legs rushing to keep up with the adult stride.

The accompanying child took Zofia aback. She hadn't been told about a child, only the woman. Likewise, there was only a set of papers for one as well as a place to stay.

Zofia had nothing for the little girl.

She approached the two, unsure if she ought to whisper or speak loudly. "Magda?" she asked, opting for a familiar, friendly volume.

The woman turned toward her, terror openly visible on her pretty face. She nodded, the muscles of her neck tight as bowstrings.

"Oh, it's a delight to see you, my friend." Zofia looped her arm around the other woman's.

It was what Janina would do in such a situation with someone in need of kindness and caring. An ache pinched at Zofia with the thought of her friend.

"What luck to run into you so soon after just meeting up last week." Zofia swallowed her nerves with the silk of her lie.

The woman gave a wobbly smile and the girl stared back with wide, solemn eyes.

"I'm heading to the park, would you both like to join me?" Zofia gave them a broad smile and nodded encouragingly so they would understand her sentiment even if they only spoke Yiddish.

"Yes." Magda's gaze darted furtively about. She wore her fear like a cloak for all to see. That fear reached inside Zofia and seized her in its grip.

She glanced around again, certain the greaser—or a new one—would approach at any moment. By some miracle, he never did. None of the people who lurked around the ghetto gates seemed to notice them as they briskly walked toward the address Zofia had been given.

Upon their arrival, a Polish woman with a drooling baby on her hip answered the door to the apartment and invited them in. The house was a mess, scattered with clothing and various odds and ends and there was a strong odor of soiled nappies filling the compressed living space. The woman's gaze flicked to Magda and the girl.

Zofia's palms prickled.

"I wasn't told there would be two." The baby began to fuss and the woman jiggled the child on her hip. "We don't have the room or food for two."

Zofia didn't mention that she didn't have papers for the girl either. No doubt that would only endanger the deal more. There was no sense in arguing.

"I understand." Zofia said no more, leading Magda and the girl from the apartment. "I have somewhere else to take you while we sort this out."

The warehouse would have to do for now. It wasn't anything Zofia wanted to use on a regular basis, as it risked exposing the location if someone was captured. It was far too valuable. But so were these two lives she held in her hands.

In a pinch, the warehouse was a necessity.

She guided them to the burned-out building. Neither hesitated as they followed behind Zofia, rushing into the demolished lending library without question. Worry crossed Magda's face for a brief moment as she pulled the girl closer, but she offered no protest as Zofia unlocked the warehouse door.

Light from an extraordinarily sunny day streamed in through the grimy windows, casting the room in an ethereal golden glow and illuminating the rows and rows and rows of books.

The girl sucked in a breath, her eyes going wide as she stepped forward slowly, reverently, then stopped as if afraid to touch anything. Magda watched her with a tender, affectionate smile.

"You can choose a book to read, if you like," Zofia offered.

The girl remained where she stood, her gaze uncertain. Magda spoke to her in Yiddish, which Zofia recognized from all the days spent in Bubbe's kitchen with Janina, days that felt a lifetime ago. Zofia shoved the thoughts away to keep the pain from impeding her task.

"We have a section of books in Yiddish and Hebrew." Zofia indicated the row of shelves and waved the child forward.

The girl slowly approached the books and looked from top to bottom, her hands clasped over her heart. Tilting her head to one side, she began to peruse the row of titles, her mouth forming the words silently as she read.

"I know she is not supposed to be with me." Magda's Polish was accented with Yiddish, which explained why she had been so reluctant to speak outside. "I could not leave my daughter behind. I worked too hard to keep her safe, hidden in the attic first and then in a hollow section of the wall. Life has been so miserable for her. Not a childhood at all."

"I heard there were no children left in the ghetto," Zofia said gravely. "I'm glad to see that is not the case. And I'm gladder still that you are both out now."

The girl pulled a book from the shelf, sank to the floor, and immediately began reading by the light of a golden sunbeam. Magda smiled, tears gleaming in her eyes. "She loves books."

"You both are welcome to them," Zofia said. "I will return soon with supplies and will see about getting papers for your daughter as well as accommodations for you both. I will make sure she continues to remain safe."

Zofia managed to deliver the bedding and some food to Magda and her daughter and still made it to the library precisely one minute before her shift. This earned her a nod of approval from whichever of the Fraus was standing at the door with the clipboard.

With Mrs. Mazur gone, Zofia was placed in charge of the warehouse. She spent hours wheeling books to and from departments while still combing through inventory lists.

The day of the library's reopening had come and gone and still the doors remained shuttered with no word of when a date might be rescheduled.

Once the inventory audit was complete, Zofia was unsure what would happen to the employees who couldn't speak German. She and the other staff who were fluent, including Kasia and Danuta, were being tasked with rewriting all Polish catalog cards into German, reordering them in a nonsensical system that was being used in Berlin. It was a mind-numbing job that would likely take years. What's more, it was useless when the previous way of cataloging was so much more efficient.

Kasia wheeled an empty cart into the warehouse. "Good morning, Zofia." Though she gave one of her brilliant, unfettered smiles, there was a wary look to her as she glanced about.

"Were you…?" She bit her lip. "I thought I saw you earlier this morning, but you didn't look like you."

Zofia lifted her brows innocently. "I don't know what you mean."

Kasia nodded as if Zofia had confirmed what she already knew. "Please be careful around that area. Someone was recently killed."

"Killed?" Zofia's pulse missed a beat.

"There has been a lot of violence near the wall. Not just with guards shooting people, but about a week ago, a man's body was discovered in the alley near my apartment. An old woman found him and immediately rushed upstairs, too afraid to notify authorities. She said his head had been struck by something heavy. The Wehrmacht or Gestapo must have done it, because a brick was lying there next to him, with no attempt made to hide it. Then the blue police came and the man just disappeared."

Zofia's head spun as she recognized exactly who that man had been. "Was he dead?"

Kasia nodded. "The woman in my building said he was gray and when she touched him, his skin was cold and stiff. He was definitely dead."

Zofia exhaled the breath she'd been holding.

He was dead.

She had killed him. The realization left a sickening twist in her stomach. But also an immense sense of relief. Yes, she had killed a man, but now Janina and her mother would not be recognized. At least they were safe.

Veronica was able to supply papers for Magda's daughter and found them a home on the outskirts of Warsaw. By that evening, the two were settled into their new safe house, both with books to keep them company until Zofia saw them again.

Knowledge of the greaser's death made her next run to guide a young man from the ghetto go far smoother without the paranoia of being recognized. As did the subsequent runs after that, especially with fresh disguises and using different routes and gates to avoid suspicion. Two weeks later, she received a box filled to the brim with złotys—payment for all those safe houses.

Two out of ten of those safe houses required no payment at all, having agreed to shelter the Jews for free. The others exacted a steep price for their "generosity." Delivering such vast sums was no easy feat, and often required Zofia to return home several times for stacks of złotys.

When she arrived at the house where Mrs. Steinman was staying, she found the elderly couple far less kind than at their initial introduction. They waved her inside, their faces red with irritation.

"It's not enough." The woman turned her nose up at the thousand złotys Zofia had extended toward her.

While most Varsovians were getting by on one or two hundred złotys for a month of work, the sum Zofia was offering for simply letting someone live with them was practically a fortune.

"Not enough?" Zofia asked.

"We need more," the man groused. "This Jew eats us out of house and home."

Zofia's pulse throbbed in her temples. "I'd like to see Mrs. Zieliński, please," she said, using Mrs. Steinman's new name.

The woman folded her arms over her chest. "She's busy."

Zofia's awareness grew sharper, her instincts suddenly on edge. "I won't take no for an answer."

The woman narrowed her small eyes and they nearly disappeared in the fleshy moon of her face.

Fear prickled down Zofia's spine. Had they done something to Mrs. Steinman? Had they turned her over to the authorities?

Zofia took a threatening step toward the woman. "You will get no money at all if you don't present her to me at once."

The older woman turned her mean stare toward her husband and nodded.

Several minutes later, Mrs. Steinman was led from a back room. Though she had been on the Polish side for nearly a month, she had not gained any weight. The sharp bones of her shoulders thrust through the worn dress that hung on her like a curtain. Her hair was lank and dirty and it was obvious some time had passed since she last bathed.

She kept her head down, not looking up at Zofia.

"What have you done?" Zofia demanded of the couple.

The woman said nothing, her arms folded belligerently over her chest.

"She won't be staying with you a moment longer." Zofia's fingers tightened on the money. Her eyes never left the couple. "Mrs. Zieliński, please gather your belongings. You don't have to remain with these people."

The man's eyes went to the stack of złotys Zofia held in her clenched hand. "We still kept her this whole month."

"Then you still get your money," Zofia said in a low voice. "But you won't get a single groszy more." She fought the urge to throw the money at them and let it scatter through the dingy apartment like fallen leaves. Instead, she thrust it into their hands, not bothering to mask her disgust.

The woman snatched the payment and a tense silence filled the room, congealing between them until Mrs. Steinman emerged again several minutes later.

Zofia left with Janina's mother and started toward the hidden warehouse two streets over. Once more, it was a temporary fix for the pressing concern.

They would need another safe house.

Chapter 27

ZOFIA MADE IT A point to check on the welfare of her wards with every delivery of payment after Mrs. Steinman's awful experience. In times of war and strife, the bad in people tended to emerge. Fortunately, there were some who were good as well, who offered their homes without cost to Jewish refugees.

Mrs. Steinman was relocated with a woman who lived alone on a quiet street. The apartment appeared sunny and clean and thus far, the woman appeared to be treating Janina's mother well. Zofia slept easier knowing Mrs. Steinman was safe again.

The days passed quickly between Zofia's efforts helping Veronica, her work at the library, and the minor sabotage she still continued to commit with the Gray Ranks. There wasn't as much room in her busy schedule for the latter as of late. However, she still tried to help with the Gray Ranks where she could by keeping watch for Gestapo or Wehrmacht while some of the more daring boys destroyed Nazi flags or drew the new symbol for the Polish Underground State and Home Army on walls whenever possible. Known as the *kotwica*, or anchor, the symbol was a *P* with a *W* at its stem, in memory of those slain in Wawer back in 1939. It was a symbol of vengeance—a symbol that promised one day they would fight back.

As the months went by, the flow of the men and women fleeing the ghetto became a trickle due to the continual roundups. The process of helping those few remaining flee grew more difficult, more dangerous, and the bribes came at a higher cost.

Zofia had not seen Janina since the day she'd helped Mrs. Steinman escape and made it a point to walk by the ghetto wall when she could. Where once the area within teemed with noise, it now fell eerily quiet.

"Isn't it a shame?" a man asked one day, pausing beside her to regard the wall. Then he lowered his head and went on his way.

Several others cast sympathetic looks at the wall as they passed, all of them too late in their concern to help.

Hanukkah was nearly upon them. It had been Zofia's hope to reunite Janina with her mother for the holiday, but ultimately it was impossible. Not without hearing from Janina or even knowing where she was in the ghetto.

Or if she was even still there at all.

One afternoon when the Bandit Book Club was trying to devise a way to obtain another copy of *War and Peace* since Kasia had spent months trying to read their single copy, Darek had asked everyone if they wished to attend a secret piano performance. Zofia had been the only one free to do so and while she'd been looking forward to it then, she now regretted making the plans. She was too busy with everything she was involved in, all of it far more important than a night listening to someone play the piano.

Still, she had agreed and tried to dress as best as she could for the event. Occasions such as these weren't the same as before the war when one attached diamonds to their ears and wore lovely dresses made of velvet and silk. Not that she'd ever been a person to enjoy such frivolities anyway.

Concertgoers had to give the appearance that this was a day like any other. But even so, Zofia managed to dress herself up somewhat, styling her waves using one of her mother's old jeweled pins, and wore one of her nicest dresses—the blue wool with a white collar. Matka tied a black ribbon around her waist as she'd grown too thin for the dress, and the addition lent the look a touch of elegance. It had been enough to make Matka smile, seeing Zofia so concerned about her appearance.

Now Zofia sat in a basement with a dozen other men and women, their chairs placed around a single piano. Candles illuminated the room and everyone left their coats on to fight off the chill. Though the pianist was not there yet, people still spoke in hushed whispers.

"Do you enjoy the piano?" Darek asked quietly.

"My father did." Zofia recalled how Papa would close his eyes as he listened, a finger tapping the rhythm on his knee as he lost himself to the music.

But Zofia had never felt that connection. She'd accompanied her family to concerts, but had always been eager to leave, to return home to comfortable clothes and a good book.

She'd said yes to attend this event for the same reason she'd finished secondary school and read books Hitler had banned. Whatever was restricted from her, she wanted it as a means of protest.

So, if listening to a secret concert in a cold basement was forbidden, then she wanted to be there.

The pianist came into the room and the audience broke into applause, giving him a standing ovation before he even began. But then, Zbigniew Drzewiecki was renowned for his artistry at the piano, especially in his performance of Chopin's pieces.

The Nazis had devoted a museum to the claim that Chopin had German roots—this after having blown up his statue in

Łazienki Park soon after the occupation. It was a lie, of course. Chopin was a proud Pole who—when he suspected his impending death while in France—insisted his heart be buried in Poland. Now, almost a hundred years later, Warsaw still held the composer's heart.

Chopin was undeniably Polish and this concert was a way to celebrate what Poland stood for: arts, creativity, learning, and—above all—freedom.

Mr. Drzewiecki bowed to the audience and sat on the bench before the piano, its black surface polished to a high shine that reflected the dozens of flickering candles. The room went completely silent. Without preamble, the pianist's fingers fluttered over the keys, the movements quick and light, each note resonating in the belly of the instrument.

The sound was delicate, teased out by the adroitness of Drzewiecki's deft fingers. Zofia didn't know what Chopin had in mind when he composed the piece, but the song carried her back to summers spent on the shores of the Vistula with Janina, long before the war had ever been a topic of discussion.

It was a whisper of a memory, one she tightened her hold on lest it tug away, like a balloon string on a windy day. She closed her eyes and locked her mind, letting herself be transported to those innocent, carefree times.

The notes undulated over her like the shifting waves of the river. *Flecks of sunlight danced off the Vistula and water lapped against their naked toes. Janina laughed at something, her brown eyes crinkling at the corners as she kicked, droplets spraying and shimmering where they hung in the air before cascading back into the river. Little ringed plovers darted around them, pausing occasionally to pluck at the sand with their beaks.*

Warmth filled Zofia's chest, bubbly and effervescent as champagne.

Happy.

She was *happy.*

The song faded away, but she clutched at the feeling so that it lingered long enough for the next piece to begin and for a new vision to unfurl.

Papa sat at the square wooden breakfast table with a cup of coffee and an open newspaper. Matka brought him a plate of toast smeared with generous amounts of creamy butter and rich, red jam. She looked beautiful, the way she did before the war, her face full and lovely. It was obvious Papa thought so too with how he smiled when he accepted the plate from her. Antek plopped into his chair at the table, the front of his hair jutting up from the cowlick that had plagued him since boyhood. When he grinned, it was directed at Zofia. "Want me to teach you how to tie a knot that won't come loose?"

She wanted to stay in those memories forever, those everyday moments that she had taken for granted. They had been boring then, her thoughts fixed on faults rather than love. It had all been so simple. So perfect.

It had been beautiful.

She let the music carry her away on the wings of her recollections. Days at school with Janina at her side, family dinners with full plates and quality food, Girl Guide meetings and laughter, playing hoops in the park amid the scent of lilies of the valley and lilacs.

All too soon, the music came to an abrupt end and Zofia found herself back in a cold, semidark basement, sitting in a hard wooden chair. People clapped around her and she did likewise, her movement automatic as her brain reeled at how transportive the music had been. And the way its absence made her suddenly bereft.

There was no intermission as with a prewar performance. The concert was over and the silent piano left an emptiness in her. *The Little Match Girl* had been one of her favorite childhood stories and it came to mind now in the way books so often filled her thoughts.

For the last hour, each song had been like a match struck, leaving Zofia to bask in the glow of a golden memory. When the concert was done, those little flames had all snuffed out, relegating her to this cold, hard world where everything had changed.

She realized then how Papa could listen for so long with his eyes closed, his finger gently tapping. He had been absorbing the music, letting it carry him away from the nightmares of the Great War and his troubles at the hospital to times of joy.

Back then, she hadn't experienced enough of life to truly appreciate music in the way Papa had. But that had been before she'd known how deep the chasm of loss could run.

Marta Krakowska's advice came back to her—to truly write emotion, one must die a thousand deaths. Perhaps this was what she meant, that in enduring the rawness of life, one could finally cherish what was so often overlooked.

That evening, Zofia had relished those moments like pearls gathered on a string of music.

When the concert finished, Darek led her out into the frigid December night. Stars winked in the silky blackness overhead, their glow made brilliant by the darkened street. Neither she nor Darek said anything for a while as they walked, their footsteps loud on the pavement as they came down from the exquisite performance.

That was one of the things Zofia appreciated about the friendship she'd developed with Darek. They could lose themselves in their thoughts together in companionable silence.

"The Department of Education and Culture wants to host an exhibit of my art." Darek's soft voice brushed aside the quiet like a curtain.

"For your paintings?" She recalled the power of his intricate canvases often, the stark difference of the before and the after and the impact they made.

"My paintings and some of my charcoal work too." He looked up at the stars as he spoke.

In truth, his charcoal work was her favorite, the detail so precise, the image might have been captured with a camera rather than a bit of charcoal. "Darek, that's incredible."

"Would you want to go?" He glanced down at her.

"Of course I would."

He nodded and though it was dark, she imagined she could make out a shy flush on his cheeks. "I'll let you know when it is."

They stopped in front of her apartment and the sounds of Nazi merriment and women laughing from Bar Podlaski was garish in the otherwise beautifully still night.

"I'm looking forward to it." Zofia smiled at him.

Being tall for a woman, she wasn't always able to look up to men. But she could with Darek and she liked that about him. In fact, there seemed to be quite a number of things she liked about him lately.

Maybe a little too much.

She stepped back, putting space between them. Life was too complicated to give in to whatever made her heart beat harder when he was around.

"Good night." She walked backward toward the door to her apartment.

"Good night, Zofia." He remained where he stood, a grin lifting the corner of his lips. It wasn't until she was safely inside that he finally turned and headed in the opposite direction down the street.

If they met before their lives had so drastically been altered, things might have been different between them. There might have been room for something more, something like love.

By January, the secret library on Traugutta Street was in full operation. Zofia enlisted Danuta's and Kasia's assistance in finding books that secret patrons requested and for discovering alternate ways to remove and return those books to the main library undetected.

Patrons came by several times a day, their presence masked

by the busy street and a shaded alcove. With illegal books suddenly available again, the man who had once requested *The Invisible Man* was now carrying it back home to read to his son.

Zofia had just closed the rear door where people came to collect their books when a bang sounded from the front of the small building.

"How have we not known about this one?" a familiar shrill voice asked.

Zofia quickly gathered up the books she'd brought from the hidden warehouse. "It's Frau Beck," she whispered to Miss Laska as she rushed to hide the books in the rear closet.

The rattle of keys jangled at the front door. Frau Beck opened the door and Frau Schmidt appeared beside her, both in their matching dark jackets, skirts, and sneers. They drew up short when they saw Miss Laska and Zofia.

"What are you doing here?" Frau Schmidt asked, her lip curling. "This building is supposed to be empty."

"It is?" Miss Laska asked, blinking behind her massive glasses.

It was and they both knew it. The order had come after inventories had been reviewed. But Miss Laska hadn't turned in her inventory sheet either.

Fortunately, they had prepared for an event such as this and thus far, Miss Laska was playing her role to perfection.

"Yes," Frau Beck snapped. Her disapproving gaze took in the reading room, its shelves mostly bare save for the books approved by the General Government and one relatively healthy plant.

Frau Schmidt nodded at Zofia. "And what are you doing here? It is your day off, is it not?" She flicked through the stack of papers on her clipboard.

"I've always come to help Miss Laska," Zofia replied with the benign innocence of someone who had done no wrong. "Even on my days off."

Miss Laska smiled at Zofia. "The help is always appreciated."

"Miss Laska," Frau Schmidt repeated, still leafing through her clipboard. "I don't recall you being employed here any longer. You aren't on my list."

"I'm not?" Miss Laska blinked again.

"Are you even being paid?" Frau Beck asked.

"No, but I assumed it was an oversight that would be corrected."

The Fraus exchanged a beleaguered look.

"You are not supposed to be here," Frau Beck said abruptly. "You must leave or we will have you arrested."

"That isn't true," Zofia said. Both women looked at her and she switched to German. "I requested her assistance for verifying the inventory of this building. She knows more than anyone about this branch. You seemed amenable to it at the time." She addressed the latter part to Frau Beck, who was sometimes easier to persuade.

The woman pursed her lips while Frau Schmidt went to the desk and rummaged through it. "There's hardly anything in here save for a few old logs and she is clearly senile. What could she possibly help with?"

Zofia picked up the 1933 logbook where they had been recording current checkouts after the new year, making it look as though she randomly selected it from the table. "She can recall historical detail with precision. Ask her anything from this checkout log."

Frau Schmidt rolled her eyes and opened the book. "Who checked out *Quo Vadis* on January 5, to be returned by January 25?" she asked in thickly accented Polish.

"Mrs. Halinka D.," Miss Laska answered without hesitation.

Frau Schmidt's brows lifted as she swiped back several random pages. "What about *Gone with the Wind* on January 3 and when would it be returned?"

"Mr. Jan G. and with a return date of January 23."

Frau Schmidt seemed impressed. Perhaps too impressed. She

picked up another book, this one dated 1929, and Zofia's stomach shrank.

Miss Laska's ruse only went as far as their current checkouts. Anything truly in the past meant Miss Laska would fail and they would both be caught.

Chapter 28

ZOFIA TENSED, WAITING FOR Frau Schmidt to open the old checkout log with books that really did date back over a decade.

"That's enough," Frau Beck said irritably.

Frau Schmidt sighed and set down the logbook from 1929. "Very well, she may remain so long as you need her assistance."

With that, the Fraus swept out of the building and the tension in Zofia's shoulders relaxed. Miss Laska was safe for the time being.

The older woman suddenly began giggling. "It's a good thing they aren't actual readers." Her eyes glinted with mischievous amusement. "Or they would have known *Gone with the Wind* wasn't published until 1936."

A knock came from the back door. Zofia opened it, half expecting the Fraus to be playing a cruel trick on them by showing up at the rear entrance with a patron. But it was a welcome face that greeted her, one with bright blue eyes and a matching scarf over red hair.

Marta Krakowska smiled and entered the library. "Ah, the future author."

Zofia gaped stupidly. "You remember me?"

"The way you handled the books we saved from Krasiński Library made you unforgettable. In fact, I used it in a scene I recently wrote for my most recent novel, *Poland's Eagle*."

"That sounds amazing."

Marta chuckled. "You've only heard the title."

Sometimes a good title and a familiar name were the only things necessary for Zofia to know she'd love a book.

Miss Laska approached with an item in her hand. "Here you are." She held out a copy of *The Bridge of San Luis Rey* by Thornton Wilder.

Miss Krakowska accepted the book and nestled it into a large woven bag at her side. "This is a good story for an aspiring author. The best way to write a character is to know who he is at his core. Thornton Wilder does a wonderful job of this in his exploration of what connection truly means to mankind. You'll have to read it." She tilted her head in consideration. "After I'm done."

"I'll add my name to check it out next." Zofia wrote Miss Krakowska's due date in the log. "February 4."

Miss Krakowska thanked them and slipped out the rear door, the entire exchange as normal as any other library patron.

"You want to be an author?" Miss Laska settled the book log back in the drawer.

"I'd considered it once." Zofia shrugged, suddenly feeling ridiculous for having ever dreamt of the possibility. Who could think of future aspirations when the focus of every day was survival? Not only hers, but those she loved and those who she had been entrusted to help.

"You don't need to worry about it now." Miss Laska patted

Zofia's forearm. "Better to take your time and do what it is that you want rather than a job you're forced into."

"Is being a librarian what you wanted?" Zofia slid the other checkout logs into the desk, placing them in order with 1933 on the top.

"It is, but..." Miss Laska looked in the distance, as though seeing a different life, a different time. "But when I was younger, I was a radical."

"A radical?"

Miss Laska shook her head to clear it and refocused on a stack of books on the desk. "All I'd ever wanted was a free Poland. I opposed the Russian oppression at every opportunity. After we were free following the Great War, I thought we would never have to live through an occupation again. You are lucky to be young, to have been born into freedom and to be able to fight."

"You could still join us." Zofia filled up the little watering can for the lone plant in the reading room.

Miss Laska laughed out loud, so caught in the humor that she forgot to cover her missing tooth. "I can scarcely lift a heavy box or water a plant. No, I think I am long past those days." But even as she said it, her eyes twinkled. "There is nothing I want more in this world than a free Poland." Pausing a moment, she let her gaze peruse the shelves in front of her and gave a contented sigh. "But I was—and am—fortunate to work with my other passion—books."

The work Veronica had done to aid the Jews was absorbed into the Polish Underground State in an organization called Żegota, which used her assistance to effectively plan out their efforts. Not long after their leadership was announced, the woman sheltering Mrs. Steinman informed Zofia that a neighbor had discovered her guest and threatened to go to the police.

Żegota immediately had Zofia relocate Mrs. Steinman to a home on the outskirts of town to reside with a widower whose husband had been killed during the Great War. Mrs. Steinman had been there nearly a month now and Zofia had worried about her ever since.

Once Zofia was finally able to spare a day to visit Mrs. Steinman, she had to do so by train. It wasn't the optimal mode of transportation. Gestapo agents were constantly checking travelers for smuggled food and money and there was always the risk of a resistance attack that might blow the train off its rails. But Zofia had no choice, not when the frozen roads were impossible to attempt by bicycle.

Though the widow had said no money was necessary, Zofia had several hundred złotys nestled in the lining of her purse. Just in case.

It was a long walk to the cottage, the effort made all the more miserable by a snowstorm that nearly blinded Zofia. By the time she arrived, she was nearly frozen through.

The widow, whom Zofia only knew as Ella, opened the door and quickly ushered her inside where it smelled like a smoky fire and roasting meat of some kind. Zofia's mouth watered.

Ella's graying red hair was braided back from her pleasant face and concern showed in her green eyes. She led Zofia to a chair by the hearth, a fire roaring steadily within. Heat prickled over Zofia's chilled flesh like needles, painful before growing pleasant. With fuel so scarce in the city, Zofia felt as though she hadn't been warm in months.

"What are you doing out in this weather?" Ella pulled the green shawl around herself a little tighter and called out over her shoulder, "Hania, it's Zofia."

Mrs. Steinman rushed out of a rear bedroom in an instant. "Zofia, what were you thinking, coming out here in the middle of winter?"

Zofia stared at Mrs. Steinman, unable to look away. Janina's mother was completely changed.

Her skeletal frame had plumped out, not only rounding her

hips, but also filling out her face. A healthy, rosy hue glowed at her cheeks and her hair was lustrous.

"I would have come to get you if we'd known." Ella tsked. "Hania, can you please bring a few extra blankets for her while I heat up some milk?"

Finally, Zofia pulled her stare from Mrs. Steinman, certain she had heard incorrectly. No one had milk these days.

But sure enough, Ella withdrew a bottle from the windowsill and poured some milk into a pan. Blankets settled over Zofia and within minutes, the milk was hot and steaming in her hands.

She drank it down quickly even though it burned her tongue, savoring the creamy goodness and the satisfaction of it settling in her stomach.

"You appear to be well and warmed up now." Ella smiled down at Zofia. "I'll leave you two to chat a bit." With that, she slipped from the room to afford Mrs. Steinman and Zofia some privacy.

"Is Janina all right?" Mrs. Steinman asked, her brow puckered with worry.

"I haven't heard from her."

Mrs. Steinman nodded, concern still crinkling her forehead. "Since you risked such weather to come out here, I thought…"

Zofia shook her head. "No, I only wanted to check on you, to make sure you were being cared for properly. It's been so cold this year, and after that horrid couple… I couldn't bear for anything to happen to you."

Mrs. Steinman reached out and stroked Zofia's hair the way she always did with Janina. "You risk too much for others."

Zofia didn't say anything. She wished she could risk more, but it wasn't possible when Nazis were watching at every turn.

Once she reassured herself that Mrs. Steinman was in a safe place and being well cared for, Zofia had to return to Warsaw. This time, Ella insisted on transporting her to the train station in a small horse-drawn cart.

Zofia waited until they were bumping over the frozen countryside, wrapped tightly in their coats and scarves. "I brought money for you."

Ella propped her foot on the wooden beam at the front of the cart. "Don't need it."

Who turned down money in times such as theirs? Zofia tried again. "Surely it can help with getting food or supplies."

Still, Ella remained facing forward, quiet for long enough that Zofia's nerves began to dance.

"There is something you can do for me," Ella said finally. "It's a big request though."

Everyone had a price and she was about to find out Ella's.

"Hania let me borrow *Gone with the Wind* when she was done reading it," Ella continued. "She also said you work for the library."

Relief released the tension in Zofia's shoulders. "Would you like me to bring books for you next time I come?"

"Not me." Ella steered the cart left, toward the train station in the distance. "The library here has nothing but books on farming. I imagine the young people are as desperate for entertaining reading as I am. Though I would like to request some Proust if you have any."

Zofia regarded Ella's profile, considering the older woman who shared every part of her life with Mrs. Steinman, from the food her small farm produced that the Nazis didn't take, to the clothes from her own wardrobe. And now, even the favor she requested was to share with others.

"In the spring when the roads are clearer, I'll bring some," Zofia replied. "That way I can ride my bike. In the meantime, why don't you put together a list of titles you might want."

The smile growing over Ella's face indicated she'd have no problem with that task.

Just after the middle of January, the sounds of war exploded in Warsaw once more, this time concentrated in the heart of the ghetto. The commotion continued through the day, and Zofia was beside herself with fear for Janina.

It was rare for Jews to escape from the ghetto anymore. From what Zofia had been told, those remaining were trapped behind a second set of walls, sealing them in the factory where they worked with barely any food or sleep.

That evening at Darek's art exhibit, the impromptu uprising was all anyone talked about.

"I heard they were successful." Kasia was by Danuta's side as usual.

Though they had not reunited to discuss books this time, it was good to have the Bandit Book Club in one place together again.

"It's about time someone fought back," Danuta said as she studied one of Darek's paintings.

It was a view of Krasiński Library before the war, with the beautiful garden fanning around the grand structure. The image blurred in the middle to show the collapsed roof on the reading room and museum with books scattered and burning on the scarred lawn.

Darek captured the scene with such realism, Zofia could practically feel the grit of smoke and dust against her fingertips from the books they'd salvaged.

"Is the uprising still going?" she asked.

"No," Kasia replied softly. "But they were able to hold the Nazis off for a while."

Darek, who had been speaking to another group, turned to join them. "The fight was enough to attract the attention of the Home Army," he said in a low voice. "I hear they are going to try to put together more arms to send into the ghetto."

Which meant there would be more battles against the Germans. Zofia's thoughts returned to Janina again, and she silently prayed her friend was safe.

"Darek, you are such an amazing artist." Kasia studied the painting of Krasiński Library. "I'm so impressed by your skill."

Danuta stepped closer to the painting, examining it in more detail. "Truly exquisite. Even my father wouldn't have been able to find fault with your work."

Though Zofia had seen these works before, she was awed by them all over again. Darek had natural talent, his style reminiscent of famed nineteenth-century Polish artist Jan Matejko. The play of light and shadow over the scene, with vivid reds and jewel tones. "If this was a different time, your work would be in the National Museum," Zofia said earnestly.

Color flushed over Darek's cheeks and she hated that she noticed how handsome he looked that night. The pomade used to slick his hair back reminded her of Janina's letters, and he was as stunning as an actor from the cinema with his sharp jaw and wide, expressive brown eyes.

"That was once a dream of mine, to have my work in the National Museum." He looked at the tips of his shoes at his admission.

"It's not your dream anymore?" Zofia asked.

He shrugged. "Who would waste a dream on something so selfish? If I could have anything, it would be for this occupation to never have happened, and for equality between Jews and Poles, exactly as it should be."

His words resonated with Zofia whose own thoughts had a hard time pushing into a future beyond having completed secondary school. That could come later. Now was for Poland.

Danuta moved on to the next painting, one of Świętokrzyska Street where the reading room over the hidden warehouse had once stood. It was the center point in Darek's painting, half stoic and proud on one side, aflame and crumbling on the other. Kasia followed Danuta for a more thorough look, but Darek didn't join them. He remained in front of Zofia, and asked, "Have you had any word from Janina?"

Zofia shook her head.

Darek's lips pressed together. "I'll let you know if I hear anything."

"I wish all this could have happened sooner," Zofia lamented, giving voice to the words aching inside her for too long. "Maybe the wall could have been prevented. Jews would not have been persecuted. Innocent men and women would not be captured and put to death."

"And your father and my parents would be alive." Danuta looked over her shoulder at Zofia, obviously eavesdropping on the conversation. "Instead of being dragged to Palmiry like they were."

Zofia frowned at the mention of the village on the outskirts of Warsaw. "My father was at Pawiak Prison."

Danuta turned around fully and looked at Zofia, her eyes filled with a mix of hurt and rage. "That's what they said about my parents too."

A cold sensation washed over Zofia.

"What do you mean?" Zofia tried to swallow but found her throat suddenly dry.

Danuta's sympathetic expression made Zofia's pulse go jagged. "Hitler was given lists of men and women with higher education, ones who might be perceived as a threat to the occupation," Danuta explained. "Dentists, lawyers, professors, like my parents. And doctors."

Doctors.

Zofia's head swam.

"You don't need to do this, Danuta." A note of warning rang in Darek's tone.

"Yes, she does," Zofia replied through numb lips. "I need to know."

Danuta flicked a challenging look at Darek before continuing. "They were arrested and taken first to Pawiak, yes, for a day or so. Then they were carted to Kampinos Forest near Palmiry where they were lined up before deep pits in the earth."

"And?" Zofia's breath locked in her chest.

"And shot." Danuta looked away.

Zofia snapped her attention to Darek, who gave a solemn nod. Something sour churned in the pit of her stomach. Dots marred her vision.

She had believed that Papa was in Pawiak, and that he'd been receiving the packages she'd made him, that he knew he was loved and cared for before dying there a year later. But this…

She shook her head to clear it, but the action only made her thoughts spin more. The room was suddenly too small, the air too still, too thick to breathe.

If that was the price exacted for merely the possibility of an uprising, what would the Nazis do to those who had actually risen up against them?

Chapter 29

THE HUM OF WAR in the air was an all too familiar tune. What had pulsed to life in the ghetto in January lay dormant for several months, fine-tuning its pitch until the eve of Passover in April, when it erupted with the rattle of gunfire.

Zofia and Matka both jumped at the table, their eyes meeting over the meager fare of boiled potatoes and a quarter loaf of hard bread as they tried to place the direction of the commotion.

Ever since Hitler had been defeated by the Soviet Union at Stalingrad two months prior, the General Government had become more aggressive in their cruelty. There were more roundups and arrests as well as public executions with bodies left swinging for days on lampposts all through Warsaw.

The elite of the Gray Ranks like Darek continued their own executions of people found guilty by the underground courts and blew up rail lines, while others including Zofia continued performing minor sabotage.

The sound of fighting seemed far enough away to not be a

police raid on their building. But whatever peace Zofia found was replaced by the sinking realization of where the battle was coming from.

"I think..." She drew in a slow breath. "Matka, I think the uprising in the ghetto has begun."

Matka reached across the table and took Zofia's hand with her warm, thin fingers. "Janina."

Another time, Zofia would have drawn away from her mother's touch, repelled by her own doubts of Matka's affection. Now, she found comfort in the clasp of their hands, two women united against the world.

The way mother and daughter ought to be.

"I'll see if I can find any information on her." Zofia's promise was halfhearted. She would ask, but knew it was likely impossible. It had been so long since Zofia had heard any news of her friend.

Matka pinched her little gold cross. "I will pray." For her, seeking divine counsel was the ultimate aid anyone could offer.

And truth be told, Zofia would prefer Matka bending over a lit candle at church than running around with secrets hidden in her handbag.

The fighting grew worse as the day wore on. Every crack of gunfire or rumbling explosion flicked at Zofia's raw nerves. Even the Fraus seemed on edge at the library, ordering everyone to stay indoors through their shift.

Not that anyone wanted to be outside anymore these days. Even before the ghetto uprising, it was far too dangerous with so many roundups and so much Nazi aggression.

When Zofia did finally leave the library that day, Darek was waiting for her, hidden in the shadows. "I know you're worried about Janina," he said by way of greeting. "I have people asking about her."

Zofia let him guide her in the direction of the reading room, where Miss Laska was on her own. "Is the uprising going well?"

Darek nodded, solemn and stoic as he so often was these days. "It's only just beginning. The Home Army is sending some men to aid their efforts. I volunteered to go, but they wouldn't let me." Bitter disappointment tinged his last statement.

That he wasn't allowed to go didn't surprise Zofia. Darek's task as an executioner for the Polish Underground State made him too valuable. She altered their path slightly so they strode by the ghetto wall.

There had been more Nazis and collaborators put to death in the last few months, and the change in Darek had been undeniable with a new hardness about him that made Zofia ache for the gentle man he'd once been. Though war made such things necessary, they were difficult to witness.

"The Jews have been preparing." Darek looked behind them as he spoke, confirming no one was following close enough to hear. "At night, they've been building bunkers and making grenades and even flamethrowers."

He drew up short and stared over the ghetto wall at the end of the street. Zofia followed his gaze and almost wept at the sight.

There, amid streams of black smoke, were two flags rising above the battle. The *flaga Polski* and another one beside it, a perfect complement with two bands of color as well, white on the top and blue on the bottom.

Four years had passed since she'd seen the brilliant white-and-red Polish flag rippling in the wind, liberated from wherever it had been stored to unfurl and stretch into freedom.

The swell of patriotism roaring through her in that moment was palpable. She had taken the appearance of that flag for granted her entire life.

Just as she had taken her freedom for granted.

"What is the other flag?" she asked.

"The ŻZW," Darek said with reverence. "The Jewish Military Union. Side by side with Poland as it should have always been."

Janina was in there, fighting beneath those flags alongside her brethren. And Zofia would have given anything to be with her.

Neither Zofia nor Darek spoke again as they walked on, both lost in the companionable silence of personal reflection. When they came to the intersection leading off to Traugutta Street, they broke away without another word, both knowing discretion was needed when it came to the secret library.

Miss Laska opened the door to Zofia more quickly than usual. "Do you hear it?" she asked, her eyes wide and blinking with excitement.

Zofia nodded, locking the door behind her. "The uprising has started."

"They're fighting back." Miss Laska peered out the window toward the ghetto. "We should be joining them, uniting our ranks and our arms." Her fist pumped into the air with emphasis as she spoke.

But Miss Laska saw it from the perspective of many Poles, that the Jews were finally going to have a chance to liberate themselves. Zofia understood the situation from Janina's experience, and from the perspective of the many men and women Zofia had guided from the ghetto to safe houses.

This was a fight the Jews knew they could not win. It was vengeance for all those who had been slain. It was reparations for the wrongs done to them. It was all of those things, yes, but it was also a chance to die with a gun in their hands, battling their enemy, and hopefully bringing a few Nazis down with them.

"I pray for them every night," Miss Laska said. "I will do so even more now, to give them courage and strength and protection."

Zofia reached up to water the little plant and noticed a parcel set beside it, too high to see from below. "What is this?"

Miss Laska turned away from the window. "A gift for you."

"Me?" Zofia drew the parcel down. The only one who might give her a gift would be Darek, and surely he would have done so already when he met up with her.

The weight of the item suggested it was precisely what it appeared to be: a book.

Perhaps a new one for the hidden library. Anticipation brightened the darkness pressing all around her, a glimmer of something to look forward to. She peeled back the paper and her eagerness dropped like a stone, dragged down from its heights by disappointment.

One Hundred Potato Dishes.

Miss Laska clapped her hands, her luminous eyes sparkling.

It was for the older woman's benefit that Zofia plastered a smile on her face as she held up the book. "I do love potatoes."

"Bah." Miss Laska waved her hand. "We all hate potatoes now. What's underneath it?"

Her question took Zofia aback until she realized the older woman meant the dust jacket. Zofia peeled the paper back from the cover and revealed a flat gray book beneath, the title printed in plain black. *Poland's Eagle* by Marta Krakowska.

Zofia's mouth fell open, but no words emerged.

Miss Laska laughed with joy.

"It's Marta Krakowska's newest novel." Zofia gaped at the gift. "How…?" Wonder filled her at the impossibility in her hands. "How was this even printed?"

"The underground press did it." Miss Laska opened the cover and pointed to KOPR on the publication information. "See there? That's how you know it was published by the Home Army. Likely here or in Krakow. And here…" She indicated the print date reflecting a publication in 1938. "That is to ensure the book looked like it was created before the war."

Zofia turned in awe toward Miss Laska. "How do you know all of this?"

"I'm not as busy as you are." Miss Laska gave a wicked grin. "And I do love a good clandestine read."

"Don't let the Fraus find out," Zofia scolded.

The playfulness of her tone was drowned out by a distant chatter of gunfire, followed by an explosion that set the windows vibrating in their frames.

Miss Laska looked in the direction of the ghetto. "Have you heard anything from Janina?"

Zofia shook her head and wished desperately that Darek could find someone to provide her with any information.

"It will be fine." Miss Laska's pleasant reassurance wasn't at all convincing. "I'm sure it will be over quickly, like their first one. Another victory to savor while the Nazis lick their wounds."

But the uprising was not over in a day. As it continued on in the next several days, people whom Żegota paid to hide Jews began to grow uneasy. Especially as the General Government increased their efforts to find Poles sheltering Jews. And make them pay.

Whole families disappeared in the night, abandoning the Jews who depended on them while others cowered in fear, reneging on agreements. Safe house rates increased to preposterous sums and even good Samaritans began to withdraw their generosity.

Which was exactly what the Reich wanted. Zofia had to work twice as hard to find new places for everyone to hide, a job that seemed to be never ending.

Thankfully, she had Marta Krakowska's newest book to read in the hours the curfew relegated her to her home. It offered some solace amid Zofia's constant worry. The story carried her through those dark days of fear for Janina and all those fighting within the ghetto. It was a reprieve from the sharp-eyed Fraus and their ever-changing rules at the library.

It would have been so easy to read in a single night. Certainly, doing so would have been well worth the haze of gritty-eyed exhaustion, the plot rolling around in her head like a ghost, haunting her lack of sleep with memories of a well-written book.

But no. Zofia wanted to relish the lyrical prose of Krakowska's talented pen, to appreciate the nuance of every character. She wanted to savor every beautiful word.

And she did.

As the days wore on and the uprising in the ghetto continued, she sank into the story of occupied Poland where a boy joined the Home Army to keep his family safe. In his travels, he managed to save a beautiful Jewish girl who loved books and salvaged many from a bombed library. It was at this point Zofia recognized a blend of herself and Janina in the heroine of the story. Together, the couple went on to defeat Hans Frank, the head of the General Government in Krakow. They settled down in a home on the outskirts of Warsaw as heroes with hope for a fresh start, a baby on the way, and—of course—a little calico cat.

That was how Krakowska always ended her novels, with a calico cat. There was no surprise to it, but the familiarity always elicited a sigh of contentment. At least for Zofia.

When the book finally came to a satisfying close, she leaned back in bed after having stayed awake far too late, and blinked the tears from her eyes with joy for the love that mended so much hurt. And with sorrow to bid farewell to the characters who had grown roots within her heart over the course of those few days.

She brought the book with her to the reading room to share with Miss Laska, who eagerly took the gift and cradled it to her own heart. "Took you long enough."

Zofia laughed at the older woman's cheeky reply, eager for her to read it. Good books were like amazing sunsets or awe-inspiring landscapes, better enjoyed with someone else. There was no greater experience in the world than sharing the love of a book, discussing its finer points, and reliving the story all over again.

It was why they had begun the Bandit Book Club after all, though it had been a while since they'd been able to meet. The

Fraus were too vigilant, and they hadn't found an additional copy of *War and Peace* which had taken Kasia five months to read before turning it over to Darek. Poor Danuta had read it first and was dying to discuss it.

The sound of shouts and gunfire rang out at Zofia's back as she left the secret library that night, making her way home as swiftly as possible. Nazi violence ran high these days as their anticipation of an easy victory against the Jews disappeared in the smoke of homemade grenades and flamethrowers.

They exacted their frustrations on the Poles, especially ones found walking alone in the evening. A warning seemed to hang in the air that day, a cold, ominous thread that wound around her like a serpent. Zofia shivered and wrapped her black shawl more tightly against her shoulders, as if she could shield herself with it, blending into the shadows to disappear. Home had never felt so far from the little reading room.

When she turned down Krucza Street, all looked as it normally did, everything quiet and still apart from Bar Podlaski, where several Nazis found reasons to stay up late, carousing. She made her way up to their apartment, where Matka had a platter of boiled potatoes and a bit of bread already on the table.

"Has something happened?" Matka asked.

Zofia shook her head, though the feeling of unease had not abated.

"Then why do you look so frightened?" Matka set aside the bowl she was holding, its contents indiscernible.

"I have a bad feeling." Zofia felt ridiculous to even be saying those words out loud. But she couldn't cast away the strange sensation running up and down her spine, like fingernails clicking over each bump of her vertebrae.

An engine rumbled to a stop outside and Zofia's heart seized in her throat. Matka's eyes went wide.

Before they could even react, boots thundered through the entry of their building, echoing up the cavernous stairwell.

They were trapped in their apartment, with no way to escape and nowhere to hide.

"Zofia." Matka beckoned her closer.

She rushed to her mother, gripping her hand. Matka was so slight these days, her thin fingers like twigs as they held Zofia with a wiry strength.

If they were caught, it would be Zofia's fault. Every aspect of her life fought against the occupation, bringing danger to their door. Yet for the books she'd salvaged, for the lives she'd saved, she would do it all again. A protective instinct surged through Zofia and she hugged her mother closer, wishing the risk did not include Matka.

Boom, boom, boom…

The boots were getting louder.

Matka's gaze locked on Zofia's as tears swam in her large gray eyes. "I'm sorry I was so domineering—"

Zofia shook her head to let her mother know these last words weren't necessary.

The boots were only one floor below theirs. No doors had been flung open yet, which meant they had not reached their destination.

"My parents," Matka continued quickly. "They never cared about me, they were too busy attending parties…" She looked desperately at Zofia. "I thought I was helping you by giving you advice and guidance. Things I never had."

Zofia pulled her mother harder against her, curling her arms into a full embrace around Matka as if she could shield her from this terror.

She had told her mother not to say those things, but now that they were out, the confession bathed Zofia's heart, a balm over her chafed soul.

Her poor mother, abandoned first in childhood and then amid a war. It must have wounded her deeply for her parents to have left for Switzerland and never even expressed concern for her.

The clap of boots on stairs thundered in front of their door.

Boom, boom, boom…

Matka shuddered.

The boots continued on, climbing one more flight.

Zofia sucked in a breath. "They didn't come for us."

Above them came the muffled sound of a door splintering open and orders barked in German. The man and woman who lived in the floor above screamed in surprise.

Zofia knew which neighbors they were: a kind couple who helped Mrs. Borkowska from time to time. The husband did small repairs around the apartment for her and the wife generously watched Mrs. Borkowska's granddaughter after Matka cut ties with her. Both visited the clandestine library often, telling jokes so bad they were funny, encouraging chuckles as much as eye rolls.

Violent thumps and slams sounded overhead amid a cry of pain. Matka inhaled a shaky breath. The boots were out in the stairwell again, this time accompanied by a low, keening wail.

Though the couple had sought to aid others in these trying times, no one was there to help them now. Doing so would be far too dangerous.

Not that it hadn't crossed Zofia's mind, but to go to their aid would put not only Zofia's life at risk, but also Matka's.

There was no right way to respond—to sacrifice a loved one and yourself, to whom others looked upon for help, or to intervene for those who saved others, and be arrested as well in the process.

The sacrifice would be for naught.

Being an impossible situation, however, didn't stop Zofia from hating herself for her silence, nor did it make her feel any less like a coward.

In the evenings, the fighting in the ghetto fell quiet. According to Darek, that was when the Jewish warriors sheltered in their bunkers, gathering what supplies they could and working through the night to replenish their stock of handmade arms.

Yet while they prepared for another day of battle, an eerie blanket of silence descended over Warsaw. Sleep eluded Zofia for some time, imagining the men and women who were already exhausted by the battle pushing on through the night to ensure they could fight again the following day.

And all the while, thoughts of Janina plagued Zofia until she fell into a restless slumber where the covers made her too hot, and yet it was too cold without them. In the end, she skimmed the surface of sleep, light enough to be aware of every creak and groan of the building. Perhaps that was how she heard the knock.

It was soft and careful—a single rap. Though it was not repeated, she knew what she'd heard. She snapped awake in an instant and rushed to the door. Whoever was there wanted discretion and was desperate enough that they were willing to risk being out past curfew. This was important and it was urgent.

Zofia unlocked the front door as quietly as possible, twisting the lock with painful slowness so it didn't give an echoing snap through the hall. When she opened the door, she found a man crouched in the hallway, hiding from the moonlight streaming in through the stairwell window until he was little more than a shadow himself.

The odors that assailed her were familiar, reminiscent of the attack on Warsaw at the start of the war: smoke and blood.

"Help." The man's hoarse voice was barely a whisper.

Zofia reached for him, assuming he was on the ground with an injury, but he rose, carrying someone in his arms. Stepping back, she opened the door wider to make room for him to enter the apartment before quickly locking the door behind him.

The curtains were drawn across the windows, the fabric thick enough to block out any light from being seen outside, which gave Zofia enough confidence to light a candle.

"I need your help," the man said again. "Without it, she'll die."

At his words, Zofia spun around, the flickering candle sheltered in the cradle of her palm. It cast its meager light on the woman lying limp in the man's arms.

She was far too thin, her neck lax, and her dark hair trailing toward the ground, falling back from her face.

Zofia gave a choked cry and nearly dropped the candle as recognition dawned.

Janina.

Chapter 30

ZOFIA COULD NOT TEAR her eyes away from Janina's face, her lovely features relaxed the way one is when asleep.

Or dead.

"On the sofa," Zofia directed, her voice trembling as she set the candle on the small table nearby, not trusting herself to hold it. The man gently laid Janina down without a sound from either of them.

Matka's door opened. "What's happen—" Her gaze landed first on the man, her eyes widening with horror before turning toward Janina. She pressed her hands to her mouth, smothering a cry.

"She needs help." Zofia knelt by Janina.

Zofia's thoughts swirled to recall those Girl Guide first aid lessons from before the war. God, it had been so long ago. Too long.

And this was Janina.

The slightest misstep and Zofia might kill her.

The cost was too dear.

"She was hit by several bullets," the man said. "One in the shoulder, one in the side, and maybe another. It was too dark. Too smoky. I couldn't..."

"I'll see to her." Matka's voice was calm but decisive. "There is food and water in the kitchen. Please help yourself to whatever you like, and be as quiet as you can. We'll see what we can do."

The man hesitated, gazing down at Janina, his face in the shadows, making his expression impossible to read.

"We'll take care of her," Zofia reassured him. "I'm sure you need to eat and rest." The man was covered in soot and streaks of blood that stood brilliant red against his dirty white shirt. Janina's blood.

"And privacy for her modesty would be appreciated," Matka offered delicately.

This finally convinced the man to relocate into the kitchen, his steps silent.

Matka tsked softly to herself as she pulled Janina's shirt up from the waist of a pair of pants to reveal a wound at her side, exactly as the man had said.

"What can I do?" Zofia asked, desperate to do something—anything.

"I'll need several items." Matka pushed aside the collar of Janina's shirt to reveal an angry hole in her shoulder, an obvious bullet wound. "Hot water, your father's surgical bag, and the medical text you have hidden under your floorboards."

Zofia didn't ask how her mother knew about the concealed books, but moved to comply as quickly as possible. When she returned, Matka had Janina's shirt unbuttoned to reveal the two bullet wounds and a third that appeared above her bra. The man who carried Janina had eaten and drank already and disappeared into Zofia's bedroom where he had been directed to sleep.

Matka took Papa's medical bag with great care, her demeanor one of reverence as she pulled it open, the old leather creak-ing. After assessing the tools inside, she looked over Janina once more, inspecting the wounds.

"It's been some time since Janina sustained these injuries," Matka explained. "Which means they will be more difficult to work with and likely painful for her." Sympathy flashed in her eyes. "Perhaps you can think of a story to tell her. A pleasant one from your childhood, like the time you tried to make Bubbe's famous cookies, but mixed the cannisters and used salt instead of sugar."

Were the situation not so serious, Zofia might have smiled as she recalled how everyone's faces had soured when they bit into those unexpectedly savory cookies. Her gaze wandered to the bullet hole just under Janina's shoulder. "That tale might be too short."

"A book retelling then," Matka encouraged. "One you could speak on for an hour, if not more."

Zofia relaxed into the request, knowing exactly which one Janina would love.

Poland's Eagle.

Matka withdrew the tetanus shot from the medical bag and expertly administered it as Zofia first explained how she'd come upon the author at the clandestine library. Then, while Matka dug the bullets from Janina's body, Zofia retold Marta Krakowska's latest book, recalling it so vividly from her memory that it might well have been real, as it often seemed with books that perfectly written.

In less than an hour, Matka had all three bullets dislodged and the wounds bandaged. "I've done all I can." She straightened from her work, hands pressed to her lower back. "Now we must wait and hope she does not develop a fever."

She cast a worried glance at Janina, who remained perfectly still, exactly as she had while Matka worked. Zofia put a hand on Janina's brow. Her skin was cool and damp.

Up until this moment, Zofia had only ever known her mother

to take care of household matters. But when she'd worked on Janina, she had been as professional and stoic as Papa. The medical text remained on the floor beside the sofa, unopened. "How did you know what to do?" Zofia asked in awe.

Matka smiled, as if she could read Zofia's thoughts. "Your father and I started with nothing after my parents disowned me when I married him. In order to open his practice, he needed a nurse, and we couldn't afford to hire one. He taught me what I needed to do."

They fell into silence, sitting by Janina's side until the gray light of dawn limned the heavy curtains drawn over the delicate lace ones.

The door to Zofia's room opened and the man stepped out. "How is she?" There was a rasp to his voice, the way one sounds when they've been breathing in smoke for too long.

"We've done all we can," Matka said. "I'll see if I can find some kind of meat or bones today to make a fortifying broth for her."

The man nodded. "I need to go back."

"You don't have to." Zofia got up from the floor where she sat beside the sofa where Janina lay. "I work with Żegota to find homes for those who escape the ghetto. I can secure you a place—"

The man swallowed, and for a moment she hoped he might agree. But his jaw clenched. "I need to go back."

"Shower first, or they'll catch you as you are." Matka indicated his appearance.

He'd washed his face and hands, but grime still showed around his hairline and at his neck. There had been nothing he could do about his clothes which were still dirty and stained, Janina's blood now rust colored.

While he showered, Matka went out and bought as much food as she could find. It wasn't much—a loaf of bread, some beets, and a few links of sausage—but the man's eyes went wide when he saw it. He packed it all to bring with him, refusing to eat any until he could share with the others.

Papa's clothes hung loose on his slender frame, but nothing that would call attention. Everyone's clothes were too big now. He was younger than he'd looked with the grime on his face, maybe a few years older than Zofia. Before he left, he paused in front of Janina, his expression tender.

Zofia wondered how they were acquainted, and it struck her suddenly how strange it was to not know anything about Janina's life. They had always shared everything.

But in these months of silence, Janina had made friends Zofia had never met and had gone about daily tasks to which Zofia was oblivious.

"Thank you," Zofia said to him. "Thank you for saving her."

"I promised her father I would." A look of pain furrowed his brow. "He was a good man."

"He was." Zofia's voice went thick with the memory of Mr. Steinman, who could whistle any tune in the world, who smiled as bright as the sun whenever he saw his daughter, and who never met a stranger.

The world was a darker place without his light.

Janina's rescuer slipped from the apartment and Zofia went to the window, peering from the side of the curtain to watch him until he turned off Krucza Street.

Matka cared for Janina while Zofia worked during the day. She miraculously managed to procure bones and meat for making thick, nutritious broth which she painstakingly dribbled into Janina's mouth. Zofia constantly checked her friend's brow for fever, each time breathing a sigh of relief as her forehead remained cool.

Finally, after three days of virtual unconsciousness, Janina stirred.

Zofia had been at her side and leaped to attention. "Janina."

"Zofia?" Janina's brows knit together and she squinted as she looked around the room.

She blinked against the light streaming in from the window. "Where am I?"

"You're in my apartment. You're safe."

During Janina's convalescence, Zofia hadn't allowed herself to think of what could happen to her friend, of how precariously Janina's life dangled by a spiderweb-thin thread.

The acknowledgment of that risk rushed over Zofia now, how Janina might have died there on the sofa, her life snuffed out. Gone forever. No more brilliant smiles or shared secrets, no more dreams or planning for the future.

"How are you feeling?" Zofia asked around the knot forming in her throat.

"I had the strangest dream." Janina's voice rasped with disuse, her eyes falling closed. "That I was in a Marta Krakowska novel."

"Did you have a cat at the end?" Zofia asked, smiling through her tears.

Janina's lips lifted at the corners. "A calico."

Zofia hurried to the reading room after an arduous day at the library, which she'd spent copying book details from Polish to German in a seemingly endless list of catalogs. Miss Laska opened the door with a worried expression. "You haven't been here in three days. What's happened?"

Zofia rushed inside, not speaking until the door was closed. "Janina's in my apartment."

Miss Laska's hand fluttered first to her mouth to stifle her gasp and then to her heart. "Thank God she is safe."

"She was wounded in the uprising."

Miss Laska cried out, her hand going back to her mouth.

"Matka attended to her with Papa's medical bag. I didn't even realize she could do that." Zofia found herself marveling again at the side of Matka she had never truly known. "I haven't been able to come by while I've been taking care of her so Matka could get some rest. But Janina woke up today and I had to let you know that she is safe."

Before Miss Laska could reply, a knock came from the rear door. Miss Laska opened it and Miss Krakowska entered, wearing her signature bright blue shawl over her red hair.

"*Poland's Eagle* was just the most incredible story," Zofia effused. "Thank you for such a precious gift."

"It was amazing," Miss Laska added. "I read it after Zofia and finished it in a day."

"A day?" Miss Krakowska's brows shot up. "It took me three years to write."

"I couldn't put it down." Miss Laska grinned. "And you know that's the mark of a good story."

"I'm so curious—why a calico?" Zofia asked. "You always have the couple end up together and happy in the country and they always have a calico."

Miss Krakowska's mouth twitched. "You noticed that?"

"Anyone who loves your books has noticed it." Zofia tilted her head in encouragement for the woman to answer the question.

Miss Krakowska, who perpetually exuded confidence, now hesitated, her lips pursed. At first, Zofia thought she wouldn't answer the question and worried it had been invasive to ask.

But after several moments Miss Krakowska finally began to speak. "I grew up in a loving home as a girl, living in the country next to a stream with a garden full of herbs and lovely flowers. We had a little calico cat named Nela who slept on the windowsill. Her fur was so soft, always warm from lying in sunbeams. During the Great War, the destruction spread toward our home and we lost everything. For me, I suppose, a calico cat is a symbol of home, of peace. Since then, I don't know that I've ever found peace enough to settle down and have a cat of my own. So I make sure that my characters do."

Zofia had anticipated a simple, easy answer, something about it merely being her favorite animal. But the response had been so unexpectedly intimate that Zofia recalled the author speaking of her own pain in regards to her writing.

"I hope someday you can have a calico cat again," Zofia said softly.

Miss Krakowska's eyes crinkled in a genuine smile and she placed her hand on Zofia's forearm. "I hope we all do."

The ghetto had fallen silent the day after Janina had been brought to Zofia's house, so Janina was not aware of how disconcerting the quiet was now.

In the absence of war sounds, she continued to heal as the days went on. But she also began to grow restless.

She paced the room, her stockinged feet silent on the floor. "I need to get back. Jakub needs me."

"Was that the man who brought you here?" Zofia asked.

Janina nodded. "He was the second-in-command of the group I was fighting with. My father worked with him at the brush factory. He said Papa saved his life and he'd vowed in return to ensure Mama and I always stayed safe." She hugged herself. "I really must go back."

Zofia watched her friend with concern. Janina didn't smile anymore; the suffering she'd endured was carved in hard lines on her face.

"You can't," Zofia said gently.

"I'll be careful," Janina pleaded. "I can still use my right arm and my aim with grenades is good. I can…"

Her eyes fell on Zofia, who had not been able to mask the painful truth.

Zofia swallowed. "It's over."

Janina pulled in a hard breath, her mouth twisted with silent grief. She didn't ask who won. There was never a question as to who would win.

Her arms curled around her midsection and she bent in half,

embracing a pain Zofia could not see, but could feel just as sharply as if it were her own.

"I should have been with them," Janina gasped. "I should have gone down with the last bullet at their sides."

Darek had told Zofia how the Home Army had tried to help. Not everyone in the organization had been in support of the effort, with staunch nationalists still clinging to their old prejudice.

The units of those eager to help were sent to the ghetto and did what they could, attacking German units externally. As they fought, two missions were launched to breach the ghetto walls to provide food and arms within. Both attempts had ended in failure.

In the end, none of it had been enough.

Janina grew despondent in the following days, her empty stare fixed toward the ghetto, where thick gray columns of smoke rose to the sky.

Darek had told Zofia the Nazis were hunting the Jews out with dogs and machines that could detect sounds. When those methods didn't work, they burned buildings to draw the hidden inhabitants out to be shot.

Zofia didn't share any of that with Janina, who already wore her survival like a cloak of shame leaden with studs of guilt.

What Janina needed was a reason to live.

What she needed was her mother.

Chapter 31

ZOFIA PREFERRED TO RIDE her bike when visiting Mrs. Steinman so she could also bring books to the village library. But with Janina in no shape to ride, the train was their only option. While all her papers were in order, Zofia worried Janina's injuries might raise questions.

During her time in the ghetto, however, Janina had learned to adapt to her surroundings. At the train station, she hustled through the crowd as if she'd never been gravely injured and during the journey assumed the same passive, bored expression as the other travelers.

The girl who never could tell a lie had become quite the consummate actress.

It was an hour's walk in the pleasant May weather, a moment to breathe in the fresh air and take in the sunlight.

Janina didn't say much, her lips pressed tight together, and her arms wrapped around her slender body. When they arrived, Zofia knocked twice in rapid succession followed by three slow raps. The code they'd used since Zofia arrived unannounced that past winter.

The door opened to reveal Ella's smiling face. "Zofia, you're early. I hope that means you've brought books—" Her gaze caught Janina and the words died in her throat. Quickly, she waved them inside. "Come in, come in. Hania. My God, Hania, come here."

Mrs. Steinman emerged from the back room and gasped. "Janina?"

Janina stiffened at Zofia's side.

"My girl." Mrs. Steinman rushed toward Janina, her face crumpling. "My baby."

"Mama." Janina's voice cracked.

Mrs. Steinman pulled Janina into her arms and a muffled sob broke from Janina. "Mama."

In the entire time of her recovery, Janina hadn't cried once. Not a single tear. It worried Zofia to see her so empty. Janina, who had always been made of sunshine and happiness, was never meant to be turned to stone by tragedy.

Ella and Zofia turned away from the mother and daughter, leaving them to their reunion in private.

"I want to help with your work," Janina said on the walk back to the train, her eyes bright with a newly awoken passion. "The way you find people homes and ensure they are cared for, like you did with Mama. I want to do that too."

"Then we have a stop on our way home." Zofia smiled at her friend, unable to suppress the overwhelming gladness to see her have a taste for life once more, no matter how small.

They stopped by the Żoliborz district when they returned to Warsaw and met with Zofia's contact in Żegota. He happily agreed to let Janina help as long as Zofia trained her and kept her safe. Something Zofia was more than eager to do.

On the way home, they strode through Wilson Square, when

a song erupted from the loudspeakers. The first notes of "Poland Is Not Yet Lost" blared from the barkers that usually issued orders and warnings.

Several Wehrmacht soldiers scowled at the patriotic music.

"Enough," one shouted. "Stop this at once."

But the passersby who had stopped to listen had no control over the speakers. Whoever was behind the prank had found a way to infiltrate the Nazis' own system.

As the words to "Poland Is Not Yet Lost" began, the man beside Zofia lifted his voice and sang along. One of the Wehrmacht soldiers darted toward him, face red with fury. Before the soldier could strike him, others stepped in front of him, shoulders squared, their voices rising to sing with him.

Almost a century and a half after the song had been written, the message still rang true. They would *never* stop fighting.

Zofia clasped Janina's hand and together they sang as loud as possible.

The soldiers looked around, no doubt doing the simple math to realize how greatly outnumbered they were. Only half a dozen Wehrmacht soldiers stood against the crowd that had amassed within seconds of the music playing. Zofia closed her eyes and let the words she once mumbled along with in school burst free with all the love and reverence she had for her country.

When the song ended and she opened her eyes, the soldiers were slinking back, their control withering beneath the power of Polish pride.

When "Rota" blasted from the speakers next, everyone cheered with public jubilation that hadn't been seen in Warsaw since the summer of 1939. Before the war, before they stopped appreciating the normal, everyday moments they never knew they would soon lose.

Eventually, the speakers went silent and the crowd dispersed, but the scene stayed with Zofia, glowing like a flame of hope in her chest.

It had been over three years since Polish music had drifted through the street and filled the souls of Varsovians.

As they resumed their journey home, Zofia considered the words in "Poland Is Not Yet Lost" and couldn't shake them from her thoughts.

So long as Poles lived, they would not stop fighting to regain what foreign occupiers had taken from them.

And Zofia would be there every step of the way.

The ghetto could be seen burning for several days as buildings were systematically set on fire, one after the other until there was nothing left.

Janina watched the distant glow with a clenched jaw. Homes were destroyed. Lives were lost. A culture teetering on the edge of extinction.

It made Zofia and Janina's efforts with Żegota all the more important. They remained busy in the following weeks and received so much money from the organization with which to pay the homes harboring Jews that they had to strap stacks of złotys to each other's bodies and bury the bulk under loose clothing.

Walking thus to the necessary locations was terrifying. But it was also exhilarating to know they were doing something to help others, to offer a modicum of right in a world that felt so hopelessly wrong.

Through their efforts with Żegota, they found familiar faces from time to time, including Mrs. Berman. She and her husband had managed to escape the ghetto and were working with the same diligence as Janina and Zofia to help keep as many Jews hidden as possible. Knowing she was safe brought Zofia great comfort.

Janina stayed in the apartment with Matka and Zofia. If Mrs. Borkowska noticed her there, she ignored it and made no further threats against Zofia. Perhaps through guilt at her former actions, exacerbated by the destruction of the ghetto and the dismal fate of the remaining inhabitants.

In the evenings, Zofia and Janina found solace in books. Rereading old favorites and exploring new tales. Unlike most people in Warsaw, they were lucky to have the hidden warehouse at their disposal. And once Janina was able to finish *War and Peace*, she insisted on attending the Bandit Book Club once more.

Darek was already waiting at the reading room on Traugutta Street, a far safer location to meet for their book club than the main library, where Janina could possibly be recognized. After all, only Zofia and Miss Laska were ever at the secret library, especially after hours.

"It's good to see you two reunited." Darek grinned at Zofia and Janina.

Before he could say anything else, Danuta and Kasia slipped through the rear door.

"Janina." Kasia ran to her, embracing her so fiercely that Zofia winced, worrying about Janina's injuries, which were not yet fully healed.

But Janina didn't seem to mind, her face glowing with joy as they began catching up. Kasia tried to share two years in two minutes, interspersed with enthusiastic embraces.

"Are you going to talk to Janina all night?" Danuta folded her arms over her chest, though even she had a smile hovering on her lips.

Kasia turned to Danuta, exasperation like a plea on her face. "We'll get to *War and Peace* soon. Just give me one more moment, please. We haven't seen Janina in years."

"I know," Danuta replied dryly. "That's why I wish for a chance to greet her as well."

Color flooded Kasia's cheeks and her eyes widened. "I'm so sorry, I was so excited, I…"

She quickly backed away to make room as Danuta embraced Janina. "The Bandit Book Club hasn't been the same without you."

Janina shrugged shyly. "I didn't really contribute much."

"You did," Danuta replied with sincerity. "More than you

realize. Welcome back." She turned to Kasia. "Now let's discuss *War and Peace* because I've been waiting about almost a year to finally talk about it."

"This was probably the most popular book in the ghetto," Janina said. "I only had one copy and by the time I left, the pages were tattered from being read so often."

"I'm still in awe that you ran a library out of your suitcase." Kasia shook her head in disbelief. "It must have been terribly heavy."

It was quite a difficult thing to imagine with how slender Janina's arms were. She had gained a few pounds since leaving the ghetto, but for friends who hadn't seen her in over two years, she was likely skeletal in their perspective.

Janina was still beautiful, and she always would be. But now lines creased her brow, premature from so much worry, and her body had wasted away under starvation rations. Her eyes, once wide and innocent, now saw the world in starker hues, no longer an opportunity, but a challenge.

"The burden of the suitcase was worth the weight to witness what pleasure those books brought to everyone." Janina smiled sadly. "The ghetto was a place where joy was in short supply."

"Why do you think *War and Peace* was such a popular book?" Darek asked. "I have my own theories, but I'm curious to hear your observations."

Janina paused, as though sampling the flavor of her words before putting them in her mouth. "I think one of the most important aspects of *War and Peace* is that no matter how successful a leader is, he is still just a man. His armies are subjected to the same circumstances as any of us. And if Napoleon could be defeated, so too can Hitler."

"He will be," Darek vowed.

"Of course he will," Danuta agreed. "No man is above fate and the natural turn of events, no matter how much they try to manipulate things no one can control."

Before she could continue on and dominate the conversation, Kasia interjected. "These characters suffered so greatly, their homes were destroyed, their families…" She swallowed hard and shook her head as if trying to cast away her own grief. "There was so much loss and hurt, but their country lived on and they survived, like Natasha. Like Pierre. It's inspiring to know that there will eventually be an end to what we are enduring."

"And it's all the more reason to fight." Something bright and determined flashed in Darek's eyes. "Hitler is only a man. The Nazis can be defeated. Poland can be free again."

It was perhaps the most robust book club discussion they'd ever had, inspired by a book that was so relatable to their own life events though it was written decades ago. The pain of loss, the suffering of war, the longing for peace. It was beautiful and heartbreaking in one bittersweet wrap and each of the bandits spoke with the passion of their soul.

"Along this same vein, I suggest we read *The Teutonic Knights* by Henryk Sienkiewicz next," Danuta said when their conversation finally tapered to a close.

"It's another long book, isn't it?" Kasia sighed and playfully rolled her eyes.

"It's about the Polish defeat of the Teutonic knights in the fifteenth century," Danuta replied. "It's relevant today in regards to the forced Germanization of Poland. It could even be helpful in our own fight."

Zofia pulled out a vodka bottle, the last of their stores with a little less than half the liquid sloshing within.

There were too many who had been lost since their last meeting. If they were to toast to Maria, they would have to toast to all those others as well. But how best to delicately phrase such pain, to honor their bravery and sacrifice?

Darek met her gaze, as though reading her thoughts. His hand went to the bottle, covering hers with his warm palm. "To Poland."

Zofia nodded and together they lifted the bottle. "To Poland."

★★★

As Janina healed, she was able to accompany Zofia to the country on their bikes, bags laden with books for the single-room library in Ella's small village. It was simply decorated with unadorned white walls, three plain bookshelves, a single table in one corner, and several hard-back wooden chairs for those interested in reading there for a short while. The books were their decoration, the librarian was fond of saying.

That noted, the building's initial "decoration" was as sad as Ella had implied. The books were primarily ones meant for farmers, offering advice on tilling fields and harvest times. In those trips, Zofia and Janina provided a rainbow of subjects that brought the sleepy library to life.

The librarian was a sweet older woman with a little blue-eyed kitten who followed her like a shadow. Zofia and Janina were always welcomed with a wide smile and a list of books her patrons hoped to receive with the next delivery.

"When do you think the Home Army will attack?" Janina asked as they biked back to Warsaw one warm July day. Perspiration glistened on her brow, and she wiped it away with her palm. A healthy pink glow graced her cheeks from the sunny bike rides and the weight she'd gained.

"I'm not sure." Zofia kept her gaze fixed on a treacherous part of the winding country road. Tires were precious commodities and a sharp rock or deep divot could derail their work for weeks.

"When the battle begins," Janina said, "I want to be there."

Zofia glanced at her friend. "We'll be there together. Fighting for Poland."

Janina narrowed her eyes, looking forward as if she could see the future. "And for vengeance."

PART THREE

Chapter 32

One Year Later
July 1944

WEHRMACHT SOLDIERS STREAMED INTO the Warsaw Library warehouse and lugged crates of books to the waiting trucks. The texts within were from the German reading room—items that were commandeered for use by Germans only and now were being taken out of the country. Stolen.

They were from the coveted collections on physics and chemistry and medicine: all the sciences, and decades of Polish knowledge.

Nausea gripped Zofia's belly to see it all disappear, helpless to stop as one box after another slipped away. Now more than ever, she was glad to have smuggled students of the secret schools into the library behind Herr Nagiel's back in those earlier years. That access to the wealth of learning was their birthright, one future generations were now being robbed of. She only regretted not being able to find a way to continue helping students once the Fraus took charge.

But at least the Nazis were fleeing. News traveled like fire, raging through the city about the advance of the Soviet Union, bent on a German defeat. Their target: Warsaw.

Finally, Poland was to receive aid after almost five long years and the Nazis were scuttling out of the city as if artillery fire was already hot in the air.

"Zofia." Frau Beck's sharp voice cut through the warehouse. "Come here at once."

The Fraus' sour demeanor had only grown more bitter at the collapse of the General Government. But the Germans refused to leave without committing a final injustice; they pillaged the art from museums and plundered rare collections and artifacts from the libraries, all with little care for the precious treasures. The large hooded trucks once used to transport men and women to public executions were now housing priceless pieces of Polish history and culture.

Zofia approached the front of the main library's warehouse, not bothering to mask her contempt for the two women who tormented the staff by cutting wages, furloughing valuable employees, and having others arrested for no legitimate reason.

They should have left at the beginning of the week when most of the General Government had slunk away, tails between their legs. The ever-present clipboard was tucked against Frau Schmidt's arm, indicating their intention to continue overseeing the removal of the final collection from the German reading room. Along with whatever else they meant to steal.

"A book with the library's stamp was found in the home of a Polish criminal." Frau Schmidt practically spit her accusation. "He confessed it came from the reading room on Traugutta Street."

A criminal.

The only criminals in Poland were the Nazis. Their roundups

had intensified in the last year, those innocent men and women held hostage in Pawiak Prison until the Home Army committed an "act of terrorism"—and all retaliation against the Nazis was seen as an "act of terrorism"—then they were executed in retribution.

These executions were public, though people were forbidden to watch. Streets were emptied and open windows were shot at if people tried to look. Initially, victims sang Polish songs before their deaths or cried out for Poland's victory, but later mouths were plastered shut or they were drugged heavily so they could scarcely walk. The names of the victims were printed on pink pages the following day, and plastered around the city. But as much as the General Government tried to cover their crimes, Warsaw bore evidence of those murders. Brick walls were chipped away by bullets and shrines were built where public executions had been. The Nazis removed those memorials, but evidence remained in the form of discarded flower petals and wax from the candles melted between the cobblestones, like tears frozen in time.

"If someone had an illegal book with the library's stamp, it was likely in their possession before the war." Zofia kept her reply serene even though her heart was about to knock out of her chest. Books from the hidden warehouse never had the new Nazi mark and still retained the old mermaid stamp.

"We aren't stupid." Frau Beck sneered. "Your city may have help from the Soviets soon, but we are still in charge. You have been stealing from the Reich—an offense punishable by death."

As much as Zofia hated to admit it, they were correct. The Soviets were not in the city yet and she was still at their mercy. Just because the mass public executions ended with the Home Army's execution of Franz Kutzchera, the SS and police leader of the General Government, that didn't mean Poles weren't still being slaughtered on a regular basis.

Smuggling books that should have been destroyed, lending

them out to patrons when the library was closed, and distributing them not only in Warsaw but also in the outskirts at little one-room country libraries—those were all punishable offenses.

Frau Schmidt held a hand toward the other woman in an effort to calm her down before turning to Zofia. "Admit to your crimes or we'll have to confront Miss Laska with our findings."

Likely they would question her regardless. Still, a sick feeling swirled in Zofia's stomach. Miss Laska would never tell the Fraus anything no matter what the Gestapo did to her in their headquarters. But nor would she survive any amount of interrogation. Her frail body would never outlive her spirit.

"She has nothing to do with it," Zofia said vehemently.

Frau Beck lifted her head with a cocky grin. "So, you confess."

Zofia recalled the week she and Janina had spent in Kampinos Forest under the guise of a camping vacation. There among the ghosts of those who were brutally slain, they trained with the other members of the Gray Ranks. Some were as young as fourteen or fifteen, others were older at twenty-two, like her and Janina.

There wasn't enough ammunition to shoot with abandon, but they each had three bullets to practice their aim. It was enough for Zofia to discover she was an excellent shot.

Right now, she wished she had the weight of that Parabellum in her hand. The 9mm German-issue sidearm fit against her palm like it'd been made for her, and she missed the weapon as soon as she'd relinquished it. That loss now was profound. That gun and just two bullets in the magazine would be all she needed.

"I confess nothing." Zofia threw her hands up, feigning innocence. "You can check everything here. You'll find nothing."

That wasn't entirely true. The invitation was intentionally given, knowing the Fraus wouldn't be able to resist seeing for themselves. Not that they actually needed real evidence to arrest her if they really wanted to.

"We probably won't find anything." Frau Beck narrowed her eyes. "But we'll check anyway."

They went to Zofia's desk and jerked open the drawers. A little gift from Darek rested in the back of the top drawer, covered by several sheets of benign paperwork, a secret intentionally stashed in anticipation of discovery.

Frau Schmidt rummaged in the top drawer, her movements rough.

Zofia took a step back and tried not to flinch, unsure how much pressure was needed to detonate the explosives. Or how far the blast would carry.

Frau Schmidt's eyes lit up. "What is this?"

Frau Beck came to her side as Frau Schmidt withdrew a box of E. Wedel chocolates, the famed "bird's milk" confections with pillowy white cream inside a delicate shell of milk chocolate.

The two exchanged a look and Zofia tensed. If they opened the box here, the blast would kill them all.

Frau Schmidt curled her long fingers over the edge of the package and Zofia's heart shuddered to a stop.

"Is that chocolate?" Frau Beck paused her efforts of tossing papers about to peek at the box.

"We'll need this." Frau Schmidt tucked the chocolates against her clipboard and Zofia's heartbeat resumed in galloping thumps.

"There is nothing in the desk." Frau Beck confirmed. "Though I'm certain we'll find something at that miserable little place on Strasse der 8 Armee."

Strasse der 8 Armee was the ridiculous name the Germans had given to Traugutta Street.

"Miss Laska is innocent," Zofia protested again.

Frau Schmidt stuck her nose in the air. "We'll see."

The Fraus departed the warehouse, Frau Beck barking an

order for a car. Within minutes they would be at Traugutta Street. Was there time to run and warn Miss Laska?

Zofia looked around and quickly slipped from the rear door. She hadn't gone more than five steps when an explosion sent the earth rumbling under her feet. A spiral of smoke ascended to the heavens from somewhere in front of the library.

Breath locked in her lungs, Zofia crept forward, edging around the building to Koszykowa Street. There, parked just before the library entrance, was a smoldering car, flames crawling from the blown-out windows, with twin figures slumped against one another within.

Most likely, over a box of E. Wedel's chocolate.

Darek's plan had worked.

Not long after, news spread that Dr. Witte, the man in charge of Warsaw's libraries, had fled the city. He'd been notified to tell the employees at the main branch to seek shelter as well, but failed to follow through in his desperation to protect himself.

A coward to the end.

Dr. Bykowski was now in charge of the library, no longer a puppet director but actually acting by his own right and authority. Pride puffed his chest as he addressed the library staff assembled before him in the reading room.

Not only was Miss Laska there, but so was Janina, able to be around the library once more without fear of being recognized now that the Germans were too frightened to assert their prejudice. It was good to have Janina back at the Warsaw Library again. And judging by the way her gaze kept passing over her surroundings with wistful appreciation, Janina was glad to be back too.

"Warsaw is preparing to fight back," Dr. Bykowski said to the room.

Cheers and jubilant shouts erupted from the group.

Zofia and Janina exchanged grins. They'd recently been issued

Home Army ID cards. The pink cards had "Armia Krajowa" printed on the top with their code names and other information handwritten in ink, all sealed with a blue stamp bearing the proud Polish eagle. They were officially part of the warriors who would force the Germans out of the city for good.

"We need to prepare the library," Dr. Bykowski continued once the room quieted. "Not only do we need to ensure as many books are transferred into the safety of the warehouse as possible, but also to host anyone seeking refuge. For our soldiers, know that we will have medical supplies and food here."

The crack of artillery could be heard on the other side of the Vistula River in the Praga district within the last day. The Soviets were coming and with them would be liberation from Hitler's grip.

Better the devil you know.

At home, Zofia carefully relocated her own small stash of books from under the floorboards in her bedroom to the hidden warehouse. At work, she labored alongside the library staff shuttling their stock to safer locations and assigning value to discern which collections should be moved first. The frenzy of activity was poignantly reminiscent of September 1939.

Only this time, they were sure to be victorious.

The Home Army attack on the General Government was ordered to begin at 5:00 p.m. on August 1—W Hour—and left the air charged with electricity.

That morning, Janina went to Miss Laska's apartment to help her to the library while Zofia helped Matka pack for the same purpose. It wasn't as safe as being in the country with Ella, but the library had been fortified in anticipation of the upcoming battle.

Matka's single suitcase sat by the door, filled with a few days' clothes, all the food they had, the remaining jewels they could use for currency, and pictures. More pictures than Zofia even realized they had.

Zofia and Antek as children, their faces grinning in grainy black and white and grays. Matka and Papa on their wedding day; happy and young. The family together on vacation by the shores of Gdynia. A lifetime of memories captured on film to remember those forever lost.

Beside the suitcase was Papa's medical bag, ready for Matka to use at the library for anyone requiring first aid. When it was time to go, however, Matka remained by the kitchen window, staring out through the lace to the street below.

"Don't do this, Zofia." Matka turned, her narrow face pinched.

"Don't fight back?" Zofia shook her head, incredulous. "After all we've suffered. After they killed Papa and after everything they've done to Janina and her family and the entire Jewish population?"

Matka tensed as if she'd been slapped.

"Think of Antek." Zofia gentled her tone.

"I think of you." Matka stepped closer. "And how you are all I have left." Her fingers found the golden cross at her throat. "I can't lose you too, Zofia. I will have nothing in this world without you."

"And I can't tolerate the oppression any longer," Zofia replied, resolute. "This is our freedom. Matka, I'm going, but first I want to make sure you are safe."

Matka didn't reply, her eyes lit with an internal fire. But then she always hated losing control.

"Nothing you can say will change my mind." Zofia shook her head.

Even Matka knew when she was defeated. They didn't speak any further on the walk over to the library where Matka would remain while Zofia fought with the Polish Home Army. Errant shots popped off through the city, accompanied by the rumble of hooded trucks. Those sounds, the reminder that the occupiers were still in the city, hurried Zofia and her mother onward.

Anticipation buzzed through the library for the battle that would soon begin. Provisions once used during the initial bombing of Warsaw were put back in place, making the library a place of refuge. The kitchens were stocked with food, sleeping quarters in the warehouses were secured for the librarians and their families. Additional care was spent this time in creating additional exits.

There were not many rare collections left, but those that remained were protectively bricked behind newly laid walls.

The library was ready for war.

Miss Laska was already there with Janina. Darek stood beside them, along with Danuta and Kasia. They all wore a variety of mismatched military gear, whatever could be salvaged from limited supplies. Janina wore a blue jumpsuit, while Danuta and Kasia paired their Girl Guide button-down tops and knotted kerchiefs with a pair of serviceable pants like Zofia did. Darek looked the most like an insurgent with a green army jacket, a metal helmet with a white-and-red band around it and a gun tucked in a holster at his hip.

On each of their right arms was the mark of the Home Army, two ribbons sewn together, a band of white on the top, and red on the bottom. Zofia touched her own armband, and pride swelled in her.

"I wish I could join you." Miss Laska's mouth was drawn tight with determination.

"We'll fight for you," Darek assured her. "But we need to hurry or we'll miss W Hour."

Zofia turned to Matka, dreading the show of her mother's irritation in front of everyone. However, when Matka looked at her, it wasn't rage in her eyes. It was heartbreak.

"Zofia." Matka's voice trembled. "I love you."

Zofia hadn't realized she'd longed for those words from her

mother until that moment, when the sweet acknowledgment of her love had been so tenderly expressed.

Matka grabbed Zofia's hands, drawing her toward her into an embrace. "I have always loved you and nothing will ever change that," she whispered fiercely.

"I love you too, Mama," Zofia replied quietly, referring to her mother with the affectionate endearment for perhaps the first time in her life.

And she did love her. Matka had risked her life to keep Zofia fed, she'd found a place for them to live when so little of Warsaw was habitable, and she had acknowledged her own wrongs and fought to correct them.

Zofia squeezed her mother with a tight grip before finally letting her go.

"I'll take care of her, Mrs. Nowak," Darek vowed. "I'll protect her with my life."

The burden of such a promise fell over Zofia's conscience like a weight. "That won't be necessary."

His gaze found hers and something in her chest went tight.

"It'll be over in three days anyway." Kasia grinned her brightest, most winning smile. "That's what everyone is saying."

"Stay safe, my Zofia." Matka wrapped her entire fist around her little cross. "And I will see you soon." Her gaze was pleading as she stared at Zofia in search of confirmation.

Zofia nodded. "You'll see me soon."

The worry did not clear from Matka's eyes, but she stood back with Miss Laska, a silent sign of her permission for Zofia to go.

Darek glanced at the watch on his right wrist, a relic from the Great War Zofia knew had once belonged to his uncle—a talisman for good luck. "It's time."

Anticipation heated Zofia's veins like a shot of vodka on a freezing day. Finally, they would take back Warsaw and make the Nazis pay.

Chapter 33

ZOFIA GATHERED AT GIBALSKIEGO STREET with Darek, Janina, Danuta, Kasia, and the others in her company in the Parasol Battalion. Theirs was a group made up primarily of Gray Ranks members, young men and women who had committed sabotage together throughout the occupation and then later trained for combat in the forest.

Energy pulsed in the air as people in less regimented units shifted this way and that, breaking their military lines to greet friends and relatives. While some insurgents were dressed in military gear, many looked ready for the victory celebration rather than the fight.

Men wore business suits, complete with dress shoes polished for the occasion, while women had donned their finest dresses, with some in sling-back wedges and others in high heels.

The seasoned soldiers among the crowds watched with shrewd looks, older men who had defended Poland and slipped into hiding after the occupation and others who had also fought in the

Great War. Those men stood off to the side, lacking the jubilation of the younger crowd, their faces expressionless.

What struck Zofia the most was how young so many men and women looked. When Antek had left to defend Warsaw, he'd been eighteen. At the time, he had seemed so grown up to Zofia—fresh out of secondary school and preparing for his first year at university to study medicine like their father.

What a difference five years made.

Now eighteen-year-olds looked like children, their faces still soft with youth and their eyes bright with innocence. They'd been so young during the attack on Warsaw in September 1939, many sheltered by parents and older siblings.

For the first time, Zofia saw Antek as their mother had. Not as a man going into battle to protect his family and his country, but as a child charging headlong into danger.

Perhaps in five years, Zofia would look back on this moment through Matka's eyes and also see herself as being far too young for war.

Darek took his place in front of Zofia's group, their illustrious leader after his efforts in the assassinations of so many collaborators and Nazi officials.

Beside them was another group, also with the Parasol Battalion. They were under Krystyna's command, who easily bore the weight of those whose lives depended on her.

A frisson of excitement rippled through Zofia.

With leaders such as theirs, this uprising would be a success. It had to be.

"For years we have tolerated abuse and hate and prejudice." Darek looked out over them as he spoke. "We will be cowed no more. Now we are armed and ready to fight. And once again, Poland will be free."

Zofia's heart thudded faster in her chest, her breath quickening. A glance at a clock jutting from the wall in front of a nearby pharmacy reflected 4:59 p.m.

A reverent silence descended over the masses as the minute hand swept to W Hour. A deafening cheer erupted. Polish flags were unfurled from windows and above buildings, five years of wrinkles from storage snapping free in the wind.

The men, women, and children who didn't intend to fight passed out cigarettes, food, vodka, and other offerings as the intrepid soldiers of the Polish Home Army rushed by.

"Grab the food," Darek instructed in a low voice. "We may need it later."

Zofia accepted several squares of sugar, perfect for fueling their energy, and filled her pack with boiled potatoes. Janina's pockets bulged from either side of her thighs as she also took as much as she could. They caught one another's eye and erupted in laughter, giddy with the thrill humming through their veins.

In the distance came the *pop, pop, pop* of gunfire. The civilians cleared out as Darek waved a hand to silently draw them toward Old Town, where they were to be stationed. Krystyna led her people in the other direction, toward the Wola district.

Music streamed from a gramophone, filling the air with patriotic songs that would have been fatal to play until this moment.

They rushed into one of the tenement houses and lay low. Once safely inside, Darek scanned them with an intense gaze. "Our orders are to protect St. John's Archcathedral once the Germans roll closer. For now, we need to find areas to set up sniper positions."

Outside, the chatter of gunfire continued, followed by shouts of other Parasol units.

Darek paired his soldiers up due to the limited number of weapons, with two people for one gun and the other person armed with handmade grenades.

It was better than some units where there was one weapon for three people. The arms they had were scavenged from wherever they could be found, meaning Great War relics were now being put to use once more.

Zofia climbed the stairs up to the third floor with Janina, who she'd been partnered with, and found a corner window. From there, they had a clear shot of the street while also remaining under the protection of a thick stone exterior.

"I'm glad we're together." Janina had the gun first and squatted low beneath the window. "But I don't want you to risk yourself for me any longer."

Zofia frowned. "We're doing this together and we're coming out of it together."

"You don't know what it's like." Janina's gaze remained locked on the empty street below, the Sten gun at the ready in her hands. "I thought I knew before the ghetto uprising. I assumed it would be like the attack on Warsaw. But active warfare is another thing. Being shot at, being hunted, knowing that no matter where you go, there is no safety; it's terrifying in a way you can't let yourself acknowledge until afterward or you'll go mad."

"All the more reason to never leave your side," Zofia declared. "I regretted every day you were in the ghetto and I couldn't fight with you."

Janina glanced back at Zofia and nodded resolutely. "Together."

Simultaneously, they returned their focus to the street. The walkways were torn up from the efforts of the Home Army earlier that day. Chunks of the broken stone were used to create a barrier that bristled with pieces of carts and chairs and tables.

Warsaw was a sorry sight compared to the beautiful city it had once been.

The sun sank into the sky and cast long shadows over Old Town. A sudden movement showed in the streets.

Zofia stiffened. Several figures scuttled along the broken walkway, their green uniforms pristine and matching.

Nazis.

Janina aimed her gun, eyes narrowed in concentration. The explosion of gunfire sounded in Zofia's ears, leaving them ring-ing as Janina's body jerked against the weapon's recoil. In the distance, one of the German soldiers crumpled to the ground.

The orderly line turned chaotic, the men scrambling like ants, their shouts filling the air as they tried to discern where the shot had come from. One man pointed up toward them.

Zofia and Janina flattened on the ground as a barrage of bullets rained through the window, showering them with splinters of glass.

The assault went on for what felt like minutes, though it likely lasted only several seconds. When the gunfire stopped, Zofia nodded toward the exit and they crawled across the floor, their thick military clothing protecting them from the glass.

Darek appeared in the doorway and offered a hand to each of them, hefting them from the room and into the relative safety of the hall. "Thank God you're safe."

Gunfire came from the floor below, followed by a volley of shots fired in return from outside. They all crouched to the ground and Darek put his arms out, blocking Janina and Zofia with his body.

He waved for them to silently follow him to the lower floor. The windows were broken in the room below the one Zofia and Janina had been in. The girl who had been propped by that window now lay in a pool of blood. The boy partnered with her continued to fight, the weapon now fully his.

Darek closed his eyes, his brows furrowed with pain. When he opened them again, his expression was fierce. "To the first floor. Make sure you stay covered."

Shots were exploding all over the street now as the Home Army fired from one side and the Nazis countered from the other. Eventually, the German troops fell back, ceding the building and the surrounding street to the Home Army, a small victory which afforded them an opportunity to rest for the evening before fighting resumed in the morning.

While some around them celebrated the win, claiming it

would be one of many on the horizon, Darek ordered their group to dig a grave for the girl who had been killed. She was too young to have been there, the sister to the boy who now had full ownership of their shared gun. They buried her in her sprigged pink dress and sandals that weren't made for fighting and set a wooden cross over her grave along with a wreath of braided flowers Kasia had woven together.

It was a reminder for those willing to pay attention that in war, even the winners lost, that they were all mortal no matter how invincible they felt.

Dinner was dished out from a large communal pot into simple bowls. Zofia and Janina inched forward in line for what felt like an eternity, their mouths watering. Once the adrenaline spike of the shooting had died down, a ravenous hunger took its place.

The fare was the same bland potato soup they had all been eating for months with a bit of hard bread, but it had never tasted so good. Thick and slightly salty, with meaty hunks of potatoes, the opaque liquid perfectly softening the bread for easier eating followed by mouthfuls of cool, clean water. Judging from the silence of those around her, she was not the only one thoroughly enjoying the meal.

After she'd finished eating, she realized Darek had not joined them. She retrieved a bowl for him and found him still by the grave, the mound of dirt casting a long shadow in the firelight.

"You need to eat." She held up the food.

His arms were crossed over his chest, his stare locked on the fresh grave like a sentry. "I know."

"Then you should take the bowl."

With a sigh, he accepted the meal from her. "I didn't want this position," he confessed. "I don't want these deaths on my conscience."

"She was here because she wanted to be," Zofia said gently.

"I'm in charge of making sure all my people live." He spooned the soup into his mouth. While most others ate with relish, he did so with resentment at his need of sustenance. "I failed her. And I'll fail others as time goes on."

Zofia didn't bother to remind him that the battle should be over in three days. The Soviets were still on the other side of the river in Praga, the sounds of their own battle echoing across the Vistula.

Was it naive to hope for the Soviets to rush to their aid?

A seed of doubt planted itself in Zofia's mind. After all, Warsaw had held out hope for aid before, and had been let down.

Why would they expect otherwise now?

As Zofia had feared, three days came and went without assistance from the Soviets. Old Town had morphed into a proper battle zone where streets couldn't be crossed without ducking behind barriers and nights were spent clinging to the edge of sleep while still being aware of one's surroundings.

Janina and Zofia were paired by a window again. This time the gun was in Zofia's possession, the weight of it considerable against her palms, where she held her right hand on the trigger and her left on the long magazine.

She trained the barrel on a single man as he slowly walked across the street, his shoulders curled protectively forward, and held her breath. It had been nearly forty-eight hours since they'd slept and the exhaustion left her mind fuzzy.

Still, she managed to keep her focus on her target and squeezed the trigger. Her forearms absorbed the recoil of the gun, but before she could see if she landed her hit, the flash of a muzzle across the street caught her attention and sent her plunging to the safety of the floor alongside Janina.

The Nazis continued to fire at them, their bullets chewing through the opposite wall, flinging bits of wood and dust on them. Janina had been right: being in combat was different than what they'd gone through when the city was bombed.

A coppery odor assaulted Zofia, a scent that had become all

too familiar these days. Warmth tickled under her palm. With a gasp, she pulled her hand up and found it covered in blood. There had been no pain on Zofia's body. It couldn't be coming from her. She looked at Janina, who stared at her wide-eyed.

Zofia's breath caught. "Janina."

When had Janina been hit? Why had she not cried out? Zofia did a quick visual sweep of her friend's body, but couldn't find the source of the blood.

The rattle of bullets came to an abrupt stop.

"Stay calm," Janina whispered.

"Where are you hit?" Zofia asked.

"It's not me." Janina edged closer, terror filling her gaze. "It's you."

Zofia's head pulled back to better survey the blood in the semidarkness. That's when she noticed the stain on her sleeve, glistening in the moonlight.

A burning pain suddenly sliced through her shoulder.

"I hadn't even felt it." Zofia's lips were numb as she spoke, her mind reeling.

"Let's get you downstairs." Janina put her helmet on her weapon and held it up to the window. When no shots came, she quickly helped Zofia to her feet and they scurried from the room to the small living room they used as a safe gathering point.

Darek snapped upright when he saw them. "What's happened?" Before they could answer, he called for Kasia.

She ran over, the small medical kit bouncing at her side, and studied Zofia's injury in the semidark.

They couldn't use light with the enemy so close. The Wehrmacht were adept at spotting any kind of illumination and firing their rocket launchers in that direction. They had seen it happen and quickly learned from the mistakes of others.

"Looks like the bullet grazed her pretty deeply," Kasia said in a hushed voice. "She'll need stitches, but I don't have any more thread."

The last of it had been used on a boy from the Żoliborz district who always had a ready joke no matter the severity of the situation. His wound had been stitched long enough for another bullet to land a fatal blow. It had been a hard loss, the same as all the others before him.

"Get her to the hospital on Długa Street," Darek ordered. "And take Danuta and Janina with you."

"It's only a graze," Zofia said irritably. "Just tie it off with a cloth. There's no need for us all to go."

Kasia considered the wound and shook her head. "It's too high. Tying it is impossible."

"Why are we all being sent?" Janina asked, her frustration evident.

Zofia regarded her friend whose eyes were blazing, as if the burning need for vengeance had manifested itself into something wholly visible.

"Because I gave you an order." Darek's voice was sharp with authority, and he softened it. "Don't worry. We won't kill all the crows before you get back."

Crows. It was how the boy from Żoliborz had referred to the Nazis. With Germany and Poland both represented by eagles and only Poland being worthy of the powerful, regal bird, he'd referred to the Germans' emblem as a crow and the whole lot of them as crows. The reference outlived him, a constant testament to his memory.

"Go get your gear." Darek jerked his head toward Danuta. "Janina, get Zofia's as well."

The three women turned away, leaving Darek and Zofia alone together briefly.

"Why are you doing this?" Zofia asked.

"I promised your mother I would keep you safe." He stared at her, the brown of his eyes shadowed in the limited visibility, letting her glimpse a flash of fear, of sorrow, and another emotion she couldn't name. "I promised myself as well," he said. "I should have..."

The shield fell over his gaze as he trailed off.

"You should have what?" she pressed.

He ran a hand through his dark hair. The grime of several days left the strands standing in all directions.

"You should have asked me to dinner?" she answered for him. "I mean a second time, after I said no."

A muscle worked in his jaw. "I didn't want you to say yes out of obligation after I helped you with Janina."

An ache welled in Zofia's chest. "I would have said yes," she rushed. "I was too serious at the start of the war, too involved to let myself live my life. All those years were wasted when they could have..." Her voice caught. "When they could have been spent with you."

Darek didn't say anything, but instead closed the distance between them and cradled her face in his hands. He smelled like gunpowder and oil, but beneath that was the slight spiciness of his scent, the one that enveloped her when she'd cried against him after the ghetto was sealed, the one that emanated off his wool coat when they went to the concert together.

She inhaled, savoring him, hating the injury to her shoulder and how it was separating them now that they were finally saying what had taken too long to confess.

He pressed his lips to hers, soft and brief. "There is still time, Zofia." He kissed her brow, his touch gentle. "I'll take you out to dinner and dance with you beneath the stars."

Kasia and Danuta appeared in the doorway with Janina behind them, their gear slung over their shoulders. Darek didn't step back from Zofia. Instead, he ran his hand tenderly down her cheek. "I'll see you soon."

Zofia took one final look at him as she followed the others into the street and wished with everything in her that he was right.

Chapter 34

THE HOSPITAL ON DŁUGA STREET was filled with men and women in far worse condition than Zofia. There were missing limbs, head trauma, and injuries that couldn't be treated.

She tried to protest that her wounds didn't warrant attention when the room began to go dim and she felt herself sliding to the floor. It wasn't until the next day that she woke, lying on clean sheets with a pristine bandage on her shoulder.

She stared at those sheets in wonder, the white so bright, it almost hurt her eyes. Had it really only been several days since she'd seen anything so clean?

"You're awake." Janina eagerly leaned over her, relief easing the tension from her features. Her dark hair was still pulled back in the updo she'd done when the uprising started, though now it was powdered slightly with dust and dirt.

"It's just a bullet graze." Guilt pulled at Zofia as she looked around those in the surrounding beds. "We should go back."

Janina shook her head. "The fighting is too bad right now in

Old Town. We've been warned away until it's under control." A flash of disappointment showed in her eyes before she turned her gaze to the ground. "Kasia and Danuta have volunteered to work here. There are too many people in need for them to return with us when we can go."

The loss of Kasia and Danuta going back into combat was bittersweet, but it made sense. Kasia had medical training from her mother and the need for her skills was apparent.

"It's for the best," Zofia said. "They will be safer here."

They were all safer in the hospital, evidently by design on Darek's part. He had, after all, promised Matka he would protect Zofia, and they remained out of immediate danger as they helped the nurses at the hospital as best they could over the next two days.

Kasia fell into an easy rhythm, following her mother's footsteps as she cared for those who could be treated, and comforted those who would not survive. Danuta even found her calling by reading aloud in her steady, smooth voice to the insurgents as they recovered. The stories so enraptured the wounded soldiers that even when bombs whistled toward them, those who could walk away remained at her side as she continued to read.

Zofia helped as much as her wound allowed and even managed to drop a letter to her mother in the hospital's new mailbox.

The Scout Mail had been active early in the uprising to transport messages to and from various districts taken over by the insurgents. The younger boys of the Gray Ranks manned these posts, and took their work very seriously, ensuring all mail was promptly delivered and even going so far as to create "stamps" out of carved potatoes for each reclaimed district.

Zofia leaned back against the wall and read through a letter from Matka, delivered just that morning. There was a painful familiarity to the looping script of her mother's neat writing, the concern for Zofia's welfare evident with each word. Thankfully, there had been no problems at the library on Koszykowa Street thus far. That was one worry off Zofia's mind for the time being.

Sadly, there was no post to or from Old Town due to the intensity of the fighting, leaving Zofia in the dark about Darek's well-being and that of their unit.

A cheer erupted outside.

"We have Krasiński Palace," a nurse cried.

Janina and Zofia ran into the sunshine amid the rush of a crowd. There, at the front of Krasiński Palace, an umbrella dangled over the entryway.

It was now officially property of the Parasol Battalion.

Zofia relocated to the palace with Janina to help the incoming soldiers find refuge and free beds in the hospital.

The men and women who staggered in from combat had eyes that didn't focus on anything, their faces so coated in layers of grime, they were indistinguishable from one another.

The front line in Old Town was still too heavy to pass into and while they all waited, rumors spread like fire. If they were to be believed, Wola had been decimated. Not only the forces defending that district, but also the civilians, with tens of thousands mercilessly slain in only a matter of days.

This news was received with the somber realization that they likely would never see Krystyna again.

Janina and Zofia left that night, disobeying orders to rejoin Darek and the rest of their unit. It wasn't uncommon as they'd seen many risk the front line fire to return to their units.

They only made it to the edge of Old Town when they were stopped by a group of ten insurgents sheltering in one of the battered tenement houses. Their ages were impossible to determine beneath the dust and dirt, especially with limited visibility.

The Parasol emblem showed on the side of their helmets, a painted Home Army anchor with an open umbrella over it. If nothing else, they were the same battalion.

"Are you our reinforcements?" the first man asked. His eyes

were bloodshot in his soot-stained face. "Can they only afford to send two?"

"No, we're trying to find our unit," Janina replied.

"Then they've sent no one." The man wiped his forearm over his eyes, blinking rapidly. "There's no one."

"We haven't slept in four days," a woman stated. "Yesterday someone brought us bread and some pills to stay awake. We've had nothing since and the tablets are fading."

As if to illustrate her words, the man staggered, eyes rolling back in his head before snapping open.

"We'll stay with you," Zofia said. "We'll keep watch while you sleep."

The soldiers scarcely replied in the affirmative before falling into a heavy slumber. Those hours on watch were difficult, when silence stretched on and on and on as the thoughts usually quieted by action were able to tumble freely in Zofia's brain. There were too many people she loved at stake in too many places to keep track of.

Matka, Miss Laska, and everyone else in the main library, Darek, and the rest of their unit, even the books tucked away in the hidden warehouse. Bombings had started again, the buzz of planes and the shriek of their dropped wrath echoing in everyone's ears at all hours, their targets unpredictable.

Zofia was on guard for only two hours when the sound of boots crunched over the pavement just outside the copse of trees where they hid. Moonlight shone on the dull rounded shape of a cluster of helmets. There was at least a dozen of them, submachine guns just barely visible beneath their heavy coats. Germans.

Zofia and Janina exchanged a look in the shadows, their silent conversation screaming in Zofia's head.

If they woke the sleeping party, there could be a fight they would not win. Especially considering how sleep deprived those now resting were. But if the Germans went by without noticing them, they at least stood a chance of surviving the night.

One of the boys in the unit curled into a ball, setting the grass beneath him rustling.

The line of soldiers froze and so did Zofia's heart.

"What was that?" someone asked in German.

No one answered as the silence filled one beat, then another. Finally, they moved forward, carrying on their way without bothering to inspect the sound. Zofia breathed out a silent sigh of relief.

They'd made it.

When the group woke almost twelve hours later, Zofia and Janina gave them their bread and water, then joined the unit as they advanced deeper into Old Town. After all, there was safety in numbers.

Cheers rose up the following day from a street over, a victorious and collective shout followed by a raucous singing of the Polish national anthem. Zofia, Janina, and the unit they attached themselves to rushed toward the sound and found a crowd of people surrounding a captured tank in the middle of the street, an actual German tank!

Children were being hoisted atop its turret as men and women climbed aboard with them, little white-and-red flags fluttering in their hands as the masses pressed in to see the tank.

"How did we get it?" Janina asked a woman clapping her hands in time to the music.

The woman stood on her toes to get a better look. "Apparently the driver fled under attack and we were able to capture it this morning."

Janina grasped Zofia's arm. "We should go."

Zofia hesitated. Amid so much death and loss, she wanted desperately to relish this victory.

"Do you think the Nazis would really let a tank fall into our hands?" Janina asked bitterly.

Zofia would not question her skepticism, not after the hell Janina had lived through. And so she allowed her friend to pull her from the celebration. They signaled the men and women they arrived with, beckoning them to come away. Most did, but the youngest boy remained, reveling in those rare, fleeting moments left of his piecemeal childhood.

They were midway down the opposite street when a great boom seemed to rattle the world, and sent the ground shuddering underfoot. Janina closed her eyes as one of the women from the unit raced back toward the street. Her return was slow, and she paused halfway to be sick.

She shook her head when she finally rejoined them. "It was a bomb," she said quietly, her eyes glistening with tears. "It was a bomb."

The fighting began again soon after, the unit burning hot with fury, eager for revenge. Zofia and Janina remained with them, constantly asking after Darek's unit to any other groups they encountered.

No one had seen them.

Worry began to knot itself in Zofia's gut with each soldier that shook their head. Days and nights went by in a blur as they ducked into dilapidated homes, fired through holes in the brickwork, and strung netting over the windows to prevent grenades from being thrown in their temporary encampments. They took turns sleeping in two-hour shifts.

As it had been with Darek's group, the people in the unit fell one by one until there were only three members left along with Zofia and Janina. In that time, Zofia grew used to things she would never have imagined possible: functioning on no sleep, shoving all thought away when focus was needed for combat, and learning the ease with which she needed to kill.

They stopped one night in a home where the living room was still largely intact, the moonlight gleaming on a shelf of books with a large, overstuffed chair to one side. Someone's personal library.

She ran her fingers along the spines, cherishing the feel of them, lamenting the darkness which would prove impossible to read by. It made her long for the life she had before, where she could lose herself in reading and escape the broken world around her.

Muted light caught on the gilt edging of one book.

The Bridge of San Luis Rey by Thornton Wilder. The very title Marta Krakowska had once recommended. Unable to help herself, Zofia slid the book from the shelf, leaving a gap in the otherwise pristine line of texts, and nudged it into her bag.

That night was particularly brutal as they came under fire again, narrowly escaping a rocket launcher that took out the building beside theirs. Several days later, a runner approached them, a boy no more than twelve with a helmet so large, it wobbled on his head. "You're being ordered back to Krasiński Palace to recover."

It was one of the most beautiful statements Zofia had ever heard.

"We could press on." Janina looked back toward the heart of Old Town where the worst of the fighting was. Her foot bounced in apparent agitation. "We might still find Darek."

It was a bad idea and they both knew it.

"How many bullets do you have?" Zofia asked.

They both had Sten guns now.

Janina unclipped the magazine and frowned. "Five. How's your shoulder?"

Zofia rotated her shoulder and was rewarded with a dull ache. "Stiff, but not as painful anymore. I only have seven bullets left."

There was no need to discuss anything further as they turned toward Krasiński Palace with the unit, skirting behind barriers of fallen walls and piles of rubble.

There was another reason that prevented them from pressing on to find Darek and the others. One neither wanted to voice, yet they both secretly feared—the very real possibility that Darek and the rest of their unit were all dead.

They didn't know how many days had passed since they first left Krasiński Palace, but they'd ventured out with hope and determination. Now they returned, staggering back, their stomachs empty, their wills depleted.

Zofia scarcely remembered tripping through the entryway and being ushered into the noisy darkness that reeked of sweat and blood. When she awoke several hours later, her bandage had been changed and Janina lay on a bed beside her, her face wiped clean as she slept deeply.

Grit seemed permanently embedded in Zofia's eyes and her temples throbbed. She wanted to sleep for a few more minutes. Or maybe a few days.

But in the back of her mind was the awareness that they were at war. That sleep was dangerous.

"Thank God you're safe."

Zofia's eyes flew open to find Kasia at her bedside with her familiar sweet smile. "I've been so worried since you both left. Old Town is getting too dangerous. There are more wounded than we can care for and scarlet fever has started to break out among the troops."

"Darek." Zofia's voice came out in a croak. Her clothes were caked with dust and dirt. Her mouth felt similar. She tried to swallow and her throat stuck together.

Kasia held a canteen toward her. Zofia took it and drank in greedy gulps. The water was cold, delicious. She couldn't swallow it fast enough. Immediately the ache in her head abated.

"Slow down," Kasia said. "We've rationed our water usage

right now. Everyone only gets so much." She held up a square of pink paper with a "1" handwritten in ink. "You get one more today and that's it."

"We're rationing water now?"

Kasia only offered a good-natured shrug, but the lines of stress across her brow told a different story. One of a battle that was not going well. If they didn't have water, how could they last much longer?

And where were the Soviets who were supposed to help liberate Poland? Still sitting on the other side of the Vistula River, watching Warsaw burn. Just like the rest of the world had in September 1939.

Once more, Poland was left to defend herself.

"Have you heard from Darek?" Zofia asked again.

Kasia shook her head and returned to the hospital. It was the same answer the next day and the one after.

In the quiet hours recovering in Krasiński Palace, Zofia opened the book she'd taken from the apartment in Old Town and lost herself in the pages. In place of the fear that hounded her every second and the horrors of death and violence that she witnessed, she instead let her mind wander through the intricate lives of the residents of San Luis Rey and how they were each connected. It was a temporary refuge, that world hovering between fantasy and reality, but in the pages of that book, she began to live again.

"Zofia. You'd asked about Darek," Kasia said one evening.

Zofia looked up from her book, her eyes taking a while to adjust from the dimly lit pages to where Kasia stood beside the bed. "Yes. Do you have news?"

"Well..." Kasia grinned.

Suddenly a bowl appeared in front of Zofia. She looked down at the dirty hand holding it, then up the strong forearm to the familiar face and those warm brown eyes she had thought of more often than she should admit.

"Are you free to join me for dinner?" Darek asked.

Zofia cried out with such delight, Janina startled awake from where she dozed against her rucksack. Kasia quickly took the bowl from Darek, cradling it like something precious—as it truly was—and Zofia flew into Darek's arms.

"You're safe." She squeezed him in an embrace. He was real. He was here.

They ate their bowls of soup together, both going slow to make the meal last as well as their time together. Only two members of Darek's unit were still alive. He didn't go into detail when he mentioned the loss of the others, but his haunted expression told her of the weight he bore for each of those deaths.

"Have you heard from your mother?" Darek asked.

"I heard from her a couple of weeks ago. The library was still safe. I'm going to send another letter tomorrow before the scouts get the mail." Zofia stirred the mixture of barley and water and plucked a few husks free.

Food had grown so scarce that they'd had to fall back on barley found in the Haberbusch i Schiele brewery. It wasn't husked, however, and the process of clearing the inedible husks from one's mouth gave it the popular name "spit soup."

She flicked a husk free and wiped her hand on the leg of her pants. "Have you heard from anyone at the university library?"

Darek set his spoon in the bowl and cleared his throat. "They aren't doing as well." A muscle worked in his jaw. "I haven't heard from them directly, but I found a copy of the *Information Bulletin* the other day. It stated the Nazis took control of the university library and have been using the staff to fetch their food and…" He pressed his lips together. "They've also been using the library employees to walk in front of the tanks."

Zofia closed her eyes against the horror. She'd seen as much herself, civilians forced to walk before German tanks as they rolled toward insurgents. It was an impossible choice for the Home Army, to kill innocent civilians in an attempt to take down the tank, or to die themselves and forfeit their position in the fight.

"Let's not talk about that anymore," Darek said. "I want to show you something." His warm hand slid around hers, his tug insistent, but gentle.

Zofia eased from her chair and followed him outside to the gardens behind the palace. The sky was an inky black, and the air smelled of ash and moist earth. In the distance were several rosebushes still blooming, battered things with their heads lifted in proud defiance. Flower beds that had once been tended to with care now lay in patches, overgrown or dead. Mingled between them were mounds of earth, marked with wooden crosses and names scratched in a hurried hand.

"Not at the garden." Darek touched the underside of her chin, encouraging her to look up. "At the sky."

She did as he asked, lifting her attention above to the flecks of stars winking overhead. "This reminds me of when we walked home from the concert," she said softly. "The stars had been so bright. And I had never been so moved by music in my life."

"I almost kissed you that night." He ducked his head.

She remembered it all too clearly. How he'd looked at her with sincerity, how her heartbeat had tripled in response. And how she'd stepped back, putting space between them, keeping him at an arm's length once again.

She leaned forward and kissed him now, a light brush of her lips against his, but enough to ignite a quiet fire within her.

"Dance with me," Darek said quietly. "Under the stars."

"Sounds fancy." She grinned, foolish and happy in the same dizzying moment.

He pulled her toward him, securing her right hand on his

broad shoulder and her left over his bicep as he shifted his palm to her waist.

He carefully stepped across the grass, leading her in a dance with an imaginary song. "This isn't the Adria, but it'll do."

Zofia smiled. The dance hall was famous in Warsaw with its rotating stage and American-style drinks.

"I'd probably have fallen on that dance floor anyway," she teased.

"It's made of rubber to keep people from slipping. You'd be fine." Still, he tightened his grip on Zofia, not that she minded one bit.

She cocked an eyebrow. "Go there often?"

He laughed, smooth and easy, and it was the most wonderful thing she'd heard in far too long.

"I've heard enough about it that I might as well have." A flush spread over his face, reminding Zofia of the way he'd looked when they first met. "That's not really my type of place."

She tilted her head, curious to learn even more about this man she already knew so well. "What is your type of place?"

"The National Museum." Darek spun her slowly beneath the stars, stopping her when they were eye to eye. "And the library. There's this really beautiful woman who works in the warehouse…"

"You really know how to talk to a woman, don't you?" Zofia wasn't much for being playful, but in that precise moment, the flirtation made her feel effervescent.

Darek shook his head. "I know how to talk to you." He dipped her low, his strong arm at her lower back holding her upright. "That's all that's ever mattered to me."

That night at Krasiński Palace, she didn't leave his side, not until sunlight spilled in through the windows. In this world of uncertainty and terror and sorrow, she would not squander one minute of joy when she'd wasted so much by keeping her distance. Not when they might all be dead tomorrow.

Chapter 35

THE NEXT MORNING BROUGHT the reality of war back to them with orders to return to the front line.

Zofia joined up with Janina, who had her gear slung over her shoulder. Kasia had given Zofia an extra bandage and some ointment for the wound at her shoulder and with a hug from both her and Danuta, Zofia and Janina finally reunited with their unit.

Darek grinned at Zofia, then ruffled Janina's hair. "It's good to have you both back with us." His demeanor shifted to one of seriousness. "We have a big task ahead of us, holding the crows back. The Nazis are one row of houses away from taking Old Town."

That meant the Germans had advanced quickly in the few days Zofia and Janina had spent recovering.

After they each received a canteen full of water and a loaf of bread, their small unit made its way back to the front.

They were met with immediate enemy fire, losing one of their few troop members within the first day. It was a man who took a bullet to the thigh, a seemingly innocuous wound that killed him within minutes. Zofia had knelt at his side, filling in as field medic with Kasia no longer able to join them.

"Duck." Before the word even registered to Zofia, Darek's body covered hers as bullets soared over his back. Exactly where her head had been.

She gaped up at him in horror. "You could have been killed."

"So could you," he said evenly.

Darek rested his forehead against hers. There had been sweet relief in giving in to the relationship they had put off for years. But no joy in this broken existence came without cost, and the way they cared for one another would likely exact a heavy toll.

Their unit sheltered for the night, but with so much shuffling and movement outside on the German line, sleep was almost impossible. The following day, the enemy's efforts were brought to light as the firepower increased tenfold.

The growl of a tank sounded, rattling above the din of warfare.

"Goliath." Darek had to shout to be heard. "Fall back."

The Goliath looked like a toy as it rolled in front of a massive tank. But the innocent-looking miniature version was packed with explosives and controlled remotely, the operator protected in the large tank trailing back a few dozen feet.

The Goliath rammed into the church Zofia's unit had once been sent to protect, a massive structure filled with civilians seeking shelter and wounded men and women. Zofia pushed Janina back behind one of the buildings and then was shoved herself by Darek, who quickly followed behind them. A wave of heat rushed past them, yanking at their hair and clothes and leaving the air burning in its wake.

A quick glance back revealed their enemy pouring from the yawning opening, amid streams of sunlight filtering through clouds of dust. Their firepower was too great, coming in waves that did not cease, splintering bricks with missed shots and eliciting moans from those that were successful. An explosion blasted nearby, close enough that another wave of heat bathed Zofia.

Janina stumbled back, crying out in pain. "I've been hit." She stared in shock at her bloody forearm.

Darek cursed and pulled Zofia and Janina back behind the building. "When I give the order, run to Krasińskiego Street."

"I'm fine," Janina said through gritted teeth. "I can still fight."

Darek shook his head. "It's your right hand, Janina."

An explosion shattered several bricks beside them and they all reflexively shrank back.

Despite Janina's protests, her pupils were mere pinpricks in her dark eyes and sweat glistened on her brow. It was something they'd all seen before, and it was not a good sign.

"People are escaping through the sewer at the next street." Darek's voice was even as he addressed Zofia, as if the enemy closing in on them didn't rattle him one bit. "You need to go there and take Janina through the sewers to safety."

"And you?"

"This is an order, Zofia."

She ignored the authority of his tone and gaped at him, not as his subordinate but as the woman who loved him. "You're not coming?" The idea of leaving him behind sent her pulse beating wild and erratic.

He continued to speak as though he hadn't heard her. "When you get to the other side, take off your armbands, find civilian clothes, and get to your mother. However you can manage it, get out of the city. Go to Mrs. Steinman and Ella and don't leave until the Soviets have kicked the crows out of Warsaw." His mouth flicked up in an easy smile. "I'll meet you there."

The way he said it, she almost believed him.

"I love you, Zofia." He reached for her, cradling the back of her head, his wide, expressive brown eyes looking at her with a sorrow that brushed her soul. "Now run." He didn't even wait for a reply as he pulled himself away and raced back around the corner.

"Darek," Zofia cried. "I love you."

But he wasn't coming back. She knew better than to expect it. Janina's wounded arm had begun to shake. There wasn't any time. They needed to leave now.

Taking Janina's good hand, Zofia forced her to sprint, putting their backs to the enemy, offering up vulnerability for speed. They rounded the corner without a shot fired at them and drew to a stop. The sewer cover in the street lay open and an insurgent was lowering himself into the black emptiness below.

A man with a blue coat waved them over. "Hurry and get in. We're closing it after you two."

Zofia went first to ensure whatever fluid sloshed below wouldn't be too deep for Janina.

The smell hit Zofia first, that raw sewage and the odor of rot, the force of it so powerful, her eyes watered. Though the waterline only came up to her ankles, the bottom of the sewer sloped down together, like the pointed top of a raindrop, and made walking difficult in the slippery muck underfoot. The ceiling was not tall enough to stand upright, and left Zofia hunched forward to keep from hitting her head.

Janina's boot-clad feet lowered into the sewer and Zofia reached up to help her friend inside.

Light filtered in from above them, highlighting Janina's bewildered expression.

"Janina," Zofia called in an attempt to get her to focus, even just for a minute. "I need you to put your good hand on me. I need to know you're behind me."

Janina nodded.

"I'll make sure the way is clear for you to walk," Zofia said.

Janina nodded again.

"Don't let go no matter what," Zofia said fiercely.

If there was another nod, Zofia didn't see it. The cover lowered over the hole, sealing them in darkness.

"I wish I had a torch," someone grumbled.

"No torches," someone else replied from up front.

"The Nazis will be looking for lights," another voice explained. "The smallest flicker or sound and they'll drop a grenade down here and we'll all be dead. So stop talking."

There was no more discussion after that.

It took a while to get the feel for walking blind. One had to trust there would be an unobstructed path for their feet to follow and nothing to hit their face. Eventually, the group found a pace, slow and steady as they inched along, their backs hunched to accommodate the short ceiling. The blackness around them made a maddening pressure build in Zofia's eyes as she attempted to see into the nothing.

After a while, she closed her eyes, willingly relinquishing her sight to focus on her other senses. The splash of the water around her, the cold rise of liquid as they went onward, creeping up her shins and then over her knees. And, most important, the light weight of Janina's hand on her back.

The odor began to ebb away, likely as they grew used to the foul smell, and the dull ache in her lower back from walking bent over grew into an insistent burn.

They stumbled about in darkness for what felt like days, the water climbing as high as Zofia's neck at one point. She tried not to think about Janina's injuries and what effect the fetid water might have. Even more, she tried not to focus on the soft objects that bumped against her as she moved through the water, though her imagination knew well what horrors had washed down the drains throughout the violence of August.

At one point, the water lowered to a trickle and rats squeaked at them, running over their feet and even biting a few in their party. And later, the tunnel narrowed considerably, forcing everyone to crawl.

Through it all, by some miracle, Janina had held on to Zofia.

When they finally reached their destination, their blindness from the dark was replaced by a blindness from the dazzling sunlight. Zofia's arms trembled with exertion and she could barely pull herself from the hole, let alone help Janina out. Strong arms grabbed her in a gentle hold and hauled her outside before reaching for Janina.

Zofia wavered on her feet, out of sorts as she tried to adjust to the brilliant daylight and orient herself. A street sign nearby proclaimed it to be Warecka Street. They were in the Śródmieście district.

They had exited hell, and entered a place in Warsaw seemingly untouched by the uprising. Civilians strode by, eyes widening at the state of those emerging from the sewer. Buildings were whole and the trees had healthy amounts of waxy green leaves stretching up to the sky. Even the windows in the storefronts were still intact.

"Warecka Street," Janina murmured in recognition.

The fact that they were in the Śródmieście district meant they were also not too far from the main library branch.

"Zofia." Janina was pale, her lips drawn tight with pain. Her lids flickered and Zofia had to hold her tightly to keep her upright.

"Please," Zofia said to a woman in a lavender dress with dainty black heels. "Where can I find a hospital? I need a doctor."

The woman gaped at them and silently pointed to a building across the street.

Zofia adjusted Janina's weight on her as they drew closer. "Just a few more steps. We're almost there."

A nurse rushed to Zofia immediately and swept Janina from her. Zofia followed, desperate to keep from being separated.

The doctor strode in without so much as a glance at Zofia, who waited outside the curtained area, on display for anyone to gawk at as they passed. She didn't care. Concern for her loved ones crowded out any level of self-conscious thoughts. She wanted to make sure Janina would survive the injury to her hand and arm, that the time in the noxious sewers hadn't sealed her fate. And she wanted Darek to come through that door and pull her into his arms.

That latter thought was shoved away as soon as it entered her mind. She couldn't think on it now. The truth was like a hammer hurtling toward whisper-thin glass, ready to break the illusion Zofia needed to keep in order to be strong for Janina.

The nurse emerged from behind the curtain. "Your friend needs to go into surgery. The showers aren't working anymore now that the water mains are cut, but I'll get you a bucket of water and sponge and some clean clothes. You can wash up and get some food and rest while the doctor is seeing to her."

Zofia chewed her lip, not wanting to agree to being sent away from Janina, but not really having a choice either.

The nurse gave a kind smile. "He's one of the best. He trained for several years under Dr. Nowak."

The name pulled the breath out of Zofia's lungs.

Her father had trained this man who would be saving Janina's life. Short of her father himself, there was no one better than his protégé.

Zofia nodded and let the nurse bring her to a private curtained area to clean. But as the water ran down her scalp, and she scrubbed away the grime and sewage, the barrier holding back her thoughts washed away too.

It all rushed back with powerful clarity. The way Darek had delivered such careful instructions, how he'd so obviously lied when he promised to be behind them, the way he declared his love as if it was not only the first time he said it, but also the last.

He'd meant to stay behind, to die with the others protecting the path for her and Janina to run to the sewer. To fulfill his promise to Matka to keep Zofia safe.

Zofia had once thought they had all the time in the world. They didn't anymore. It had slipped through their fingers like sand gliding through an hourglass. Squandered on pride and waylaid by cowardice.

There in the curtained-off area, Zofia found herself alone for the first time in almost a month, save for the ghosts and regrets that were her constant companions. She curled her arms around her back as if doing so would hold herself together, and gritted her teeth to keep her tears from slipping free.

Janina made it through the surgery without issue. Her hand was swathed in a massive wrap of cotton, completely immobile. After a day of rest and food, the color even came back into her cheeks.

Zofia now wore a navy blue dress with a plain collar and sandals that were slightly too tight. She'd procured another dress for Janina, this one the same shade of purple as a May lilac in full bloom, and sandals she hoped would fit.

When the doctor and nurse were out of earshot, Zofia leaned toward Janina. "We need to leave."

Determination glinted in Janina's dark gaze. "I'm going back to Old Town."

An ache welled in Zofia's throat that she couldn't swallow away. "There is no Old Town anymore."

Janina didn't say anything for a while, her left fist opening and closing, her eyes glossy with tears. "I want to make them pay."

"We need to save Matka and leave Warsaw. It's why Darek—" Zofia broke off, unable to finish the sentence. "We need to focus now on those we love, not those we hate."

The blaze in Janina's gaze dimmed.

"Our mothers need us, Janina." Zofia pulled in a pained breath. "We are all they have left."

Finally, Janina nodded. "Let's get to the library."

It was not an easy journey to get to Koszykowa Street. All around them, the beauty of Warsaw had been shattered to rubble, with homes reduced to little more than shells with frames of windows and doors gaping like empty sockets. A massive hole had been knocked from the front edifice of the library, but aside from that, the main library branch appeared to be fully intact.

The front door would be bolted, so Zofia helped Janina toward one of the newer entrances they'd created. The barrier flew open before they arrived and Miss Laska beckoned them inside, her blue eyes larger and rounder than Zofia had ever seen before.

"You're alive." Miss Laska rushed them in and worked to lock the door behind them, her hands fumbling in her efforts as she couldn't seem to pull her gaze from Zofia and Janina. "My God, you're alive. They told us Old Town…" Miss Laska swept her hand in the air, wiping away the thought. "Never mind any of that. Come, this way."

She tucked the key in the pocket of a pink sweater and led them back to the warehouse where people had set up makeshift beds among the many shelves and stacks of books.

"Zofia."

She turned toward the sound of her name and went still. Matka stood only feet away from her, blond hair perfectly coifed, still elegant and beautiful as she'd always been. A moment hung in the air between them, the power of their reunion trapped in that span of time as if suspended in amber.

Matka opened her arms and Zofia longed to run into them, but her legs suddenly didn't seem to work. All the energy that had been propelling her forward, getting her through just one more day, suddenly bled out to nothing.

"Mama," she whimpered, her voice more that of a child than a grown woman who had seen combat, who had killed men, who had fought for Poland's freedom and now felt hopelessly defeated.

In an instant, Matka's arms were around her, pulling her close, cradling her in a maternal embrace that had become familiar in that last year, one of comfort and love, unconditional and all consuming.

That's when the tears finally came. The ones Zofia hadn't let fall after Darek sacrificed himself for their escape, the ones for Papa and the man he'd trained who saved Janina's life, for her fear that Kasia and Danuta might have met a fate similar to all those in the Parasol Battalion in Old Town. Once the tears began, they could not stop. She sagged against her mother, weeping.

And Matka simply held her.

More than the initial fifty people now sheltered within the library's walls, including many civilians who had sought refuge. The library fared well through the fighting, though Dr. Bykowski might have been inclined to disagree. He'd been erroneously charged with coercion with the enemy and was arrested for several days. During that time, he was shot at by a German sniper while working as forced labor for the Home Army. His bitterness was evident.

There had been several changes since Zofia and Janina had left. Wells had been dug in the first courtyard to provide water when the mains stopped working. The front gate had been fortified and a cemetery had been established in the second courtyard.

Several employees had been killed, one of them a janitor who had always been kind. Zofia heard about how he'd bravely fixed the barrier being used to block bullets from getting into the library after the explosion had knocked it askew and fell victim to enemy gunfire.

Though it was Zofia's intent to bring Matka, Janina and Miss Laska to Ella's home in the country, too many bombs continued to drop to make such an attempt safe. Slowly, Germans began to retake the districts the Home Army had fought so hard to reclaim and Zofia found they were trapped inside the library.

The *Information Bulletin* was still printing its daily paper and

Lightning Radio had relocated into the main library branch where it now broadcast updates on the outside world. But even that biased reporting could not mask what everyone knew.

The Home Army was losing.

Through the *Information Bulletin*, Zofia received written confirmation not only of the battle for Old Town being a terrible defeat with hundreds dead or left behind, but also the loss of Krasiński Palace and the hospital on Długa Street.

Kasia would never have left patients behind. Likewise, Danuta would never abandon Kasia. Much in the way Janina and Zofia had never separated through the uprising.

The haven that had been the library suddenly felt hollow, haunted by everything they had lost.

Zofia drifted through her tasks to maintain the safety of the building, as well as the people and materials within. Everywhere she went, she was reminded of those who were now gone, of Mrs. Mazur and her perpetually busy state, of Danuta and her overly complex way of speaking, of Kasia with smiles that could light a room like sunshine.

And of Darek.

The pain was more than she could bear, robbing her of breath and replacing oxygen with something else that blazed like fire in her breast.

She had a better understanding now of what Janina had gone through after the fall of the ghetto uprising. At the time, Zofia had thought she knew, but no assumptions can touch the true chasm of such loss until it is experienced.

Nostalgic and desperate for a connection with those no longer with them, she went to the back of the rear warehouse where they once sat for their Bandit Book Club and leaned her head back against the shelf.

Then she saw it.

The familiar red cover of a book she'd once cradled in her hands. She got to her feet and lifted *All Quiet on the Western Front* from where it had been hidden, nestled against two larger books on the bottom shelf. Whatever contempt might have embittered her toward the German author was quelled by the memory that it was Darek who had suggested the book. She drew the cover open and ran her finger along the page.

It whispered to her in the silence, a promise only a book can make to a reader, to offer a journey unique to them, tailored to the path that life had led them.

Zofia settled on the ground and turned to the first chapter.

When she first read the book, she had been innocent to war and blinded by hate. In reading it again with the experience of a soldier, she connected to the protagonist. The book touched her in a way that brought back so much about war. Not only the horror, the fear, the uncertainty, and bravery, but also the confusion of where lines were drawn and how humanity had to be held at an arm's length.

Once, this book had not so much as grazed her interest, and now…now it punched into her heart like a sniper's bullet.

But that wasn't all she realized in poring over those pages. The dire importance of their Bandit Book Club struck her anew. And why Hitler so feared the books he banned.

There was power in literature. Brilliant and undeniable.

Books inspired free thought and empathy, an overall understanding and acceptance of everyone. In the pages of books that were burned and banned and ripped apart for pulping, Zofia had found herself. These were the parts of her that were human and strong and loving, parts that understood lives she had never led.

And that was how her newest path opened to her, unveiled in the pages of a story written by someone who might have been her enemy. She had to ensure those books she'd saved reached every hand possible, to encourage Poland's youth to fight in the most effective way. With their hearts and with their minds.

That determination was what got her through that brutally hard September of bombings and attacks as Janina's hand healed and Zofia's soul knit back together. Finally on October 1, a ceasefire was called for several hours so civilians could flee. She, Matka, Janina, and Miss Laska left the forsaken city behind them and went to Ella's cottage as Warsaw fell once more into the hands of the Nazis.

On October 2 at 8:00 p.m., the capitulation agreement was signed in an effort to afford the insurgents protection under the Geneva Convention.

After sixty-three days of fighting and bravery and sacrifice, the Poles had lost Warsaw.

Chapter 36

Four Months Later…
February 1945

ZOFIA'S HOME ON KRUCZA STREET was gone, just another pile of beams and bricks amid a sea of similarly ruined homes. Their city that had once heralded buildings of art and beauty, that dated back hundreds of years ago, was now almost completely razed.

The Soviets renewed their advance once the Poles were defeated. The Nazis knew the city was lost to them and left a path of destruction in retaliation as they fled. Holes were drilled into the remains of Warsaw's architectural gems and stuffed with explosives that reduced the last of the city's splendor into powdered dust and broken debris.

Museums, monuments, the city's palace in all its opulence, and the libraries—all were targeted for demolition.

Zofia wrapped her hand around Janina's good one as they explored the city, each wounded by what could not be saved.

Mrs. Steinman and Matka had remained back at Ella's with Miss Laska. While the four women wanted to go to the city as well, Zofia refused until she and Janina had made entirely sure it was safe.

Zofia thought about how she had once made a sandcastle on the beaches of Gdynia, but as the waves rolled higher onto the shore, the water swept most of the structure away. What remained sagged in on itself in ruin. The city looked that way now, as if it had all been made of sand and was swept away by a vicious tide.

The Warsaw Library that had once survived the ruthless attack in September 1939 had not been spared from this recent atrocity. No matter how hard the library staff worked to protect the books from being damaged, nothing could have stopped the Nazis bent on destruction in those final days.

The main branch on Koszykowa was heavily damaged. Shells of the warehouse thrust up into the sky like bones from barren soil. In the back, windowless holes gaped and were blackened by the damage of flames and graves of insurgents still filled the courtyard.

Zofia and Janina had helped dig most of those graves.

"Zofia?" a voice called. "Janina?"

Zofia strained, staring toward the open window where someone waved frantically at them. Wanda Dabrowska, who had run the art reading room, told them to wait a moment before disappearing and opening a rear door a minute later.

"Come, come." She beckoned them.

Zofia and Janina ran over. "How are you here?" Janina asked in genuine surprise. "I thought everyone had left Warsaw."

"We only left for a while." Mrs. Dabrowska's pale blue skirt was streaked with soot and a smudge showed on her forehead, just over her left eyebrow. "Until the Soviets came in and we rushed back to find it like this."

She led them through the library. The acrid aroma of smoke was pervasive throughout the building. "The Nazis set fire to the ground floor before they left." Mrs. Dabrowska turned to look at them as she walked. "When the above floors burned, they collapsed and poured the books directly into the flames." She paused and sighed, the quiet breath of one in pain.

The tightness in Zofia's chest suddenly had little to do with the thick odor of smoke. "Are the books all gone?"

She and Janina followed her to the door of the main reading room.

"That's what I meant to tell you." Mrs. Dabrowska stopped before the door. "It's why we came back. There were only several of us, but we put out the flames and we salvaged what we could."

Janina sucked in a breath. "You mean…"

"Yes." Mrs. Dabrowska smiled and pushed open the door. The light coming in from the glass ceiling was slightly fractured from damage sustained in August, but still created enough light to reveal the stacks and stacks of books. "It didn't all burn," she announced proudly. "There is more in the attic as well."

Emotion snagged at the back of Zofia's throat and for a moment, she couldn't speak.

"It isn't much, I know." Mrs. Dabrowska looked at the collection of salvaged books, most filthy from debris and smoke. "The fires were so great and we had so little to—"

"You saved so many," Janina breathed as she surveyed the books.

"It's incredible," Zofia choked out. "You are rebuilding the library then?"

Mrs. Dabrowska nodded. "Of course. Not all of the rooms were completely damaged. We hope to reopen again soon."

For the first time in months, Zofia experienced a flicker of hope. "Then I have something that might help…at least, if it is still there."

She hadn't been to the hidden warehouse on Świętokrzyska Street since before the uprising. It could have been blown to pieces by a bomb. Or perhaps soldiers had stumbled upon it, kicking open the flimsy door for a place to hide and used the books as fuel.

She pulled the key from the chain at her neck, kept there for safekeeping since she managed to escape the city. "If it hasn't been destroyed."

The key suddenly felt heavy where it lay against her palm. So many had worked to save those books, to smuggle them to safety, and see them protected. But now she was the only one left alive.

She alone was their keeper.

She led the way to Świętokrzyska Street, through streets that now held only rubble and shells of buildings, ghosts of what had once been. In the distance, the Prudential Building that was regarded with such esteem still stood, but its exterior was punched through with gaping holes and its frame jutted from the stonework like ribs.

Her heartbeat quickened.

How could the hidden warehouse have survived this?

It was difficult to even discern exactly which building was which, but Zofia finally found the one she was looking for. The frame had already been weakened by the bombings and several of the upper floors had crumpled into the lower ones.

Key in hand, Zofia strode toward the structure.

Janina caught her arm. "Zofia, it's not safe."

But Zofia didn't take her gaze off the building. "I have to know. Stay here with Mrs. Dabrowska."

Janina didn't listen. The part of her that always heeded others and followed every rule had been broken long ago by suffering. Through the months in Ella's home that were filled with love and light, Janina's smiles had begun to slowly return, the shine filling her lovely brown eyes once more.

Together they entered the former lending library and picked their way carefully through the debris littering the ground. They stepped over beams and edged around fallen chunks of stone to where the staircase was, only to find it filled with rubble.

Zofia was not so easily deterred and began to dig. One brick tossed aside at a time, one hunk of the rafters hefted between her and Janina, they slowly revealed the door, more warped than ever before.

Breath held in her chest, Zofia inserted the key and the lock gave way with a grating click. The door remained stuck fast. Zofia pushed at the handle with all her strength and the door finally gave, swinging inward.

Chapter 37

THE SCENT OF OLD books wafted toward Zofia, the most cherished aroma there ever was, a prelude to the most beautiful sight there ever was.

Rows and rows of shelved books, salvaged from beneath Nazi noses and kept safe in the heart of a ruined library that still had one precious gift left to give to the readers of Warsaw.

The books were safe.

While the hidden warehouse had survived the uprising and subsequent destruction, the reading room on Traugutta Street had not. Like Zofia's home and so many other buildings in the city, there was nothing left of it but a charred pile of rubble.

Box by box, they delivered the secreted stash of books back to the library, reuniting them once more with the main library stock as the arduous task of sorting them into some kind of order began in earnest.

After a week in the city—and much pestering from Miss Laska—Zofia and Janina brought her and their mothers back to

Warsaw. Both Janina's former home on Mazowiecka Street and Zofia's home on Szucha Street had survived, both with residents locked tight within who refused to open the door to the original owners. With nowhere else to stay, they took up residence within the library again, sleeping on cots in the warehouses that had not sustained too much damage as they all worked to rebuild what they could.

They were in the damaged main reading room going through a fresh stack of books with a newly created catalog half-full of titles when Miss Laska crossed her arms over her chest. "We need to put out a call for people to donate their books."

There was almost no one in the city. Yes, survivors of the war were trickling in, but those sorry few had only the clothes on their back, and most returned to homes that no longer existed. No one had anything extra to give anymore.

Zofia pressed her lips to keep from speaking up. They had faced enough disappointments without her added pessimism.

"It's how the library started in 1907." Miss Laska ran a loving hand over a stack of smoke-stained texts. "People donated books from their homes. Walenty Dutkiewicz donated collections on law, Ignacy Bernstein offered his stores to the Judaic collections, and even Bołeslaw Prus offered his own original manuscripts. It's how we ended up with the vast collections we did. The people." She thrust out her jaw. "We can do that again."

"I think that's an excellent idea." Janina nodded, her eyes glinting with eagerness in the way they once did.

Perhaps it was seeing that enthusiasm revisit Janina's demeanor that sent excitement running through Zofia. "The community can help rebuild what the community began."

"Precisely." Miss Laska grinned. "I'll put a flyer out for people to begin gathering their books to deliver to us."

"I've found offering precise details is an ideal way to ensure compliance." Matka rose from where she'd been sitting in one of the surviving chairs.

Mrs. Steinman nodded in agreement from where she stood by a window. Though she had maintained the healthy glow since living with Ella, there was a sadness that never quite left her eyes. Zofia didn't imagine it ever would, not with all the war had cost her.

Matka cast a tentative look toward Zofia as she approached, silently seeking permission to offer more information.

Since being reunited amid the uprising, Matka had been much gentler with her advice, always carefully considering how her words might be received.

"Perhaps give people notice that in a month we will be collecting books in front of the library," Matka went on. "Then offer a specific set of hours."

Mrs. Steinman joined them, standing beside Matka. "We can set up a table to collect donations."

"Yes," Matka agreed. "We'll all do it together."

A month later, at precisely nine in the morning, they waited outside behind a table with a red-and-white tablecloth fluttering in an icy March morning breeze. Miss Laska sat at the head with a clipboard, ready to record people's names and addresses to deliver thank-you notes later. Janina and Zofia were present to heft the boxes they anticipated would soon be overflowing with books, and Matka and Mrs. Steinman were there to direct all the patrons. Even Ella had set aside her work on the farm for the day to join them, jaunty with red-and-white ribbons tied at the end of her braid.

And no one came.

Disappointment crushed in at Zofia as the minutes ticked by and the streets remained empty. The denuded trees offered no protection against the bitter wind and they all wrapped their arms around themselves in an effort to stay warm.

"Perhaps give it another hour." Despite Miss Laska's cheerful tone, she lowered her head in apparent distress.

It was a quarter to ten when Matka sighed. "Perhaps we ought to bring the table inside where we can at least be warmer." She had never been able to put weight back on, not even with the milk and eggs on Ella's small farm. As a result, Matka was always cold, even when she stood directly next to the hearth.

Her face was white now and Zofia knew she must be chilled to the bone.

Miss Laska sat up straighter. "Look."

They all turned in the direction she stared to find several people coming down the street.

Zofia strained to see, trying her best to hold on to a wisp of hope.

A woman arrived first, three books hugged against her chest. "It isn't much." Her cheeks went red. "But I couldn't keep these to myself knowing the rest of Warsaw could benefit from them."

Miss Laska accepted them. "We'll ensure they are well loved and cared for. Thank you."

"Thank *you*." The woman reached out and took Miss Laska's gloved hand. "You lent books on Traugutta Street when the library closed. I could never have made it through so many cold, lonely days without those books to keep me company. Not when my husband was dead and my children..." Her voice caught. She paused to compose herself. "Thank you."

Noticing someone behind her, she moved on with one last grateful nod.

More people were coming from both sides of the street now. A man stepped forward with a single book. "I'm glad I'm not too early." He extended a copy of *Sanatorium Under the Sign of the Hourglass* by Bruno Schulz toward them.

"Too early?" Janina asked.

"Yes." The man withdrew one of the flyers they'd printed using the dusty old duplicating machine and indicated the time. "It was supposed to begin at ten."

All eyes turned to Miss Laska, whose mouth opened and

closed, her eyes blinking behind her round spectacles. She had written the wrong time.

"Well," she huffed. "I suppose I'm not perfect after all."

They all laughed, partially at the humor of the situation, but also with immense relief.

The line of patrons continued to grow in the next hour, snaking along the ruins of Koszykowa Street. Most had only a few books to deliver, personal collections held through the dark days of the occupation. Many had continued to be patrons of the clandestine library on Traugutta Street, and expressed their appreciation for the books that were secretly lent to them, and for the escape they offered through terror and loss and pain.

A familiar face was among them, the gentleman who had been so eager to receive H. G. Wells's *The Invisible Man*. He set a full sack of books on the table, the contents landing with a heavy thud.

"Somewhere, someone may be impacted by one of these books and want to share the story with their child." He smiled at Zofia. "As I did with *The Invisible Man*. My son loved it, by the way." With a lift of his hat in her direction, he was gone, leaving the bounty of books behind.

Slowly but surely, their collection grew as the boxes were all filled. When Zofia returned for another box, she caught sight of someone else she recognized in line. Ewa, the girl she'd taught to read. She was taller now, her hair longer and bound back in a simple braid that reminded Zofia of Danuta. Ewa waited patiently with her four sisters in tow, three books held in her arms.

Zofia arrived as Ewa stepped toward the table. "These are the two library books I checked out from the reading room before the uprising began." She placed the copies onto the table with great care and then slowly extended the other book forward, a battered copy of *Gulliver's Travels*. The cover was worn from what appeared to be a lifetime of use. "I know it's old," she said softly. "It was our mother's book."

There was sad reverence in the way she said it, a familiar sorrow so many of them possessed in mourning for those who had not survived the war.

Zofia shook her head. "We can't take this. It's too precious."

The girl pushed the book toward her. "Before we started going to the library, this book was the only one we had. And before you taught me how to read, I never understood the story. We want to share this book with the city, the way you helped share so much with me." She put her arms around her sisters, drawing them closer. "With us. And we can always come visit the book whenever we want after you've opened."

Zofia accepted the precious gift, cradling it to her chest with the same affection Ewa had only moments before, its cover still warm to the touch. "Thank you."

It took several months to sort through all the donated books as well as all those that had survived the fire. They were organized into their original categories while new catalogs were made, written in Miss Laska's neat print.

During that time, the fates of their friends from the uprising finally emerged as more people returned to Warsaw.

Krystyna died with her unit, fighting to defend the civilians of Wola. Surviving insurgents who escaped from the hospital on Długa Street confirmed that Kasia had indeed stayed with the wounded who could not leave, sacrificing herself to bring them comfort in their greatest hour of need. Danuta had been at her side with a Sten gun in one hand, and a book in the other.

There had been no news of Darek, though anyone who might have been there was no longer alive to tell his story. All Zofia had left was her final memory of him confessing his love before he sprinted back into the fray, defending them so they could run to safety.

Zofia's memories of her lost friends were forefront as she stood before the doors of the library on Saturday, May 26. Opening day. The library had only one reading room to offer the city, but it was a start.

In that reading room were the books the Bandit Book Club had read and discussed as well as Papa's and Antek's collections from under Zofia's floorboards and so many other books that held sentiment to Varsovians, that were donated to the library for use by others.

This reading room not only represented the beginning of a rebuilt Warsaw, it also encapsulated books and memories and love all bundled into one perfect gift.

Bullet holes still marred the entrance to the library, intentionally left there to remind all of how Poland had fought back. The Minister of Education, Mr. Skrzeszewski, stood with the librarians, present to offer a speech commemorating the efforts to revive the library and to highlight the importance of what those books meant to Warsaw.

Zofia looked behind her. Every person gathered there already knew the importance of those books. The stories had cradled them through difficult times, offered light and hope when all felt dark and lost. They were there to celebrate reading and a community brought together by a love of those books.

The fight for a free Poland had not been entirely successful, as the Soviets now held control over their country. Once more the Polish eagle was held in a cage.

But their efforts had not been in vain. Looking around at the men and women and children in the crowd, she knew that in this way, they had still won.

"Zofia." A male voice called her name, a familiar one she'd never thought to hear again.

She swung around toward the sound and a sob stuck in her throat.

A tall figure moved through the crowd.

"Antek," Matka whispered. Janina spun in his direction.

No one moved, each afraid to trust what their eyes saw. If it wasn't Antek, if it was just a taller, thinner apparition of him, their hearts could not handle the devastation of such disappointment.

"Mama." He opened his thin arms and Matka ran to him, followed by Zofia and Janina. Laughing and crying, they all embraced, keeping one another upright.

When they finally released him and stepped back, Zofia studied her brother. Lines etched his face, making him decades older than his twenty-three years. White scars dotted his arms and hands and spoke of a hard life.

He was looking at all of them too, examining first one face, then another, then the next, and back again, as if he could not get his fill. His chin quivered, but he didn't look away. "I thought I'd never see any of you again."

"We thought the same." Matka reached for his hand, holding it like a lifeline. "Where have you been?"

"At a labor camp in Germany." Antek swiped at his eyes with his sleeves and sniffed, the tip of his nose red. "Not many of us survived. I don't even know how I did, but I believe it was through my memories of all of you. Through love." He shot a shy glance at Janina and she flushed.

"After being released, I made my way back home. But when I arrived last week, there were strangers living in our apartment and I had no idea how I'd find you." He nodded toward the entrance of the library. "But when I saw the notice in the newspaper of the library reopening. I knew that if Zofia was still in Warsaw, she would likely have had something to do with this." He gave a wide grin, revealing several missing molars. "I was right."

"More than you know." Pride shone in Matka's eyes as she regarded Zofia.

Heat warmed Zofia's cheeks at the praise. Something she hadn't realized she had so desperately craved her entire life. "That is a story for later."

"There are many stories for later." Antek offered an arm to Matka and one to Janina. "For now, lead the way into the library. I am eager to see your H. G. Wells collection. It's been far too long since I've read *The Time Machine.*"

"You may even recognize the copy." Zofia led the way, knowing with certainty Antek's old book was on the shelf, waiting to fall back into his hands. Returned to him the way he had so miraculously been returned to them.

They entered the library together, followed by scores of readers ready to celebrate how their love of books helped them through the terrible days of the occupation. For it truly was an event to celebrate when a library whose existence had originated in donated collections almost forty years ago, had now risen from the ashes of war and oppression by virtue of donations once more.

This was how they would rebuild the beauty of Warsaw, through the community, one book at a time in a city of readers with open hearts and learned minds.

Epilogue

November 1989
Warsaw, Poland

POLAND IS FINALLY FREE.

I weep as I write what I feared may never be possible to say again. Yet even after nearly forty-five years, the words don't feel foreign. They feel right.

This is the first time I've stepped on Polish soil since the end of 1945 when the Soviets began hunting down the surviving insurgents from the uprising. Janina and I left with our families, going first to London, which was immersed in its own postwar rebuilding efforts.

From there, we moved to Paris and honored Maria's memory by living the life she'd dreamed of for so long. Eventually, we all took to the French countryside, where the sun shone down more days than not, and butterflies flitted lazily through the warm summer air.

I feel it was fitting that I waited until Poland was free again to return.

At the end of October, Joanna Szczepkowska announced on Dziennik Television that on June 4 when Poland voted in overwhelming numbers for Solidarity, the anti-Communist trade union, that communism had finally come to an end. It was then we knew we had to return home.

We found Warsaw rebuilt, large pieces of rubble pocked with bullet holes and scorched from smoke used as a frame for new construction until the entire city was a completed puzzle of new and old. Familiar and yet foreign all at once.

Janina and Antek recently enjoyed their forty-third anniversary, having wed within the first year of being reunited. Last month, their fifth grandson celebrated his bar mitzvah, a proud moment for us all to witness. As a boy who loves learning, he will likely follow in his grandmother's footsteps and also become a teacher.

My own husband, Pierre Dupont, passed away two winters ago. We buried him near the apple tree he loved so much, the one that is always bathed in sunshine and bears the sweetest fruit. Our daughter, Cosette, had married just before the heart attack took him from us.

She's a beautiful young woman who carries herself with the grace and elegance Matka displayed all the way into her twilight years. But while Cosette has Pierre's dark hair, her warm hazel eyes remind me of Papa. I tell her all the time that she has her grandfather's eyes. She says she knows with the same flippancy I used to disregard Papa's comments.

But she doesn't know. Not like I do. Not like Papa did. Not like anyone who has experienced loss and sees the beauty of their loved ones brought to life once more in every smile, every glance of their descendants.

I only had thirty years to share with my Pierre before I lost him, but it had taken me quite some time to find love again after Darek. Even after all these years, memories of my first love still inhabit my heart, just as vivid and passionate as they were in my youth.

One of the first things I did when I returned to Poland was go to the National Museum, to the exhibit of art through the uprising. I'd gone with the hope of finding some of Darek's work.

I was there for an hour, worrying Matka's little gold cross on its chain between my fingertips as I searched. With great care, I examined every piece, looking for the distinctively elaborate *D* with the rest of his name scribbled after. It was a signature I knew as well as my own.

In the center of the gallery, in a place of honor, was a sketch with that very signature. The edges were curled and burned, but the main piece of art was intact. When I lifted my focus to the image and adjusted my spectacles, tears filled my eyes.

The drawing was of me, wearing that military jacket from the first weeks of the uprising, my helmet tipped back so my face was fully visible, a smile lifting the edges of my lips. In that drawing, I saw myself as he had seen me. Symmetrical and perfect.

Beautiful.

But more importantly, his dream had been realized.

Darek's art was hanging in the National Museum. The dream he'd always had, the dream he felt was too foolish to wish for. It had come true.

Marta Krakowska once told me that when a story was ready to be told, it would pour out, that my pen would not be able to keep up. After that day in the National Museum, I went directly to my hotel and that is precisely what happened. I filled a notepad with my words, then phoned the concierge to deliver more.

Page after page filled with my writing until the story had spilled from me in its entirety.

But Marta Krakowska was not entirely correct in everything she'd told me about writing.

She had said that I had to die a thousand deaths to truly appreciate the depth of emotion and capture it on the page. But that is not what happened to me.

I *did* die a thousand deaths. In the siege, in the occupation, in the uprising, even with those who time later stole away afterward. How can anyone live through such loss and still not touch the bottom of sorrow?

And yet, I could not write.

Instead, I lived.

Going to Paris for Maria awoke the idea in me that I should live a life with experiences that honored those I had lost.

Once I was settled in the French countryside and let my roots run deep into the rich soil there, I brought home a small calico cat with a black patch over one eye and orange splotches that covered each of her ears. Exactly the kind that Marta Krakowska would have written into one of her books. I, of course, named her Nela.

For Danuta, I read every classic I could get my hands on. In Polish and in French, then later in English. The thicker the better, exactly as she would have liked. And when I read those texts, I looked for the deeper meaning in them, the hidden message intended to expand one's soul in the way vocabulary expands the mind.

Kasia's gift was the greatest of all. For her, I had my daughter—my sweet Cosette. I breathed in the milky newness of infancy and lost countless hours staring into those large hazel eyes. For Kasia, I savored the sensation of motherhood just a little more, enjoying every exquisite moment for the both of us.

Once I was fluent in French, I took on the role of being a Girl Guide captain to the girls of our small town. Thinking of Krystyna at every meeting, I imbued those impressionable young women with knowledge that would make them strong enough to know when to fight to protect their rights and those of others. I was moved to tears when one of them was so inspired that she became an architect, exactly as Krystyna had hoped to be.

I also fulfilled my vow to Mrs. Mazur to ensure the books we so lovingly hid away from Nazi destruction once more found their way into the hands of readers. Not only on that opening day of the library in May of 1945, but also now that Poland is free, exactly as intended.

I went to the library to see if Ewa's book was still there, as well as the collection of texts from Papa's and Antek's personal libraries. Not only was the battered copy of *Gulliver's Travels* on the shelves, bound with new thread, but so too was Ewa, working as a librarian in the youth reading room, where she helped teach children how to read. Exactly as she had been taught by me all those many years ago.

Speaking of a free Poland, that final dream for Miss Laska was not fulfilled until this year. But now here I stand, a voice being heard for the first time in decades. Once again, we have freedom with democracy on the horizon. Finally, we are again the Polish Republic.

The words for my story didn't come to me until I stepped foot onto soil as a free Pole, until I saw Darek's artwork grace the collection at the National Museum. I think I had to complete the quest I set for myself in its entirety. To realize every dream that could not be fulfilled.

Now that it is done, I know I must share these stories so they can never be forgotten. We cannot let the atrocities and persecution of the Jews slip between the cracks of history. We cannot allow education to be stifled or cultures to be erased or books to be banned. Nor can we let the memory of those brave men and women who fought for freedom and what is right disappear in the turning pages of time.

The world also needs to remember to never take for granted what has been gifted to us through the sacrifice of others: the right to an education and learning, the power and luxury of freedom, and the beauty to appreciate the routine of simple, everyday life.

I have died a thousand deaths, but that did not define me. Instead, I lived a thousand lives and it is for that reason that I now can write our story for future generations to always remember.

★ ★ ★ ★ ★

Author Note

WHEN HITLER FIRST TOOK Poland, his intent was to relocate or murder 85 percent of Poles, leaving around 15 percent to be used for slave labor, along with completely eradicating the Jewish population. This was part of his *Generalplan Ost* and *Lebensraum* plans for genocide and German settlement in Eastern Europe, which resulted in the murder of almost three million Polish Jews and almost two million non-Jewish Polish civilians.

Almost immediately upon Poland's occupation, Nazis implemented *Intelligenzaktion*—the murder of Poland's intelligent and/or influential people in an attempt to quell any potential uprisings before they could start. One hundred thousand doctors, lawyers, professors, scientists, politicians, and other social elites were put to death. Near Warsaw, they were arrested and taken to Kampinos Forest on the outskirts of Palmiry, where they were shot over open mass graves. People who worked in the forest were told not to go to work that day, but several brave souls suspected foul play and spied on the Nazis. They were horrified by what happened and marked trees by imbedding bullets in them so the mass graves could be located and exhumed once the Nazi occupation was over. Now there is a poignant and powerful museum-memorial built there to honor the men and women who were murdered there.

In addition to killing off so many of Poland's leaders, the Nazis sought to crush Polish and Jewish culture. Museums and schools were closed, art galleries were looted, music was banned, and Polish and Jewish literature was stripped from bookshelves. Valuable books were stolen or poorly treated, and books removed from libraries, bookstores, and personal collections were sent to pulping mills where the General Government received a mere nineteen reichsmarks per *ton* of precious books. Initially, these books sent for pulping were stolen by the truck drivers and sold on the black market. When the Nazis realized this, they ordered the local Hitler Youth in Warsaw to ensure all the books were ripped in half prior to being sent for pulping so they wouldn't have any street value.

But the power of books still endured.

In my research, I happened to stumble upon the efforts of men and women on the Polish side and within the Warsaw ghetto who still managed to bring books to people to distract them amid such horrible times. I followed this vein and was truly amazed at how much I was able to uncover about how hard men and women fought for literature.

In the ghetto, suitcases were used to lend out books from private libraries. One particularly extraordinary man named Leyb Shur amassed so many books in Yiddish that he had to sleep in the hallway of his three-bedroom apartment and then hanged himself when he was told he would be forced to move and could not bring his books. Another amazing person was Basia Berman, the librarian mentioned in *The Keeper of Hidden Books.* She worked for the Warsaw Public Library. After being forced into the ghetto, she created and ran a secret children's library, which she referred to as CENTOS, a center to help care for orphaned children. Before libraries were allowed in the ghetto again, she modeled the clandestine library to look like a play area where shelves with dollhouses could be flipped around to reveal hidden books inside. Though she carried books in Polish and Yiddish, she encouraged the children who did not know Yiddish to learn. Later she managed to escape to the Polish side, where she then helped other escaped Jews remain hidden and safe until the end of the Nazi occupation.

On the Polish side, I found incredible archives about the Warsaw Public Library's secret activities throughout the occupation. As these were written during those dangerous years, much of what was recorded had to be discreet with details on the off chance they were discovered. Before the siege of Warsaw, there were over fifty-seven branch offices, reading rooms, and lending libraries connected to the main Warsaw library branch. For a portion of the occupation, the main branch was the only library in all of Warsaw that was even open, and when that closed, the lending library on Traugutta Street was turned into a secret library. There, Varsovians could request and check out books through a secret book log librarians kept. Sadly, the building was destroyed after the uprising and there were very few details on its operation. There was also a hidden warehouse where books slated for destruction were stored, but the address of that was omitted from the documents for safety purposes, so I had to make up my own location.

In addition to the secret library, the Warsaw Public Library also provided books to towns on the outskirts of the city, with people bringing books in their backpacks the way Zofia and Janina did for Ella. This continued on even after the war, and eventually a lending library bus in the '60s delivered regularly to rural areas. Though the book bus was too late in history to incorporate into my story, it so fondly reminded me of the Cincy Book Bus today that I had to mention it here in my author's note. Cincy Book Bus (Instagram @cincybookbus) sells books to readers in Ohio, and all proceeds go to purchasing children's books for low-income-area schools and organizations.

During the course of the Nazi occupation in Warsaw, the lending libraries and reading rooms were opened and closed often. Employees were hired and let go and then rehired again, just to be furloughed again. There was also a more complex hierarchy of German librarians in place to oversee the various libraries in Poland and in Warsaw. I've simplified a lot within the library operations in the book for ease of reading. And I feel like it bears stating here due to the nature of how close their names read, Dr. Bykowski and Dr. Bachulski were two separate people and both were the library's directors at separate times—that was not a typo. Dr. Bachulski was a director for the library during the occupation and fought desperately to keep the Social Museum in place at the library and was arrested for his efforts. It should be said that the items from the Social Museum were never seen again after it was removed from the library. Dr. Bykowski was one of the librarians who also taught library studies and wrote for the library's paper. Toward the end of the occupation, he, too, eventually became the library's director, though being erroneously arrested during the uprising (and accidentally shot) left him bitter and he was no longer with the library when it reopened in May 1945.

The Polish Underground State was the most organized resistance group in Europe during the Nazi occupation. They had various departments set up to oversee everything from education to propaganda to underground courts that tried particularly brutal Nazis and collaborators in absentia. It was through the Polish Underground State that clandestine schools were operated and even books were printed on secret printing presses that backdated publications in the event of discovery. In 1942, Żegota was formed, a branch that helped Jews escape from the ghetto and worked to keep them safely hidden on the Polish side.

In this book, Mrs. Steinman was forced to relocate safe houses several times. Sadly, this was not at all unusual. The average safe house usually only lasted a month or two before requiring relocation. This could be due to neighbors threatening to report the person operating the safe house, greasers uncovering the residence, or even an increase in cost (or the person in hiding running out of money), thus making it unaffordable. The efforts to find new locations and the increased fees for payment were endless. As time wore on, costs became so steep for these safe houses that members working with Żegota had to strap stacks of bills over their entire bodies to bring enough money for payment.

The Polish Underground State and Home Army (the military branch of the Polish Underground State) were what coordinated the official Warsaw Uprising (or Rising, as it is referred to in Poland). In late July 1944, the Soviet Union promised to help the Home Army defeat their Nazi oppressors. When the Red Army was visible on the other side of the Vistula River in the Praga district, the Home Army assumed their support to be fully ready and decided to attack on August 1 at 5:00 p.m. (a day and time still celebrated in Warsaw today). It was believed by many that it would be a quick battle lasting only one to three days. As the Polish Home Army and the Nazis fought, however, the Soviets remained in place without offering aid, abandoning the Poles so that they could easily defeat the beleaguered victor and absorb Poland into the Soviet Union. When I was in Warsaw, I was amazed to find the Vistula River was less than a mile wide. I can't even imagine how terrible it must have been to know help was so close and yet never came.

In the end, the Polish Warsaw Uprising that was supposed to last one to three days went on for just over two months. During this time, 150,000 civilians were killed by German troops (40,000 to 50,000 of those were slain in just a few days in the Wola district), with around 20,000 soldiers killed. Of the soldiers fighting with the Home Army, this also included the Gray

Ranks, the boys and girls belonging to Poland's Girl Guides and Boy Scouts, meaning many of these soldiers were between the ages of eleven and eighteen.

When the Nazis fled Warsaw, they drilled holes into walls, put explosives inside, and blew up Warsaw's valuable buildings and remaining libraries. During the attack on Poland and through the Nazi occupation, it is estimated that fifteen million books were destroyed or stolen from all of Poland. Once the occupation ended, large chunks of buildings were gathered from the debris and Warsaw was pieced together to resemble the city it had once been—a giant citywide jigsaw puzzle where stained and pockmarked old was combined with pristine new to restore Warsaw's beauty.

Many of the fictional characters I created in my book were inspired by people whom I read about in my research. I've tried to include some real people in this book as well to highlight the many brave efforts done in such dangerous times. Some notable people mentioned who are real: Mayor Starzyński, Basia Berman, Dr. Bachulski, Dr. Bykowski, Dr. Weigl, Veronica (Zofia Kossak-Szczucka—code name Veronica), and Wanda Dabrowska.

Research for this book was not always easy. First of all, with the Soviet influence in Poland continuing until 1989, I had to be careful in the publications I selected to ensure they originated outside Poland, as Soviet Union censorship might have offered skewed facts. In several cases, nonfiction books gave conflicting dates, times, and spellings (especially for names of people and streets). In cases such as these, I went with what seemed most consistent between my research materials. In regards to name spellings, I did not incorporate Polish nicknames for my characters to avoid possible confusion. For example, Zofia would also be referred to as Zosia, and Janina would also be Nina or Janka. In other cases, I used nicknames and never referred to the formal names (like Kasia instead of Katarzyna and Darek instead of Dariusz). Additionally, I used the American courtesy titles for Mr. and Miss and Mrs. rather than the Polish Pan and Pani.

I was very fortunate to travel to Poland for research on this book, and stayed in Old Town, which had been destroyed during the uprising. Unlike Zofia, I've always had a wonderful relationship with my mother, and she accompanied me on my two-week trip. She reads all my books, and so it was especially wonderful to have her accompany me, as I know she'll be reliving our trip together when she reads this book. Our tour guide, Ewa Bratosiewicz, put together an informative and truly incredible series of tours for all the places I needed to see for my research and patiently answered my endless stream of questions. I realized after I returned to the US that I wanted to write about the Warsaw Public Library. The building is still standing and the staff there was enormously helpful with my research. I especially want to thank Filip S´witaj who was so helpful. Additionally all the details of life in Warsaw from my friend, Gosia Kuc Ferris, who grew up there were so enormously helpful. It was through all of their guidance and details along with the countless nonfiction books I read on Poland during WWII that allowed me to bring *The Keeper of Hidden Books* to life. Please note that any mistakes are unintentional and completely my own.

Resistance comes in many ways, whether in a civilian making homemade grenades and flamethrowers in a basement, or an insurgent fighting back against an enemy they know they can't defeat, or even intrepid librarians smuggling books and fighting bans to offer people something to look forward to in desolate times. It is my hope that *The Keeper of Hidden Books* sheds light on the desperation faced by the people of Warsaw during the Nazi occupation and displays the amount of bravery shown by the men and women who dared to fight back.

Acknowledgments

PUTTING A NEW BOOK out into the world takes a team of people behind every author, not only for the logistics, but also for support and encouragement. I'm so grateful to have so many people in my corner. Thank you to my editors Peter Joseph and Grace Towery for asking questions and catching details that make my book stronger and leave it shining, and to Eden Railsback for all her constant support and assistance. Thank you to my incredible agent, Kevan Lyon, for her immense and constant support. It's been such a dream come true to be represented by her. Thank you to Kathleen Carter for all her hard work in helping *The Keeper of Hidden Books* be seen and into the hands of readers.

I'm so lucky to have an incredible support network of friends and family as well. Eliza Knight, Lori Ann Bailey, and Brenna Ash—the Princess Crew—are my constant cheerleaders and are the best besties ever! Thank you to Tracy Emro for being there every step of the way in the creation and writing of this book, offering incredible insight and encouragement. And through Tracy Emro, I was so fortunate to be introduced to Gosia Kuc Ferris who was invaluable in providing information about life in Poland and for introducing me to Basia Le Nart who was so helpful in my visit to Warsaw—they were both so generous with their knowledge and time. While in Warsaw, I had the most incredible tour guide, Ewa Bratosiewicz, who put together several days' worth of tours that provided me with such valuable information. Not only that, but she was always so patient with my questions—and they were endless!

And always an enormous thank you to my wonderful mother, Janet Kazmirski, for not only coming to Poland with me and spending hours and hours (and hours…) in museums, but also for always reading through my books before they're published to help make them even better.

None of this would be possible without my second half, John Somar, my amazing husband who is always willing to step up with whatever is needed, so I could write *The Keeper of Hidden Books* and travel to Poland for research. And thank you to my girls who are always so proud of me and so supportive of my writing. It means the world to me!

And an enormous, heartfelt thank you to all the readers out there who read my books. Your emails and reviews keep me going when I'm having rough days and your beautiful and creative book pics on social media make me smile and always make my day. I'm so grateful for the love and support of everyone who has helped make this book possible.